DARKSIDE

— OF —

DEBONAIR

The Bushmeat Trade

To: Alf & Julie,

Hoot for the chimps!

Enjoy

Bhlara Davis-Wieland

DARKSIDE
OF
DEBONAIR

The Bushmeat Trade

Barbara Davis

Red Barn Press
Fenton, Missouri

Cover designed by Robert Aulicino
Aulicino Design
http://www.aulicinodesign.com

Interior designed by Patricia Kistler
Shady Hollow Graphics
http://www.shadyhollow.com

www.redbarnpress.com

Library of Congress Control Number 200209410

Davis, Barbara S.
Darkside of Debonair - The Bushmeat Trade

ISBN 0-9717731-0-6

Red Barn Press, Fenton, Missouri
First U.S. Edition: July 2002
10 9 8 7 6 5 4 3 2 1

Printed in Canada

Bushmeat: The meat of wild animals, including threatened and endangered animals that are protected by law, killed for profit by commercial hunters.

I don't want to end up simply having visited the world.
-Mary Oliver

Authors note

I was surfing the web, looking for a vacation spot, considering revisiting Africa. The word 'Bushmeat' appeared over and over in the search window. Curiosity forced me to begin reading about the horrors of the bushmeat crisis. Deforestation, the human consumption of our closest living relative, the search for a cure for AIDS, and the lack of media coverage all weighed heavily on my soul. That evening, I prayed, asking for a way that I could help. I dreamt this novel in whole that night.

Over the next three days I began collecting information, organizing and reading every thing the web offered about the subject. Then on the fourth night, I awoke at two o'clock in the morning with my heart pounding; I had dreamt the first chapter in more detail. This happened again a week later with the second chapter and every week afterwards, throughout the first quarter of the book.

Over the course of the next two years, I worked on this book. My quest for information and understanding opened doors for me that I never imaged. Divine guidance? Possibly. Over-active imagination? Possibly. Combination of the two? Probably. Regardless, the story was in me and had to come out. I wanted to help spread the word of the bushmeat crisis to others.

I have never personally experienced any portion of the bushmeat crisis, but the foundation for this story, with its catastrophic events is very real, though I have taken some literary leeway on the story location.

I would like to thank my parents, Edward and Margaret, and many friends for really believing in this book and me. Particularly my sister Patricia, my truest friend, whose neverending energy always goes far beyond regular family duties. And to Pauline, my editor, who's patience, gentle teachings and kind words flowed as consistently as the red ink.

On the technical side, a special 'Thank you' goes to Dr. Michael Huffman, D. Sc. (primatologist), for sharing his professional experiences of studying the medical uses of plants by chimpanzees with me, and to Terry Wieland, for sharing his knowledge, love of Africa, hunting and weapons, and also for his ongoing support and advice beyond friendship.

Chapter 1

The morning sun cast a lazy hue through the branches of the tall forest trees. Sprinkles of light scattered across the ground, splashing the ferns and moss. Cool mist gathered on the greenery in pearls that rolled to the leaf's edge and soaked into the mossy woodland floor. The jungle's high canopy rang with the melodies of brightly colored birds. The music floated down through the trees and softened into a soothing lullaby.

A small family of chimpanzees moved through the forest in single file. A female led the way. Clinging to her back was her young daughter of just three months. The old matriarch knew this would be her last baby; the two before were born lifeless. She was tired and weak from the hard pace she was setting.

Just behind her limped an older daughter. She helped with the raising of her little sister, caring for the infant while their mother rested or foraged for food. The long trek had worn down her youthful energy, and her younger brother who frolicked behind frayed her patience.

At first, the hike into the unknown was quite exciting to the young male. The unfamiliar landscape offered a new array of odors, but this time the group would not tolerate him exploring the strange jungle. The family took turns keeping the youngster in line, while he waited for them to drop their guard so he could sprint off and explore. Even his rather terrifying old father could not keep a grip on the young renegade.

Reaching a shady opening, the old male stopped and listened for the now familiar threat that pushed them ever forward. As the others continued on ahead, he made a low grunting noise. Stopping and looking back, they saw that he was beginning to forage. Taking their lead from him, they also began to feed on moist vegetation covered with dew.

Once they had eaten their fill, exhaustion overcame them. The big male nested down away from the others. Stress and worry covered his face, as danger had been their shadow for the last three days. The pursuer had chased them many miles out of their home territory, pushing them continuously, leaving no time for foraging or rest. Now in this strange part of the forest, with no apparent signs of danger, the gray harried male closed his eyes and fell into a deep dreamless sleep.

Up in a tree, the young chimpanzee's mother folded over the leafy branches, creating a bed for her and her baby. Slowing her progress, the infant tried to climb to her mother's swollen breast. The velvet-faced matriarch, finally satisfied with her construction, settled in and allowed her tiny daughter to nurse. With a gentle touch, she smoothed the fine hair of her suckling child. A few minutes of feeding would sustain the youngster for several hours. She soon fell asleep in the safety and comfort of her mother's arms.

In a bed built high in the neighboring tree, the older daughter lay on her side watching her adolescent brother below. Sounds of deep slumber were coming from her weary mother. She struggled to stay awake, but finally passed into a peaceful sleep.

At the base of what once was a massive oak tree, a long wiry arm reached deep into the decaying trunk and pulled out a plump white larva. The dark hands gently cradled the grub as it wiggled about in the unfamiliar surroundings. The chimp watched it with delight until the temptation became too much and the juicy grub became his midmorning snack.

Looking around, the chimp selected a stout blade of grass. Using his lips and teeth, he skillfully transformed the long blade into a useful tool. A slobbering lick moistened the fishing tool with the sweet juices from the grub. He then slowly and carefully inserted the prepared tool into a tiny hole that tunneled deep into the ground.

The scent of the grub on the invading blade of grass drove the worker ants mad. They attacked wildly with full force. When the chimp removed his dipstick, the ants clung to it, fighting against their invader. Their masses created a sweet stick of candy for the young chimp to enjoy. Over and over again, the chimp dipped the saliva-covered stick into the hole, each time withdrawing it covered with tiny sweet morsels of black ants.

Becoming bored with fishing for bugs, the ambitious youngster wandered a few yards away. Glancing back over his shoulder, he checked to see if his movements had awakened his family. They all slept peacefully in the cool shade of the morning as the young chimp began climbing up a tall wild-fig tree.

Near the end of a long limb he settled into a thick clump of leafy branches densely packed with ripe figs. As he looked down over his family, he chewed the sweet wild fruit, dropping half-eaten pieces to the ground far below. The limb gently rocked up and down with the chimp's movement as he reached out farther and farther for the ruby-red fruit.

A strong breeze caressed the chimp as he relaxed high above the ground, cradled in the fork of the branch. The limb slowly rocked and swayed with the added weight. The gentle swinging soothed and relaxed him. Having eaten his fill, the young male chimpanzee finally closed his eyes. Fatigue had overcome his youthful resistance to nap.

The tall slim black man, wearing camouflage pants and a dirty olive-green tee shirt, blended perfectly with the jungle foliage. The double-barreled shotgun Valli had received from the watchman at the logging concession seemed heavier now than when he started three days ago. Increasingly dense bush made it more difficult to follow the traces of the chimps.

Stopping for a moment, the hunter heard a soft murmur; it was close, very close. Looking around, he saw the bulk of an animal lying quietly in the shadows of large ferns. Allowing his eyes to adjust to the darkness, he focused on the large chimpanzee curled on the ground. Slowly, silently, he crept up to where the big male lay. He thought, is it already dead? Has there been another hunter following this group? Just then the old male let out another rumble of a soft snore. Raising his gun, he aimed the barrel at the chimp. At point blank range he pulled one of the triggers. The nine lead balls of the Chevrotine cartridge entered the old alpha's chest creating a hole large enough for a man's thumb. Completely relaxed in his sleep, the chimpanzee did not twitch with the arrival of his death.

At the startling sound of gunfire, the young female chimp jumped up from her nest, terrified and confused by what had suddenly awakened her. Her quick movement caught the hunter's attention, and he turned and fired the other barrel. The lead pellets caught her squarely in the face. Her body was thrown backwards, into the lap of her graceful old mother. Consumed by the hunting frenzy, Valli quickly reloaded both barrels.

The old female leaped up into a sitting position, still cradling her small infant. Looking down at her faceless daughter, the old mother released a blood-curdling scream and kicked the lifeless body out of the bed. Carrying her tiny daughter, she jumped down from the tree. The third shot rang out as she ran into the bush. The buckshot entered the old female's back and, as it exited, her blood splattered over the lush green foliage that covered the forest floor.

It was all over in less than a minute. Killing these small human-like creatures sent a sudden charge of orgasmic satisfaction through Valli. Drenched with a throbbing ache, the poacher's breathing became rapid and shallow. A hot pressure flowed across his midriff, creating a rising sensation that filled his trembling manhood. It was the same desperate desire that he felt when he was with his lover. She could make his body pulsate the same way.

But there was much work to be done, and no time for the hunter to enjoy his spoils. His younger brother, Khoza, was trailing along behind him by half a day or more. It would take both of them several days to process the meat and carry it back to the logging road. There they would meet the lorry driver who would take them to collect their pay.

Still feeling the sensational rush, Valli dragged the large old chimp over to where his second victim lay. This one would bring a big price, probably fifty United States dollars. Pity the other one was hit in the face, he thought. It ruined the skull. Still, she should bring twenty dollars.

As he worked the numbers over in his head, he grabbed the old female by one foot and started dragging her to the collection pile. A small mouse-like noise caught his attention. Turning back, he found the bloody infant that had been lying underneath the old female. She had been hit by some of the exiting buckshot, and she lay whimpering and squirming in a pool of her mother's blood. Reaching down, he picked the infant up by both her feet. Her arms waved violently in the air, reaching out, trying to grab some type of support. Blood oozed from her nostrils and mouth. Swinging the frail tiny body, Valli smashed the infant's head against the

4

tree. At the impact the little skull collapsed, and all sound of the little voice subsided. Valli thought about how much money he could have received for the baby had it lived. But the children in the village could play house with it now. They would cut it up and cook it.

Setting up his camp, Valli began by building a fire. Fresh green limbs would provide the heavy smoke needed to preserve the meat for traveling. Reaching into his pack, he pulled out a small cardboard box of matchsticks and a deep aluminum pot. Once the fire was established, he poured what water was left from his canteen into the pot to boil.

He reached into his pocket for the folded gutting knife. Valli tested it for sharpness by skimming the edge across the back of his hand. The sharp stainless steel blade yielded skin smooth as silk. Kneeling by the largest chimpanzee, he forced the knife through the dark leathery hide at the sternum. Pulling backwards, he cut open the rib cage and carefully removed the intestines. Placing the innards in the pot of boiling water, he made his dinner of sour stew.

Next he cut the arms, legs and head off, then moved on to crudely butcher the other chimps. He leaned the limbs up against the log allowing the blood to drain completely. Upon the log, he lined up the severed heads next to the body of the infant. Wiping his knife blade clean, he watched as a colony of ants swarmed around the blood soaked earth.

Lifeless empty eyes stared at him as he ate. When his brother arrived, they would finish skinning, butchering and smoking the fresh meat. Until then he would rest and try to bring back the throbbing ecstasy of his day's work.

As the movement in the camp subsided, the birds once again began their choir. The other jungle noises slowly returned, and a shocked young male chimpanzee lay motionless. Unable to comprehend, unable to flee, he watched from high above, safely covered by the thick branches of the wild fig tree.

Chapter 2

A musky smell hung in the air of the dimly lit airport terminal. The duty-free shops and food courts were closed as the first plane full of tourists arrived.

Following along, MacKenzie Blankenship walked with the crowd of people, trusting that they knew the way to the baggage claim. The multi-lingual signs hanging from the ceiling all had arrows pointing down the same gray vinyl-tiled hallway. At the end of the passage, a stairway led down to a large room divided in two by a tall chain link fence and gate. The three exterior walls were constructed of roll-up metal doors. Armed men in uniform paced back and forth, guarding each doorway. Near the bottom of the stairs, a wide metal conveyer belt wound its way in and out of plastic-covered openings in the wall. The passengers waited for their luggage to ride by. Once the baggage was claimed, they lined up beside the chain link fence, waiting for the security officer to inspect their papers.

Sitting at an elevated desk, Simon Kuldip asked each tourist several questions. He inspected and stamped each passport, and checked baggage claim tickets before allowing anyone through the gate to officially enter Kenya.

MacKenzie approached the desk with a backpack and a small red duffel bag. She had to reach high to hand her passport to the officer dressed in a drab green uniform. His shiny bald head was partially covered by a red beret decorated with a round military insignia patch. His eyes were as dark as his black skin. She had never seen skin or eyes so dark back home in the United States. The whites of his huge olive shaped eyes seemed to jump out. He read her name out loud, "MacKenzie Blankenship? What brings you to Kenya?" His English was perfect, with just a hint of a British accent.

Standing on the tips of her toes to see him, MacKenzie replied, "I'm here on business. The company I work for sent me to pick up research information."

After stamping her passport, Simon crossed his huge black hands over the book. "What type of research and where will you be going?"

She held onto the edge of the desk for balance. "Biological. We have a group of scientists in the Tinet forest studying what chimpanzees are eating that makes them resistant or," she said, shrugging her shoulders, "suppresses AIDS type virus."

Looking past her, Simon asked, "How much cash are you carrying?"

"Six hundred dollars."

"What type of electronic devices are you bringing into this country?"

"I have a laptop computer, GPS receiver, and a camera."

He moved her passport out of her reach and said, "Wait here." He pointed to an empty chair alongside his desk.

"Is there something wrong? I need to meet my travel agent."

Reaching for the next person's passport, he replied, "No, nothing is wrong. Just wait here." MacKenzie watched as the officer turned his attention to the other passengers, slowly processing their papers. One at a time they moved through the gate to meet their various travel agents and field guides before loading into wildly painted vans.

When everyone else had cleared the loading area, MacKenzie stood and picked up her bags. Without looking up from the prominent desk, a large pink palm motioned for her to be reseated. Simon took time to finish the paper work from the other passengers.

After reading and signing each sheet, he placed the papers in a yellowed folder and handed them to one of the guards. He pushed himself away from his desk, stood and stretched. He was a mountain of a man. MacKenzie thought that he would dwarf any American football lineman. The great power of this man was easily seen through the uniform that was too small for his bulk. The short sleeves had been snipped to allow for the expansion of his massive biceps. As he looked down at her from his raised desk, MacKenzie felt as if she were a small child gazing up at a giant. He stepped down and picked up her bags. "Follow me."

They walked down an empty hallway with closed doors on both sides. MacKenzie had to hurry to keep pace with him. Her slender frame did not reach to the man's shoulder, yet this giant walked with the gliding grace of a dancer. His hard-soled shoes made only the slightest noise with each step. In contrast, her soft soled hiking shoes squeaked and echoed between the concrete block walls.

At the end of the hallway, he opened a door that led into a tiny office. As she entered, she read the brass nameplate: *Colonel Simon Kuldip.* He motioned her to a wooden chair with a handmade seat cushion. He placed her bags on the floor next to her feet, and then asked, "Would you like to join me for a cup of tea?"

Still unsure what was going on or why she was there, she accepted. He put a small kettle of water on a hot plate to boil. Seating himself behind his desk, he dialed a number on the telephone. "Hi Colleen? She's here. Okay, bye." The teakettle began to whistle. "Do you like honey or cream with your tea?"

"Honey, please. But what I would really like is to know why I am being held?"

As he prepared her tea, he replied, "My dear, you are not being held. Say when . . . ." He began to squeeze honey out of a plastic bear-shaped bottle.

"When. So what am I doing here?"

Bringing her the mug, he said, "My wife, Colleen, is the owner of C.R.K. Wilderness Travels. She's your tour agent and will take you to meet the man who will help you find the researchers."

Stirring her tea with a plastic straw, she asked, "You know that they are missing?"

As the colonel prepared his own tea, he said, "Of course. It is part of my job, and my wife is your travel agent. I helped her choose the right man to assist you."

Returning to his desk, he explained, "You see, had I let you go out onto the passenger pickup area, you would still be standing out there, being pestered by the taxi drivers. This is much more pleasant, don't you agree?"

Setting her tea on the corner of the desk, she reached into her pack. She pulled out a small plastic bag with homemade sugar cookies and offered them to him. "I wish you had told me what was going on. I was afraid I was being arrested or something."

Accepting a cookie, he replied, "Oh, no, you have done nothing wrong. I have just been sitting behind a desk for too long. I am bored with this meaningless job, the uniform, and the tourists. In less than a week I will be off restricted duty and off medical leave and back to my normal duties."

"What are your normal duties?"

"I am a colonel in the army, assigned to a special division that assists Kenya's Wildlife Service Anti-Poaching Unit. In a nut shell, I catch poachers."

"Sounds very dangerous. And very interesting."

"Yes, very dangerous. The criminals are becoming highly organized and exceedingly well-armed, as in any expanding business. Although it is not as common here in Kenya as in neighboring countries, occasionally a tourist runs across their trail. It is a sad thing, what is happening across Africa. I received a bullet wound in my lung last fall, which is why I am behind this desk until I am released by the doctor next week."

"You mentioned that you helped to choose the man who will help me find the researchers."

"Yes. Jon Corbett. On the wall behind you is a picture of the two of us. He is a very good man. You can trust your life to him. I have done so. We grew up together and have worked with each other many times. He is like my own blood."

MacKenzie went over to get a better look at the photo. She saw two men in dinner jackets saluting each other with their drinks.

He continued, laughing, "If you cannot tell, I am the big dark handsome one on the left, he is the small pale one on the right." His voice softened, "He stood by me at my wedding, and my oldest son bears his name."

The door to the office opened and a tall, elegant woman walked into the room. She wore a simple lavender blouse that matched her long walking shorts and flat, soft, leather sandals. Her hair, cut very short and left natural, promoted large dark eyes that glowed over high cheekbones and a brilliant smile. Her skin was silky smooth and so black it seemed to reflect the lavender highlights from her blouse.

The richness in her voice added to her striking beauty. "Hello. You must be MacKenzie Blankenship." She had just a touch of a British accent, yet more distinct than her husband's. "I'm Colleen," she said holding out her hand. "I trust that my husband has been treating you well."

"Yes. It's nice to meet you." She shook Colleen's hand and said, "Your husband was just telling me about his work and the man who will be my guide."

"Oh, he has told you of Jon? Don't worry; you will be quite safe with him. He is a bit . . . unfinished, but nothing you should be concerned about. It comes from living out in the bush. If you are ready, we should be going. It is quite a long drive out there. Oh, your boxes of supplies arrived yesterday. I have them loaded in the truck."

Coming out from behind the desk, Simon shook MacKenzie's hand. "Godspeed on your search and your research."

Turning to Colleen, Simon gave his wife a proper kiss on the cheek, "See you later, my dear. Drive safely and don't let that blue-eyed devil charm you into staying longer." Turning back to his desk, he added, "And tell him to keep me posted. I'll be back at it next week."

A flash of disapproval swept across Colleen's face as she remembered the danger of his job and the recent episode that nearly made her a widow. Regaining her composure, she asked calmly, "Ready MacKenzie?"

MacKenzie picked up her bags and said, "Ready, and please call me Mac."

Chapter 3

A cool breeze chilled the tourists as they lined up to place their luggage in the back of a zebra-striped pop-top van. In the shadow of the van, a handsome man with a strong square jaw was saying his farewells and helping the passengers on board. For ten days they had followed this tall broad-shouldered stranger through the brush land of the

Ewaso River Valley, deep in the heart of Kenya. Jon Corbett's cobalt-blue eyes and the black, curly locks that fluffed out from the edge of his tan cap betrayed his family's British heritage.

As the van pulled out of the thatch-hutted base camp, waving arms were barely seen through the cloud of dust that trailed behind. Each long dry season brought people from all over the world for a short escape from city life, surrounded by concrete and steel. The rainy season found this quiet leader of hiking tourists guiding hunting expeditions across miles of rugged terrain, in the neighboring countries where hunting was still permitted.

Jon's loud whistle brought a big, liver-colored Rhodesian Ridgeback to his side. Buster's face and neck were dotted with dried drops of blood. In a recent quarrel with an angry baboon, the dog lost half of his left ear, and received a deep cut down his left hip. The injury kept him from accompanying his owner with the last several tour groups. Separation was hard for both the man and the dog. The ugly wound on his hip had to be stitched, and had since healed nicely. The ear had not. Playfully, Buster wiggled circles around Jon as they entered the hut.

Built on the edge of a bluff, the large octagonal hut was open on four sides, giving a full view of the grassy valley below and of the white-water rapids of the muddy Ewaso River. The thatched roof provided shade from the hot African sun. The back wall contained a long narrow bookshelf filled with manuals and textbooks for the do-it-yourselfer. Next to it was a small white gas-powered refrigerator, always well-stocked with cold bottles of water, soda, beer, and a variety of medications. The shelves above were neatly stacked with jars and boxes filled with a variety of nuts and bolts, nails, plumbing fittings, and other spare parts needed to keep his little rural resort running smoothly. Reaching up, he grabbed the handle of a large metal box marked with a bold red cross centered over a white circle. Tucking the box under his arm, he reached into the refrigerator and pulled out a cold Tusker beer.

In the center of the hut was a long metal table surrounded by a dozen wooden folding chairs. Placing the first-aid kit on the table, Jon snapped the cap off the beer bottle, pulled out a chair, and whistled again to Buster. The big dog laid his chin on Jon's thigh. The bitten edge of the ear was raw, and flies and gnats had feasted on the bloody scab. Digging around inside the metal box, Jon pulled out a tube of fly-resistant healing ointment. The bright pink would clash with the dog's deep color but would help keep the flies off. As the ointment was being applied, Jon's soothing voice could not quiet the dog's whimpering or ease the pain that showed in his eyes. The wound was healing very slowly.

The stitches running down the dog's hip came out easily, with just a snip and tug. The nylon threads pulled out cleanly, with no sign of infection. With the first aid completed, the well-mannered ninety-pound patient zestfully jumped into his doctor's lap. With both front paws over his shoulders, Jon was trapped and being fully attacked by Buster's ambitious wet tongue. The weight of the dog and Jon's six-foot six inch muscular frame was too much for the chair. The wooden dowel pins holding the seat to the frame collapsed, sending the pair backwards, landing hard on the braided rag rug that covered the stone floor. Still playing, the two friends continued rolling around childlike.

"*Bwana, Bwana* Jon," Mhinga stood in perfect posture at the hut's opening. "*Bwana,* a truck is coming down the road. Are you expecting visitors?"

Still playing hard with Buster, Jon was almost out of breath. "No, who is it? Can you see?"

"No, *Bwana,* I have never seen this truck before."

Having a hard time getting up off the floor with the feisty dog still wanting to play, Jon said, "Okay, put Buster back in his kennel. Wash that dried blood from his face. We must try to keep the flies from eating on his ear. See about stringing up a mosquito net over the kennel." The poised young man gave a shallow bow and led the playful dog away.

The small white truck came to a stop in the shade of the large hut. Stepping out, Jon brushed the dust off his shirt and placed the tan cap over his ruffled hair. Painted on the truck's doors, familiar bold lettering '*C.R.K. Wilderness Travels, International*' brought a grin to Jon's rugged face.

Resting a finely chiseled chin upon her ebony arms, Colleen Kuldip gave a bright smile as she watched the handsome man approaching.

Leaning on the side view mirror, Jon looked lovingly into the woman's dark doe eyes. "What brings the world's most beautiful travel agent all the way out here, so far from the bright lights of the big city?"

"Jon, you speak so sweetly to me when my husband isn't around. I have come to show off my new truck and to bring you an important client!" Leaning back in the truck seat she continued, "Jon, this is MacKenzie Blankenship from Los Angeles. The company she works for just hired you for a special assignment."

Across the cab of the truck a young woman smiled warmly at Jon. Her thick auburn hair was neatly braided and just long enough to reach the shoulder of her baby-blue tee shirt. The sun was reflecting off the truck's rear view mirror, catching sparkles of the cinnamon highlights woven within the woman's thick hair. A long, slim nose supported large dark, plastic-rimmed sunglasses, and also prevented him from seeing her eyes. When she smiled, her mouth seemed too wide for her small oval face, yet her lips were full, and Jon wondered if they would be soft to kiss.

Reaching across to shake her hand, he noticed her small firm breasts. The callused palm confirmed the steadfast handshake of a woman who was not afraid of hard work, yet the back of her hand was soft and luxurious.

"Hello Jon. Colleen has told me much about your business here."

Intrigued by her low quiet voice, Jon flashed a devilish grin, "Well, I know nothing about you, that company you work for, or what they want from me. Why don't you two ladies come in, have a cool drink, and tell me all about it."

Opening the truck door, Colleen called over to Mhinga, who was tending the dog kennel, "*Jambo,* Mhinga, please unload the boxes from the truck and be very careful with them, little brother." Mhinga stopped working and bowed very deep and long at his sister's request.

The women followed Jon into the thatched hut and sat down, while Jon got their cold drinks. Sitting at the head of the table, pushing the first-aid kit aside, he asked, "So, Ms. Blankenship, what can I do for you?" Jon studied her as she removed her sunglasses. Her eyes were dark hazel green with glittering gold outlining the pupil, all surrounded by a black band halo. The fine lines at the corners of her eyes directed his attention to this kaleidoscope of colors.

He was so captivated, he hardly noticed she had begun talking.

13

"First of all, call me Mac." Pulling an accordion-style map from her back pocket, she began to open it. "Several months ago the company I work for, Sperry Pharmaceutical Research Laboratories, sent a group of four researchers to an area west of here near the Uganda border. They were to meet with their ground transportation and be taken to this location." She pointed to a circle marked on the map. "There they were to set up a base camp and begin a field botanical study. After a few weeks there, they were scheduled to move farther into the old forest, establish a new base camp, and resume the study. It was here," she said, pointing to another circle on the map, "that I was to meet up with them, collect their data, and replenish their supplies. It was during this move that we lost all contact with them -- radio, computers, and GPS signals. Their last known position was here." She pointed to an area deep inside the forest. "I need you to help me find them and deliver the supplies."

While listening to her story and studying the map, a shadow crossed over Jon's face. "It could be very dangerous. That area is being heavily logged. The logging companies are hiring poachers to feed their workers. It is very possible your group of researchers ran into these hunters, and you may never find any trace of them."

"Sperry knows about the logging going on in that area. The French-Canadian logging company, Camino Timber Enterprises, is a co-sponsor of our study. They have given us permission to go onto their leased land ahead of the loggers to do the field study. It's good for their public image. They even supplied the porters, so it is unlikely that any foul play is involved."

"Then why do you need me? The porters Camino supplied would know right where to take you."

"The logging manager has refused to help. He says he cannot spare any more men to act as porters. The ones he originally sent out have not returned to work and now he is behind schedule. He also claims he doesn't know where the researchers are. His corporate people are supporting him. I am on my own."

Reaching across the table, Colleen laid her hand on Jon's arm. "Jon, I have reassigned all of your groups to other guides. Sperry is picking up all your expenses. It is very good money." She sighed lightly, "Simon agrees you are the best man for the job. When can you be ready to leave?"

Jon had never been able to say no to Colleen. Perhaps it was his loyalty to her and her little brother, who supported and helped him build his business, or the kinship and history that he shared with Simon. They had never steered him wrong, "All right. We can start tomorrow. I'm still not convinced we won't run into any trouble. But, we will take all the time we need to find your four researchers."

Mhinga came across the hut and gave his sister a kiss on the cheek. "You are always so beautiful! And you have a new truck too! How are mother and papa?"

"They are fine. They miss you and send their love. You should take some time off, ride back with me, and stay for a while. It will do you good to come back to the city."

Jon intervened. "Actually, I will need him for this little project of yours. We will leave Mac's supplies here, and once we find the researchers, I will send Mhinga back to oversee the loading of the pack camels and make the delivery."

"Jon, you can't send my little brother out in the bush alone; he is not a Maasai plainsman."

"Colleen, you know I will take care of Mhinga. We will also take Zawawi; he will be useful for tracking down the researchers. I'll have him escort Mhinga back here safely."

"See big sister, Jon takes very good care of me. I will visit our parents at the end of the season."

"Mhinga, why don't you show Mac to hut six. It is close to the shower hut, and I'm sure she would like to clean up and rest before dinner. I'd like to talk your sister for awhile."

Getting up from the table, Mhinga bowed at Jon and kissed his sister on the cheek. "Yes, of course. Ms. Mac, please follow me." He picked up her bags and she followed him out of the large open hut.

As soon as they were gone, Colleen ripped into Jon. "I should have never let Simon and you talk me into allowing Mhinga to come out here and work for you. He would have been better off staying in school, in the city with me."

"Colleen, really he is fine, he is learning so much here. Why, he practically runs the whole operation: the books, supplies, and the payroll. Besides, the guests love his cooking and stories. He is happy here. For Pete's sake, he is nineteen years old. He is better off here than with that group your husband works for. That job would get him killed for sure."

Her voice softened, "You are right about that Jon. After almost losing Simon last fall . . . ." Regaining her composure, she said, "He returns to his outfit next week; he wants you to report in every night. If you do run into trouble, you may need his help."

"I will try to call each night if it is possible. You know what it is like out there."

Dropping her eyes, she said softly, "Yes, I remember." She looked back at Jon. "I should be getting back."

"I'll radio the old dog and let him know that his beautiful doe is returning home."

❖ ❖ ❖

The glow of the candles lit the metal table covered with dirty dinner dishes. The two diners were trying to relax after stuffing themselves with the delicious meal that Mhinga had prepared for them. The aroma of hot coffee entered the silent hut long before Mhinga appeared with the tray. He interpreted the silence as a compliment to his culinary work. Without asking, he set the tray down and began pouring two cups of steaming hot java.

MacKenzie accepted the cup. "Mhinga, I've never tasted anything like that before. The herbs and the spices were unique, and flavorful! I didn't want to stop eating."

"You are very kind, Ms. Mac. These are special herbs grown only in Africa. I have a small garden in the back where I pick them fresh from the plant."

"Mhinga's parents," Jon began, "are employed at the Uganda Presidential Estates. His mother is from India and works as the chef there. His father is the master gardener and beekeeper. He is descended from the Okiek tribe deep in the Tinet forest where your researchers are lost."

"Really! So, Mhinga, you know this forest very well?"

"No, Ms. Mac I have never been there. My father's people are considered squatters by the Kenya government. They have been removed from their homeland many times. Some of them returned or moved deeper into the forest when the government promises were not kept, but not my father. The skills that he learned from his father helped him find work at the presidential estate where he met my mother."

"Do you know much about your father's people?"

"I only know what my father has taught me about them and their ways. They are a very small peaceful tribe of wild fruit, nut, and honey harvesters. They live in this country's largest remaining area of indigenous forest. Some of the trees there are 500 to 800 years old. It was amongst those old trees that my father learned the art of herbs."

"Well, if the President eats like this regularly, then he must be one fat and happy man," MacKenzie giggled.

Stacking the dinner dishes on the tray, Mhinga muttered, "Yes, foods that are served there, at one time were only found in the deep forest. Now this food is a delicacy for the wealthy."

Sipping her hot coffee, MacKenzie asked, "Did your father bring the recipes from the forest?"

Mhinga seemed a bit agitated. "No, he would never be disloyal to the ways of his people. The recipes were developed, my father only had knowledge of the herbs."

As Mhinga left the area with the dirty dishes, MacKenzie looked puzzled at Jon. "Okay, what did I say to upset him?"

Leaning across the table, Jon was slow to answer her question because he watched the gold flecks in her eyes glittering with the movement of the candle flames. "You said nothing wrong. He is just very close to his father and sometimes over-protective of him and his people's beliefs. It's really very complicated, nothing for you to worry about. He will be fine tomorrow."

MacKenzie let out a big yawn. "So, what about your folks? How do they feel about their son living out in the wilderness?"

"My folks," Jon flashed his boyish grin at Mac, "think it's great! They left the cities of England when I was just five, and have lived the last 30 years working in the bush. My dad is a veterinarian for the parks department and when my mother isn't assisting him, she is usually helping to teach the native kids to read and write. They love the land and the people. They've never considered going back."

Letting out another yawn, MacKenzie said, "Sorry. It isn't the company, just a long day. Any brothers or sisters?"

"Okay, last question before I walk you to your hut; you have a long hike ahead of you tomorrow. I have three brothers. Jace is my blood brother and is in college in South Africa. Simon is Colleen's husband; he is just like an older brother to me. His father was a game warden that my father worked with. Then there is Zawawi, Simon's half brother. The three of us were inseparable as kids."

"I bet you guys had an interesting childhood."

"Yes. Sometime I might tell you about it, but now you must get some rest. Come on, sleepy head. I will walk you back to your hut."

Chapter 4

The harsh flat landscape stretched to the horizon, occasionally broken up by the skeleton form of the baobab trees. Losing its leaves during the dry season gave it the appearance of being plucked from the earth and replanted upside-down. The long bare branches offered no protection from the hot African sun. Scrub brush grew throughout the veld of tall brown grass that flourished in the dry dusty soil.

Traveling in single file along the winding path, Buster trotted happily a few feet in front of Jon. His bright pink medicine-covered ear stood out sharply against the natural earthy colors. The narrow trail appeared to have been swept clean of all pebbles. Each step made by either man or beast left a perfect impression in the dusty earth.

This was such a drastic difference from the green valley that the thatch-hutted base camp overlooked. For MacKenzie, the novelty of being in Africa had worn off. The countless hours spent in the company's gym were not helping her to keep up with the labor-hardened men that she trekked between. The afternoon sun, the weight of her backpack, and jet lag were taking their toll on her. After just five hours on the trail, she was tired and slowing down. An earlier nosebleed had been a much-welcomed excuse for a break, after which the pace slowed to accommodate her.

The air was so still they could hear the insects' wings as they buzzed around in the tall grasses. Off in the distance, a dirt devil whirled up a skinny column of dust. Dancing across the grasslands, it propelled itself seemingly without any meaning or direction.

Mhinga recited an old Maasai folktale of a woman searching for her children who were lost in a great storm. "The woman sought help from a powerful witch doctor, the Laibon, who turned the woman into dust, forever binding her soul to search for her missing children. It is the angry spirit of that woman, which drives the dirt devils across the land."

MacKenzie let the legend fill her mind. It kept her from thinking about the heaviness in her legs and the effort necessary to take each step.

Strolling in front of her, Jon was unaffected by the weight of his gear. He carried a small backpack with bedroll and the .375 caliber Winchester rifle that he balanced casually across his right shoulder, holding on to the end of its barrel. The long sharp blades of grass left no scratches on the rugged tanned skin that covered the muscular legs extending from his tan cotton shorts.

Watching the rocking swing of his hips, MacKenzie was able to pull herself along in an almost hypnotic state. This kept her from caving into the weariness that was slowly taking over. Jon's stop came as a sudden surprise. MacKenzie walked right into his back. "Oh, sorry. I wasn't paying much attention."

Looking down at her upturned dusty face engulfed with fatigue, he wished he could see her eyes, those green eyes that were hidden behind those dark sunglasses she always wore. "We don't have much farther to go. The *kraal* is straight ahead, about a kilometer."

MacKenzie looked across the mirage. The heat vapors rising from the sun-baked earth made the *kraal* materialize and seemingly float above the savanna. "I can't imagine how this barren land can support a community of people."

Standing alongside her, Mhinga answered, "That is simple: just smell the air."

Closing her eyes, MacKenzie took in a deep breath of air holding it while her senses separated and analyzed each individual scent. The strongest smell was of the sweet purity of unjaded air. There was no hint of car exhaust or chemical pollution. Next she wrinkled her nose at the earthy smell of the land: dirt, clay and rock. The sweetness of the tall brown grasses filled her. Then she noticed the scent of moisture as it evaporated from all living things with the heat of the afternoon sun. As the sour scent tingled her senses, she sorted through the odors, detecting one light, but unfamiliar smell. "Okay, I smell something, but I don't know what it is. It is very faint and foul."

Mhinga's wide smile showed his perfect set of white teeth. "That, Ms. Mac, is the smell of Maasai wealth. Their cattle." Immediately, the smell became recognizable.

Reaching into her pocket, MacKenzie pulled out a small black rectangular plastic box. "Where are we anyway? I feel like I have just walked fifty miles." As she twisted a small lever on the side of the box to an upright position and pushed a small blue button, the digital screen lit up.

The men watched what she was doing with the computerized handheld device. Jon asked, "What is that thing?"

While watching the screen, she explained, "It's a GPS receiver. It bounces signals off different satellites and gives a global coordinate location of where we are. It can store the information that can be downloaded into a computer for mapping. According to this, we have gone about six miles." Looking up at Jon, she continued, "We've gone a long way off course from the researchers' first base camp to pick-up your tracker friend."

Jon flashed his boyish grin. "You didn't need a fancy little box for that information. I could have told you that. Zawawi is a seasoned tracker. He knows the land better than anyone and can follow a spoor days old over the hardest ground." Then he added sarcastically, "We need him."

MacKenzie returned the grin and ridicule, "Perhaps I should just fire you and hire Zawawi."

"Yes, you could do that, but you should know that he doesn't think much of white people and particularly white women."

She interrupted, "But he likes you?"

"Yes, I earned his respect many years ago. If you were to anger him, he would just leave you for the lions. It's not going to be easy to convince him to come along with us. He won't want to travel with you. His services will be expensive."

"But we need him, right?"

Mhinga agreed, "Right, and we are wasting time. We should be going."

Falling back into line behind Buster, the three trudged on toward the smell of cattle.

Hardly anyone noticed the dog, the two white people, and Mhinga as they entered the *kraal*. Protecting the tribe and their animals from predators, the thick round fence was made from sharp thorn bushes. Scattered around the interior, a dozen squat huts made up the sleeping quarters. The huts were constructed from branches, and pasted together with fresh cowdung that baked hard as brick under the hot African sun.

Several women wearing brightly colored waist wraps tended cooking fires near the center of the *kraal*. Strings of bright beads hung around their necks, and each wore multiple bangle earrings. The heat and smoke from the fires engulfed the women, who were stirring big pots of steaming liquid or turning roasting meat.

As Jon approached, one woman carrying firewood spoke, "*Jambo, Bwana* Jon. *Habari?*"

Speaking fluent Swahili, Jon smiled, "*Mzuri sana. Na wewe?*"

Almost whispering in Mhinga's ear, MacKenzie asked, "What are they saying?"

He whispered back, "They are saying hello, how are you. He is now asking the whereabouts of Zawawi."

The conversation between Jon and the woman continued for several minutes, and ended with the woman pointing towards the cattle.

Turning to Mhinga and MacKenzie, Jon relayed what the woman had told him. "Zawawi has gone out to check on the boys tending the cattle. He will be back soon. We can wait over there," he said, pointing to a small open hut with short poles supporting a thatched roof. It was just big enough for the three of them to stretch out comfortably. Buster had run off and was playing fetch with several of the village children who were throwing a long white bone.

To sit in the cool shade was a blissful release for MacKenzie. On the woven grass mat, she stretched out her slender legs and with two quick zips, transformed her canvas pants into cool shorts. Again, she took out the GPS receiver and electronically recorded their location, then placed the instrument back in her snap-covered pocket. Opening her backpack she pulled out her camera, loaded it with film, and took several pictures of the women cooking.

Mhinga informed her, "It is permissible to photograph these people here. They are used to Jon bringing tourists. But I must warn you not to photograph any Maasai outside of this *kraal*. It could become very unhealthy for you. They believe a camera may steal their soul."

"Or more likely," Jon added, "that you'll exploit them and use their photographs to make money."

"Yes, that too," agreed Mhinga.

A change in direction brought a warm breeze across the open hut where the group rested, bringing with it the smell of roasting meat. The odor made them realize how hungry they were.

Leaning forward, MacKenzie muttered, "Gosh, that smells good. I wonder what they are cooking?"

Lying down against his pack, Jon closed his eyes and said, "Go on over there and ask them. Take some pictures too. Your friends will love them when you get home."

She stood up, hesitating. "How do I ask?"

Sitting up, Jon took his cap off and scratched his head. "Say, *'Tafadhli nataka bia pombe baridi'.*"

Sharply Mhinga scolded Jon, "*Bwana,* you teach her the wrong words!"

Alarmed MacKenzie asked, "What did he say? What was he going to have me ask those women?"

Jon chuckled, "All right, it was just a little joke. No harm. What I said was, 'I'd like a cold beer'."

A smile came across MacKenzie's face. "I'd like one too, and do they have any here?"

Still laughing, Jon lay back down, "Not cold and not suitable for the American palate." He closed his eyes, and placed his cap over his face.

Looking over at Mhinga, MacKenzie asked, "Tell me the right words to say?"

"Repeat slowly after me, *'Samahani, hini chakula garu?'* then point at the meat."

She had to repeat it several times before the vowels sounded correct. Then she asked, "What am I saying?"

"Very simple. 'Excuse me, what is this food?' Remember what they say. I will translate when you return."

As MacKenzie approached the women, they stopped and looked at her uncertainly. Raising her camera she gave them a kindly smile. The women understood, replying with a smile and returning to their duties. She took several photographs of the women working, and then stood there in the hot sun with the heat of the cooking fires, watching them prepare the meal.

Without moving, Jon asked Mhinga, "How is she doing?"

Watching from the shade of the open hut, Mhinga said, "She is doing very well. Took some photos and is now just watching them cooking the meat."

Kindly Jon added, "She's got more gumption than I gave her credit for. She hasn't complained all day."

"Is that the reason for the fast pace this morning? To test her?" Mhinga could see a crooked grin on Jon's face under the bill of his cap. "Oh, I see. *Bwana,* I do not think this woman will become an easily smitten tourist. She is much different than the others."

Tilting back his cap, he grinned at Mhinga. "Yes, she will be a challenge."

"*Bwana,* go back to your dreams. She is returning."

Jon covered his face with the cap as MacKenzie plunked down next to Mhinga. The young man asked her, "Did you speak their words? What was their response?"

She leaned back on her backpack and replied, "Yes, I tried. I believe they said *'chui na hirola'.*"

23

Pushing his cap up on his head, Jon rolled over on his side and propped himself up on one elbow. "Say that again?"

MacKenzie tried the words again, "*Chui na hirola.*"

Jon and Mhinga stared at each other for several seconds. "Well, what do you make of that." It was more of a statement than a question to Mhinga. Jon rolled back over and replaced his hat over his eyes.

Looking back and forth between the two men, MacKenzie asked, "What is it Mhinga? What kind of meat is it?"

Before he had a chance to answer her, Jon interrupted, "It's bushmeat. Wild game."

"Do you mean some type of deer?"

Confirming Jon's answer by nodding his head, Mhinga laid back and closed his eyes.

MacKenzie quietly repeated the words to herself. Then following the others' actions, she laid back and closed her eyes, softly repeating the words again, "*Chui na hirola.*"

Before dozing off, Jon speculated to himself. Perhaps the antelope had already been brought down. A long bow in the hands of a skilled hunter could easily take out a leopard. But taking two very rare animals at one time would be an unusual opportunity. Zawawi would not have taken either animal except in an extreme situation. He should have a good story to tell.

Chapter 5

Kacha Ngozi, you sleep like a woman." Zawawi used Jon's nickname meaning "tough hide." Dressed in a blood-red shoulder *shuka,* the tall muscular Maasai kicked Jon's foot. "Get up, you pale baboon and stand like a man."

Pushing the cap off his head, Jon sat up and joked back, "Zawawi, you stink like elephant dung." Getting up, Jon shook his friend's hand in the traditional Maasai way of gripping one's hand near the other's elbow. "I hope your cattle are well."

"It is good to see you. My cattle are slick and fat. My youngest sons tend to them very well."

"And your older sons, Valli and Khosa, what has become of them?"

"They have left, gone off to work for the white Europeans at the logging concessions."

MacKenzie started to rise, but was stopped by Mhinga. Very softly he uttered, "Wait until Jon calls to you." She quietly remained seated and listened to the two old friends conversing.

"Why do the loggers need such fine Maasai warriors?" Jon teased. "Do they fear an attack from the falling trees?"

Zawawi laughed. "No, *Kacha Ngozi*, my sons have turned away from their Maasai legacy. They work like the dogs, that is what they have become."

"Perhaps they will see the truth and return to being a true Maasai."

"Perhaps . . . until then they are no longer my sons, and I spit at the thought of them." With that Zawawi spat onto the ground, kicked dust over it and stamped it with his sandal made from an old tire tread. "Valli had always questioned our ways. Always causing trouble. Khosa worships him, following him all around. Followed him into the pale baboon's camp."

"They sound a bit like us," Jon added cheerfully, "but you have two other fine sons. Sons who love your cattle as much as you."

Zawawi's smile showed a big gap filed in between his front lower row of teeth, an old Maasai tradition. "Yes, they are becoming tall and very strong, and they do love the cattle."

"My friend, sit with us, there is much to discuss." Jon pointed to the shade of the small hut.

Looking in the hut, Zawawi ignored MacKenzie, and nodded at Mhinga, "I see you, Mhinga."

Returning the acknowledgement, Mhinga said, "I see you Zawawi. I hope that your cattle are well."

With a nod, Zawawi chose a corner of the mat next to Mhinga and across from MacKenzie. Jon seated himself in the opposite corner of the mat.

"*Kacha Ngozi,* your business is not going well? You have only one lamb today, or has the flock wandered off again and you need me to find them?" Zawawi smiled at Jon.

Jon's smile faded as he became very business-like, getting right to the point. "Yes, some have wandered. There are four American scientists lost in the Tinet area. You will be very well paid. Will you come?"

Sitting in a squat position, Zawawi dropped his chin on his folded arms around his knees. "Tinet is not a safe place, and I have cattle to attend to."

"Tending cattle is a boy's job, not a job for a senior Maasai warrior who is famous across the land for his tracking abilities." Jon flattered Zawawi, "Your cattle are slick and fat and they have two fine boys to tend them. Those are your words. Come with us to find these scientists who search for a cure of slims disease, the illness that killed your father and mother."

"Your tongue is quick today, *Kacha Ngozi.* Tell me how this comes to you."

Zawawi listened to Jon recite the story of the loggers, porters, Colleen, and Mac. He listened to the entire story without moving or looking up. When Jon had finished, he just sat there silently for quite a long while before asking, "What of Simon?"

"Simon is due to be released back to his duties very soon. He has requested regular check-ins and has offered his help."

Speaking almost to himself, Zawawi whispered, "My brother believes there could be trouble."

"Yes, I suppose so," Jon agreed quietly.

"What of this woman?" For the first time Zawawi acknowledged MacKenzie.

Mhinga laid a gentle hand on her shoulder as she was beginning to reply to Zawawi. A quiet nod was enough warning for her to remain silent. MacKenzie glared back at Mhinga, not understanding his reasons.

"She works for the same company. It is her duty to find the scientists."

Zawawi stared long and hard at MacKenzie. Uncomfortably she glanced back and forth between Jon and Mhinga, not returning Zawawi's stare. "If I am to be hired, she will not come."

Rolling her eyes up, MacKenzie showed that her patience was just about to reach its end.

"See, Jon," Zawawi pointed out, "She is a weak child. She will hold us back. Interfere with our work. If we were to run into trouble, you know what would become of her. No, she must stay."

Having heard enough, MacKenzie leaned toward Jon, "This is the great man you told me about? A great tracker? A warrior?" Now leaning towards Zawawi, her temper began to rise, "I see a boy afraid of taking on a challenge. Because I am a woman, he is unwilling to accept that I may be able to contribute!"

She spoke with so much anger and so quickly that neither Mhinga nor Jon could stop her. Louder she continued, "What I see is a small boy in a man's body with a small mind." Throwing her hands up in the air, she concluded, "Living in a small world!" Fuming, she glared over at Zawawi. She held his stare as silence filled the entire *kraal*. The women at the cooking fire had stopped. The children playing fetch with Buster had stopped. All eyes were on the hut with the four people, watching the white woman's fury.

Still holding her stare, Zawawi spoke very firmly, "It will cost you double for my fees. I will show you no mercy and when I find your scientists, you will show me great penitence and respect."

Struggling to regain her composure, MacKenzie's skin turned bright red. She added, "I will gladly pay you double fees, and I shall gain your respect. Then you shall show me great penitence."

The challenge was set. Jon and Mhinga looked across the little hut at each other knowing that this was not going to be easy. Jon broke the silence as he rose quickly. Grabbing MacKenzie by the arm, he jerked her to her feet. "I'd like to talk to you." Roughly he dragged her out of the Kraal. "What the hell was that all about? Do you know what you have just started?"

Yanking her arm out of Jon's firm grip, she yelled "Yeah! I got that egotistical tracker friend of yours to agree to go with us!" Her face flushed with a bright red coloring giving an almost sunburned glow.

"No! What you have done was set yourself up for a gauntlet of pun-

27

ishment. A challenge that you can't possibly survive, let alone win."

"Oh, please! I think that you are overreacting just a bit!"

"I know this man. You've challenged his manhood, his pride. Maasai are very stubborn, fierce and noble people. He is going to make your life a living hell just to prove his point."

"Well, I'll do whatever is necessary. I am not afraid."

"You should be. You were struggling this morning trying to keep up with us."

"Have you ever heard of jet lag? I had just gotten here. Twenty hours of flight time. I was tired!"

He boomed over her, "You don't seem tired now!"

She raised her voice to meet his, "I'm mad now!"

Taking his hat off, Jon wiped his brow on his sleeve. "What aren't you telling me? This seems way too personal. What is going on?" Replacing his hat, he grabbed her by both arms, nearly picking her up off the ground. His face was so close to hers, he could feel her hot breath on his cheeks. "Tell me."

"One of the researchers is my father. He is getting old and his health is not great." Jon felt the tension in her body release. "I'm worried about him."

Setting her down, he saw the pain in her eyes, those magnetic hazel eyes. In the natural light of the sun, they were even more intense, so he softened. "Well, you should be worried, but for now you need to worry about Zawawi."

"Is it really going to be that bad?"

"Oh yes! You'd better believe it."

Turning from Jon, she crossed her arms and looked into the lowering afternoon sun. "Would it help if I went back in there and played the distraught woman pleading for his forgiveness?"

"He might buy it if you were a native, but he doesn't trust white women. You had better get prepared for some rough times. Mhinga will help you as long as Zawawi doesn't see him. I'll run interference whenever I can. Just stay away from him. Stay near Mhinga or myself. Whatever you do, don't let him see you weaken. He will squash you like a bug."

Mhinga was running out of the *kraal* towards them carrying all of their gear, "We must hurry! Zawawi has gathered his gear. He has left the *kraal* and his pace is swift." Stopping in front of MacKenzie, he said, "Ms. Mac, do not look Zawawi in his eyes. It will only fuel his anger. Stay very quiet and close to me. I've taken your bedroll to lighten your pack."

"Thank you, Mhinga. Help me through this and I will find a way to repay you."

"Just say nothing else, hold your tongue. Hurry, we must catch up with Zawawi."

The rest under the cool hut and the angry outburst had rekindled MacKenzie's energy. She had no trouble jogging in line between Jon and Mhinga with Buster bringing up the rear.

As they drew near to Zawawi, Jon sped up and jogged shoulder to shoulder with his old friend. A familiar awakening was occurring between them, a feeling of youthful strength and *deja vu*.

The slow steady jogging pace lasted for well over an hour. The barren landscape had changed little when they reached the crest of a hill, finally coming to the logging road. It was little more than two parallel dirt-rutted trails winding through the tall dry grass. The setting sun was just reaching the jagged horizon of the distant forest.

Totally unaffected by the long jog, Zawawi spoke to Jon, "There is a good camping spot overlooking a river just beyond those trees. We will camp there tonight, and tomorrow the woman will pay for us to ride on one of the lorry trucks to Tinet." Seeing Jon a bit winded, Zawawi made fun of him, "You have gotten soft, my friend. Mhinga's cooking has done you in."

Jon caught his breath. "You remember his special ways with food. You will not be disappointed tonight. Now show us to this good camping spot."

Zawawi walked ahead. Jon waited for Mhinga and MacKenzie to catch up. Seeing the grief on her face, he asked, "How are you doing?"

Looking quite pale, she tried to catch her breath. "I think I'm going to throw up."

"Go pick herbs with Mhinga. Do it then. Don't let Zawawi see you.

He will be watching you very carefully looking for stress, so don't show any. Pull yourself together before you get through those trees. That is where we will be camping tonight."

Still panting, MacKenzie gasped sarcastically, "Great, I can hardly wait."

"Do not worry, *Bwana,* I will see to her. Now go and keep him occupied."

Jon ran to catch up with Zawawi who had made it almost half way across the field.

MacKenzie followed Mhinga around the clump of trees to a small trail that led down the steep embankment to the river's edge. The small boulders that littered the narrow gorge were rubbed smooth by the rushing water. A long shallow pool calmed the muddy water before it rushed into the next obstruction of stones. The tiny particles of mud settled into the sand and gravel bottom of the pool. The quiet water gave the illusion of being only inches deep.

For MacKenzie, the gentle wind hit her like a wall of freezing arctic air, and she basked in it. The warmth of the sun and the uplifting breath of cool air revitalized her skin into tiny goose pimples.

At the edge of the river, Mhinga had removed his pack and was searching the green weedy bank for herbs. The sound of the rushing water over the scattered boulders was so loud that MacKenzie had to yell at Mhinga to be heard, "Is it safe to go in the water?"

"Yes, but don't go above the rocks."

Sitting down on one of the small sun-baked rocks, she removed her pack from her aching back and shoulders. After stretching and bending about, she emptied her pockets. MacKenzie removed her wristwatch and shoes, then slowly walked into the cool clear pool. She waded out until the icy water was just above her knees. The contrast in temperatures was amazing. Above the water line the cloudless sky allowed the sun to bake all that it touched. But below the water line, the temperature seemed to be just above freezing. The temptation to dive in and refresh her hot upper body was an ongoing debate with the sensation of coldness that surrounded her lower legs.

Mhinga had gathered his plants and seated himself on a shady rock watching her. She yelled over to him, "Come on in Mhinga, the water feels great." Then joking she added, "You're not afraid of a little cold water, are you?"

Seeing her revived, he joked back, "No, Ms. Mac, I'm not afraid of cold water. But very much afraid of crocodiles."

Quickly twisting around she scanned the banks and the rushing muddy waters looking for crocodiles. Trying to comfort her, Mhinga yelled back, "Not much to worry about, Ms. Mac, they usually do not come into the rapids. You should be fine. Trust me, I will warn you of any approaching troubles."

"Great. He will warn me." She muttered to herself. Removing the brightly colored elastic band from the end of her braided hair, she smiled and waved across the river to him. Her body temperature had adjusted to the initial harshness of the cold. With a deep breath, she threw herself into the clear shallow river. The iciness shot through her body with an explosion of shivering cold. As she rose out of the water, her thick dark hair had untangled itself and lay like a wet blanket down her back. The sun's enormous heat rapidly engulfed her. She played in the water for just a short time more before returning to the rock where her pack lay.

Mhinga watched the water-soaked woman as she waded back across the river. Resting in the shade of a white barked river tree, she could not see his inquisitive review. Her wet white tee shirt clearly showed the complete outline of her lacy bra and her slim narrow waist. Reaching back she squeezed the water from her hair. She appeared now more like a child than the feisty woman who matched the stare of a Maasai warrior just a few hours ago. She will be a challenge, he thought, but more of a challenge for Jon than Zawawi. The prospects of watching this unfold before him brought a grin across his face. Perhaps, he thought, Jon is the one who is in the most danger.

Once on the bank, she crawled upon a large, sun-baked boulder to warm herself. Feeling her body relax she started to fall asleep in the warmth of the late afternoon sun. The popping noise of distant gunfire broke through the soothing sound of the river. Startled, MacKenzie sat up looking over at Mhinga, who had not moved an inch. "Did you hear that?"

"Yes, it is Jon getting our dinner. We should be going back to the camp soon." The sun hovered over the top of the tree-lined river. "It gets dark very quickly here."

Putting on her shoes MacKenzie looked up at the bluff where they would be camping. Along the edge she caught a glimpse of movement, but could not determine what she saw. Pointing, she asked, "Mhinga, what is moving around up there?"

Turning to look, Mhinga's voice sank, "Baboons."

"Are they dangerous?"

"Mostly they are not. They sleep at the edge of the bluffs to discourage leopards from attacking them at night. It was a fight with a baboon that wounded Buster. They can be quite aggressive."

Picking up her pack, MacKenzie felt her muscles stiffening with pain. Noticing her expression, Mhinga offered her what appeared to be a small piece of moist white bark, "Chew on this. It will become like a chewing gum. The juices will ease your pain."

Taking the morsel from him, she asked, "What is this?"

"My people call it *Canellaceae*. It is like an aspirin. Leave a piece of this under your tongue tonight while you sleep. In the morning you will feel much better."

The white bark had a bitter taste and a sour look came upon her face. "Thanks, Mhinga."

"The bitterness will go away. Don't let Zawawi find you with this. He will know that I am helping you, and it will be rough for both of us."

"Don't you think he suspects that anyway?"

"Yes. But he is a very fair judge and will not act upon it until he sees it for himself. So show no weakness, Ms. Mac."

Darkness fell quickly, taking with it the heat of the day. In the chilly night air, beside a small, open fire, they ate roasted dik-dik, a tiny antelope, seasoned with Mhinga's special herbs and steamed wild spinach. After dinner, Jon and Zawawi carried on a long conversation in Swahili just to ensure that MacKenzie could not join in. The thought annoyed her, but she remained quiet. She added notes of her journey into her laptop computer while Mhinga tended to the camp clean up. Buster curled up next to Jon and fell into a deep slumber. His hind leg twitched as he ran across the African prairie in his dream.

Finishing her notes, MacKenzie closed her computer and crawled into her sleeping bag with a tired, "Good night all." Heads turned her way and nodded in response. Rolling over on her side so no one would see, she placed the piece of bark under her tongue. A smile of contentment spread over her face, and she felt confident that she had won round one.

Mhinga had tossed a few more logs on the fire before turning in. The new wood snapped and popped. The rising internal temperature softened the sap deep within the limbs. Seeping out, the burning sap created a brilliant show of bright bursting reds, blues and greens in the fire. The cool night air was filled with the sound of locusts from the field they had crossed earlier that day. A wood owl in a nearby tree called across the wooded bluff to another. From some distance away, the return call was faintly heard over the continuous sound of the rushing waters in the river below the bluff.

The two old friends sat quietly, absorbed in the primal feel of the African wild. The silence between them bothered neither one but seemingly fed and bonded their souls together.

Very softly, as if in a sacred place, Jon broke the silence. "Zawawi, back at the *kraal* your women were cooking quite a bit of meat. Are you now hunting for sport?"

"*Kacha Ngozi,* you have known me most of your life. You know that I never hunt for sport. That is the way of the whites, not the Maasai. If you have something to ask, then just ask, old friend."

"I was a bit surprised to find *Hirola* antelope and leopard smoking over your fires."

"Yes, Khosa brought the meat in."

"Khosa! I didn't realize that he had gotten so good with a long bow."

"No. It was not Khosa who made the kill. It was Valli. Khosa is just his little puppy. Valli sent Khosa in with the meat to show the women what their job is with the logging concession. Valli is not yet man enough to do it himself. Khosa came and went while I was away, or you would not have seen the meat at all. It will not happen again. They have brought shame upon themselves. I do not understand how Khosa can be so blind when it comes to his older brother."

"Perhaps someday he will see."

"Yes, perhaps he will learn before it is too late for him. I feel a terrible omen around him."

❖   ❖   ❖

Curiosity was getting the best of him. Who were these strangers using the same bluff for safety? He had seen these creatures only at a distance; fear had always kept him from getting closer. But now they were here on the same ledge; he was close enough to see the outline of one of them asleep in moonlight. Their fire had died down, and there was only a glow of warm orange embers. He crept slowly toward them. He moved just a few feet at a time, nerves on edge, always ready to sprint back to his troupe.

He had managed to sneak up to the campsite without awakening them. Bravery and fear filled every inch of his body as he sat there, studying the strange pale-skinned creatures that walked upright. Sitting on his hunches, the young baboon reached out and touched the long dark hair that stretched out towards him. He moved the tips of the soft fine hair around with his finger as it lay on the rocky ground. The rising sun fueled his interest. He was so engrossed with the new beast that he did not notice the small movement happening across the camp.

Lying on his side with his head in the crook of his arm, Zawawi watched the curious baboon for several minutes as it played with MacKenzie's long hair.

Jon lay asleep next to him, with his back towards MacKenzie and the baboon. With a light puff of air, Zawawi blew into Jon's face. He opened his eyes slowly and looked over at the smiling Zawawi, knowing something was up. Zawawi raised his eyes, pointing towards MacKenzie. Jon slowly rolled over onto his side to see where Zawawi was pointing.

The movement of Jon's body caught the baboon's attention. The animal froze with an expression like a kid caught with his hand in the cookie jar. The primate looked around the camp, still holding a lock of long soft hair.

Jon's stirs awakened Buster, who was sleeping next to him, back to back. Both dog and man saw the baboon at the same time. Before Jon could grab Buster, the dog had jumped up and was leaping towards the baboon.

At the same instant the baboon gave a loud shriek above MacKenzie's head. She was startled out of a deep sleep just as Buster was making his final leap towards the baboon. Springing to his feet in fright, the baboon had not released the lock of auburn hair. Pulling the hair with him, the baboon jerked MacKenzie backwards, pinning her between himself and Buster's landing.

The dog's hind foot nearly landed on MacKenzie's face. As he leaped again, his claws left a long scratch down her neck.

The young baboon made its way up the nearest tree with a clutch of long hair still dangling from his hand.

Afraid to move, MacKenzie lay very still inside her sleeping bag with her hands covering her face. Jon knelt down beside her and touched her shoulder. He could feel her body shivering with fear. Her reaction was so fast that he barely missed her flying fists. There was no aiming. Her fierce wild swings were striking out at anything that might get in their way. Catching her brutal strikes, he tried to calm her down, "Hey, it's all right. You're safe now. You're okay."

Panting with fear, she looked at Jon with wild eyes. "What the hell happened?" Looking around the camp she saw Buster bouncing around the base of a nearby tree. Zawawi was still laying on his bedroll, not trying very hard to control his laughter. Mhinga, suddenly awakened by all the commotion, looked as confused as she.

Jon could still feel her pulse racing as he released her arms. "A baboon wandered into the camp near you. Buster ran him up the tree."

Now sitting, the dog looked back and forth between Jon and the baboon. Wagging his thick tail, he waited for Jon's approval for a job well done. Following the dog's gaze up the tree, MacKenzie saw the primate clinging to a thin branch high above.

As she turned her head, Jon noticed the scratch down her neck that was starting to bleed. To get a better look, he brushed back the long hair that lay down her shoulder. His touch surprised her, and she jumped.

Trying to comfort her, his voice was soft, "It's all right, really, just a little scratch. A couple of small bandages should do the trick." Before he could say the words, Mhinga was there with the first aid kit.

Zawawi began to rebuild the fire. Over his shoulder he watched as Jon delicately attended to MacKenzie. Turning back to the fire, he muttered, "Trouble. She is going to bring us great trouble." Now chuckling, he added, "I should call her that, *Sumbua,* it suits her, trouble."

Overhearing his quietly spoken words, Jon briefly paused from his doctoring. MacKenzie leaned toward Jon, and whispered in his ear, "Could he have had anything to do with this?"

Looking back over his shoulder at his friend starting a fire, he answered, "No." Turning back to her, he continued, "Baboons are curious animals. He probably rambled in here on his own. But I do know that Zawawi is taking great pleasure from your fright. Even though it was not his doing, he will take it as a gain."

Chapter 6

Road dust filled the air like a heavy blanket of fog as the big truck came to a halt near a small gnarly tree. In the brown haze, visibility was only a few feet. Silhouettes of two boys rose from the shade of the tree. Across their shoulders they carried a thick branch that spanned between them, and dangling from the branch were three large obviously heavy canvas bags. Their weight bowed the sturdy timber.

The driver called back to his four passengers, "Okay. This is as far as I can take you."

Jon was the first to dismount from the truck. With great ease he landed on the soft shoulder of the road. Mhinga handed him his rifle and pack, which he swung easily across his shoulder. Zawawi was the next off the truck and began coaxing Buster to make the leap to the ground. Mhinga's jump landed him as supple as a gymnast. MacKenzie handed her pack down to Mhinga as she sat on the hot metal edge of the truck's bed. She was about to push off when Jon reached up offering to help steady her. Looking into his face for the first time, she realized how very handsome he was. She thought it ironic that she had just noticed.

Her hesitation to accept Jon's offer brought a perplexed look to his rugged face, "Don't you trust me?"

MacKenzie chuckled, "Well, I guess I should." Perhaps she was only now noticing his good looks because of the gentle way he had tended to her earlier that morning. Or perhaps it was the way he was sheltering her from Zawawi. Or maybe it was because she was rested and felt strong and vibrant. Regardless, his touch felt good as his hands gripped her small waist. She reached out for his shoulders. Jon's strong arms guided her easily to the ground, landing her directly in front of and very near to him. As she touched the ground, her hands slid down his shoulders onto his arms. Looking up into his face, she marveled at the brilliant blue of his eyes, the same blue as the cloudless African sky. A feminine awareness swept over her body. "Thank you," she murmured.

Jon gazed down at her upturned face. Feeling the warmth of her body in his hands, he longed to look into the eyes that were hidden behind her dark sunglasses, and kiss her soft full lips and stroke her hair. "Hey," the truck driver yelled back, "How about paying me my fare."

Brought back to reality, releasing each other, MacKenzie reached into her back pocket and removed a small, zippered cloth change purse. She counted out and handed Jon two twenty-dollar bills.

The truck driver was talking with the two young black boys who carried the white canvas bags. Approaching from behind, Jon overheard part of their conversation.

The taller one said, "Let him know of the two small bulls in the valley below the bluff where the river bends before the fork. We saw the spoor of a third one that was much larger, but we did not see him."

"Who does this go to?" The driver pointed at the three heavy bags. The smaller of the two boys knelt down to untie the bags from the pole.

"Special delivery for *Bwana* Dubois, all cut and smoked just the way he likes them. We got three *sokwe* for him to take to his King."

Passing the American money around the tall man to the driver, Jon said, "Chimpanzees are protected animals."

The tall black boy looked bitterly at Jon, "The government has granted us permission to hunt this ground, to feed the logger's workers. Do you now bring your tour groups out to see the fallen forest?"

Finished with freeing the bags from the pole, the smaller boy recognized Jon's voice. Standing up, he reached eagerly to shake Jon's hand, smiling and saying, "I see you, Jon."

"I see you, Khosa," Jon replied, taking the young boy's arm in the Maasai traditional handshake. "You have grown very tall since I saw you last. You are looking more like a man."

"He is a man," Valli interrupted, "and now he works a man's job alongside me."

"Yes, Valli," Jon offered his hand, "I see that you are both doing very well." Reluctantly, Valli accepted Jon's handshake. "Who has hired such prominent junior Maasai warriors to hunt for them?"

Excited, Khosa jumped in, "We work for the European logging company, but we are on a special detail for *Bwana* Dubois."

Valli glared down at his little brother. Interrupting him, he explained, "It is true we are the best trackers and hunters the company has. That allows us to make extra money on the side."

Not realizing the tension between his brother and the white man, Khosa eagerly continued, "Look at the fine rifle they loaned us, just to hunt *sokwe*."

Looking down at the bundles, Jon asked, "And you got three *sokwe?*"

Very proudly, Khosa answered, "It was Valli. He has learned the art of tracking very well from our father. I am his assistant."

Stepping up to the group, Zawawi looked into the eyes of his oldest son. For several seconds they held each other's glare. Finally, unable to last, Valli glanced at Khosa. Zawawi said, "They have learned nothing from me, for I do not know these two boys. We should be going." Swinging his bedroll over his shoulder, he gave Khosa one last look. His young son's face was clouded with regret. Compassionately, Zawawi said, "You can come back. Come with us now, Khosa."

Hearing his father tenderly say his name, Khosa lifted his face and looked into his father's eyes. He started to speak but stopped when Valli placed his hand on his shoulder. Hatefully, Valli glared at his father, "Khosa has made his choice, and he chose to stay with me." Reluctantly, Khosa nodded his head in agreement.

Zawawi turned and started to walk away. Pausing next to his young son, he said, "Remember, little one, a true man makes his own decisions." Then with Buster by his side, he walked off.

A new voice bellowed from within Valli, one filled with malice and hate, "You know it is not safe for you to be here, Jon."

"Valli, leave your hatred for your father with him, I am not your enemy. We are searching for four American scientists. Camino Timber Industries has allowed them to go into the forest ahead of the loggers to study the plants. Have you seen any traces of them?"

"No. No trace and if they had come across any of the other hunters, you will not either."

"Valli," Jon lowered his voice so only he could hear him, "Simon will be back to work very soon. I'm advising you and Khosa not to take any more special assignments from *Bwana* Dubois. Simon will not tolerate any type of poaching, even from his nephews."

"Here is some advice for you, Jon. Watch your back, for the forest is full of hunters who are paid by the pound. There are many hungry loggers to feed and they do not question the type of meat." The boys tossed their canvas bags on the truck's flat bed, and then climbed aboard.

As the truck pulled away, leaving a cloud of brown dust in the air, Mhinga said sadly, "Zawawi is right. We need to be going. We should put many miles between us and Valli before he can become a problem."

"I have a feeling he already is a problem," Jon said, watching the truck being swallowed in a cloud of dust.

The truck disappeared over a hill. "There isn't anything he can do to stop us. We have permission from Camino Timber to be here." MacKenzie insisted.

Looking at her sadly, Mhinga explained, "Ms. Mac, this is Africa, where the wild creates its own laws."

"What is *sokwe?*" she asked Jon. "You seemed concerned with what they had been hunting."

39

Looking down into her dark sunglasses, he could see his own reflection with worry etched onto his face. He quietly uttered the same word he had used back at the *kraal:* "Bushmeat."

"So what they had been hunting was the same type of animal that the women back at Zawawi's *kraal* were cooking?"

"Mhinga is right." Jon attempted to change the subject. "We should catch up with Zawawi. The traveling will be slow and dangerous for the next couple of days."

Alarmed, MacKenzie asked, "Dangerous? How? Hey, you are changing the subject. Tell me about the meat."

"The meat isn't important now." Jon pointed. As far as the eye could see, the land was shredded with the remains of what once had been a forest. Tree limbs littered a field of stumps that once held them high in the sky. There was only the sound of the wind rustling the dead dried leaves that still clung to the fallen branches. It gave an eerie feeling of death. As he started to walk on, he looked down at MacKenzie and said, "Watch where you place each step. This area could be crawling with snakes."

"Are they poisonous?"

Mhinga answered for Jon, "Yes, some are, but you should not worry, Ms. Mac. Jon carries antivenin in the first aid kit, or if you prefer, Zawawi has the black stones."

"Black stones?"

"Yes, Ms. Mac. They believe that by placing a stone over each puncture, the poison will vanish."

"Oh, does it work?"

"They believe so and faith can be a powerful tool."

"But Jon has a real antidote?"

"Yes and a radio to call for an emergency helicopter. We should go now. Step only where I step."

Following behind Mhinga, MacKenzie carefully placed each of her steps in the exact spot that he had used. She watched the ground for any movement of a snake. "Mhinga, what kind of meat were the women cooking? What is the English word for *chui?*"

Without looking back MacKenzie could tell that her question bothered Mhinga. "Ms. Mac, *chui* means leopard."

"And what does *hirola* mean?"

"It is a kind of antelope that is very rare."

"And *sokwe,* what does it mean?"

"You have learned the words well, Ms. Mac."

"I have a good teacher. *Sokwe* means what?"

"It is Swahili for chimpanzee."

Stunned at his answers, MacKenzie stopped in her tracks. No longer hearing her footsteps behind him, Mhinga stopped and turned back to her. "We must keep going, Ms. Mac." The shadow of her cap and her dark sunglasses could not hide the horror and disbelief that showed on her face.

"People here are eating primates?"

"Please come, and tonight I will explain. We mustn't lag too far behind the others."

Chapter 7

The ugliness and devastation of the fallen trees seemed never to end. Late in the afternoon they cut across a dirt road that had been used by big trucks to remove the fallen logs. The overgrown track indicated that the road's usefulness had ended when the tree supply had been depleted. They followed the rutted road until it ended at the entrance of an area thick with thorny brush.

Jon and Zawawi had stopped by the thicket and waited for Mhinga and MacKenzie to come up with them. Buster rolled around in the dust before stretching out and basking in the cool grass. Removing their packs, the two men began gathering wood for a fire.

Letting her pack fall beside the others, she asked, "It is still early; we've got at least three more hours of daylight. Why are you gathering firewood?"

Dropping an armload of wood at her feet, Zawawi bent down and looked MacKenzie cordially in her eyes. "You speak words of wisdom," he said, "and perhaps I passed judgment on you too soon."

Pleasantly surprised by his response, MacKenzie smiled. "That is really very kind of you, Zawawi. Perhaps I prejudged you."

"Jon," Zawawi called as he straightened up, "this is woman's work." He continued, using his pet name meaning trouble, "*Sumbua* will clean the area, and gather the wood and build the fires. Let us go and do man's work, and hunt for our meal."

"Hey! That's not what I meant at all!" MacKenzie crossed her arms staring at the tall Maasai. "I guess I had you pegged right after all."

Smiling down at her, Zawawi responded, "Your peg is not even close to the center of truth!"

Before she could respond, Jon had dropped his load of wood directly behind her. He could see the back of her neck turning red as she started to lose her temper. "Mac."

Caught off guard she jumped and turned around, snapping, "What?!"

Very calmly Jon spoke, "We will need two fires tonight. Build one where the road ruts stop before the brush, and the other ten paces this side of it. Mhinga will help you set up the camp. We will be back shortly."

The men whistled for Buster to follow. As the three walked into the thorny grove, MacKenzie stamped her foot in the dusty soil. "I do not believe those egotistical men! Both of them! I can't believe that Jon just let him walk all over me like that!"

"Ms. Mac," Mhinga called softly to her.

"What?!"

"*Bwana* Jon was protecting you. Zawawi had found one of your weak spots, and he knows how to anger you. Now you must find a way to reverse, it or he will continue to feed that fire until you burn yourself up and he will win."

"I just wanted to know why we were stopping so early!"

"The thicket is many miles across, and we would not be able to reach the other side before nightfall."

"Couldn't we have just camped in there?"

"Very dangerous, Ms. Mac. The Cape buffalo are many. It is safer to camp here and cross the thicket tomorrow."

"So why two fires tonight?"

"Safety from the buffalo and other animals. Tonight we must all take a turn as guard."

"Even me?"

"Yes, Ms. Mac, even you. Especially if you continue to challenge Zawawi."

"But I know nothing about being a guard or guns."

"Jon will help you with that. I will help with Zawawi. But for now we must clear the area for our camp." Grabbing a sturdy limb about three feet long, Mhinga removed his belt and looped it around one end of the pole. "Ms. Mac, we will need your belt also." Removing her belt she handed it to him and watched as he looped it around the other end of the stick.

"What you do with this is," he began, while demonstrating, "put your foot here in the center. Hold a belt strap in each hand. Now lift your foot from the pole and the pole with your arms. Take a small step forward moving the pole with your foot, flattening the grass down. Do the area between where the two fires are going to be."

MacKenzie caught on quickly and, as she walked around flattening the tall grass, Mhinga re-stacked the wood and gathered more.

"What do you think we will be having for dinner? I'm starved," she asked.

Dragging a large branch over to the pile, Mhinga answered, "If we are really lucky we could have antelope steaks; or rabbit would be quite tasty. Whatever comes across Jon's path first." Dropping the end of the limb, he continued, "Or snake. Have you ever eaten snake?"

"No, can't say that I have. Some people I know in Texas say that rattlesnake tastes like chicken." Turning around she saw Mhinga stabbing at the ground with a long stick.

Holding the stick very straight and still, he called over to her, "Would you like to try it?"

"Sure. But what are you doing?"

Reaching into his pocket he drew out a folded knife. Flipping his wrist snapped open a shiny silver blade. "I have found us a tasty appetizer for dinner."

43

Laying down her tool, she wandered over to see what Mhinga was doing. He had the head of a large brownish-gray snake caught in the fork of a stick. The sharp horns protruding above the snake's eyes were lodged in the wooded branch, pinning the reptile.

"What kind of snake is it?" she asked.

Aggressively, it wrapped its stout, rough body around the hold of the stick and Mhinga's arm. "This is a horned viper, the image of Satan himself. They are very common in this area."

"A viper! Is it poisonous?" She watched as Mhinga struggled with the hissing and puffing snake struggling wildly to free itself.

With one swift strike of the sharp knife, the snake's head was severed from its body. "I don't think so." Still twitching, the four-foot-long body covered with dark semicircles held its wrapped position until Mhinga untangled the long body from his arms and stick. "You should not touch the head for at least one hour. It may still be dangerous."

"But it is dead. How could it hurt me?"

"Reflexes, Ms. Mac, and even if the snake is not poisonous it could make you very ill." Jokingly, "But if you would like to sample Zawawi's black stones," his voice trailed off.

"No. Really, there is no reason for that."

He smiled over his shoulder at her. "This will be very tasty."

Several hours had passed since the killing of the snake. MacKenzie dozed on her bedroll on the soft grass she had flattened down earlier. Mhinga had finished skinning and preparing the snake for dinner. The watch fires were built and ready for lighting. The cooking fire was lit and the camp ready. Out of the thicket, Jon and Zawawi slowly walked into camp, empty-handed. Both men were covered with sweat and exhausted from the heavy moist heat inside the dense brush. As they sat down on the log, Mhinga brought them both a canteen of cool water.

Buster trotted over and began licking MacKenzie in the face before lying down next to her. Rolling over on her side, she propped herself up on her elbow. "Had a hard day at the office, boys?" she snickered.

Unsuccessful in their hunt, sweaty and hungry, neither man was in the mood for a sarcastic comment. A half grin came across Jon's face as he scornfully replied, "Why, yes, dear. What's for dinner?"

She got up from her bedroll. "Well as soon as you two hard working men clean up," she said, as she tossed them a hand towel and bar of soap, "we can eat."

Catching the towel and soap, the men looked at each other, bewildered. Without saying another word, they got up from their resting places and headed off toward a small stream.

As soon as they were out of sight, MacKenzie asked, "How was that, Mhinga?"

"You did very well, just as I instructed you. It will take some more time, but you will have them both under control soon."

MacKenzie giggled, "How did you know that they would come back empty-handed and broken-hearted?"

"Ms. Mac, I believe that those two, paired together, are the finest hunting team in all of Africa. After the first hour and I heard no shots, I figured that the logging had scared off the animals and that they had not yet moved back into the area. Just listen, you have only heard the wind over the dried leaves, and you have not seen a bird all day. The area is dead. They both knew that when they started out. That is why they traveled so far and are so tired."

"Mhinga, you are a genius! Shall we start our little meal?"

"Yes, I have the herbs all ready to start."

The meal was very simple -- small flame-broiled snake steaks covered with gravy from the drippings and wild herbs. The white flaky meat had the texture of juicy chicken and the richness of an Alaskan lobster. Every bit of the four-foot long snake was quickly devoured. Their hunger was not totally satisfied, but at least it was quieted as the setting sun started to kiss the horizon.

"Jon," MacKenzie began sweetly, "Mhinga said we should all take turns guarding the camp tonight. Well, I had a refreshing little nap earlier, and I would like to take the first watch."

"I really don't think that will be necessary. I doubt that we'll have any visitors tonight."

"Maybe not, but I want to do my share and stand guard. Will you show me how to work your gun?"

Prodding him in the side, Zawawi encouraged Jon, "Go on and show Sumbua how to work your gun."

Mhinga agreed, "Yes *Bwana,* it would be good for her to have this skill."

"Okay," Jon sighed. The cool dip in the creek and the food had mellowed his mood. Standing up, he surveyed the area. "You can take the first two hours. Watch the face of the thicket," he said, pointing, "there at the trail opening. If there are any buffalo in there, that is where they are most likely to come out."

Standing up next to him, she asked, "What about from that direction over by the creek?"

"Unlikely. The hill is very steep for a buffalo to climb."

"And behind us? Across the land of stumps."

"Doubtful, they are too easily prey for lions in the open field and it is too hard to escape running over the fallen underbrush."

"Do I need to be worried about lions too?"

"Not if you keep the fires built up and stay between them. Don't wander out past the light."

"Got it! Now, how do I work the gun?"

Heckling came from the rear, "Yes, *Kacha Ngozi,* show *Sumbua* how to work the gun." The wide smile on the Maasai's face showed how much he was enjoying Jon's instructions.

Ignoring his friend's comments, Jon handed her the rifle and explained, "First of all, it's not a gun. It's a rifle."

"Oh sorry. A rifle. Okay got it." As she took the weapon from Jon, "Oh, my, it is heavier than I thought."

Zawawi was not containing his laughter. Jon looked over his shoulder annoyed. "Maybe this isn't such a great idea. You can just wake me up if you think you see something."

"No! Really, I want to learn." She looked up at him with her hazel eyes glowing through a dark banded halo. Softly, she added, "Please go on."

Mocking MacKenzie, Zawawi said in a high-pitched girly voice, "Yes, oh please go on, Jon." Then he laughed out loud.

Leaning towards Jon, MacKenzie placed her hand on his arm. "I can't back down now, can I? I can do this with your help. I'm sure of it!"

Her full lips parted and gave a warm smile. He could no longer resist when she started stroking his forearm.

"All right, let's try something else. Sit down on the ground and face towards the thicket. Bend your knees up." He called out, "Mhinga, lean a branch up on that stump so she has something to aim at."

Kneeling down beside her, he adjusted her sitting position, tilting her shoulders back to the proper angle. He rested her left elbow on her raised left knee. He placed the rifle barrel in her left hand and the butt end of the stock against her right shoulder. "How does that feel?" His warm breath stroked her cheek.

"Better, not as heavy, but still wobbly."

Sitting down behind her, he straddled her with his legs. Leaning forward, her back was surprisingly warm against his chest. Reaching around her shoulder, he steadied her left hand. He guided her thumb to the safety catch at the rear of the bolt. Her soft hands felt fragile and delicate supported inside his strong-callused palms.

The sensation of being surrounded by his body was making it hard for her to concentrate. The soft hairs on his thighs fluffed lightly against her legs, flashing a tingling awareness across her skin. The strength of his hands cradling hers ravished her imagination in uncontrollable swirls. As he whispered in her ear, her mind was swept into a spinning vortex. The warmth of his breath caressed her smooth cheek. The seductive tones of his voice controlled her every move as her subconscious followed his directions and absorbed his encouragement.

Tilting her head over, he explained how to line up the cross hairs in the scope with the target. Strands of her silky hair wisped out of her braid tickling the stubbly growth on his cheeks. He inhaled the scent of her skin, enhanced by the dainty fragrance of the soap. Softly he spoke, giving her directions. His breathing deepened and slowed as he felt her body relax and give into his hold. He tightened up the butt of the rifle into the soft cushion of her shoulder. "That's it. When you feel steady, push the safety button."

With her back up against his chest, he felt the rising and falling of her breathing slowly become calm. With his arms around her and his face so near to hers, he sensed her heart pounding and beating forcefully, pumping with excitement. A small click alerted him that she had pushed the safety off. "Now, when your hand is steady," he said, as he removed his grip from her, "slowly squeeze the trigger. Don't pull back with your hand. Don't jerk your finger. Just slowly squeeze it. Firmly, but gently."

Together in rhythm they breathed very deeply and slowly. Their hearts pounded in unison while anticipation and tingling electricity flowed between them. With each inhalation he filled his senses with the essence of her. He felt the slightest movement of her muscles tightening in her right arm. Almost inaudibly, he whispered in her ear, "Slowly now, gently." His voice softened and was as thick and warm as melted chocolate. "That's right, darling. Gently now, just squeeze it."

The force of the recoil shocked MacKenzie and slammed her back tightly into Jon's embrace. He had been ready for the feel of her body jolting into his at the moment of firing, and he caught her easily. Feeling her lose her grip on the rifle, he reached out and grabbed it before it bucked into her face.

The ringing in her ears masked all other sounds. MacKenzie could not hear Mhinga cheering her perfect hit. When she turned and gazed into Jon's face, cradled there in his arms, their faces just inches apart, she could not hear his words, but was able to read his lips. "You hit your mark!"

Holding her like a child in his arms, he was overwhelmed with emotions. He could not tear himself away from her hazel eyes and the gold flecks, sparkling in the setting sun. A row of perfect white teeth was framed by a trembling smile as her full lips parted, drawing him near. He ached to feel them press against his. Her essence pulled him forward, consuming and commanding his body's will to hers. He could hear the tiny rise and fall of her breathing. He felt the rapid concussions of her pounding heart, and he could see the tiny trembling movements in her lips, calling him forward to submit.

She responded to the same irresistible power. Tilting her head slightly, her eyes dropped from his, watching as his lips slowly parted and he neared her.

Anticipating her touch, Jon was completely consumed by the

woman he held in his arms. He was absorbed into the sound of her breathing, the silky feel of her hair and skin and her delicate scent that filled every crevice of his being. The thundering pounding vibration went unnoticed, melting into the composite of their embrace. Jon did not respond or recognize the shouts of warnings from Mhinga. Zawawi threw a stone hitting Jon on the shoulder snapping him out of his dream-like state. Turning to snap at his friends, Jon caught a glimpse of a dark object bellowing through the dense thicket. His nerves and senses already heightened, he quickly focused on the noise that was barreling towards them.

A dark shape plowed through the thick underbrush of the thicket with amazing speed and force. Less than fifteen yards away, bursting out of the brush and halting for just a second, an old bull buffalo looked for his opponents. Angry hate filled his large black eyes and streams of bloody saliva flowed from his mouth. His labored breathing was rough and graveled. Lowering his head, he tossed his wide spread C-shaped horns from side to side. The heavy black boss fused together on top of his skull as one large curved piece of armor. As bloody mucus pooled around his feet, the old buffalo sprang forward. In just one stride he covered half the distance to his enemy.

With MacKenzie straddled between his legs, just fifteen yards from the wounded bull, Jon had no time to shoulder the rifle. As the massive black animal leaped, Jon bounded forward throwing MacKenzie into the dusty, grass-laden earth. There were only seconds before the old bull would be upon them. There was time for only one shot. With a protective movement to cover the woman, Jon fired on the charging bull that was now only a few feet away. Ducking his head into his arms, he shielded himself and MacKenzie the best he could.

The ground trembled as the beast slammed into it from midstride. The bulky mass slid to rest just inches from where Jon and MacKenzie lay. Dust filled the area over them, and the thundering sound of hooves stopped. Covering her body with his, Jon could feel MacKenzie's whole body shaking with fear. Peeking up over the crook of his arm, he stared into the bull's lifeless eye. Releasing his grip on MacKenzie, Jon raised himself up. "Are you all right?" he asked.

Slowly, trembling, she opened her eyes. Looking first at Jon with a wolfish grin, she glanced out the corner of her eyes at the bloody face of the dead bull. Unable to speak, she nodded her head.

Jon tenderly wiped the fallen strands of hair from her face. "Looks like you've gotten us dinner."

The laughter in his voice brought her around. "Did I do that?" she asked shakily.

"I would say so!" he replied, helping her up from the dusty soil. "The shot you made went into the thicket and hit the bull. You hit him hard, you got him in the lungs." Jon pointed to the stream of blood that ran from the bull's ribs.

"How about that, Zawawi!" Mhinga exclaimed. "*Sumbua* has brought us fresh steaks for our dinner. Help me with the butchering."

"She had a moment of luck." Zawawi waved the woman off. "It was Jon who made the blind head shot from only four feet. That was impressive." And he slapped Jon across the back.

Mhinga roasted the fresh steaks until they were tough but edible. Night fell quickly; the watch fires lit the overfed party of campers. Even Buster had eaten his fill. The tiny voices of insects and the crackling of burning wood were a serenade in the night air. Jon and Zawawi lay on their bedrolls half asleep. Mhinga had just prepared his and was lying on his back looking up at the star-filled sky. MacKenzie sat with confidence on a log with the rifle laying across her lap staring out into the darkness. Softly she spoke so she did not disturb the sleeping men, "Mhinga?"

A quiet voice answered back, "Yes?"

Without looking back at him, she asked, "Tell me about bushmeat. Why do people here eat chimpanzees and other endangered animals?"

Mhinga looked over at Jon. Without speaking, Jon nodded his head, giving approval to answer her question.

"In the past it had not been a common practice to eat primates. Only a very few rural tribes did. The animals were plentiful then and many used the meat only as medicines." Mhinga sighed sadly. "They claimed that if your child was sickly you simply feed him gorilla meat to make him strong. The hand of a chimpanzee was thought to cure stomach pains. These tribes took only what was needed to sustain themselves, and any meat that was not used was taken to the market to aid others. With other tribes it was taboo to eat the meat of the great apes. That was the way of our world for many, many years."

Mhinga paused to gather his thoughts before continuing. "Now the human population is growing and their wants are growing as well. The cost of cash crops, coffee and cocoa, have fallen while the cost of lumber has soared. As the loggers cut new roads into the forest, more of this type of meat is being made available at the markets." Aggravated, his voice rose slightly, "Now it is the very wealthy who are buying it and at three to six times the cost of beef or pork. It has become a sign of high status." Mhinga rolled over and looked at MacKenzie, saying, "I've even heard that the meat of primates has become so popular that it is being smuggled out of Africa and is on the menu at some restaurants in Europe."

Rolling onto his back he went on, "It's not just the primates that are being targeted. Elephant steaks are very popular and are sold in the butcher sections of some supermarket chains. In another part of Africa, there have been severe droughts lasting many years and the people can not grow crops and are simply just eating whatever meat they can find in order not to starve to death."

MacKenzie silently listened as Mhinga spoke, processing all that he had just told her. "What about the governments and the organization that Simon works with? Or the police?"

Jon sat up and gazed into the fire. "Many of the rifles and cartridges are supplied by the police, government officials, or the logging companies. Remember back where the lorry driver dropped us off? Khosa spoke about the fine rifle that was loaned to them to hunt. Some poachers are better armed than the police are. With a small bribe, they can get through roadblocks. Many government officials have no will to stop it since they serve the meat at their own banquets."

"And what about Simon?"

"He despises it, but since he has been away, the market has grown rapidly. It's becoming very organized."

"What about the media? Surely this must surpass the ivory crisis of the 1980's."

"From what I understand, the media doesn't know how to publicize what is going on, and it is much worse in some other central and western

African countries where the governments are less stable."

"Perhaps Sperry Pharmaceutical knew this was happening and that is why they sent the researchers so swiftly. If all of the chimps are being slaughtered for meat," her voice broke off. "Oh God! If all of the Pan Troglodytes Troglodytes are killed off, the world may never have a cure for AIDS."

Mhinga looked across at MacKenzie. "Pan Troglodytes Troglodytes?"

"A subspecies of chimpanzee. You see the chimps are carriers of the SIVcpz virus, which is the grandfather of the HIV-1. But for some reason the wild chimps don't get sick, they don't develop AIDS. It is believed that the virus was passed on to humans when hunters nicked themselves skinning their kills. Or eating their meat." It all seemed so clear to her now.

Zawawi was mumbling in his sleep. His gibberish allowed for a break in their conversation. Under a blanket of stars, MacKenzie's mind drifted off with the deep thoughts of new information Mhinga had shared with her. The feel of the cold steel rifle barrel leaning against her shoulder, her back blazing warm from the fire, she stared out into the vast blackness of the African night.

Chapter 8

The thicket towered over the trail. High branches clustered with small slender leaves covered the path, encasing a tunnel. The upper branches, tightly woven and full of leaves, would not allow air to circulate, so there was no breeze. Moisture was drawn by the inter-twined root system that spread unseen below the rocky soilless ground. Creating its own hothouse effect was the thicket's secret of survival.

The moist shady heat provided a haven for an abundance of insect life. Relentlessly attracted to any kind of wetness, they were a consistent source of annoyance to any living creature passing within this shady refuge. The insects buzzed around, trying to land and drink from facial openings that were easy targets. Speaking was nearly impossible without swallowing some type of flying insect, so the group traveled silently.

Buster suffered the greatest. The bright pink medicine applied to his severed ear simply melted in the humid heat leaving the wounded ear unprotected and swarming with insects. The constant irritation on the soft healing scabs prompted the raw edge to bleed, attracting more flies. Shaking his head brought no relief, as the feeding flies clung to the ear like glue. But his tribulations did not end there. With each body-cooling pant, swarming insects would try to suck moisture from his saliva, causing the dog to occasionally choke and cough.

Leading the way, Zawawi hacked at branches supporting sharp thorns with his long double-edged *simi*. Mhinga followed behind him, carrying a small bundle of drying buffalo meat tied to the end of a sturdy limb. It was balanced over his shoulder, giving the young man the appearance of a railroad hobo. MacKenzie and Buster, then Jon, followed in line.

Traveling in the early morning had been quite pleasant and fast paced, but by late afternoon the heavy moist heat was taking its toll and slowing their stride.

It was late afternoon when the dense canopy began to open. The humidity was decreasing, and the sinking sun reduced the temperature. From the thicket they emerged into what appeared to be another world. Large trees with wide limbs spread high over a carpet of short fine grass. A few yards into the wooded area, a cool breeze gently kissed their salty, sweaty skins, stopping them dead in their tracks. Buster wandered on a few feet ahead of them. Sniffing the ground, he found the perfect spot and dug a shallow hole. It was just deep enough to remove the warm top layer of dirt and expose the soft, cool earth that lay just below the surface. After rolling in the dust, he stretched out and closed his eyes.

Simultaneously, without saying a word, the weary group took their lead from Buster. Dropping their packs to the ground, they rested in the cool shade of the tall trees.

The rock path, along with the heat and humidity, had drained them of their energy. After a few hours of rest, the group gathered firewood. Supper was a few mouthfuls of dried buffalo. They made an early night of it, each taking a two-hour watch.

The morning was as slow to rise as they were. It was late when they had cleared camp and began moving, heading northwest towards the Tinet forest. The new environment and the rest had done them all good. Buster finally gained some relief from the insects.

The forest was like a park. The traveling was easier on the grassy tree-covered ridge. A cool, steady breeze kept them refreshed. The area was alive with the sounds of nature. Birds of many colors flew between the trees, and cries of larks, swallows, and robins were all distinguishable. Somewhere deep in the wooded area, woodpeckers were busy creating new homes. A small troop of blue monkeys watched from high in the treetops as the group of five passed below.

The day felt more like a picnic than a journey with a serious purpose. The new territory filled them with wonder and joy. Even Zawawi showed his enjoyment of the tranquil place by occasionally joshing Mhinga while he identified the different birds and plants that MacKenzie photographed.

They stopped to watch a small clan of wart hogs feeding on the short grass. One by one, each family member lifted its enormous head, showing his or her pair of huge curved upper canines. The largest of the group, the male, was distinguishable by the two pairs of warts on his cheeks. The hogs had dried clumps of mud hanging from the coarse hair that thinly covered their backs. With a grunt and a squeal, their tails raised straight up like flagpoles, the family turned and trotted off into the forest.

Zawawi and Jon were like two young boys as they pointed out and identified tracks made by the different animals. There were fresh tracks of a large cat and many forked prints of antelopes.

Around the base of a fig tree were signs of monkeys. While investigating the spoors, loud noises of branches and leaves being violently shaken came from above. Looking up, they spotted a black and white colobus monkey. Alarmed by the intruders, he made such a racket that a clump of wild figs broke loose. The group scattered as the wild fruit rained to the ground.

Mhinga picked up the wild figs and thanked the monkey for its gift. Turning to the group, he said, "This will sweeten the meat tonight."

As they traveled on, the peaceful woods changed. The underbrush thickened and the ridge began to slope upward before leveling out into a small meadow surrounded by trees. Butterflies filled the air, fluttering above the tall grasses and wild flowers. The brightly colored dainty wings danced over the field, spreading pollen and collecting nectar.

Crossing the little field, Buster was enthralled with the many fluttering butterflies. They were attracted to the bright pink color of the medicine on his ear. He jumped and snapped his jaws at any that flew close to his face. His reactions were quite comical. There were so many butterflies, the dog did not know where to look or snap next.

The wooded area across the field inclined steeply. They followed a narrow and rocky animal path for more than half a mile to where the hill crested. Beyond the peak, the tiny trail descended to a long-standing twisted tree, and appeared to end there. Low thick branches reached out towards them, balancing the ancient root system that anchored the old tree to the edge of the high bluff. The trail continued on, wrapping itself around in front of the tree. The exposed roots, tightly holding in the rocky earth, created a mixture of odd steps leading onto a trail that hugged the face of the cliff.

The splendor of all they had seen earlier that day could not compare to the spectacular view of the valley below. A series of bluffs lined one quarter of the crater-like canyon. Near the foot of the vertical wall of exposed rocks a river flowed south. The banks curved around the field in a semi-circle before splitting into two separate rivers. The west side was lined with white-barked birch trees. The east side of the river was mainly littered with boulders that had fallen from the bluff. Dense greenery grew among the rocks camouflaging the river's edge. Past the treeline, a large grassy field stretched out to a compacted barrier of fertile green underbrush that bordered tall timber. The tops of the trees became a rich sea of green that reached out below the late afternoon sun, hovering over the horizon.

Stopping at the twisted old tree, the group stared at the lush green valley that opened below them. Resting in the shade of a gnarly branch near the edge of the bluff, MacKenzie took a series of photographs trying to capture the panorama. When she had finished, she smiled at Jon.

"Welcome to the beginning of the Tinet forest." As he spoke he felt a calm warmth toward this woman, something oddly secure. It confused and comforted him at the same time. Pointing across the field, he continued, "Just beyond is the Mount Elgon escarpment, and just past that is the Uganda border. South of here is Lake Victoria."

"It's so beautiful and . . . untouched. Like going back in time." Her voice carried the wonder of a young child.

Mhinga added, "This area is difficult for the tourists to reach as there are no roads. It is known only to a few serious hunters and the locals."

Almost to himself, Zawawi muttered, "Until the loggers reach it. Then it will be gone forever."

It saddened them all to think of this paradise being stripped of its trees. Jon lightened the mood when he noticed two young bull elephants coming out from a group of trees lining the river. Pointing down, he exclaimed, "Look there!"

Their backs were shiny black from water that they sprayed, cooling themselves from the hot afternoon. Their short ivory tusks gleamed white against the open field of green. They frolicked and played, entangling their trunks and tossing clumps of grass at each other. Butting heads, they tested each other's strength with a game of push and shove. They carried on for quite some time until something in the treeline caught their attention and they stopped. They stood side-by-side, large ears spanned out, watching.

Slowly, quietly, there emerged an enormous ancient bull elephant. His yellowed ivory showed his age, and it nearly reached the ground before curving up, the tips tilted inward. His thick hide, draped across his back, showed the ridge of each vertebra. He was wet from his bath under the shady outstretched branches covering the river.

From high atop the bluff, his size mesmerized the watching party. In all the years and thousands of miles traveled across African soil, Jon, Mhinga, or Zawawi had never seen an elephant so large. He was the kind of animal the old hunters talked about hunting as young men, the likes of which had not graced the African plains in a century. Yet there he stood, towering over the two adolescents, pausing to reach out with his thick trunk, touching, smelling, and communicating with them. He blessed them with his presence for just a short while before continuing on his way toward the setting sun.

Chapter 9

Two young black boys came running into the camp. The taller one called out, "*Bwana! Bwana* Dubois, they are here; they have returned!"

Seated in a canvas-folding chair, Dubois folded the topographical map that he had been studying. Removing his reading glasses as the two boys stopped in front of him, he asked, "What is it, Valli? Who has returned?"

Slightly winded, Valli tried to catch his breath, "The elephants! Just like I said. They have returned to the field where we saw them last."

Standing up, Dubois laid his hand on Valli's shoulder. "Good work, Son! I can always trust you to find me fitting sport!" Looking down at the smaller of the two boys, he continued, "You too, Khosa, good work! Now let's go see what we're about to add to our little food bank." Picking up his Mark V Deluxe Weatherby magnum rifle, he followed behind the two boys.

Approaching the clearing, the three crawled through the weedy underbrush. As he peered past the edge, Dubois twirled the end of his handlebar mustache, delighted at the size of the two adolescent bulls. He was slightly disappointed at the small tusks they were carrying, but he consoled himself with the thought of the high price that he would be paid for the young trunk steaks.

Valli whispered in his ear, "See, *Bwana,* big and young. Tomorrow night when the butchering and cooking is done we will feast on the juicy meat of one of those feet. The pit and hot coals will be ready for the roasting and the celebration of your hunt!"

Not wanting to dampen his enthusiasm, Dubois let Valli quietly rattle on. He had proven himself very useful over the last couple of months as a good tracker. With just a bit of fatherly encouragement and praise, Valli was as loyal and eager to please as a well-trained dog. He was committed to Dubois and easy to manage. The little one, Khosa, was Valli's shadow. He was just happy to go along for the ride, stroking his big brother's growing ego.

A bit of good luck happened for the poachers as one of the elephants turned and started walking directly towards them. The other one followed closely behind.

Staying quiet, concealed by the brush, Dubois lined up the rear v-notch with the front blade sight on the ramp, centering on the elephant's forehead. Waiting for the elephant to come very close before firing, the three lay as still as logs in the green leafy underbrush. They waited and watched as the two young bull elephants silently crossed the field of grass.

Showing great patience, Dubois did not fire until the animals were at the perfect distance for his .460-caliber rifle. As the first animal came within twenty-five yards of the Frenchman, Dubois' finger tightened against the trigger. He felt the tension in the cold steel slightly resist his touch before giving way. In less than a fraction of a second, the five-hundred-grain bullet entered the skull of the bull. As it struck the brain, the young male collapsed to the ground, exposing the elephant following behind.

The second elephant, alarmed and confused, moved around the still body of his companion. He rubbed his trunk over the area where the bullet entered and smelled the unfamiliar scent of blood. Kneeling down, he butted his head against the other's back, trying to help it rise.

In the quiet of the brush, Dubois waited patiently for a clear shot of the confused elephant's forehead. Rifle ready, he was steady and focused on the elephant. Nervous tension built in the Frenchman's hand, waiting for the split-second opening when he could clearly take the other down.

A rush of excitement filled the three poachers. The taking of any animal with one shot is the finesse of the hunt every hunter strives for. But the taking of one of the Big Five game animals of Africa in one shot is an admirable feat. The adrenaline flowing through Dubois' veins pumped his heart strong with pride at his shot. Yet he remained calm and steady, totally focused on the actions of the young bull that was desperately trying to bring his companion back to its feet. The seconds stretched out like hours. Khosa began fidgeting to his left, and then the young boy jumped to his knees yelling, "Look there!" His arm flashed across the rifle's barrel, bumping it out of Dubois' grip.

With one quick sweeping motion, Dubois knocked Khosa back into the bush. "Get down, you fool!" he snapped.

The small elephant trumpeted and turned to face the three hiding in the bushes. Dubois stood, steadying the long, heavy rifle barrel the best he could, aiming toward the approaching animal. The bull's quick bouncy, pace made it a much harder target. The shot rang out, striking the moving animal high on the broad forehead, missing the brain. The stunned animal slowed his pace. Now an easier target, the second shot checked the elephant's approach. He shook his big head and wobbled a few feet forward, still determined to reach the man. Quickly Dubois reloaded and took aim. The third shot brought the unsteady beast quickly down to the earth.

Standing between the two boys, Dubois snapped at Valli, "Let's go and finish the job. Leave the boy here so he can't cause any more trouble." Khosa still lay in the brush where the big white man had knocked him. Wide-eyed and near tears, he looked towards his brother for support. Valli scornfully gazed down at his little brother as he followed Dubois out into the field.

Jumping up, Khosa started running after them, shouting, "You don't understand! Look!" He pointed again to the west side of the field.

At the same time the frantic boy got their attention, an old bull elephant trumpeted. The roaring blast poured from the creature sending a sound wave that vibrated in their chests. He raised his head high, picking up his massive ivory tusks and charged.

The surprise of the old bull delayed Dubois' reactions. The length and girth of the ivory captivated his attention, prolonging his aim.

As the man came to his senses and shouldered his rifle, the old bull smartly checked his stride. Just as the rifle was fired, the elephant turned and lumbered back into the forest.

Without hesitating, Dubois turned and smiled at Khosa. His handlebar mustache rose wide and no longer hid his stained teeth. Laying his hand on the boy's narrow shoulder, his voice gently stroked the young boy, "You did well, my son. Now hurry back to camp and bring the others to start butchering the first kill." Turning back to Valli, Dubois saw the fire of the hunt burning brightly in the young man's eyes. The Frenchman exclaimed, "Let's go find that old bugger."

Running up to the spot where the elephant had turned, Valli inspected the ground and weeds looking for any sign of blood, an indication that he had been hit. Following its path to the forest edge, high on a branch a drop of red sparkled on a leaf. "Got him!" Moving into the shadows of the trees, Valli knelt down looking at the prints in the soft woodland floor. "Look here, he is injured. See how one step is slightly deeper than the others are? He is lame."

"Good man, Valli," Dubois said as he twirled his mustache. "Now follow his spoor as far as you can and report back to me later tonight. I must get back and finish off the other one and see to the butchering." A pat on the back sent Valli trotting into the forest.

Walking back towards the two gray humps lying in the field, Dubois watched the men and women hacking away at the carcass. They carried the meat back to camp to carve it into strips and hang it to dry. He thought they looked like a group of black ants swarming over a bowl of food left on the ground after a picnic.

The other elephant was mortally wounded but was still stirring. Reaching out with his trunk, he tried to grab anyone who walked close by. His trumpeting had quieted, but still he called out with a deep pitiful rumble.

As Dubois crossed the field, a sparkle of light caught his attention from high above the black and yellow-streaked bluff. Raising his hand, he shielded his eyes from the harsh noon sun as he looked across the edge of the cliff. With the naked eye he could see nothing unusual. He decided that he had just imagined it or that it was the sun reflecting off mica rock, a common rock made up of thin sheets that glisten like glass in the sun's light.

The wounded elephant lay quietly now, just the slight rise and fall of his side indicated that he was still breathing. A stream of blood was leaking from the openings at the end of his trunk. The three bullet wounds trickled bright red blood down his forehead encircling his eyes. His will to avenge his pain on the human was still great. As Dubois stood over the elephant, it raised its trunk weakly trying to reach him. To pull the man down and squash him into the dirt was his only desire. His massive strength was failing him. Coughing, he blew splatters of blood over Dubois' pant legs.

Dubois rolled his eyes in disgust at the dying animal. As he did so, another sparkle of light caught his attention from the same spot on the bluff. This time he knew it was not his imagination. He called out, "Khosa! Come here."

The young boy hurried his way, "Yes, *Bwana?*"

Not taking his eyes from the bluff's edge, he said, "Hurry back and fetch my binoculars and the radio."

As the boy ran off, Dubois pointed his rifle a few inches from the adolescent bull's head. A crooked smiled rose under the long handlebars as he thought about the huge profit he would make trading the elephant meat for timber-cutting rights in Uganda. Pulling the trigger, he ended the elephant's suffering.

"Base camp, come in base camp. Dubois here, do you read me? Over."

Static distorted the French-accented voice answering the radio call, "Base camp here. You're coming in loud and clear. Are the packages ready for pick-up?"

"We're wrapping them up now, and we're trailing a third with a lot of decoration."

"Copy that. We'll prepare transport for the first two packages."

"Wait on the transport. I've got a special project for the sentries."

"Go ahead."

"Bring them on in. Drop them on top of the middle bluff. We have a live audience up there that needs to be taken care of."

"Affirmative. Sending the sentries to bluff for scouting and securing. Out."

Looking through his binoculars, Dubois watched the four figures resting in the shade of a tree. They had not realized they had been spotted. Several minutes had passed before a faint rumbling was audible over the forest canopy. The helicopter was on its way.

The workers skillfully carved the flesh off the face of the elephants, exposing the white fatty tissue around the embedded root of the long teeth. They carved carefully and slowly, avoiding marring the surface of the ivory. The meat from the trunk was crudely cut into big chunks and carried to the campsite for carving into dinner steaks. Some of it would be dried for later use and some packaged for immediate sale. Sections of the hide behind the ears were pulled for tanning and would be used for leather goods. A doorway in the elephant's belly was cut and, when the skin fell open, the entrails slid out in a messy stream of hot blood and fluid. Barefooted, one of the butchers stepped gingerly among the tangled web of intestines into the ribbed room, removing the liver and heart.

The first elephant was nearly completed when the helicopter's rotors could clearly be distinguished. As the helicopter became visible over the forest, Dubois glassed the bluff through his binoculars once again. There was movement.

"Ground to airborne. We have movement on the bluff. Do you spot? Over."

"Affirmative ground. Movement spotted. We'll look for a clearing to drop lives. Out."

As the helicopter flew overhead towards the bluff, "Airborne to ground. We have a clear view, there are two blacks, two whites and a dog." The helicopter hovered over the top of the bluff. "One of the whites is a female. Over."

"I don't give a damn! Just drop the sentries and make them disappear. Copy? Out."

"Copy. Will make them disappear." Gunfire was barely heard over the boisterous beating of the rotors. "Approaching small clearing preparing for delivery. Out."

At the first sight of the helicopter, the group on top of the bluff got up, exposing themselves and running back into the forest. Minutes later they were back at the bluff coming down a narrow path along its face. The trail led underneath overhangs and behind large boulders, occasionally blocking them from sight from above the cliff's top and the valley below.

The gunmen finally arrived at the edge of the bluff. Not seeing the trail that wrapped around the gnarly old tree, they paced back and forth along the edge looking for a sign showing which way the group ran.

"Ground to airborne. Viewers are on the trail climbing down the face of the bluff beginning at the twisted tree. Signal the men."

"Roger ground."

The helicopter hovered near the face of the bluff at the twisted tree. From there the pilot was able to motion to the gunmen on the ground. They soon found the narrow trail and began their descent.

"Khosa!" Dubois yelled.

Running over, Khosa replied, "Yes sir?"

"Find four warriors with sharp spears and long bows. Send them to find where the trail ends. Tell them not to take any prisoners alive, but to set their souls free. Do you understand?"

"Yes sir!" Pride swelled in his chest as he ran off to carry out Dubois' special orders.

The helicopter hovered in front of the bluff's face occasionally getting close and stirring up dust. The flinging dirt hampered the gunmen's ability to follow the group's trail.

"Ground to airborne. Get the hell away from there. Proceed to designated landing area and prepare for package pick-up. Over."

"Copy ground. Proceeding to base camp. Over."

Dubois watched the four senior warriors that Khosa had chosen, swiftly run across the field. As they were disappearing into the tree-lined riverbank he thought, "Now we have them. Nobody is going to spoil the operation for me this time."

Chapter 10

With her 300mm lens, MacKenzie had photographed the young bull elephants at play and interacting with the old bull. A fresh roll of film captured the old bull wandering off toward the forest in the west. The young bulls did not follow the old one. Instead they marched single file to the north. From above the top of the bluff, the group watched in silence. The only sound was the camera motor as it advanced the film.

When the elephants were midway across the field, one dropped to the ground. A second later, they heard a loud pop.

"What happened?" MacKenzie asked as she continued viewing the area through her camera lens.

"What do you think, Jon? .450? .500?" Zawawi asked.

"It had to be. That was a seriously loud boom."

Lowering her camera, MacKenzie asked, "What are you two talking about?"

"Poachers, Ms. Mac. The caliber of their rifle."

"Oh God. No, not here!" Looking through her camera, she asked, "Where are they?"

They watched from high above at the edge of the bluff as the other elephant moved around his companion. He tried to lift his friend by butting his head up against its back. Not understanding why there was no response, he moved around to the head, rubbing his trunk over the still body. Lingering over the bloody forehead, the tip of his trunk fingered the stream of blood. Placing the tip in his mouth, he sampled death. MacKenzie photographed the tender gestures made by the young bull.

Movement in the brush had caught Jon's attention. "There!" he pointed.

Swinging her camera over, MacKenzie was able to get a couple of frames of a black boy who jumped up from the brush and pointed to the west. As she continued to shoot, she captured a white man standing up and striking the boy across the jaw. Speaking just above the hum of the camera's motor, she asked, "What is he doing?"

Mhinga quietly said, "The old one has returned, and the small poacher has spotted him."

Elbowing Jon in the side, MacKenzie lashed out, "Do something!"

"Like what? It is already over."

The men's movement in the brush caught the young elephant's attention. With a forceful trumpet, he began his charge at the men. A shot rang out slowing the elephant's stride. A second shot stopped the elephant, and he stood there, stunned, shaking his head.

"Are you just going to sit there and watch him die?" MacKenzie's face was starting to turn red with anger.

"What do you want me to do? Stand up here and yell down at him, 'Don't do that. It's against the law'? "

"Ms. Mac. Any interference could put our lives in danger." Mhinga tried to smooth over the tension between her and Jon.

"Well, if you're not going to stop the killing, then call Simon on that radio of yours and have him get out here and arrest them! Will you at least do that much?"

With a nod of approval, Jon retrieved the radio from his pack. Dialing the correct frequency, he pushed in the long button and spoke into the speaker, "Big Dog, come in. This is Little Pup. Over." After several seconds carrying nothing but static, Jon repeated his call.

Finally a woman's voice broke through strongly, "Little Pup, this is Travel One, are you all right?" Colleen's voice was filled with worry.

"Yes, Travel One, but we have a situation. Where is the Big Dog?"

"He is here. I will get him. Over."

While they waited for Simon to come to the radio, a third shot had dropped the elephant to the ground.

"Big Dog here. What's your situation, Little Pup?" The distance of the radio waves could not mask the sound of concern in Simon's voice.

"We are watching two, possibly three tuskers being taken."

"Are you in danger?"

"Negative, we haven't been spotted."

"What is your location?"

"Do you remember the valley where the Suam River forked below the bluffs?"

"Where we used to fish when we were kids?" Simon was unsure of the location.

"Negative Big Dog. Much further up stream, below the Mt. Elgon escarpment."

Butting in, MacKenzie exclaimed, "Oh for Pete's sake! Give him these coordinates!" MacKenzie handed Jon her GPS receiver. Showing on the digital screen was a small satellite map indicating their longitude and latitude coordinates.

"Big Dog, U.S. *Sumbua* has given me the map coordinates. They are . . . ." As Jon began to relay the information to Simon, two men emerged from the brush, soon followed by a third. The old bull released a trumpet blast, getting all of their attention.

Over the radio, Simon heard the noise. "What the hell was that?"

"The biggest old elephant that you ever saw."

Simon was alarmed, "I thought you said you weren't very close!"

"We're not. We're on top of a 300 foot cliff, and the elephants are in the valley below."

"My God." Simon continued, "How many poachers do you see?"

They watched as another shot rang out, looking up just in time to see the old bull dart back into the forest. "Looks like just three of them. One of them is white."

"Do you recognize any of them, Little Pup?"

"Negative, Big Dog. But Sumbua has them on film."

"I have mapped your location. Our helicopter is down waiting for parts. I will load the truck with a few men. We won't be able to get there until tomorrow evening."

"Affirmative, Big Dog. I will check in with you later. Over."

"Affirmative, Little Pup. Out."

Quickly, Jon tried to catch Simon again, "Big Dog, are you still there?"

"Affirmative, Little Pup."

"Correction on the number, add a dozen or so natives. This white guy is well organized."

"Roger. Out."

Turning off the radio to conserve the battery, Jon smiled at MacKenzie. "There, do you feel better now? Now that the cavalry is on the way?"

"No, not until I get a good photo of that poaching bastard to help Simon throw the book at him! At least the big old bull got away."

In the shade of the old tree high above the valley, they watched as the black man scouted the area where the old bull had turned. Running off into the forest, the scout left the white man to return to the kills.

Zawawi finally spoke, "The old bull may have gotten away, but he is injured."

MacKenzie asked, "How do you know that?"

"Did you see them looking at the branches in the tree and the foot prints on the ground? The old bull was hit high near his right shoulder."

Jon reached up and slowly lowered MacKenzie's camera. "He may have seen us."

"From this distance? What makes you think so?" MacKenzie asked.

"See what he is doing? He is viewing the bluff. He saw something. My guess is he caught a reflection of the sun hitting your camera lens."

They watched the white man return to the mortally wounded animal. They saw how even in the shadow of death, the elephant reached out with his trunk trying to grab at the man. Powerless, they viewed the gunman point his rifle at the wounded animal. MacKenzie raised her camera and photographed the elephant's final moments, spraying blood over the poacher in his last effort at defense. After a pause, the white man fired his last shot.

The black who had given away their position earlier in the hunt approached the white man. Then he ran off into the woods in the north, heading back in the same direction that the other natives carried large chunks of meat. He returned a few minutes later to the white man carrying two small items. It was soon clear that one item was a pair of binoculars, as the white man scanned the edge of the bluff again.

"We might not be so lucky now, *Kacha Ngozi,*" Zawawi added. "He saw something."

"Yeah, I think you are right. Looks like he is radioing for support."

MacKenzie asked, "Are we in trouble now?"

Looking into her eyes, he wanted to lie, but could not. "We could be. Are you ready for a hard run?"

"If my life depends on it, of course, I can do it!"

Jon started to speak but was interrupted by Zawawi, "Listen! Do you hear the rumble?"

MacKenzie answered, "Sounds like distant thunder."

"No thunder, Ms. Mac. It's too consistent." They listened to the noise, trying to decipher its origin. "Sounds like a helicopter."

In the western sky, a black dot appeared above the tree line in the horizon. As it drew near, its shape became clear. It was indeed a helicopter, and it was coming straight at them.

Jon took charge, "We've got to make it back to the thicket before they land."

Without waiting for replies, he was up and running, leading the others along the trail through the thick woods. They had just crested the mountaintop when the helicopter flew directly overhead and hovered. Looking up, Jon could see the code numbers on the fuselage were masked over with tape. Through the window he could see a man looking down at him.

Sliding the window open, the man pointed his rifle down at the ground and opened fired. *Rat-a-tat-tat,* the bullets flew wildly. Instinctively, Zawawi grabbed Mhinga and flung him to the ground. Jon grabbed onto MacKenzie and dived protectively alongside a fallen log.

The helicopter circled, trying to get a clear view. The gunman continued firing. Bullets slammed into the forest floor, splintering leaves, sticks, and small bits of stones, showering them in every direction. The strong wind from the rotors whipped the rising splinters into shrapnel, spinning the debris as if caught up in a tornado.

The rattling noise of the gun subsided as the gunman emptied the clip. Jon raised his head over the top of the log. The blowing debris stung his face as he searched for Zawawi and Mhinga.

Zawawi too had seized the brief break in the assault to look around the trunk of the large forked tree he and Mhinga were huddled behind. Each man flashed an okay sign.

The helicopter still hovered overhead. The canopy of trees prevented it from landing. Their height and leafy branches kept the gunmen from getting a clear view or jumping out. Slowly the helicopter circled, and then, raising a bit, it moved off towards the east.

Jon watched it move out of sight, and then shouted loudly over the roar of the engine. "They are going to land in the butterfly field! Quick, back to the bluff!" From their hiding spots they ran back to the tiny trail that led in front of the old twisted tree.

"Buster! Where's Buster?" Jon's cries carried throughout the woods. Buster heard his name called and turned back towards Jon's voice. Fear showed in his eyes as he ran towards them.

The rocky path along the face of the bluff slowed them down, but the overhang gave them protection from above. The path wound its way behind large boulders, hiding them from view of the valley below. They stopped for a quick breather. Mhinga noticed armed native men crossing the river. "Look *Bwana!* They are coming up the hill too. We are trapped!"

Jon could hear the helicopter coming back over the mountaintop. Quickly he gauged their position. It wouldn't be long before their enemies would find their trail and would be firing down upon them. The four men coming up the trail could be taken easily since they carried only spears and bows. Jon was the only one with a gun. With MacKenzie in the group, a gun or hand-to-hand battle would be a last resort and they could not win against the men coming down the hill.

The helicopter had cleared the bluff and was slowly moving back and forth across the face looking at them. As Jon looked back up the trail from where they had come, he noticed a wide A-shaped opening in the face of the bluff along the trail. It was only about three feet tall before it began to pinch off and taper into just a tiny crack. It was not at all noticeable coming down the trail and would be barely noticed by someone running up the trail.

Pointing to the crevasse, he ordered, "MacKenzie, you first. Take Buster with you. Mhinga, you follow, then Zawawi."

On her hands and knees, MacKenzie crawled into the crack calling to Buster, who followed her willingly. The crack went back half a dozen yards before making a series of hairpin turns back on itself. The height of the crack had lessened and she had to remove her backpack, scooting it in front of her as she went along. It was more like a tiny dark tunnel now that the sunlight from the top of the crack had become a pencil-thin line. She kept moving over the dusty, pebbly, narrow space, scooting on her stomach and elbows. The light reflecting off the stone walls was barely enough for them to see by. The walls were so close together, her shoulders scraped against the sides. Around a bend, the tunnel ended. She called back, "It has stopped!"

The message was relayed down the line. Moving backwards, Jon had been brushing away their markings left behind in the dirt with a small dried scrub brush hoping to discourage any of the gunmen from looking down the tiny crack that they had crawled into. Helping them to conceal their trail, the wind from the helicopter's rotors was stirring up dust along the cliff trail erasing all traces of their tracks on the path.

If the gunmen did find their hiding place, Jon thought he might be able to take a few of them out and hold them back for a little while before being taken out himself. The idea of openly firing on men, face to face, brought a sick feeling to his stomach. There was nothing else he could do but wait and hope that the gunmen did not find them.

As the helicopter pulled away from the bluff, Jon could hear the voices of the men searching for them along the trail. It was just a matter of time before the gunmen coming down and the warriors coming up the trail would meet. Checking that his rifle was fully loaded, he clicked off the safety. One cartridge in the chamber and three in reserve, four shots before reloading. The odds were not very good. But if he were close to them before firing, the big, heavy .375 bullets would pass directly through the first man, and take out the second. He would have to be lucky.

At the end of the crawl space, MacKenzie stared at the rock formation in front of her. Something did not quite look right. The stones were of a different color and texture than the walls she had been crawling between. Propping herself up on one elbow she reached over her pack and dusted the orange red wall in front of her. She was right; it was not a natural formation. The colored rocks had been carefully mortared in place. Pulling out her knife, she opened it up where the sturdy needle-nose locked into place. With shaky hands she began hacking at the mortar. Her reach over the pack was not long enough to allow her any strength. In a demanding voice she called back, "Zawawi, send up your spear. I may have found something."

Without hesitating, his spear was passed up to her. She could now easily reach ahead to the wall and pick at the mortar. With just a few good strong pricks, the mortar started crumbling away. As she pushed, the melon-sized stones fell inward, exposing a small cavern. As the first light entered the cave, the squealing sounds of bats echoed through the opening. "I found a cave!" She slid her pack into the hole first. There was a small drop to the floor, which was cluttered with the rocks she had pushed in.

Buster balked at going into the dark hole. MacKenzie coaxed him from inside while Mhinga pushed him from the behind. Once inside the cave, MacKenzie held the dog tightly in her shaky arms and stroked his smooth coat as the others crawled in. Buster, too, was quivering with fear and he licked her face for comfort.

Jon was still dragging the brush behind him. With everyone safely inside, he and Zawawi quickly replaced the stones in the opening, leaving the brush propped up outside to mask the freshly opened doorway.

In the dark again, the bats quieted. The ceiling inside the little cavern was dome-shaped and tall enough for standing upright. The uneven floor was covered with a thick, soft layer of bat guano, and stinky stale air filled their safe haven. MacKenzie felt in the darkness for her pack. Scraping off the guano, she rummaged around for her small flashlight. Just as she switched it on, Jon found his, too, and passed out the two spares to Mhinga and Zawawi. The dim beams of light waved over the wall of the cave, soothing their anxiety and, fortunately, having little adverse effect on the bats.

Feeling secure in the darkness of the cave, MacKenzie broke the silence, "Why would that little opening have been sealed shut?"

Shining his light around the walls, Zawawi answered, "Because of him."

Everyone turned to look at the small spot of light that wavered on the crumbled remains of a guano-covered skeleton. Lying on a narrow natural shelf on the back wall of the cave, the bones coated in black filth were hardly recognizable as being human.

Mhinga asked in a quite respectful hush, "Do you know who it is? Or from what tribe?"

"No. I know of no tales of a Maasai King being placed in these hills. It means nothing to me."

MacKenzie joined in the conversation. "Well, whoever wanted him in here sure went to a lot of work crawling around those curves dragging a stiff body behind them."

"You know, Mac, you're right," Jon spoke up. "I bet there is another opening, and they sealed this little one to keep any animals out. But where?" They all shone their lights at the walls, but found no openings.

Mhinga cried out, "The bats! They were not going in and out through the doorway that we used." Shining his light up, he searched the ceiling. "There! In the ceiling, an opening!"

"It sure is big enough to get a body through it." MacKenzie was thinking out loud.

"It doesn't look like it goes very far," Zawawi added.

"Mhinga," Jon started directing, "climb up on my shoulders and have a look around."

Sitting on Jon's shoulders, Mhinga was able to see that the hole in the ceiling opened up into another smaller room over the burial room. "Can you crawl up into it?" Jon asked.

"Yes, but I will need to stand on your shoulders to reach the top of the ledge."

Clinching his flashlight between his teeth, Mhinga grabbed hold of the top ledge for balance. Then, steadying himself, he was able to pull up where he could get a foothold on Jon's shoulders. The ledge was just high enough that he could wiggle his upper body over the edge. "Okay, I'm up."

"Okay, Mac, you're next." Getting MacKenzie to his shoulders, Jon asked, "Do you think that you could lift Buster up to Mhinga?"

"I can try." There wasn't a lot of enthusiasm in her voice, but Zawawi picked up the muddy-pawed dog and handed him to her.

Lying on the floor, Mhinga leaned over the hole. Reaching down he was able to grab the dog around his barrel chest. Buster whimpered as he was pulled from MacKenzie's arms.

As the pooch left MacKenzie's grip and rolled over onto the ledge next to Mhinga, she called down, "Zawawi, hand me the packs." One by one he handed her the gear, and she passed it up to Mhinga. Finally she reached up, taking Mhinga's hand. Steadying herself, she lifted her foot on top of Jon's shoulders, and wiggled up onto the ledge.

From outside the lower cave, voices were echoing between the walls of the crawl space. The gunmen were crawling towards them. Zawawi offered cupped hands to give Jon a boost up to the hole. "Don't argue with me, just go. We are running out of time. Trust me I will be right behind you." A second later Jon was on the ledge.

The voices were growing louder as the gunmen arrived at the hidden doorway. "Quickly!" Zawawi ordered in almost a whisper. "Place my spear across the opening, hold it steady or wedge it under a rock so it doesn't move."

Zawawi could hear the voices outside talking about the dead end of the crawl way. He jumped up reaching out for the spear's staff, just missing it by inches. He jumped again, still a bit short.

One of the gunmen had discovered the cut bush and the rocks that were neatly stacked behind it. Zawawi jumped again, his fingers just swiping the underneath side of the staff.

The first rock was pushed in. The light from outside riled up the bats into a squealing fit. Zawawi jumped again just as the second rock fell to the cavern floor. The tips of his fingers nearly reached around the diameter of the spear's pole.

The voices outside were growing louder, and the rocks now easily fell to the floor. Again Zawawi jumped, and this time he had a firm hold on the wood. "Lights!" he whispered, and the flashlights were immediately clicked off.

As more of the rock wall tumbled in, Zawawi tucked his knees up to his chest, then hooked them over the spear, inching his way closer to the ledge. Once there, Jon and Mhinga pulled him up and over. Quietly they removed the spear and backed away from the opening. Hiding in the darkness of the upper room they huddled together, listening as the men below knocked in the remaining rocks.

Chapter 11

The gunmen entered the cavern firing their weapons. The crashing of their automatic rifles inside the peaceful burial chamber sent the bats into an uproarious fury. Thousands of the small winged creatures swarmed around the men's heads in panicked flight.

A few of the bats were able to get past the noise and confusion, finding their way up through the ceiling into the tiny room above. Flying in reckless, confused terror, they were striking whatever happened to be in their way. The swarm of mad bats pinned the four fugitives down on the hard stone floor, in the darkness of the upper cavern.

In the area known as the twilight zone, where total darkness meets dim natural light, Buster was struck several times by the terrified bats. The frightened dog leaped towards the dim light glowing from the room below. As the dog brushed by, MacKenzie grabbed the supple skin of his neck. The momentum of the clutched tackle pulled them backwards into the darkness. The added weight of her body started the pair into a sliding roll. Fearful, the dog snapped his powerful teeth, and struggled violently to free himself from the girl's arms. She strained to gain a better grip on him. The reverberation from the gunfire and the high-pitched squeals of the bats completely concealed all sounds of the threatening growls.

Pulling herself on top of Buster's back, MacKenzie had the dog pinned to the floor. Reaching up she felt for the dog's head as he tried to reach back and bite whatever was holding him from escaping. Finally she was able to clamp one hand around the dog's muzzle and wrap her arm around Buster's stomach. They wrestled in the blackness, bumping into Mhinga.

Laying face down on the rough cold floor with his hands protecting his face, Mhinga felt something scrape the length of his forearms. Instinctively he reached out into the darkness and grabbed for whatever was attacking him. Once firmly in his grip, he recognized the feel of the dog's hind legs struggling about wildly for freedom. Feeling around he was able to grip both hind legs in one hand. With the other he switched on his flashlight for just a second shining it towards the dog's head, immediately quieting Buster's fighting. Both the dog and the girl were panting with fright.

The gunfire had stopped. Seeing an empty room, the armed men found humor in the small number of bats that lay dead or flopping wounded on the cavern floor. Hundreds of empty shells lay in the midst of their few tiny victims. Many more bats were settling back to their inverted roost on the ceiling, squealing their protest at the invaders. Clowning around, one of the gunmen changed to a fresh clip and opened fire on the bats overhead. In one bulky cloud the bats swooped off their perch, sweeping down onto the gunmen before rising towards the opening in the ceiling. Standing in the center of the cavern, the armed men watched the massive flock of bats fall and rise upwards. The others opened fired too, this time knowing their intended victims. Their massive rapid firing hammered into the gritty limestone ceiling of the cavern. The gunmen, consumed with foolishness, ignored the earthy shower they were bringing upon themselves.

Once again, the roar of gunfire masked all noise. Through the floor Jon felt the high velocity-bullets gouging into the soft rock below where he lay. In the dim light he watched the dense cluster of bats scattering overhead into the darkness of a small low passageway in the back wall. Crawling on his hands and knees he followed below the thick cloud of panic-stricken bats. Once he had passed the others, he switched on his flashlight, and they followed quickly.

After a short distance, the passageway enlarged into a tall, bell-shaped tunnel. They were nearly able to stand upright. The gunfire behind them had quieted. Jon motioned for the others to move past him around a corner for protection.

Standing by Jon's side, Buster pricked up his ears. Tilting his head, he began to whimper. Jon reached down and stroked him on his back, wondering what it was that Buster was hearing that he could not. At nearly that same moment, his question was answered by a low rumbling noise that quickly grew louder. Buster barked out just seconds before the tunnel began to tremble. Small bits of rock were loosened and fell from the low ceiling. There was no place to take cover. The best they could do was cluster together, placing their packs over their heads for a little protection. The disturbance lasted only for a few long seconds before a large cloud of dust came barreling down the tunnel from where they had just escaped.

Gagging and coughing from the dust, Jon checked on the group. Then pulling the edge of his tee shirt up over his nose and mouth he said, "Wait here, I'm going back to see what happened." He crawled back into the low passageway with his flashlight clenched in his teeth. The beam of light glared into hazy brown air. Unable to see more than a few inches ahead, he had to feel his way through the tunnel. His progress was slowed as he pushed aside and maneuvered over the newly fallen rocks.

Reaching out with his hand, feeling the ground for his next crawling stride, he felt only open space. He was on the verge of falling forward. Regaining his balance he settled down, switching off his light to conserve the batteries, waiting in pitch-blackness for the dust to settle. Sitting there alone near the edge, he listened for sounds of anyone who might have survived the cave-in.

In a short time his breathing was easier and the air less gritty, the heavy cave soot was settling. Clicking on his flashlight, he was amazed at the devastation.

The small burial cavern had doubled in size. The floor was littered with large boulders. The bullets penetrating into the ceiling had weakened the thin limestone shelf that had made up the floor of the upper room where they had sought sanctuary. It had completely collapsed; bringing down with it the ceiling the bats had been roosting on. The entranceway they had found mortared closed could not be seen. The newly fallen rocks now solidly protected the low natural shelf that held the blackened bones of the unknown native. There was an eerie sound of silence in the freshly sealed tomb that brought both the relief of safety and, at the same time, a sense of terrifying turmoil. Turning around, Jon crawled back to the group.

"What did you find, *Bwana?*" Mhinga asked for them all.

"Total destruction. The upper room has fallen in and taken the dome ceiling with it." His voice lowered, "We're not getting out that way."

"So we're trapped in here?" MacKenzie whispered.

Mhinga tried to cheer her up. "If the bats found a way out, we can too."

Smiling over at him, MacKenzie laid her hand on Mhinga's shoulder, saying, "Bats are very tiny, and they can fly." Her voice dropped, "We are trapped."

"Ms. Mac, remember, whoever brought in the body of that dead chief had to enter somehow." Mhinga's words calmed her a bit.

"Do you think the people in the valley will send up a search party? We could wait." As the words left her mouth, MacKenzie realized how silly it sounded.

Zawawi rolled his eyes, "Yes, why don't you just sit here and wait for the search party." He moved closer to her, and she took a step backwards. His voice deepened, "Perhaps they will find you before you die of starvation or you freeze to death." Leaning over, he looked down at her and continued almost in a whisper, "And while you're waiting you can let your mind imagine how they will torture you once they get you out of here."

Realizing he was right, her mind raced over the possibilities. She fought back the urge to cry. Too scared to move, she stared back at him, not knowing what to say.

In the small brightness of the flashlights, Zawawi could see he was getting to her. Her skin grew very pale and her shoulders slumped. The lack of a quick response gave proof that he was winning the battle. His voice dropped even lower, "You're a spoiled, stupid, white woman, who has brought this fate on all of us."

She didn't know what he was going to do next; she was afraid of him. She had lost a lot of ground, and he knew it. Somehow she had to gain it back. From deep inside herself, she pulled up strength. Her shoulders squared as her back straightened and she looked him square in the eyes. "Okay, Chief, then you get us the hell out of here! Go on and lead the way."

Zawawi waved his index finger in MacKenzie's face. As he took in a deep breath to unleash upon her, Jon intercepted. Forcing himself between the two, he pushed them apart. "Stop it, both of you." Anger filled his voice, as he said, "I've had enough of this!" Pointing his finger at MacKenzie, he spoke slowly, gritting through his teeth, "You just keep quiet." His eyes widened and his face trembled, "Not another word out of you." His patience had reached its breaking point. "You do as you are told. Follow along and keep your mouth shut." He turned away from her just as tears started to fill her eyes.

Jon's voice was a knife-edge, slashing out at Zawawi, "From now on, you leave her alone." The authority in his voice was not one that even the brave Maasai warrior would challenge. Jon pointed down the dark tunnel, and his voice lightened a little, "Now let's see where this tunnel goes. Zawawi, you lead the way. Mhinga, you and I will conserve our flashlights for later. We will follow in-between these two to keep them apart."

As they walked quietly through the bell-shaped tunnel, the tension traveled down the line. Buster tuned into it too, and followed ever so quietly next to Mhinga.

MacKenzie had wiped her tears on the dusty sleeve of her tee shirt, leaving dark streaks of brown dirt across her cheeks. She knew she had to pull herself together. To take her mind off the tension and fright, she forced herself to think of happier times. Her mind wandered back over her college days, remembering courses, friends and professors. She thought that her geology professor would be envious of her now as she roamed through this unexplored cave. The short session on underground study came back to her quickly as she looked about, recognizing standard formations and types of minerals. She was starting to feel better.

Suddenly the tan sandpapered walls expanded in height and width before forking into a much larger tunnel. Zawawi stopped at the intersection. Looking back at Jon, he asked, "Which way?"

Pulling out his compass, Jon determined that the section of the big tunnel they were in ran north and south, parallel to the bluff that overlooked the river.

MacKenzie walked about the intersection of the connecting tunnel. It was large enough for a small car to drive through. The walls and floors were sandy smooth. Speaking quietly to herself she said, "I bet this is a karst cavern."

As they all turned to her, Jon asked, "What is that?"

She hesitated, remembering the tongue lashing Jon had given her an hour earlier. Turning away from them, she answered very softly. "A karst cavern carries a stream, often showing smooth bottoms. But this looks dead, like there hasn't been any flowing water in here for a very long time."

Sarcastically, Zawawi said, "Now she is an expert on caves!"

Twirling around, her anger flared fast, "No! Not an expert, Zawawi," MacKenzie glared at him and her voice toughened, "Just a college course in geography."

He snapped back quickly, "Fine, since you are so well educated, you lead the way out of here."

"Will you two stop it?" Jon growled. "We've got to stick together." Trying to hold his temper, he said, "Mac, do you know anything else about caves that might help us get out of here?"

Anger flushed her face, and she tried to force a smile. "Oh! Is it okay for me to talk now? Are you giving me permission?"

Walking over to her, Jon fumed, "I've had enough of the sarcastic remarks from you two." He turned away from her and took a deep breath attempting to regain his composure. Slowly, he added, "Mac, do you know anything that would help get us out of here?"

She felt so frightened and confused. Jon turned back, looking at her, waiting for a reply. The pale blank expression on her face and dark streaks of dirt under her eyes made his heart sink to the pit of his stomach. It bothered him seeing her like that. He crossed over to her, cupping her face in the palms of his hands. His thumbs whipped the dirty tear marks from her cheeks. Very softly he spoke to her, "We are all afraid of being trapped in here. And we must find a way out before we run out of food and water." He felt her starting to tremble. "If you know anything that could help, I for one would like to hear it."

The gentleness in Jon's voice brought a tiny smile to MacKenzie's face. She took a long deep breath and relaxed a little. His hands touching her gave her a feeling of hope and protection. They slid down to her shoulders, allowing her space to compose herself. "I don't know much about caves. We studied them for just a few weeks. General stuff. But a karst cavern usually opens up at a river, creek, or underground spring.

The river outside may have once run through here."

Mhinga approached, adding, "If she is right, *Bwana,* the gradual slope of the floor would indicate that the water flowed down to the valley."

"We're wasting time here. We should be moving on." Zawawi turned and walked on down the tunnel. Mhinga and Buster followed.

Alone together, Jon put his arms around MacKenzie and pulled her close. She did not resist, but allowed herself to melt into the safety and comfort of his arms. He felt the tension across her back and shoulders. He rocked her, swaying back and forth. "Oh Mac, we're going to be okay. We're going to get out of here and find your father and the other scientists." He gently squeezed her tight, and he felt her body relax a little bit. She felt so delicate in his arms. "Do you believe me?" he whispered.

Her shoulders began to tremble and she sniffled back, fighting the urge to cry. Her face was buried in the soft cushion of his shoulder.

"I need for you to believe in me and be strong." He pulled her away, looking down into her tear-filled eyes. Embarrassed, she looked down at the ground. Jon tilted her face upwards, wiping tears from her cheeks. "Can you do that? Will you be strong and believe in me?"

MacKenzie could not speak, but she gave a tiny nod.

"I need to hear you say the words."

Choking back the tears, her trembling lips whispered, "I can be strong."

Cupping her face in his hands, Jon was drawn into her glossy eyes. Ever so slowly he leaned down and softly kissed MacKenzie on the forehead.

"Say the other words," Jon whispered. "I need to hear you say them."

Feeling slightly dizzy, she softly sighed and whispered back, "And I believe in you."

Tenderly, he kissed her salty-moist cheeks. "Always. Say you will always believe in me."

Tilting her head back she could feel his stubbly growth against the smooth skin of her cheek. Her voice was so low and tiny, he barely heard her. Instead, he felt the breath of her words escaping. The moisture caressed his lips as she whispered to him, "Always." And he covered her lips fully in a long deep tender kiss.

Chapter 12

Zawawi's flashlight batteries had gone dead. He was now using one of the spares to lead the way. They traveled in silence down the main tunnel as it gently snaked back and forth. When a branch was found, Mhinga and MacKenzie waited as Jon and Zawawi explored. Each time the offshoot tapered down to an impassable crack. After several hours of traveling in the faint light, the tunnel still showed no formations or any characteristics of a live cave.

The floor began a series of short steep ramps, each longer and steeper than the one before. The last one in the series plunged down very steeply. They had to sit and slide down the ramp to reach the bottom. At its base there was a large opening in the floor. Crowding around the hole they gazed down into its darkness. Their flashlight's beam was not powerful enough to reach the bottom. Searching around, Jon found a loose stone and dropped it down the cavity. After several long seconds, the tiny ping of a splash barely echoed up the tall chimney.

Zawawi broke the silence, "That's a long way down."

Quietly, MacKenzie added, "About one hundred and eighty feet."

"How do you know that?" Mhinga asked.

"Simple. Acceleration due to gravity multiplied by the length of time squared gives you the distance."

Mhinga was puzzled. "What?"

"Oh, it's just basic physics."

"One hundred and eighty feet to the water below." Jon was thinking out loud. Looking at Zawawi, "Do you recall any underground springs along the river?"

"Jon, it has been so long ago since we last fished that river." Zawawi closed his eyes trying to visualize his childhood memories of when they had last camped and fished in the area. The group remained silent as he concentrated.

Opening his eyes, he smiled at Jon, "I do recall a bubbling spring along the east bank downstream from the bluff. About half a mile or so."

Jon dropped another pebble down the shaft. They sat and listened until they heard the tiny splash in the water. Jon repeated, "One hundred and eighty feet."

"Too far to jump," Zawawi muttered out loud, "and we don't have a rope."

He and Jon seemed to be working from the same mind as Jon finished Zawawi's thought, "and the shaft is too wide to scale down."

"Even if we were to get to the water, we still don't know where it goes."

"Or if it comes out at the river."

"Or how far under water it might come out."

"Back to plan A?"

"Yes, *Kacha Ngozi,* back to plan A."

The two men looked at each other with a whimsical grimace, and they began to snicker. Jon's voice cracked, "Just like old times, my friend."

"Yes, just like old times."

The two men settled back still thinking over the situation.

Looking back between the two, MacKenzie asked, "And what is plan A?"

Jon answered, "We continue on the same way until we meet up with C."

"Plan C?" she questioned. "What was plan B?"

"That, my dear," Jon smiled warmly at her, "is one hundred and eighty feet too deep."

As Zawawi rose, he sarcastically muttered under his breath, "College educated."

They traveled on for several hours. The slant of the tunnel's floor took them ever downward. Their spirits leapt each time the floor would abruptly drop or a new chimney was discovered. Dropping a small rock down each shaft confirmed that the distance to the stream below was becoming progressively shorter.

Finally the flashlight's beam was able to reach the bottom of a shaft. A clear shallow stream was a mere fifty feet below. Still too far for the untrained group to scale the walls without safety gear, so they continued on.

Another of the flashlights had lived out its life. They were down to just two. But their spirits remained high, knowing they might soon escape the confines of the gloomy cave.

The cave's ceiling was gradually getting lower and the walls were narrowing as well. Jon and Zawawi had to stoop down to avoid bumping their heads. The cavern floor was sloping very steeply and then abruptly fell away in a sheer rough wall about twelve feet high. At the base of the wall was another chimney. The edge was as sway-backed as an old pack mule. For years water had rushed over its edge, falling into the shaft. Both sides of the concave center were jagged with rocks jutting out, creating good holds to climb down.

Coaxing Buster to make the long leap was the most difficult part. A little persuading with buffalo jerky did the trick. Buster followed his hunger, lunging from the high point into Mhinga's arms, knocking the young man onto the old stony floor. The grateful dog gobbled down the piece of meat as his cold nose sniffed and prodded Mhinga's hands and face for another piece. Not finding anything but a strong scent, the appreciative animal licked his friend's face until he cried out with laughter, "Jon, please get your silly dog off of me." His words were barely audible through the laughter.

Jon's call to Buster went unnoticed. "I guess he is very hungry."

"Get him off!" Mhinga's, voice was failing.

The sight of Mhinga trying to wiggle out from under the big dog that was showing his great appreciation for the nibble of food made it all the funnier to the others. The cave was echoing with the sounds of their laughter.

"Make him stop!" Mhinga was out of breath.

Jon finally reached over and grabbed the dog by the loose skin on his withers, pulling him off the young man. With his other hand he offered to help his friend up. "I'm a little hungry too. Got any more of that buffalo?"

Dusting himself off, Mhinga answered breathlessly. "Some, but you must promise not to jump me like Buster." He gathered up his pack and pulled out the remaining pieces of meat. "There's not a lot left, so we must ration it." He handed one long strip to each member and another small piece to Buster.

The strips of meat awakened their hunger. Knowing that this would be the only food for a while, they ate very slowly, savoring each bite. Resting on the cave floor, they passed the canteen of water around, each taking one big swallow. The water was rationed, too.

Zawawi was the first one to stand. "We must keep going."

The others took their lead from him. Getting up, Jon knocked some loose pebbles over the edge of the shaft. With all the commotions of Buster, Mhinga, and their meal, they had forgotten to check this chimney's depth.

"Mac, how far?" Jon asked.

"I wasn't paying any attention. Drop another one in." There was no splash just a ping from the pebble hitting the floor. MacKenzie did the math in her head. "About twelve feet. No, that can't be right. All the others were so long. Drop another one in."

They all gathered around the opening. Silently, they shined their flashlights down the shaft. They could easily see the dry, rocky floor below. It was very close indeed. Mhinga broke the hush, looking puzzled at MacKenzie, "What could have happened to the stream?"

"I guess it could have branched off in another direction. Or the stream could have found another chimney and gone down to a lower elevation. It could have even gone further underground to the river." Looking at Jon, she said, "It's not very deep. It might be worth exploring."

Zawawi added his opinion, "I think that we should just keep going in the same direction. If this pinches out, we can return here. If we all go down there without any climbing gear, we would not get back up here if that," he pointed down the hole, "goes nowhere. We know that this tunnel is running downhill and is turning towards the bluff and river. I believe this will lead us to a way out."

"Well, what if someone went down there and took a look around, backtracking and possibly finding the stream of water? We could at least get the canteens filled," MacKenzie added.

"You are full of foolish ideas. White women should remain quiet."

"Hey, you two," Jon intervened, "don't start in on each other now."

"*Bwana,*" Mhinga spoke up, "though Zawawi speaks the logic, Ms. Mac does have a good point. We will need water to go on."

"Mhinga, I knew that you would side with the woman." Zawawi crossed his arms over his chest.

"Wait a minute, you two," Jon cut in. "You both have good points. How about this? Mhinga and Mac climb down the chimney and backtrack the lower tunnel looking for the stream, and refill the canteens. Zawawi and I will go on down this tunnel and see what becomes of it. We will all meet back here in two hours. He and I will be able to pull you back up the shaft using his spear."

Zawawi grumbled something under his breath so low that the others understood his meaning without hearing what he had said. MacKenzie looked down the shaft. The walls were only about ten feet long, leaving the headroom height in the lower tunnel about four feet. They would have to crawl once they reached the lower level.

Without any hesitation, Mhinga shed his backpack and lowered himself into the egg-shaped vertical passage. With his back up against the semi-smooth wall he braced his weight with his feet on the opposite side of the tube. First he worked his feet in two small backward steps down the tunnel. Then pushing his forearms against the wall behind him, he lifted his body away from the wall. Gravity began to work and his torso moved down the shaft a couple of inches. Then he pushed with his legs again and braced the weight of his body up against the wall. He continued slowly down the shaft until he reached the bottom edge. There he leaned forward, reaching out with one hand to the opposite side. With each hand braced against opposite sides of the shaft, he released the pressure in his legs, untwisted his body, and fell straight down the remaining few feet. The rocky uneven floor disrupted his smooth landing. Limber as a cat, Mhinga took the unbalanced stop with a roll, avoiding a sprained or broken ankle.

MacKenzie came down the tunnel the same way, only without the steady grace that Mhinga had exhibited. At the end of the shaft, he was able to help her make the transition to the cave's floor.

Jon dropped one of the flashlights and the canteens down to them. "Set up a pile of rocks to mark the spot. We will meet you back here in two hours." Jon's face disappeared from the hole's opening.

Clearing the area under the opening, they piled a large stack of rocks in a pyramid form. They would not miss this marker on their return. Down on their hands and knees, canteens hung around their necks and tossed onto their backs, they crawled off into the flashlight's glowing beam.

Rising away from the edge of the hole, Jon grinned at Zawawi, "Now it is truly like old times, my friend."

Grinning back at Jon, Zawawi said, "Yes, except we don't have Simon's life to save this time."

"No, we have our own."

Looking down, Zawawi's voice lowered, "Yes." Picking up his spear and pack he brightened, "Let's go and find our way outside."

The two men walked down the main tunnel, hunched over to avoid the low ceiling. Buster followed close behind. With only one flashlight to light the way, the tunnel felt smaller.

The floor retained its gradual slope. As the roof got lower and lower, they were soon on their knees crawling. They came across several more chimneys; each one was about the same distance down but smaller in diameter. They were quickly approaching the one-hour mark when the tunnel pinched down to a narrow squeeze. They were about to turn back when the passageway started to change. They first noticed a strange light scent of ammonia. As they prodded along, the smell became stronger. Then they crawled into a black sticky film of dampness that covered the floor of the tiny chute.

"Jon, we must be near an opening. This is bat guano." There was joy in Zawawi's voice.

"Shine the light up. Can you see any bats?"

Deep in the crevices above where they crawled, Zawawi shined the flashlight. Green glowing eyes looked back. "Yes, I can see them, a small colony. There must be a . . . Oh damn it!"

"What happened? Are you all right?"

"Yes, the little bastards just shit on me. They got me on the fore-head."

Jon could not hold back the laughter. "You should be very hopeful that Mac and Mhinga find the stream and bring back the water, my friend."

"And you as well, *Kacha Ngozi,* as we are both going to be quite rank after crawling in this shit. How are we on time?"

"We've only got a few more minutes before we need to turn back. Keep going. We must be near an exit."

The trough-sized tunnel was so small that Jon could barely see Zawawi ahead of him. He made his way by feeling in front of himself, occasionally reaching forward and touching the soles of Zawawi's sandals. Buster had not given up either. In the darkness, the dog crawled between Jon's feet.

The smell of ammonia was clearing and the floor had dried of moisture. The tiny squeeze made several sharp turns. Ahead of them dim gray shadows formed on the floor and walls. "I'm seeing shadows! We have reached an opening." Around the next sharp curve the tunnel opened into a deep mouth on the side of a bluff. The muted light of the setting sun was so strong it instantly blinded the two men and the dog.

They basked in the warm breeze that whisked across their cool dampened bodies while they waited for their eyes to adjust to the strong natural light. After a short while they were not so sensitive to the light and were able to look around at their position. The mouth of the opening was high on a bluff. There didn't appear to be any way down.

Rising above the surrounding treetops were several columns of gray smoke in a line swaying in the evening breeze. Rising with the smoke was the smell of fresh meat cooking. The two men, muddied with black bat guano, looked at each other with dread across their faces. In unity they mumbled, "The poacher's camp."

Chapter 13

This is the last one." MacKenzie's voice echoed softy across the small cavern stream. The flashlight was lying next to Mhinga as he leaned over a small ledge and reached down into an icy stream to fill the canteen. The light reflected across the swift-moving shallow stream, shining waving images of rings and streaks onto the opposite wall and low ceiling. The damp, chilly air spread goose pimples across their exposed skin. When the last of the gurgling noise quieted, Mhinga handed the wet canteen back to MacKenzie. After fastening the lid tightly, she placed it with the other three. Sitting down on the floor, leaning up against the cold stone wall of the cave, she waited for Mhinga to wriggle back from the ledge. Dusting himself off, he noticed a strange look on MacKenzie's face. He laid his hand on her shoulder, "Is something troubling you?" he asked.

"Oh, I was just thinking about how Zawawi is always objecting to my advice. What makes him so bitter towards white women?"

Sitting down across the small tunnel from her, Mhinga sighed, "I don't know all of the details, but I will tell you what I do know. You will have to accept it as I tell you."

MacKenzie gave a little nod.

Mhinga continued, "Zawawi's first wife was Moyo. She is the mother of Valli and Khosa."

"The two poaching kids we met back at the logging road?"

"Yes. Moyo lost her life because of a white woman Jon was involved with."

"That's terrible. How did it happen?"

"I don't know. Neither Zawawi, Jon, Simon, nor Colleen will talk about it. It is a forbidden subject for all of them."

"Simon and Colleen were involved too?"

"Involved? I don't know about that. I was still quite young when it happened. But, yes, they were there. They will not discuss it. My respect for them tells me I don't need or want to know. You see, for a long time after her death, Zawawi distanced himself from the others. He turned his back on them, not seeing them as family and blood brothers. They would still be this way today if it had not been for Colleen begging them to work together to help rescue Simon. His life was in grave danger last year, and they needed each other's help to save him."

"While I was at the airport, Simon told me about the lung wound he received from a poacher."

"Yes, but it was much worse than just a single gunshot wound in the lung. Simon was with a small group of men on a routine scouting drive when they stumbled across a very large poaching operation. They were overpowered and many men died. Simon barely escaped with his own life, and would not have if Jon and Zawawi had not worked together to save him. During that rescue mission, a bridge was rebuilt. It is still a bit shaky, because Zawawi still clings to the past, but it is growing stronger each day of this trek."

"I guess I'm not making it easier on the two of them."

"Perhaps you are just what they both need. Only time will tell." Glancing at his watch, he said, "We should be getting back."

"Wait." She grabbed his arm. "What do you mean by, 'I might just be what they both need'?"

Thinking for a moment, choosing his words carefully, he said, "You may have started the rebuilding of Zawawi's trust in white people." Mhinga turned and started to crawl down the tunnel.

"And Jon?"

With his back towards her, MacKenzie could not see the wide grin on Mhinga's face, but there was a joyous tone to his voice. "You may have started building a bridge of respect for women in Jon. No more questions on that subject, we must get back to the chimney."

"Wait, I've got one more."

Mhinga's shoulders slumped. "Okay, what?"

"What happened to the poacher who nearly killed Simon? Did they get him?"

"No. He escaped and Simon has sworn to bring him in. Colleen calls it 'his deal with the devil'."

"Do you think he will do it?"

"It is unlikely. They know nothing about the man except he is white, speaks French, and has a long mustache. He just disappeared from the landscape like the animals he killed. Judging by the equipment they seized, Simon believes he had some very powerful friends. Really now, we must get back."

MacKenzie crawled quietly behind Mhinga. Her mind swarmed back over all that Mhinga had told her about Zawawi and Jon. Just the thought of Jon rekindled the feelings of his embrace. She could recall his breath on the sensitive skin of her cheek and the soft touch of his lips covering hers. A blushing rush came over her. She was glad that Mhinga was not looking back at her to see the glowing smile on her face.

They did not have far to crawl before reaching the rock pyramid that marked their chimney. Looking at her watch, she said, "You know, we've got forty-five minutes to waste before the guys will be back. What do you think about leaving the canteens here and exploring down the tunnel the other way?"

"I think that would be fine as long as we are back here on time. Otherwise, Jon will be upset and Zawawi will have more to complain about." They arranged the canteens and the shoulders straps to form an arrow, pointing in the direction they were headed.

The tunnel twisted and turned more than the big upper tunnel they had been passing through. More chimneys rose up through the ceiling and down into the floor. They dropped pebbles down each one. The distance varied greatly.

"How are we doing on time?" Mhinga asked.

"We are almost at the halfway mark. Do you want to head back?"

"I see another chimney in the floor up ahead. Let's check it out first." Crawling on, Mhinga stopped by the edge and tossed in a pebble.

MacKenzie worked the math in her head, calculating the distance. Yawning, she said, "About twenty or thirty feet."

"Which? That is quite some difference."

"You are such a perfectionist, Mhinga," MacKenzie joked. "Okay, drop another one in."

Reaching his hand over the center of the hole, Mhinga released another pebble. "Hey!"

MacKenzie interrupted him, "You'll have to do it again. I lost track when you spoke."

"Ms. Mac, I feel warm air rising up through the chimney!"

Astonished MacKenzie asked, "What did you say?"

"I feel a breeze!" Mhinga leaned over the edge and looked down the stony tube. "And I see faint shadows! We may have found the way out!"

New life filled MacKenzie's voice, "Drop another pebble. We must know how far it is to the bottom." She did the calculations in her head. "About thirty feet. We could climb down that!"

Pulling her away from the edge, Mhinga cautioned, "Ms. Mac, we must go back and wait for Jon and Zawawi, perhaps they have found an easier way out."

They marked the opening with a pile of loose stones before crawling back to where they had left the canteens.

❖ ❖ ❖

"All we can do is wait for them to come back."

"Jon, they should not have gone off to explore."

"They probably didn't have far to go to reach the stream and fill up the canteens. We told them two hours. They will be back soon. At least they left us a sign which way they went."

"That must had been Mhinga's idea," Zawawi said.

"Mac could have thought of it. She's pretty smart," Jon protested.

"Why must you defend that stupid *mzunau?* She is nothing but trouble." Zawawi chuckled, "I have given her a good name, *'Sumbua'.*" Seriousness took over and his voice dropped, "They are all so stupid."

"Zawawi, Mac is not stupid, Nor is she a bad woman."

Looking deeply at his friend, Zawawi asked, *"Kacha Ngozi,* do you have feelings for this woman? If so, then I must correct my opinion of your judgment."

Jon smiled and looked down. "I'll admit that I am attracted to her," he replied.

"And?" Zawawi prodded.

"And, well . . . I don't know. She is somehow different from the others."

"She is the same as the others. Perhaps a little smarter; but the same. She will bring you trouble and great grief. It has already started."

"How?"

"She has Mhinga wrapped up in the palm of her hand. His heart is still so pure. He doesn't see her as the white demon that she is. I fear the same is growing true for you."

"Zawawi, you are my blood brother. But I think you are letting the past cloud your judgment."

"Jon, you are my blood brother, and I remember the past so I can prevent the same demons from reappearing in the future."

Reaching over, Jon lay his hand on Zawawi's forearm. "Mac is not the demon from your past. Yes, she is strong-willed, and she is educated in ways unknown to us . . ."

Zawawi interrupted, saying gently, "And she has blinded you, my old friend. Good thing that I am your friend and will try and protect you from such a demon."

"And I will try to help you let go of your past."

"Jon, she is what she is and soon you will see it for yourself."

The two men sat in the dim silence, no longer challenging each other's opinion of MacKenzie. Buster had curled up next to Jon resting his head on Jon's lap. The cool damp air of the cave had allowed the raw edge of his wounded ear to scab over. As Jon stroked Buster's side, he let his mind wander back to when he held MacKenzie's trembling face and felt her smooth skin and her soft lips on his.

The daydream was broken when tiny voices echoed up the chimney. Mhinga and MacKenzie had finally returned. Standing upright inside the chimney, Mhinga stretched his stiff back, calling up, "*Bwana?* Are you back yet?"

Looking over the top of the opening, Jon replied, "Yes, Mhinga. We have been back for a short time. Where have you been?"

"We found the stream and filled the canteens. Then we went off in the opposite direction. We have seen shadows made by the outside light. It may be a way out."

Leaning over the hole, Zawawi looked down at Mhinga. "We have also found an opening to the outside, but it is up high on the face of the bluff. Is your way accessible without a rope?"

"We don't know. It is down a crevice about thirty feet. At this hour the sun is setting, and the light will be gone soon."

The two heads that were peering down at him suddenly disappeared. Mhinga could not hear clearly what Jon and Zawawi were discussing. After a couple of minutes, Jon's head reappeared. "Okay, we're coming down. We'll drop the packs down to you first."

Zawawi leaned over the hole as far as he could reach and dropped the packs down. Mhinga caught each item and passed it on to MacKenzie. She dragged the packs a short distance down the little tunnel.

"Stand back, Mhinga, I'm coming down." Hanging from the edge of the opening, Zawawi released his grip and dropped the short distance. Reaching back up into the tunnel, Zawawi called to Jon, "Okay, drop Buster down to me."

Jon had one arm wrapped around the dog's chest, and with the other he was scratching Buster's stomach. The delightful rubbing put Buster in an ecstatic trance, so he was totally unaware of being held over the opening in the floor. Jon released his grip and the dog quietly dropped into Zawawi's arms. At impact, he whimpered just a tiny bit, licking Zawawi's face before being set down on the floor. Ducking down, Zawawi crawled out of the stack so Jon could make his drop.

Mhinga took charge. "It's not far, but we must hurry before the light leaves us."

They crawled quickly over the tunnel's rough terrain. Mhinga led the way, followed by MacKenzie, Buster, Zawawi, and then Jon. They passed all the unmarked chimneys until they reached the one marked with the pile of rocks. "This is the one," Mhinga said proudly.

Crowding around the entrance, they all looked down into the darkness. There was just a hint of light showing at the bottom of the hole. Reaching over to shine the flashlight down the crevice, Jon felt the updraft of warm dry air. Turning to MacKenzie, Jon asked, "How far to the bottom?"

MacKenzie sneezed. "About thirty feet. What is that smell? It is making me sneeze!"

Zawawi ignored her, "Looks like the wall is a little over half of that distance."

The shaft was oval in shape, long and narrow. The sides pinched off into tiny cracks. It was about three feet wide. Jon said, "The rocky sides will make it easier to scale down."

"And then just a short drop to the bottom," Zawawi added.

Still sneezing, MacKenzie interrupted again, "What is that smell? Is something dead down there?"

Jon looked at Zawawi. The Maasai's face was smeared with fresh bat guano and frustration. "Zawawi, why don't you go down first and look around?"

"Good idea, Jon," he replied, glaring at MacKenzie. "When I get to the bottom, drop my spear and a flashlight." With his bedroll strapped to his back, Zawawi quickly lowered himself into the opening. Using the exposed rocks as foot and handholds, he straddled the opening and climbed down the shaft. Once he neared the bottom, he eased the tension in his legs and dropped to the uneven floor. The loose stones wobbled his landing and he fell on his butt.

Jon called, "Are you okay?"

"Yes, just a rough landing." Standing up, he said, "Drop the spear and flashlight." Zawawi caught them in free flight. "I'll be right back. I can see the night sky."

The twilight of dusk allowed just enough light to glow around the cave's opening. There were thousands of brittle white bones crunching under his feet. Large cats must have used this cave as a den. As the Maasai neared the opening of the cave, he switched the flashlight off. Rounding large boulders that partially concealed the opening, Zawawi could smell the aroma of roasting meat. Squatting at the opening, he could hear muffled voices, and he knew they were near the poacher's camp. Silently he crept passed the boulders and scrub bushes that hid a narrow animal path, following along the face of bluff. Only a skilled and artful tracker would have seen and recognized it in the dark shadows of dusk. The sun was disappearing behind the tall mountain and treetops. The stars were beginning to show a bright array of colors as Zawawi turned and made his way back around the boulders. Turning on his flashlight, he passed over the scattered bones that had been long ago stripped of their meat. Zawawi gave a soft light whistle, and Jon recognized it as a sign of friend approaching and to remain quiet.

Soon Zawawi's light was seen at the bottom of the long shaft. Softly, Jon said, "What did you find?"

Zawawi spoke very quietly, his voice muted in the echo, "Exit found, near poachers. Come down quietly."

Chapter 14

Everyone was settling down for the evening. Dubois allowed the cooking fires to blaze a bit larger than normal. The laborers had gotten their work completed in record time. Not just one elephant butchered, but two. Dubois was very proud of this little well-organized group that he had formed.

It was all running so smoothly, until today when the four strangers were spotted on top of the bluff. One quarter of his men were lost in a cave-in trying to remedy the situation. It was because of that loss that he allowed the workers to celebrate the day's hard work and mourn the loss of their co-workers. They would soon be forgotten, for the new replacements were on their way.

The women passed around clay pots filled with warm, freshly brewed beer. Two of the elephant's feet and lower legs had been buried in hot coals and had been slow-baking all afternoon. The meat was so tender and moist it fell apart in big juicy chunks. The food and drink turned the solemn evening into a small festivity of dance and songs.

The fresh chunks of the roughly butchered meat had been shipped by helicopter across the border into Uganda just before dusk. In the deserted mining town of Lifi, Dubois maintained the hub of his secret trade. There the meat was further processed and packaged before being transported to either a presidential palace or to a large rented freezer warehouse located in the Congolese city of Ouesso, the heart of the bush-meat commerce.

All of the prime tender cuts from the elephant trunks would go into the various government palaces of central and western Africa. There the meat would be served to only the most important guests and many of Africa's top government officials. In return Mr. Dubois' family timber business would receive special recognition for timber-cutting across these countries.

The surplus and lesser cuts of meat were often shipped out of the country to restaurants in Western Europe. The demand for bushmeat in Europe was growing steadily stronger as it became part of the trendy food scene.

The junior CEO's of Camino Timber Enterprises had no idea how Dubois was bringing in such large lucrative contracts, and they did not care. Business had never been better, and the profits were allowing each board member to live high. When Dubois was questioned about it, he simply explained, "It is like an old boys' club. It is all about who your friends are." After that, no one questioned his expense reports again. No one questioned the cost of or need for leasing helicopters, or a warehouse, or paying cash for laborers or porters. It could all be justified as company overhead during and in-between production operations. Dubois was bringing in big contracts and big profits, thus keeping everyone happy back home.

No one involved kept records of the kind or the amount of meat, nor where it went. Promoting his family's timber business between hunting trips, Dubois spent his time visiting presidential palaces. There, some high-ranking official would always mention when an important banquet was scheduled. With just a word, Dubois would then ensure that a special carrier delivered the supplies.

The bushmeat was always a delight for the host to serve at his dinner parties. It was understood that in exchange for the meat, a few thousand acres of timber clearing rights would be available at a small price. After all, it was for the good of the general public. New jobs were created for thousands of people, and afterwards the roads supplied easy access to new rich, fertile farmland. The bushmeat trade appeared to be a win-

win situation for the country as a whole.

Dubois sat outside his small canvas tent sipping a warm brandy, watching and studying his workers. Mostly they were men, but a few women worked as cooks and caretakers. The laborers were from a variety of places. Some came from cities and others from vastly different countryside, all from different tribes. They left their tribal loyalties behind, joining to create their own tribe. Their King was Dubois, and he thrived on being the supreme ruler and lawmaker. Mostly, there were no problems. The laborers were paid twice as much as they would be making back where they came from. For this reason alone, they willingly gave him their respect and loyalties. All stayed for the money, and that included Petrus.

A pretty young woman in her late teens, Petrus worked as Dubois' personal cook and servant. She had long slender legs, a narrow waist, and shapely full breasts. Her quick bright smile brought a childlike appearance to her hardened soul. She had run away from home before her father was able to trade her off in marriage for three goats and a cow. At thirteen she found herself alone in a big city. There she met Ms. Bowie, who ran the presidential harem. The madam was street smart and wise in the ways of men. Thus she took in young pretty girls and taught them the trade.

That is where Dubois first met Petrus, working as a high-priced prostitute in the presidential palace in the Congo. He had come to like her smart wit and professionalism about her work. She knew the cost of unprotected sex, the disease known locally as 'Slims disease' or more commonly known to the rest of the world as AIDS. Dubois would always bring with him a case of condoms as a gift for Petrus whenever he would visit. They became friendly, and soon Dubois discovered that Petrus was a useful ally. During their visits she would often discuss privileged, private information about the palace guests and goings on. The information was always made available for a fee, and it was always worth the price. She was smart, confident, and had a sly streak. Most of all, Petrus was a grand actress. Dubois loved to watch her work her talents to get the things she wanted and the information he needed.

Once, while visiting the palace, Dubois requested a visit from Petrus. Ms. Bowie informed him that Petrus had been barred from the palace when she refused to carry out a guest's special request. For insulting the guest, she had been severely beaten and dumped out on the street. "It was regrettable," she had said, "Petrus was a good earner. But . . . ."

Enraged, Dubois searched the streets until he found her. Her face was badly bruised, her left eye was barely able to open, and her soft lips were cut and swollen. Dubois carried her to a doctor's office. After a few days of care, she started to come around and be herself again.

Dubois offered her a position on his personal staff. After some negotiations, she accepted. She was given a monthly salary for cooking and tending to his clothing and personal gear. She was to be given free rein to continue her business, keeping all proceeds and choosing whom she wanted. Any valuable information that she could uncover would be paid for as a bonus. Dubois accepted her terms, and her employment quickly proved to be quite beneficial.

Over the past several months, however, Dubois had given Petrus a special assignment. He wanted her to keep Valli happy, to bring him into full manhood, and keep him loyal and feeling indebted to Dubois. Petrus got him to open up to her about the goings on within the laborers group. This information was often relayed through Valli's little brother, Khosa.

The whole camp seemed to be taken with Khosa, so all talked freely to him. He would talk to his brother, and Valli, in turn, told Petrus. She secretly reported all to Dubois, who in everyone's eyes, always stayed on top of things. The Frenchman magically provided what was wanted or needed before things got out of control. With advance knowledge, Dubois also stopped any conflicts among his workers before they got out of hand.

It was an easy assignment for Petrus, and one that she enjoyed, taking a young man just growing into puberty and teaching him how to properly touch and make love to a woman. The only drawback for her was his inability to separate love and sex. It hampered her time spent with other men, the ones Valli and Khosa were unaware of. Quietly and slowly, she dropped all but her favorite, Taveta. When she brought this to Dubois' attention, he subsidized her income to encourage her.

Valli's charming boyishness faded away. His desire to please himself first took over. Petrus became bored, for he lacked control and stamina. He believed he could take on the world and please all women. Petrus, the actress, kept him believing, while she found her own satisfaction in the arms of another.

Khosa became aware of the change in Valli, although he did not understand it. Together, they were as they had always been, two brothers exploring the world, looking out for each other. But the evenings were different now that Valli spent more and more time with Petrus. So Khosa spent his extra time with the laborers. They took him in as a member of their extended group, and he was happy, as always.

Petrus was keeping a special eye on Khosa tonight, for Valli had not yet returned from tracking the wounded elephant. She watched him from across the camp while she prepared Dubois' meal. He had a wide friendly smile and a gentle nature. She thought that he would not become as tall as his older brother, but would be equally as strong. She smiled at the thought of getting to train this puppy, too.

Dubois watched her as she carried the plate of food over to him. As she sat the plate down, his eyes caught hers. As if he could read her mind, he said, "Don't go getting any bright ideas about Khosa. He's too young yet, and we need to keep the brothers together for now. You've got Valli on top of the world, and I want him to stay there. He works much better now that you two have paired up."

Looking back over her shoulder at Khosa, she replied, "I've got no plans for the puppy. Though it might be an interesting project to start one so young."

Dubois leaned forward in his canvas chair. "Listen, Pet," he said, looking hard at her, "you will wait until I say the time is right. *Comprenez?*"

Her eyes narrowed. "I will wait, but you will not call me Pet. My name is Petrus. Understand?"

Dubois leaned back in his chair, a crooked smile cracked along his thin lips. Slipping into his native French, "If it pleases my little pet," he knew that she did not understand. She smiled back at him with the same devilish grin before turning to leave. The rustling noise from the brush behind the tent stopped her. Valli was jogging in, winded from the elephant pursuit.

"Ah! You have finally returned, my son," Dubois said, delighted to see Valli. "Tell me about the elephant's spoor."

While Valli tried to catch his breath, Dubois turned to Petrus, "Be a sweet and get this noble tracker a cool drink and a plate of food." With a nod and a kind smile she was off.

Valli sat on the ground at Dubois' feet panting from the long run. Slowly he began telling the story of the elephant's trail. "It had been hit high as we thought, but not severely. The old bull ran hard and fast. After a couple of hours there were no signs of blood to be found. You may have only grazed his back."

Dubois did not like to hear that he had made a bad shot. He had hoped the wounded animal would not have been able to run far. He watched Valli's face as he told the story. Neither man noticed when Petrus brought the water and plate of hot meat. She sat the plate down and stood back, listening to the story and awaiting her next order.

Valli continued, "At last light, I could see that the big beast was growing tired. There were marks on the soft ground where his long tusk marked the earth, and his lameness was still showing. If he rests tonight, he will be stronger by tomorrow, and we will have lost much ground on him."

Without speaking, Dubois sat back in his chair pondering his limited resources to aid in tracking the big tusker. The helicopter would be busy transporting the packaged meat from Uganda to Congo. The transport trucks would be of no use to them in the dense jungle, and they would be loaded with the laborers anyway. They would have to go out on foot. By the time they tracked the old tusker down, the helicopter would be available to bring in both the meat and those rare, long ivory tusks. The meat on such an old bull would be useless. The ivory was the only prize, perhaps the grandest prize of all. He could make a small fortune on those tusks in the oriental black market. He allowed himself the pleasure of basking in the large numbers for just a second longer, for there was much work yet to be done. He was brought out of his dreamland when Petrus broke the silence.

With the sweet sincerity of a young schoolgirl, Petrus exclaimed, "You are wounded!" The shock and concern in her voice was so real that for just a moment even Dubois was taken in.

Reaching over his own shoulder, Valli could feel a long narrow tear down the back of his shirt. A branch must have snagged it when he was running through the woods. His skin had a tiny scratch and a dried bloody scab. "It is nothing," he said in his newly found man-voice.

Dubois watched in awe as Petrus once again transformed into a talented actress playing the young girl. With concern and softness in her voice, she lowered her eyes, "I worry it may become infected, if it is not treated." Her voice dropped again, "Your shirt will need mending."

"Go on, man," Dubois encouraged. "This pretty girl wants to tend to your wound. You don't want to disappoint such a nice girl, do you?"

Valli was unaware that Dubois knew about his relationship with Petrus. Shyly, he rose. "No, sir, I don't want to disappoint her."

"Good man," Dubois continued, "but don't let her keep you up late. You will need to be rested and ready to move out right after day-break if you are going to lead me to that old tusker."

"Yes, sir. Day-break. I'll be ready." Valli grinned with embarrassment as he turned and walked away with Petrus. Softly he spoke to her, "You heard our King. I must not disappoint you tonight."

Still carrying on in her role, Petrus giggled as they walked across the campgrounds. The laborers were just about all down for the night, and only a few guards wandered about changing post. As they passed one of the guards, she caught a nod from Taveta. He would be waiting for her in the wooded area just beyond the bushes. Not letting on, she looked up, smiling at Valli. "You have such an important job with *Bwana* Dubois. There are so many men that work for him. They would love to be in such an important position as you. Do you realize how lucky you are?"

"Quiet now, my little pet," he placed his finger softly over her lips and she kissed it.

She hated to be called pet. But he thought it was cute, so she went along with it as part of her job to keep him happy.

"I am very good at tracking. That is why *Bwana* Dubois has hired me. I feel only lucky to have you all to myself."

Not truly listening, her mind wandered off. Knowing that she would be in Taveta's arms soon made this act bearable.

As they made their way out of view from the others, Valli pulled her closer and walked with his arm over her shoulder. He continued, "You heard that I must get plenty of rest tonight, so I can lead him to the old elephant tomorrow."

Snapping back into her role, she began, "Does that mean . . . ."

"No, my little pet." He continued, "My black mamba snake is rising and hissing for you as we speak. He will strike out swiftly for you tonight." With that his hand dropped and started tickling her narrow waist. Unable to resist the sensation, she laughed uncontrollably. Her knees buckled and he gently guided her collapsing body to the ground. "My dancing snake makes you happy?" Valli boasted, as he lay nearly on top of her in the long grass of the clearing.

"Oh yes," she answered breathily. She was not sure if it was a question or a statement. "I've never known about such a thing before you came along. You make me so happy. You are all I think about while you are gone hunting with *Bwana* Dubois."

"Soon my little pet, I will tell *Bwana* about our love, and we will be joined in marriage and have many children."

She had to fight herself from showing her true feelings. She was thankful for the cover of darkness and for the full moon casting its shadow over her face, concealing the look of disgust that must have shown. She wanted to get away from this boy and his foolish dreams. She must end this time with Valli quickly, so she reached down and giggled in her girlish role, "Where is this snake you brag to me about?"

"I will show you, my Pet." He guided her hand down below the belt of his shorts.

She giggled again, carrying on in her role as sweetheart. "We will need a muzzle for your snake's venom." Reaching into her pocket, she removed a small cellophane wrapped condom, all the while thinking about being in Taveta's arms where she would not have to act.

Chapter 15

Shoulder to shoulder, concealed by scrub brush and the falling darkness, Jon and Zawawi lay quietly in the mouth of the cave. They listened to the singing voices of the workers in the poachers' camp muffled by the thick forest. The nearly full moon cast shadows, completely concealing the small animal path that lay within a few feet of them. Whispering, Jon asked, "Can you make out anything? What are they singing about?"

Zawawi whispered back, "No. Not a word. They are too far away."

"That is to our advantage," Jon said mostly to himself.

"Yes, especially if they think we are dead from the cave-in. Their guard will be down."

"I think we should wait until the camp quiets down for the night before we head out."

"Yes, we could use the rest too. I'll take the first watch."

"Good. I'll bring you some water to wash your face and see what Mhinga has left over for a meal." Jon crawled back around the large boulders, finding that a small fire had been built. MacKenzie had begun warming up the leftovers and boiling water to make tea. Mhinga was applying medicine to Buster's scabby ear. Kneeling down beside him, Jon asked, "How's it doing?"

"Oh, much better. The moist air has really helped it. Will we be leaving soon?"

"In a few hours. We are just above the poachers' camp. We will wait until they settle down for the night."

"Good. The bright moon will help light our path." Mhinga pointed over his shoulder towards MacKenzie. "She is heating up all that is left of the food. I'm afraid there isn't much."

The mention of food made a rumbling noise in Jon's stomach. "If we can get far enough away before first light, we will be able to hunt again. I'll take Zawawi up a plate."

"*Bwana,*" Mhinga reached into his pack, removing a bar of soap, "take this to him and a canteen of water to loosen the guano from his face and hair."

A boyish grin flashed across Jon's face. "Thanks, Mhinga, I don't know what I would do without you."

Mhinga returned his attention to Buster, "You would do just fine, *Bwana*." Grinning from ear to ear, he added, "You would be doing a lot more." He looked at Jon. "Much more. But you would be fine. Bring me back his shirt. I'll take yours too. I will rinse them out and dry them by the fire. If there are any guards posted tonight, we don't want them to find us by the pungent stink of bat guano."

Jon chuckled at his young friend as he unbuttoned his olive green shirt. After emptying the pockets, he picked up the soap and handed his shirt over. Bare-chested, he moved over to MacKenzie squatting by the little fire. Strategically placed behind two of the largest boulders and next to the cave's wall, the firelight was screened from outside. She noticed his chiseled bare chest as he knelt next to her. Blushing, she raised one eyebrow in question. Jon answered, "Mhinga is going to rinse out the bat guano. Zawawi's too. He didn't want the guards to smell us if we passed too close to them."

"Oh! Is that what I smelled? Bat guano?" MacKenzie chuckled.

"We're going to wait here until their camp quiets down for the evening." Jon continued, "I'll take Zawawi a plate of food. He is taking the first watch. You had better eat your share, then get some rest too. We will have to march hard and fast. We've got to put as many miles as possible between us and them before daybreak."

Sitting at the edge of the fire, the small metal pot of water began to boil. Instinctively both Jon and MacKenzie reached for it at the same time. As their hands arrived on the wooden handle, Jon's covered hers. Caught in the moment, they both froze, hands touching, and they looked up at each other. Their eyes met shyly. MacKenzie dropped hers, breaking the stare. Quietly she spoke as she began pulling her hand out from under his, "You make the tea, and I'll make a plate for you."

He squeezed her hand, drawing her eyes back. "For Zawawi. A plate for Zawawi."

Releasing his grip on her hand, she spoke softly, "A plate for

Zawawi and a plate for you too." Forcing her hand away, she reached for the sturdy plastic plates. She placed several pieces of warmed buffalo strips and a half dozen hot sweet figs on each plate. Jon poured the hot tea into the four cups. Silently, they worked in unison. After Jon had refilled the pot, he replaced it on the fire's edge. His bare arm brushed against her knee.

The touch once again brought their eyes together. He could clearly see the reflection of the flames dancing in the depths of her pupils. The thin ring of glittering gold flecks sparkled like a halo. He tried, but could not break the stare. Her eyes held his gaze. She watched his eyes follow the contour of her face, quietly absorbing each detail. The sharp differ-ence between the fire's dim light and the darkness of the cave intensified the dark rings under her eyes. Tiredness and fatigue showed on her face. Regretfully, he broke the spell, softly speaking to her, "You need rest. Eat, then get some sleep." He placed his hands over hers. "I need for you to be strong and ready when the time comes to leave. Tell me you will rest."

Gently she squeezed his hand and replied, "I promise you." Her voice was low and husky from the moist cave air.

He sat there a moment longer before picking up two cups of the strong hot tea and the plates of food. As he rose, he said, "I will wake you later."

A little nod of her head sent him on his way. She looked back into the fire as she reached for a piece of meat with her fork. A strange rush flashed through her body. She wondered, "What is going on?" She felt like a young schoolgirl experiencing her first crush. She ate very slowly, gazing into the fire. It set her mind free to roam over all the feelings she was experiencing. So much had happened that the day felt like a long week. Staring into the fire, she felt her body becoming very heavy. Mesmerized by the hot dancing colors of the fire, she was unable to move, feeling drugged, as visions of the day's events rolled across the bright blue light that rose over the hottest coals. Again she saw the wood-ed area, the small field of butterflies, the valley with the elephants, the poachers and helicopter with the gunmen firing down on them. Crawling into the stone crevice, hiding in the cave with all those bats, the sound of gunfire, it was all there again, happening again, right before her eyes. The fights with Zawawi squeezed her chest with fear. The sound of Jon's harsh voice raised the hairs on the back of her neck. The feel of his tender lips on hers when they kissed soothed her fears. Carried away by it all, she did not notice that Mhinga and Buster had approached.

Mhinga laid out the two wet shirts on the boulder above the fire. Turning around, he looked down at MacKenzie squatting by the fire with a piece of meat and a glazed look on her face. "Ms. Mac?" There was no response, just a small peaceful smile growing across her face. Mhinga crossed over next to her. He knelt down and looked directly into her eyes. Very softly he whispered again, "Ms. Mac?" Ever so slowly her eyes moved and met his. "What have you seen?"

Her voice was so tiny he could barely hear her, though they were only inches apart. She simply answered, "Today." Her heavy eyes fell shut, and she collapsed into Mhinga's arms, sound asleep. Gently, he laid her onto her side near the fire, removing the half-eaten piece of meat from her hand and covering her with a warm bedroll.

Warming up a cup of tea, Mhinga sat down and leaned against the cave's wall. Stretching out his legs, he ate his meal. Jon came around the boulder carrying two empty plates. "She finally went to sleep?" he asked quietly.

"Yes, *Bwana,* she fell hard and quickly."

"You look like you could use some sleep, too."

"As do you."

"I've got two hours, then I will relieve Zawawi. We will move out at midnight. I'm afraid that we have another long hard day ahead of us. Rest well, Mhinga."

Mhinga sat his cup down, leaned his head back, and closed his eyes. Shortly, his breathing deepened, and his head flopped to one side.

Jon lay down across the fire from MacKenzie. She was so deeply asleep her chest barely moved with each breath. The fire's warm glow illuminated her. That was the last thing he remembered before being shaken awake by Zawawi. As Jon's eyes came into focus, Zawawi said quietly, "Your turn," and handed him a fresh cup of sweet hot tea.

Sitting up, Jon took the cup, "Was that two hours?"

The heaviness of fatigue weathered on Zawawi's face. "Yes, now it's your turn."

The caffeine in the tea and the hot steam rising from the cup began jarring Jon's senses. "I guess now you want two hours of sleep," he tried to joke.

"Or three if you are feeling generous." Zawawi forced a grin back. He did not try to hide his tiredness.

As Jon got up, he promised, "Okay, three it is."

Jon stirring the fire and the aroma of the tea boiling woke Mhinga. As his eyes opened, Jon handed him a scalding hot cup of the sweetness. After pouring another cup, Jon reached over and stroked MacKenzie gently on her arm. Slowly, she awakened. As she rose from under her bedroll the cool damp air refreshed her skin, raising tiny goose pimples across her arms. She happily accepted the cup of hot brew from Jon. "Did you sleep well?" he asked her.

The bags under her eyes were not as dark or heavy as before. Nodding her head, she took the first sip of tea. "Yeah, I feel really rested." Then she chuckled, "For a twenty-minute nap."

"It's been almost five hours," Jon explained.

She wiped her eyes. "Maybe so, but it doesn't feel like it."

Mhinga handed her the rest of her dinner, as Jon poured Zawawi a cup of tea. Then as he reached over to wake his Maasai friend from his deep slumber MacKenzie interrupted, "Oh, can't you just let him sleep? He is so nice to be around this way." She flashed a weary smile at Jon.

"We've got to get moving, Mac," Jon said as he pushed his friend a little harder. "It's two o'clock. Wake up, Zawawi."

He stretched as he awoke; the smell of the strong tea quickly brought him around. Mhinga divided the few remaining pieces of meat. Buster got the final fatty pieces from the bottom of the bag. After eating, they gathered their gear, put out the fire, and in the darkness made their way towards the mouth of the cave.

Huddling at the edge of the trail, Jon gave instructions, "Zawawi, you lead. Mhinga, you follow, then Mac, Buster, and me. No flashlights.

The moon is bright enough. Mac, watch where you put each hand or step. Try to avoid breaking any branches or making any noise. Do whatever Mhinga does. If he drops to the ground, then you drop. Got it?"

"Got it," she answered.

With spear in hand, Zawawi, followed by the others, crawled out onto the brush-covered animal trail.

Chapter 16

Nature's blessing put them in the most danger. The moon's bright light shone intensely on the narrow trail as it snaked along the face of the bluff. With very little vegetation to conceal them from below, they remained nearly in full view of the poachers' glowing camp-fires. Their shadows were a constant reminder of the danger they would face if a sharp-eyed guard looked up. At this close range, any man with a good rifle could easily pick them off, one by one. There was no place to take shelter until they reached the ground level.

The loose rocks on the steep incline made dangerous footing. They moved quietly, slowly, in single file down the narrow trail, often with their bodies scraping against the vertical face of the bluff. In places where the trail had eroded with time or broken free from a rockslide, they had just a few inches of width for a foothold. Only Buster traveled without fear.

An hour had passed since they first crawled out of the cave. The tiny trail widened, and more plant life appeared alongside the steep hillside. The sound of the river's rushing water rose to meet them as they neared ground level. A thick cloud of fog hovered just below the treetops lining the riverbanks.

A steep slide of loose pebbles ended the trail along the bluff. Crouching low, one by one each member came down the long descent quickly. The loose pebbles acted as ball bearings, tumbling wildly beneath them. The large boulders at the base of the slide and the heavy fog shielded them. They were no longer exposed in the bright light of the moon, nor could they see the smoldering fires in the poachers' camp.

Zawawi leaned over and whispered in Mhinga's ear, "Wait here while I find a safe place to cross the river." Not waiting for a response, he was off, swallowed up in the thick fog that diffused the moon's light to a ghostly haze.

Mhinga looked back at MacKenzie. She, following his lead, had not moved. Quietly she sat in the damp coolness of the fog, grateful for the rest and for being off the narrow trail. She crooked her arm up against a large boulder, leaned her head over, and closed her eyes.

Jon was tending to Buster, examining each paw and removing small pebbles that had gotten deeply embedded between the pads of his feet. He knew that Zawawi would carefully search the riverbank, looking for a safe place to cross and watching for any signs of posted guards. He also knew that they must cross the river before first light, under the cover that darkness and fog provided. They must put as much distance as possible between them and the poachers before the break of day. If the poachers found their trail, they would know that someone had survived the cave-in and would send men out to hunt them down. Mhinga turned back and peered through the shadowy darkness, watching for any signs of Zawawi's return.

In less than an hour, the tall Maasai reappeared dripping wet and totally naked, carrying his clothing. Mhinga quickly produced a small hand towel and handed it to him as he walked by. Squatting down next to Jon, Zawawi began drying himself off as he softly spoke, "The poachers' camp is directly across the stream from where we are, off from the river by two hundred yards in a small clearing." Zawawi draped his clothing over his shoulder.

Jon looked back over his shoulder across the river as MacKenzie joined the huddle of the three men. She kept her eyes focused on the men's faces for Zawawi made no attempt to cover himself.

Zawawi continued, "There is a safe place to cross the river, not far downstream, but the water is thigh deep and very cold." He handed the towel back to Mhinga. "The water becomes deeper and very swift further upstream. I did not see any traces of crocs, hippos, or guards along the bank, but there is a well-used path on the opposite side. A little way in it forks. One fork goes to the campsite, the other goes on up the hillside."

Jon looked down at his watch. It was fifteen minutes until four in the morning, and they had less than one and a half hours until the sun broke into the sky and soaked up the fog. "Let's get going, then." He stood and reached for his pack and rifle.

Zawawi stood directly in front of MacKenzie. He looked down at her and stared. His stance was like a dare for her to look at him.

As she rose, she accepted his dare as her eyes followed the long muscular length of his wet body. There was no modesty within this man, as he stood naked in front of her. The cold temperature of the water and the morning damp air had no effect on him that she could see, though her exposed arms were covered with goose pimples. The grimace on his face told her that he was going to enjoy her suffering when she crossed the river. The thigh-deep water on Zawawi would be waist-deep on her and there would be no protection from the coldness. This was a challenge from Zawawi that neither Jon nor Mhinga could help her with. Standing there looking at him, she mustered all the courage she could find. Trying to cover her true feelings, she grinned sweetly and said nothing. He turned, and Jon followed.

Mhinga approached her, leaning over to whisper in her ear, "You did very well this time." He laid his hand on her shoulder as he passed.

Traveling over the large boulders and small rocks was proving to be more difficult than coming down the tiny trail that clung to the edge of the bluff. Goat-hopping from the top of one boulder to the next was the easiest method. Mhinga and Buster followed behind Zawawi, while Jon lagged behind with MacKenzie.

Jon crossed from one boulder to another. MacKenzie stopped. The gap was too wide for her to step across easily. "Psst," she said. Jon stopped and looked back at her. She shrugged her shoulders helplessly.

Seeing that she was unable to make it across on her own, he spanned one leg across the gap, anchoring his foot sideways on the other boulder for her to use as a step. Reaching out, he offered his hand.

Perplexity showed on her face. He looked around, worried that someone might hear his words. Very quietly, he said, "Don't you trust me?"

The fog was growing thicker with the coming of morning and even at this relatively short distance, she could not clearly see his face. Yet her mind's eye brought back all the fine details of his sparkling blue eyes, soft tender lips, and curly black hair. She took a deep breath and nodded slowly. Inching her way down, she placed her left foot against his. Reaching out, she took his hand. When their eyes met, she pushed off. Steadily, he pulled her across into his arms.

In the safety of his embrace, she was able to clearly see the depth of his blue eyes and the boyish grin that emerged from the new growth of his beard. Feeling the warmth of his body wrapped around her sent her mind racing back to the cave when he had held her like this. Was it just yesterday? Or was it the day before? In the wilds of Africa, the measurement of time did not seem to exist.

Looking down into MacKenzie's eyes, Jon knew that the answer to his question was yes, she did trust him. He leaned down, slowly parting his lips as she tilted her head slightly, offering hers. Slowly they moved closer toward each other. Just as their lips touched, the faint call of a wood owl broke the spell. Hesitating, Jon stopped. Looking up, he tilted his head, hearing the call of the owl again. Zawawi was calling to him. Jon let out a sigh, and his arms fell from MacKenzie. "We've got to catch up." With a small grin, she nodded her head, and they were off into the dense fog to find the others.

As Jon and MacKenzie emerged from the fog, Zawawi, carrying Buster, took his first steps into the cold river. Mhinga had stripped down to just his shirt. He balanced his neatly folded pants and his pack on top of his head. Bare bottomed, he waded out into the water.

Jon wasted no time undressing. Tying his shoes together by the strings, he swung them over his shoulder. As he started to unbutton the tops of his shorts, MacKenzie turned her back to him. Noticing, he stopped. Turning her around, he saw the look of modesty on her face. He cupped her face in his hands, speaking softly, "I'll tell you what." He looked across the river, seeing the others about halfway. "Can you cross alone? You will have to carry your pack high."

Looking over the river, she could see Mhinga fading into the fog. "Yes, I can make it," she answered.

"Okay, here's what we'll do. Wait until I get halfway across then you start. When I reach the other side, I will leave the towel for you on a branch and take the others into the woods so you can dry and dress yourself in private. Will that work for you?"

She nodded, "Yes," and turned around while Jon undressed and waded into the stream. She turned back in time to watch as Jon's lily-white buttocks faded into the fog. Setting down her pack she took off her shoes and socks. Stuffing the socks into the toes of her shoes and then tying the strings together, she swung them over her shoulder as Jon had done. Removing her pants and panties, she folded them and placed them inside her backpack. Rolling up the tail of her tee shirt, she tucked it in her bra. Picking up the pack, she rested it on top of her head. She balanced it with one hand as she made her way into the frigid waters.

With her first step into the water, she gasped as the iciness shot up her body. Hesitating, she remembered how Zawawi looked at her earlier, so arrogant. The men had made it across and so would she. Taking another step forward, the water rose higher on her legs. She kept going, trying to go a bit faster, lessening the time she spent in the icy water that flowed swiftly around the soft skin of her thighs.

At midstream the water was nearing her crotch and she began walking on the tips of her toes. Her steps were smaller as the speeding water was rushing to meet her tender flesh. She stopped, trying to summon up the courage to continue on. The memory of Zawawi's proud grin did not do it for her this time. The thought of Jon's embrace was not warming her now. A picture of her father flashed before her eyes. Oh Daddy, she sadly thought. Biting her tongue, she took a big step forward landing solidly on her foot. The cold water engulfed her up to mid-hip, and she gasped as the wet cold contacted her most sensitive area. She forced herself to think of her father again. Not knowing his whereabouts and condition moved her forward in the fast-running, cold, muddy stream.

The bank began to materialize in the fog ahead of her as she hurried. On the bank a dark silhouette arose. She stopped. Jon had promised to clear the area. The figure raised his arm and waved. She returned the wave with her free hand. The man turned and melted into the misty forms of the bushes and trees. It was Jon. He had been waiting to see that she made it across safely.

As she neared the bank, she could see that it was short but quite steep. A small sapling had been bent over and used by the others to pull themselves up the steep bank. Standing in the icy water up to her waist, she tossed her backpack and then her shoes up onto the bank in the bushes where the towel hung. She then took a good grip on the small tree and started to pull herself up. The young roots of the sapling were loosened from the weight of the others, and the moist dirt of the bank gave way. MacKenzie was halfway up the embankment when the roots broke free, sending her splashing back into the icy water.

She submerged completely. The swift current carried her several yards down stream before she was able to find her footing. Standing at last, shivering with cold, the dense fog obstructed her view of the bank. Cursing under her breath, she started making her way upstream towards the embankment.

A splash in the water startled, her and she stopped. Visibility was only a few feet when she first noticed a string of bubbles rising to the surface. Hiding in the murky stream, something was swimming towards her.

She stood frozen in the waist deep muddy water, not knowing what to do. Her eyes widened and stared out as the gurgling sound of air rushing to the surface was nearly upon her. Though distorted by the murky water, a long narrow pale body swam just a few inches below the surface. Her heart pounded with the rush of adrenaline, filling her shivering body with energy. Turning quickly toward the bank, she saw a sturdy low limb hanging over the river's edge.

Reaching out, she lunged for the limb. Her fingers clinched down on the branch as she was struck in the legs by a strong force. It buckled around her knees, pulling her backwards, and forcing her under the surface. The bark and leaves ripped through her tight grip, and the brown gritty water filled her mouth, silencing her screams.

She struggled, fighting for her freedom while drifting further down stream. With all of her strength, she kicked and pushed. Her lungs ached for a fresh breath. In the turmoil, she lost all sense of direction. Which way was up? She tried to break out of the squeeze that was encompassing her body, wrapping around tightly, halting her every move. She was completely helpless as the creature covered her mouth and arms. Then entwined around her legs.

At the first feel of cold air striking her face, her eyes flew open. Her head was above the water. A gritty voice growled in her ear, "Stop it!"

Devoured by fear, she continued to fight. The voice hissed at her again, "It's me, Jon." This time she heard the voice and immediately ended the struggle. Breathing heavily, she lowered her eyes. It was a man's arm wrapped around her, not the scaly body of a giant snake.

He whispered softly in her ear, "Shhh. Are you all right?"

She nodded, and he released his grip. Again he whispered in her ear, so faintly that she barely heard him, "Someone is coming." With her wrapped tightly in his arms, he lowered their bodies below the water level and slowly made their way to the bank where a small willow tree leaned dangerously over the river. The fog was still heavy and the skimpy leaf-covered branches helped to conceal their exposed heads. He kept his body snuggled up against hers to share what body heat there was between them. He could feel her body shaking from cold and fear. Quietly, he whispered in her ear, "Where's your pack?"

She felt the soft wet growth of his beard on her cheek when he spoke to her. Leaning her head back, she answered, "In the bushes, back where the towel is." Her voice was shaky and low.

The warmth of her breath on his cheek drew his attention away from the bank. He turned towards her just as she tilted her head forward. By chance her lips brushed against his cheek. Their eyes did not part. Entwined in his arms, she had a sense of safety, though she was scared beyond words.

A noise came from above. Someone was approaching the edge of the bank. Holding MacKenzie tightly, Jon could feel her heart pounding, affirming the fear that showed in her eyes. Cuddled together in the icy waters under the willow tree, they waited and listened for an all-clear call from Zawawi.

Jon tore his eyes away from MacKenzie, focusing on the sound of human footsteps above them. There was only one person, walking slowly.

Perhaps it was a guard coming to the river to relieve himself. Jon could only hope that the darkness and the early morning fog would conceal MacKenzie's pack and the marks they had left in the soft embankment.

Zawawi and Mhinga crouched in the shadowy overcast of tall bushes as a young woman walked by. Mhinga gently gripped Buster's jaws together to quiet his panting. The woman passed within feet of them. The darkness of the forest hid her face; still they were able to see her shapely figure.

Reaching the edge of the river, the woman searched the ground until she found a small stone. She stuffed it inside the spent condom and tied the end into a knot. With a small chuckling sound, the woman tossed it into the murky water, then turned and walked back into the forest, once again passing near Zawawi, Mhinga, and Buster.

After a long ten minutes, Zawawi gave the "all-clear" -- the call of an egret. Jon returned the whistle and looked back at MacKenzie. "Let's get out of here." Shivering, she forced a smile as he helped her walk upstream to the embankment. Pulling down another sapling, he turned to her. His stomach knotted as he watched her shivering, her tanned skin pale against the muddy water. He spoke softly, "Do you want me to help you up?"

Bravely, she shook her head. Lifting her chin, she said, "And you don't have to wait for me either. I can do it."

Jon gave her an encouraging smile. He understood. "I'll be waiting just inside the treeline for you." She smiled back at him. Leaning down, he kissed her forehead before climbing up the embankment.

She waited a few more numbing seconds before slowly climbing out of the water. Searching around she found her pack and shoes hidden in the brush. Under it was the towel. She must have struck it when she tossed her pack up. Quickly she dried herself off and put on her clothes. For just a brief moment she felt like a warm wool blanket had been wrapped over her. She twisted the water from her long braid before heading into the woods. Jon stood where he said he would be. Mhinga had brought him his pack, and he had changed into his only other set of clothing. She reached down and bundled his wet clothes with hers, wrapping them together in the small towel.

Mhinga took the bundle from her as he softly said, "I will carry these for you. Zawawi wants to travel quickly to avoid any more run-ins with the poachers. Are you up for the swift pace, Ms. Mac?"

She shrugged off a shiver. In a quiet voice, she answered, "The sooner we get moving, the sooner we will warm up." Turning to Jon, she took his hand and said, "Thank you. If you hadn't jumped in the water when you did, I would have crawled up that embankment just as that guy came out of the woods." Her voice trailed off, and she began to tremble. "Oh God. Jon, I thought you were a giant snake or a crocodile."

Jon wrapped his arms around her, pulling her close, comforting her. Mhinga butted in, "It wasn't a man." They both looked at him with astonishment. He continued, "It was a young woman. She was at the river's edge only a very short time."

Jon said, "Yes, we saw something very small." He cupped his hand showing the size. "It was tossed into the river, and it sank."

Another birdcall came from the woods. Mhinga shrugged his head. "We better go; Zawawi grows impatient."

Chapter 17

Zawawi scouted ahead of the others. Ghost-like, he swiftly moved through the thick forest undergrowth without making a sound. His natural hunting skills took over, and his senses were greatly intensified by some primitive intuition that even he did not fully understand. It was as if his soul absorbed the surroundings. He instantly recognized every sound, whether it was mammal, bird, or insect. He noticed the smallest movement of a leaf, or a tiny blink of an eye that would give away the hiding spot of his prey. This time avoiding the prey was the necessity. They had not come to this area looking for a confrontation with poachers. They had come to locate the missing scientists.

Following him, Jon set the pace for the others. Moving the group quickly, he kept Zawawi in sight, but stayed far enough back not to hamper his effectiveness as a tracker. They needed to get out of the valley and onto the hillside as quickly as possible. Their survival depended on placing as many miles between them and the poachers as they could.

The chill was leaving Jon's body when Zawawi suddenly dropped to the ground. One by one, each member of the group dropped to the ground. Jon motioned back to Mhinga and MacKenzie to stay put, before crawling up to Zawawi.

Propped on his elbows, the Maasai lay on his stomach, perfectly still, eyes searching the brush for what had alarmed him. Strangely, Zawawi breathed in deep breaths of air. It was not a sight or sound that had alerted him to danger but an unnatural scent. Jon breathed in deeply, too. There was something out of place, yet he could not instantly identify it.

In a flash, they both saw a tiny orange glow flicker to the ground, followed by a small gray puff of smoke. Motionless, the two men lay in the underbrush watching for a glimpse of the stranger who had been smoking a cigarette. A rustling noise in the bushes beyond him brought the stranger out from behind a tree.

The shadows outlined the form of a man with a rifle casually hung over his shoulder. He wore military camouflage fatigues. Only the scent of the burning tobacco and the glow of the cigarette butt gave him away.

A woman appeared from the bushes. Her shapely figure told them that she was the same woman who had passed by them just a short time ago near the river's edge. As she approached the man, she giggled, "There you are! I've been looking for you. Did you give up on me and think I wasn't coming back?"

He took her in his arms. "It took you such a long time to get rid of the condom. Where did you go?"

Petrus reached up and straightened Taveta's cap. "To the river. I placed a rock in the condom and tossed it in. Then I went back to check on my project boy. He will be awake soon, and I needed to repair his torn shirt. But good news, Lover. My little boy-toy and his brother will be leaving at first light to go off with Dubois to find that old elephant."

Zawawi and Jon looked at each other. They now knew the poacher's name: *Dubois*. It was the same name as the man Khosa had said they were working for when they crossed paths at the logging road. Jon saw that Zawawi's face had hardened. They remained still, listening to the lovers' conversation.

Taveta leaned over and kissed Petrus' forehead. "How is that good news, my beauty?"

She pulled back, hitting him fondly on the shoulder. "Don't you see? Dubois, Valli, and his little brother will be gone for a day or two, maybe longer, until they find that old bull."

Pulling her close again, he asked, "And?"

"And," she said as she walked her fingers up his shoulders, "We will have entire nights all to ourselves before we have to pull up camp and move closer to the kill. No sharing with Valli. Dubois will want him all to himself during the hunt. A few days off work! It's sort of like a holiday for you and me."

He kissed the back of her hand. "And I will be on guard duty each night."

She giggled again. "And I will do my best to make sure that you stay awake. All night long." Her hands ran down his sides, and over his crotch.

"Oh, my beauty, I do love the way you think," Taveta groaned as he leaned over kissing her fully on the mouth. Pulling away, he looked down at her. "Tell me something." She pulled back and tilted her head slightly. "Don't you enjoy being with him?"

"With who? Valli? Listen to me." She stepped back, still holding his hands. "Valli is my job. Dubois pays me to keep him happy. He is just a growing boy with an overactive snake. You know what? That's what he calls his penis, a dancing black mamba. It's more like an earthworm. He wants to be married and have children with me! Can you imagine? I just want to be free. To have great sex with you makes up for the hideous performance of that boy. His talents only lie out in the wilderness, tracking animals." She looked up at Taveta. "Don't go and get all mushy with me. This is my job, my life, who I am, and what I'm good at. When Dubois is done with this trading bushmeat for tree business, you will go back to your wives. I will return to the streets and have my own group of girls who will work for me. Understand?"

He pulled Petrus close. "I understand, and I wouldn't have it any other way. Now you had better get back before your boy-toy starts looking for you." He kissed her one more time.

As she turned, he smacked her bottom. Looking back over her shoulder, she smiled at him. "See you tonight, lover." She disappeared into the bushes.

The man lit another cigarette and looked up at the daylight breaking through the tall canopy of trees. Zawawi and Jon had not moved. Out of the corner of his eye, Jon could see his friend's face harden with disappointment. Slowly Zawawi closed his eyes and dropped his head. What he had learned about his oldest son made his shoulders slump with grief.

As they lay side by side, Jon silently watched the gunman finish his smoke and walk into the bush. Zawawi finally looked over at Jon. A burning intensity showed in his eyes. Very softly he broke the silence with a whisper, "Valli has made bad, very bad, choices." Looking up at the sky, he tried to focus on the task at hand. "Daylight. We must get moving." He rose and melted into the lush foliage. Jon waved to the others, and they followed.

The disappointment turned into an anger that fueled Zawawi and drove him on relentlessly. Farther and farther they marched through the valleys of the foothills. They stopped only briefly at noon to nibble on wild berries that MacKenzie and Mhinga were able to gather as they followed behind the trackers.

Resting on a fallen log, the tartness of the fresh root tea curbed the rumbling coming from their bellies. In silence each person drank several cups, while Buster lay close to Jon with his eyes closed. Between cups of tea, MacKenzie had unbraided her thick auburn hair. It was still damp from her dunking in the river earlier that morning. She carefully separated the long dark waves in the wet braid, and she spread her hair over her shoulders to dry.

Jon watched MacKenzie as she tended her hair. It was the first time he had seen it loose, cascading over her shoulders. He thought back to another woman he knew with long hair.

Sharon's hair was not as thick, but much longer. Seemingly translucent, absorbing the sun's light, it seem to glow with sparkles of gold. He let his mind wander back to when they made love, how she would stroke

119

the length of his body, caressing him with her long fine hair. He remembered how her voice, sweetened with a deep southern belle accent, coaxed him against his better judgment. She could charm any man, and had him submerged in her spell. This woman had been pure poison, and severely damaged his life and Zawawi's. Jon's experience with her had changed his whole outlook on women. Until now.

Watching MacKenzie, he thought back over his conversation with Zawawi in the cave. He was feeling something different, not just an attraction, but also something stronger. He could not fully explain it to himself, nor expect Zawawi to understand it either. Though he understood his friend's mistrust, he was partially to blame for it.

Setting down his empty cup, Zawawi saw the far-away look on Jon's face. Nudging him, he said, "We should try to contact Simon."

Jon snapped out of his thoughts. "Yeah. We'll get a better signal on top of the hill." They picked up their weapons. "You two wait here."

"I will search the area for something edible." Mhinga rose too.

MacKenzie stood and started to speak, "Can . . . ."

"NO! You are not coming," Zawawi cut her off. "This is man's work. You would just be in the way."

"Mac," Jon said affectionately, "Zawawi is right. You had better stay here with Mhinga and help him search for mushrooms or berries."

Her face flushed with redness. She placed her hands on her hips and stood her ground. Gritting her teeth, she snapped, "If you had let me finish, you'd know I wasn't going to ask to come along." The two men looked guiltily at each other. MacKenzie continued, "I think you should take the GPS receiver and get our location recorded."

Jon winced. Crossing over to her, he looked down into her upturned face. The redness drained from her skin as she looked into his blue eyes. "You're right," he said, "we shouldn't have cut you off like that."

"Do not speak words for me, Jon," Zawawi said, crossing his arms over his chest.

Ignoring his friend, Jon continued, "Can you show me how to work the receiver?"

Standing close to Jon, MacKenzie's anger melted away. She looked past him at Zawawi, wanting an apology, but knowing it was not going to happen. Zawawi shook his head, knowing that Jon had weakened. Turning her attention back to Jon, she said, "It's really very simple," MacKenzie said, smiling warmly at Zawawi, "even a Maasai could do it."

Zawawi took a step towards her. Jon held up his hand, keeping him at arm's length. "Okay!" he said, "You two are even here." Turning back to MacKenzie, Jon asked, "Now, how do you work it?"

"Very simple," she began, "just lift this antenna and push the blue button." Jon watched her closely, standing next to her with their arms touching. "Then wait for a few seconds for the signals to bounce back from the satellites." She looked up at him with her gold-flecked green eyes, capturing his attention. "When the digital screen changes, showing the coordinates, push this button marked Save." Looking up at him, she smiled warmly. "That's all there is to it."

This time when she looked into his eyes, though, she felt him looking into her. Caught off guard, she finished her instructions very slowly, "Pushing the blue button again turns it off."

Holding her gaze, Jon took the receiver and placed it in his shirt pocket.

Zawawi walked past Jon, bumping him in the shoulder as he went. "Let's get going." Buster followed the two men from the area.

Mhinga had turned his back to MacKenzie to hide his wide smile. As he looked about for food, laughter began to rumble from deep inside him. His shoulders shook, and he moved his head back and forth. Finally he could resist no longer. Laughing out loud, he sputtered, "That was very clever and very funny, Ms. Mac."

"What are you talking about?"

His eyes watered, and he sucked in a deep breath of air trying to gain control of his laughter. "What you said." He mocked her voice " 'It's so easy that even a Maasai could do it!' Very funny!" Holding his stomach, he chuckled, "You are a bold one!"

MacKenzie's face lit into a brilliant smile. Full of pride, she said, "Thank you, Mhinga."

Reaching down, Mhinga plucked firm ripe fungi. Looking back over his shoulder, he said, "It is not a true compliment, because it is not something that Zawawi will soon forget."

"Yeah, I know . . . ." MacKenzie sat down, crossing her legs under her. Her shoulders slumped as she sighed, "I just get so tired of his arrogant attitude."

"Yes." Mhinga crossed over to her. "And he feeds off that." Kneeling down in front of her, dropping the mushrooms in her lap, he said, "But Jon is always there to defend you, isn't he?"

The mention of Jon started a warm sensation rushing over MacKenzie. Mhinga left her there to continue his search. Holding the mushrooms in her lap, she stared off with a dazed look on her face.

"Big Dog, come in. This is Little Pup. Over." The sound of static filtered across the radio signal. Jon repeated his call to Simon. "Big Dog, come in. This is Little Pup. Over."

"Big Dog here. Where in the hell have you been?" Hearing the concern in Simon's voice brought grins to Jon and Zawawi. Simon continued, "You were supposed to radio in at twenty-one hundred hours yesterday!"

Zawawi laughed. "He sounds like a mother hen calling to her lost chicks."

"Big Dog, or should we now call you Mother Hen?" Jon broke into laughter, too.

Simon's temper rose. "What's your situation?"

Sobering, Jon said, "The big bad guy spotted us. We've been lying low and very deep. But all is well now. They think we are dead. Where are you?"

"We are marching towards the open field where you saw the tuskers go down. Another four hours south of it. What's your location?"

Jon turned on MacKenzie's GPS receiver and pushed the blue button as she had instructed. The digital screen lit up. While Jon waited for the coordinate information to be retrieved from the satellites, he answered, "We're in the foothills on the northeastern slope of Mount Elgon. About ten miles north of your position." Looking at the GPS receiver, he repeated the coordinates to Simon.

Simon's voice returned to normal as he asked, "Do you have any idea how many there are?"

"A dozen or so. Not more than two-dozen. A chap that goes by the name of Dubois heads them up. Ever hear of him?"

"Negative, but I've been away for awhile."

"He has some dealings with the loggers, trading the bushmeat for timber rights. He and his two scouts have gone out chasing the old bull. His followers are having a camp in the woods on the north side of the clearing, about three hundred yards west of the river." Jon looked to Zawawi for confirmation that he had given the right location.

Zawawi nodded. "Close enough."

Jon continued, "They have a few armed guards and there are some women in the camp too. They also have a helicopter and military rifles, possibly from Uganda."

"How in the hell did you get all that information?"

"They think we're dead, remember?"

"Right, you are more useful as a dead man," Simon joked. "Which way did Dubois and his two scouts go?"

"West of the field. They followed that old bull into the eastern foothills of Mount Elgon."

"So, you are on the same damn mountain as him?"

"Yeah, pretty close. But we're heading north towards the area where the last coordinate reading was received from the scientists. Dubois appeared to be going more towards the west."

"Anything else I should know?" Simon asked.

Jon hesitated for a moment. Zawawi nodded, "Tell him, Jon."

"Little Pup? Is there anything else?"

"Go on, Jon, tell Simon about the boys." Zawawi looked down and scuffed his tire-tread sandal in a pile of leaf litter.

"Yes." Jon's voice dropped, "The two scouts that are with Dubois . . . they are Valli and Khosa. They are working for him."

"Oh Christ!" Simon's voice fell, "Anything else?"

"When you get to their camp, find a shapely young girl named Petrus. She is Dubois' right hand and Valli's whore. You might get some valuable information out of her."

"Roger, I will keep the radio on, and you do the same. We'll make contact with you later, after we take the poachers' camp. Out."

"Roger. Out." Jon turned to Zawawi. "Let's get the others and get going."

Chapter 18

Four faded green tents formed a semi-circle around the open-sided nylon pavilion which served as the research center. Scattered under its roof, several metal folding tables bore the weight of microscopes, clear vas bottles, notebooks, plant specimens, lamps, measuring devices, laptop computers, countless batteries, and many yards of interconnecting wires and cables. Four men wearing identical khaki shorts and tee shirts bearing the logo of a stylistic S, shaped like a chemist's bottle, worked in silence. Gloom hung heavily; their porters were now armed guards.

There were eight of them. Though they spoke French to each other, they were quite capable of communicating in English when needed. Their language, and the scarred tattoo lines across their faces, revealed their Congo heritage.

Only four armed men remained in camp at a time. They switched with the other group every four days or so. The scientists had no idea why they left and returned several days later, exchanging places with their comrades. Often returning filthy and exhausted, they almost always carried fresh meat of some sort. This was seldom shared with the Americans, who were left with their canned rations. The guards, who had little taste for vegetables and canned meat, had already devoured the sweet treats of pudding, candy bars, and diced fruit.

Three of the armed guards watched the scientists during the day; the fourth man came on duty at night while the others slept. Communication between the guards and the scientists was civil at best. When a researcher needed to collect plant species for his study, one of the three guards would follow him into the forest, never letting him out of sight.

The first few weeks had been the most tense, but the guards soon learned that the scientists were unskilled in the forest. Their biggest weapons were small pen knives used for cutting the foliage they studied. The Americans, fearing for their lives, never spoke harshly or challenged the gunmen. They concentrated their energies, trying to find a cure for AIDS.

This part of the forest gave no indication of chimpanzee inhabitants, the foundation for their study. However, many other primates lived in the canopy. The break of day brought out the beautiful black and white colobus monkey, as well as the blue monkey. The elusive bush baby could be heard at night, but was rarely ever seen. It was the need to study the chimpanzee that brought these men to the other side of the world. Now hostages, they still were allowed to study the plants, but were unable to determine which plant a chimpanzee might choose to eat. So the researchers continued their study the best they could.

Sitting at his microscope, Dr. Blankenship leaned back in his chair. Crossing his arms over his chest, he bowed his scruffy chin and closed his eyes. In his mind he reenacted their steps, again and again. What clues did he miss? At first it was all so easy, with everything going according to plan. The logging company, Camino Timber Enterprises, had granted them permission for the field study as well as partially funded the trip. The company also supplied the porters, who now held them captive.

The first several weeks had gone smoothly. They reached their first designated campsite without any problems. Though the porters kept to themselves, they seemed to enjoy watching and assisting the scientists gathering plants and setting up the equipment. It was, overall, a happy, productive atmosphere. During their next move farther up-country, things started to go wrong.

At the time, it appeared to be an accident; the man carrying the radio transmitting equipment lost his footing and fell to his knees on a steep rocky hillside. He reached out to cushion his fall, losing his grip on the bundle he carried. The bright yellow watertight container tumbled down the hillside. The sturdy case cracked and chunks of it broke free, splintering off with each bouncing impact. As it struck large boulders, big holes tore through the molded rubberized styrofoam insulation that coated the inside of the rigid carton. The mangled box came to a splashing pause in the muddy river. Then, caught in the undercurrent, the shattered case disappeared, taking with it the high-tech equipment inside.

That porter left soon after, presumably out of shame, but he returned several days later. He told Dr. Blankenship that he had gone ahead to scout the trail. A rockslide had occurred making the trail impassable. They would have to take another route. The new trail ended at their present location, far from where they needed to be to study chimpanzees.

After being forced to set up a new campsite, Dr. Blankenship received an unsigned letter, presented by one of the guards. It contained an apology for the inconvenience, but confirmed that they would be allowed to continue their studies providing they followed orders and caused no trouble. The letter warned them that anyone attempting to escape would be shot on the spot. It went on to say, if they cooperated, they would be allowed to return to the United States with their research.

Time passed quietly in the guarded camp. With eyes closed, Dr. Blankenship rocked his head slowly back and forth. He felt responsible for the situation. It was he who had made all their travel arrangements. He should have known from his years of experience that these field expeditions never went smoothly nor easily. He should have known something was not right. Something in that Frenchman's voice triggered a warning -- greed, and an odd eagerness to help a group that contradicted his own purpose. Was it in his voice, his words, his actions, or a combination of the three? But the biggest question Dr. Blankenship asked himself was, "Why didn't I see it?"

The stress was taking its toll. His doctor had advised him strongly against going, saying that a trek through the African bush would wear down his strength and that, in turn, would weaken his immune system. He knew when he left his home in California, that the disease he hoped to help find a cure for was going to kill him. He never dreamed that he would be held as a prisoner and possibly shot.

He remembered his daughter begging him not to go. MacKenzie

was the light of his dim life, his only true companion since the death of her mother ten years back in that awful car accident. Since then, they had bonded closely, supporting each other in their grief. Then, a year later, while Dr. Blankenship was working in the lab drawing blood from an AIDS patient, the Sierra Madre fault decided to release some stored up tensions.

The unexpected shock of the high-rise building swaying about on its earthquake rollers jolted the doctor. Losing his light grip on the syringe full of contaminated blood, he dropped it. The needle pierced his thigh. He infected himself. Not long afterward, his test came back positive. He hid this from his daughter and co-workers for several years, until the disease became obvious, then he confessed.

Leaning forward, Dr. Blankenship rested his snowy white head on the palms of his hands. His gut told him they would all die at the hands of these gunmen. He was not so concerned for himself as he was the other scientists. They were still young men with pretty wives and small children waiting for them to return home, hopefully bringing back with them a clue to cure this plague. A tear formed in his eye when he thought of the possibility he might never see his daughter again or be able to tell her he loved her. The tear rolled down his hollow cheek. He had grown weaker and lost much weight since he arrived in Africa. He knew, one way or the other, death for him would be soon.

Henry had been watching Dr. Blankenship for the past several minutes. He thought how awful his mentor looked, so very pale and weak. When the first tear started to fall, Henry went to him. Leaning over, he placed his hands on the bony shoulders of his colleague. "Hey, doc," he said, "Why don't you lie down for awhile? Take a little nap. This will be here when you wake up."

Dr. Blankenship reached up and patted Henry's hand. He nodded his head, "You are right, I do need more rest."

Henry helped his friend up from the table. Together they walked to the tent they shared. In it were two small cots and a little table with a battery-powered lamp. Dr. Blankenship sat on the edge of his cot. "You know I haven't much useful time left," he said.

Kneeling beside the cot, Henry looked at his friend and tried to smile. He knew Doc was right. "Is there anything you want me to do for you?"

Closing his eyes, Dr. Blankenship hung his head, thinking for a few moments. He mumbled, "I've got us in such a terrible mess."

"You couldn't have known this was going to happen. None of us had a clue."

Still hanging his head, Dr. Blankenship said, "I wish I could believe that." Finally, looking up at Henry, he continued, "When you get out of here, there are two things I would like." He lay back on his cot. "One, look in on MacKenzie from time to time and see if she needs anything. See how she is doing." His voice was filled with a loving sadness. "Two," rolling over, he propped himself up on his elbow and with much more strength in his voice, he said, "find those damn chimps and figure this out!"

Henry grinned brightly, "Yes sir," he answered with gusto. "Consider it done!"

Leaning back, Dr. Blankenship broke a smile. "Good. Now get out of here so this old man can rest."

Henry stepped out of the tent. All the guards watched him cross the campsite to where the other scientists worked. He sat down between them and hung his head.

Don said, "He doesn't look very good."

"No, he doesn't," Henry replied. "He blames himself for us being here." His voiced dropped very low, "For us being held captive."

Tshombe, one of the guards, walked back toward the table. The scientists went back to their work, but after a few moments, they continued their conversation. Mitch picked up where they left off, "That's just nonsense. He had no way of knowing any of this was going to happen."

"I know that. We all know that," Henry explained, "but there's nothing we can do about it."

Mitch looked around the camp. The guards paid little attention to the scientists, huddled at the end of the table. Softly he spoke, "I've been watching them. When the other four come back and exchange places with these guys . . . ." His voice trailed off as he looked around the camp again. Tshombe was moving closer, watching and listening. Mitch smoothly changed the subject. Pointing to a page in the open notebook on the table in front of him, he said, "Look at that footnote in this report. What do you think it means?"

As the others leaned over to see where Mitch was pointing, he glanced out of the corner of his eye and saw that Tshombe had turned his back. In a whisper Mitch said, "That tall skinny one watches us more closely than the others." He glanced back again before he continued, still whispering, "As I was saying, I've been watching. When they change with the other group every four days or so, the new guys are always very tired. Whoever is on duty that first night always has a hard time staying awake."

Henry butted in loudly, "I thought we had cleared that on the other report." He shuffled through the pile of papers just as Gbenya, another one of the guards, walked softly by. "Oh, where is it?"

"Wait, maybe it is in this pile." Don played along until the guard had passed by.

Mitch continued, "That first night, after the guard change, I think I can sneak out of here and go for help."

Not thinking, Henry said rather loudly, "Oh Mitch, that's just stupid." By he time he realized how loudly he had spoken, it was too late. The guards were taking more notice of them.

Trying to smooth over the situation, Don played along, "Well, Henry, think about it for a moment. We know that there are two hundred and twenty-five varieties of *Aspalathus* . . . ." Tshombe, the tall skinny guard seemed a bit suspicious and stood next to the group listening to their conversation. Henry continued on, using big complicated words about plant species in scientific terms, certain the guard would know nothing of which they spoke. It worked. A few minutes later, the guard walked away. Sitting down next to Gbenya and his other comrades, he joined their card game.

Quietly Don picked up where he left off, "Mitch, you'll get lost out there. You'll have no weapon to protect yourself against wild animals. And what about food? How will you know which way to go? We don't even have a compass!" Looking back and forth at his two partners he concluded, "They will come after you. Hunt you down and shoot you in that thick skull of yours. I vote no."

Mitch turned to Henry, who said, "I agree. We're deep in an African forest, not an American campground. Even if you do find a village, the odds are against you being able to communicate with them. Hell, they might just bring you back here. As far as we know, these men are running drugs out of here and have hired the locals to farm it. We can't take any chances. I vote no, too."

Mitch looked across the camp at Dr. Blankenship's tent. "If he doesn't get medical help soon . . . ."

Henry laid his hand on Mitch's shoulder. "Hell, Mitch, he knew that when he chose to come here. This was his choice; we all tried to talk him out of coming. Remember? He didn't want MacKenzie to see him like this."

"Okay, so what about us?" Mitch continued his plea. "Are we just going to hang out here until they decide it's time to end it for us?" Looking back at Tshombe and Gbenya, he added, "Do you really think that they are going to just let us waltz out of here with all of this stuff?" He stood from the table and his voice grew stronger, "Well I don't think so! And if you are honest with yourselves, you know that I'm right." His rage got the guards' attention again.

Mitch walked over to the dining table. Pouring a glass of water, he said to Tshombe who was staring at him. "Can you believe those two?" He pointed at the other researchers. "They think we need to do far more applied research with the white *Lignotublers of Synaptolepis kirkii* than the *Myrothamnus flabellifolius*. Isn't that just crazy?"

Gbenya and Tshombe chuckled to themselves as they watched what they believed to be the scientists disputing what to study.

Later the next day, four tired, armed men dragged themselves from the thick bush. On a pole stretched between them hung a long rack of smoked ribs. Mitch watched the gunmen as they built up the fire, preparing to heat their dinner. He could easily see their exhaustion. They chatted very little in French with the other guards before they left the camp.

After eating, the muddy foursome grew very quiet. With full bellies, three of them lay back where they sat and quickly fell asleep. The fourth man walked around the open-sided tent, gnawing on a barbecued rib, sizing up the three scientists who were eating cold canned meat and vegetables. Mitch's trained eyes noticed the heavy bags under the man's eyes and the sluggish steps that he made as he passed.

Dr. Blankenship had already turned in for the evening. Henry and Don rose from the table, calling back to Mitch, "Working late?"

Mitch had turned to his microscope. Without looking up, he said, "Yeah, I want to finish this. It will be just a few more minutes. Good night."

"Good night," Don called back. He turned to Henry, raised his eyebrow asking the same question that was on Henry's mind.

Shrugging his shoulders, Henry looked back before entering the tent, "God help him if he does try it, and us too." Don shook his head in agreement and went on to the tent that he shared with Mitch.

As Henry entered the tent, he looked down at Dr. Blankenship, sleeping so quietly that he wondered if his mentor had passed away. Then with a gruff mumble, the frail man rolled over onto his side. Through the mosquito netting he could see that Dr. Blankenship had his arm wrapped around his pillow, cuddling it like a teddy bear. Sitting on the edge of his own cot, Henry flicked off the light, muttering, "Godspeed to you both."

Chapter 19

Simon left his men behind to rest from the long hard march, and to prepare for the night raid. As graceful and silent as a predator cat, he hid among the dark shadows. Lurking around the outskirts of the poachers' camp, he memorized its layout. There were four rust-spotted AK-47 rifles leaning together outside a small green canvas tent. Outside its door, a wooden folding chair sat empty. Alongside, a small matching table was cluttered with papers. The cool evening breeze curled the loose sheets around the stone that held them in place. Seeing no movement near the tent, Simon assumed it was Dubois', who was out pursuing the old bull. He counted six men and two women altogether.

The group was relaxed and appeared to be expecting no trouble. They were quiet and settling in for the night. A heavy log was pushed into the fire to warm the chilly night air, and bedrolls lay open around the golden blaze. Simon studied the two women, looking for the girl that Jon had described. These mature females with long flat breasts and marks of multiple births did not fit the description of the shapely young woman Jon had described as Dubois' right hand and Valli's girlfriend.

Soundlessly, Simon crept away from the laborers' campsite and made his way back across the clearing to his men. Thick clouds drifted slowly across the moon's face, temporarily darkening the area into total blackness. In their aimless float across the sky, the clouds parted, lighting the yellow and black-streaked bluffs and bringing painful memories from the year before. As he walked in the darkness, he noticed that his time away had reduced his endurance. The spray of bullet wounds had healed quickly, for he had been in top condition. But scar tissue had formed in his lungs while he recovered at a desk job, processing tourists as they entered his country. His muscles ached slightly around the bones that had snapped when he hit the tree limbs as he fell from an overhanging bluff. He shrugged off the feeling as it all clearly came back to him. It had happened over a year ago, and he smiled, knowing that his body had recovered. His body; yes. But psychologically -- that was something else.

His mind could not release the riveting feel of bullets slamming into his body nor the feel of each individual hot tip piercing his skin. He could still recall the sensation of the earth separating from the soles of his black combat boots as he toppled over the edge of the cliff. He had plummeted backwards, dazed and helpless, seeing only the peaceful blue sky and white fluffy clouds overhead. There was a long peaceful silence during the freefall. The sound of the whistling wind had followed him into the tops of the trees. Shattering limbs slowed his fall and broke his body.

That was the last time he had been in the wilderness. Chasing a highly skilled poacher, he had been out-smarted, led into a trap and nearly lost his life. That case was never closed. The poacher, with his long handle-bar mustache, wire-framed glasses, and thick French accent was now just a ghost that haunted Simon's mind.

It felt good to be back in the wilds again, facing some of the night-mares that had dogged him over the past year. The sweet smell of the grasses and the pure air seemed to cleanse and rejuvenate his body. The weight of the rifle balanced easily on his broad shoulder. Feeling its cold hard steel in the palm of his hand gave a sense of pride and meaning to his job and the dangers it held. Hanging at his hip, the loaded pistol was balanced by the two spare clips, a small flashlight with spare batteries, and a heavy clasp knife.

As he walked, his mind roved back over the layout of the poachers' camp. He visualized the relation of the tent and rifles to the fire and the perimeter of light. This was his favorite part of an operation, calculating the raid and the possible scenarios that could occur. He and his men were outnumbered two to one, but they had a big advantage: the trump card of surprise. If the men in camp reached their weapons, spoiling the attack, Simon and his men would be outgunned but not overpowered. He shook the thought out of his mind.

By the time Simon reached his men, he had all the details worked out, but for now he could only wait until the dark hours of the early morn-ing. He adjusted the alarm on his digital watch to wake him at two o'clock. He calculated it would take at least one and half hours to gather the men and their equipment, conduct a briefing, make the return march across the field, and set up their positions.

Next to the small fire, Simon lay down on the cold ground and closed his eyes, but was unable to fall sleep. His mind replayed the plan, working and refining it until he felt completely satisfied with all the details. At some point during the night, however, he fell deeply asleep, for the alarm on his watch startled him awake. It was time to begin.

❖ ❖ ❖

Cumulus clouds, heavy-laden with moisture, floated slowly over-head, diffusing the moon's glow, casting an eerie brightness around the haunting clouds. The midnight blue glowed against the blackened silhouette of the forest trees and branches that towered overhead. Entangled in each other's arms, Petrus and Taveta lay panting on a soft tanned buffalo hide. Their lungs heaved heavily for fresh cool air. Rolling his head to the side, Taveta sweetly kissed her on the forehead. She smiled and said, "Your heart beats strong and wild like a lion."

Gently he quieted her, placing his fingers to her lips, "Shh, my little lioness, your king of beasts will rest now."

She giggled softly, snuggled in closer, and closed her eyes. Their exhausted bodies glistened with sweat from their fierce sex. Her energized mind began to wonder. Again she spoke, "Just think about it."

"What?" He was beginning to doze off.

"For the next few days, possibly even a week or two, there will be no Dubois, Khosa, or Valli to interrupt us! We can make love as often as we please. Every day, three or four times! I don't want to leave this spot, here in your arms. We are free!"

"Only for a short time," Taveta reminded her. Rolling onto his side he pulled her to his chest. Holding her close, he continued, "When Dubois is finished with us, you will go back to the city, and I will return to my wife and children."

"Do you love her?"

Taveta was struggling to stay awake. "Who? My wife?"

"Yes."

"She is a good woman, giving me four fine sons in as many years."

Petrus thought about his words. A woman who gives her husband sons is a much-prized wife. She pushed against Taveta's shoulders rolling him onto his back. Getting up she straddled her legs across his waist. She then leaned over his chest supporting her upper body with her hands on the ground at each side of his head. One thick pointy breast dangled across his lips tickling him as she swayed back and forth.

Pretending to be asleep, he played the game with her until the tension began to grow and he could not stand the teasing any more. With the reflexes of a cobra, he struck at her rosebud nipple, sucking it into his mouth. As it filled and hardened with excitement, she moaned and cooed, "Taveta, I've been thinking. When I open my own brothel, you will come to the city with me and work as our protector and guard. You can send your pay home as you do now, to support your wife and four fine sons. I will even allow you to visit them once a year to ensure you more fine sons." With one hand she reached down between her thighs and took hold of him. He was hard and stiff. Expertly, she caressed his masculinity. "And that," she continued simply, "is the way it is going to be. Understand?"

Rocking his hips, yearning for her, he moaned, "Oh yes, Petrus, if that is how it must be."

With him now agreeing, she slid over his erection and lowered onto him. He moaned again with pleasure. She rode him long and hard until he neared his end. As one entity, they rolled over with him on top. He bucked deeply inside her until he felt her body give. They reached their zenith together, he collapsing on top of her sweaty body. With the last of his strength he whispered in her ear, "That is how it must be."

Exhausted from their sex, they slept in each other's arms until the cool night air chilled them awake. Taveta reached over for the edge of the hide, wrapping it around them for warmth. The sound of footsteps nearby brought his instincts fully on guard. He placed his hand protectively over Petrus' mouth, awakening her. The whites of her large eyes clearly showed alarm in the dim shadowy light. Taveta leaned over and ever so softly whispered in her ear, "Someone is nearby."

She nodded that she understood, and he released his grip. Bundled up in the buffalo hide, the two naked bodies lay motionless in the darkness, listening. The sound of one man walking quietly in the woods soon became the sound of several men equally spaced apart.

Taveta held Petrus securely in his arms. Neither one of them moved as the five strangers quietly stalked past them. When the sounds of the footsteps faded, Taveta whispered again, "We must dress quickly and get away from here."

As quickly as they could, they got out of their love nest and gathered up their clothing. Rolling up the skin, they sneaked off into the blackness of the forest.

After some distance, Taveta stopped to let Petrus catch her breath. "Where are we going?" she asked, between deep gasps of air.

"We must find Dubois." The sound of a distant gunshot echoed up the hillside, interrupting him. "We must find Dubois and warn him that his camp has been raided."

"I heard Valli describe the direction the old bull took flight in," Petrus said. "We must go back around to the west edge of the large field to pick up their trail."

By first light Petrus' good sense of direction had led them to the spoor of the old bull elephant with three sets of human footprints. Taveta took over from there and led Petrus up the side of the mountain.

Simon and his men waited patiently in the bushes, camouflaged and well-hidden just beyond the perimeter of light. They blended into the forest flora so well that Simon had a hard time distinguishing each man's position. Experienced, well-trained, and hardened soldiers, they had worked together many times and trusted each other as family. They waited motionless for Simon's signal to begin the raid on the laborers' camp.

The muscles in Simon's back tensed tightly. He cupped his hand over his watch and pushed a tiny button on the side of the dial. The digital watch glowed. It would be light in less than two hours. They needed to move before the break of dawn ruined their chance for a surprise attack.

Emerging from the black shadows into the dim fire's glow, Simon took his first steps into the light. The four members of the anti-poaching team, equally spaced around the camp, took their lead from Simon and followed suit. With all aspects of the camp covered and the natives sleeping soundly, Simon rummaged through the papers stacked neatly on the small metal table outside the tent. Under the rock used as a paperweight, he found a topical map of the region. The location of this campsite was clearly marked with a red circle. Farther west, over the Uganda border, there were two other areas marked.

One mark was just east of Lifi. Now just a small shantytown, at one time it had been a growing community of miner's before the government forced the European owners out. The mining operations were turned over to the local people, and the collapse of the prosperous copper mines soon followed. Now, the area was bare of all business and people, nothing more than a ghost town sprawling at the intersection of a paved road and a dirt trail. Forgotten by most, its remote location was too isolated to attract attention.

The other red mark on the map indicated a small plateau closer to the present location, only deeper inside the forest. To the northwest, the area was covered with virgin forest. Many miles and much rugged terrain separated the plateau from the ghost town. Just the kind of place, Simon thought, an organized and resourceful poacher could easily work from with a minimal crew.

The noise of the rustling papers slowly awakened one of the sleeping men. The man, drugged with sleep, rose halfway from his bed of skins. Wiping the sleep from his eyes, he called in almost a whisper, "Taveta? Petrus? Is that you?"

Simon moved back to the dark shadows alongside the tent, squatting just a few feet away from where the man was awakening. Again the man softly called out, "Taveta? Petrus? Is that you?"

Feeling a surge of energy, Simon played the man like a cat chasing a string. Softly he giggled like a schoolgirl.

The man's body relaxed and he dropped back down to his warm bed. "Don't tease me like that, girl. Get back to sleep." The man rolled over onto his side.

Simon stuffed the map into his shirt pocket. Tearing off a strip of duct tape, he spoke aloud, "Let's get this over with." The sound of his voice broke the silence with a boom. The sleeping was man startled fully awake and rolled over. Simon sprang from his hiding place alongside the tent. The movement drew the man's attention, and he quickly spun around.

Simon knocked the man flat on his sleeping mat and securely placed the wide band of duct tape across his mouth. Caught off guard, the man was easily maneuvered onto his stomach. Straddling him like a rider on a horse, Simon pulled the man's hands together behind his back. From his shirt pocket, he pulled out a long plastic cable tie, looping it around the man's crossed wrists. Pulling tight, Simon drew the man's hands together in cowboy fashion.

Another man, sleeping close by, awoke and jumped to help his friend. As Simon began to rise from his tied prisoner, the man charged. Looking up, Simon prepared for the body slam.

As the two men's bodies collided, Simon reached out to lock his powerful arms around his opponent. As they were knocked off balance, falling with limbs entangled, they crashed hard on the ground breaking Simon's hold. Falling apart, both men quickly jumped to their feet.

Fists flew past Simon's head, first the left, then the right, and then the left again. The man soon realized he was no match for Simon's massive body.

With little effort and with lightening speed, Simon ducked away from the man's punches. Having played long enough, the mighty Colonel sent a powerful karate kick into the man's stomach.

Bent over, holding his stomach, the man gasped for air as he stumbled backwards, unbalanced. Simon followed him toward the center of the camp. Catching his breath, the guard stood unsteadily, and stared at this enormous stranger. Silently Simon watched and waited for his next move.

With reckless courage, the man charged again. Simon met him half way and ducked low at the last second, rising with precise timing. The man's acceleration propelled him up and over Simon's back, sending the man backwards, cartwheeling in the air. Landing flat on his back, the man lay quietly for a few long seconds. Then his hands began to move, and he rolled over onto his side. Simon faced him again as the winded man once more rose and stared at his opponent.

His body trembled as he coughed and gasped for wind, never taking his eyes off Simon. He slowly took a step toward the towering man in military fatigues. Sparking a menacing grin, the man was still several feet away from Simon when he began his swing. As the man's fist reached its apex, he released a handful of soft dry earth. Simon's response spun him around, protecting his eyes from the flying dust. As he whirled, he dropped to the ground and kicked out with a sweeping motion, knocking the man off his feet. Rolling on top of him, Simon's weight pinned his opponent to the ground. Simon then cowboy-tied this man's hands behind his back with another plastic cable tie.

When Simon rose and looked around him, he found that his men had carried on their work. The other prisoners were secured.

Speaking loudly and clearly, first in his native language and then again in English, Simon addressed the group of prisoners. "I am Colonel Simon Kuldip with the Kenya Wildlife Anti-poaching Division. You are all under arrest and are prisoners until you can be tried for the crimes of poaching protected animals and associating with the illegal trade of bush-meat. Anyone resisting arrest or attempting to escape will be shot. Have I made myself clear?" The prisoners nodded their heads. This he thought, was an easy raid -- a good initiation for coming back to work after his long medical leave.

Simon walked over to the first man he had so taken. He lifted him by the shirt and forced him into a sitting position. Kneeling in front of him, Simon picked at the corner of the gray duct tape that covered the man's mouth. Slowly, jerking, to inflict more pain, Simon pulled the tape from the man's full lips and asked, "Who and where are Taveta and Petrus? You called to them."

The man dropped his eyes. Simon jerked his chin up, "I asked you a question."

"I do not know what you speak about." His English was rough.

Removing his pistol from his holster, Simon waved the gun in front of the man's face. Steady as a rock the man showed no signs of intimidation. Simon dropped the clip and casually inspected the inch long cartridge. The man's eyes widened as he watched the officer inspect the gaping hole in the hollow-point bullets.

Slowly Simon returned the clip to the pistol and switched the safety off. Once more he asked the man, "Who and where are Taveta and Petrus?"

Stupidly, the man shrugged his shoulders. Simon placed the cold steel of the muzzle to the man's temple. "Do you remember, now?"

The man closed his eyes and shook his head.

Simon quietly and patiently waited for the man to open his eyes again. Then he said, "Well, if you don't have any information for me, I don't have any real use for you." As Simon rotated the muzzle of the pistol, the man cringed, feeling the cold hard steel roll into a deadly position.

In a deep, but calm voice, Simon commanded, "Look at me! I want to see your eyes."

Very slowly the man rolled his eyes up to meet Simon's. Small beads of perspiration dotted his forehead. Gathering along his eyebrows, the wetness rolled dirty streaks down his dark cheeks. Simon gave the man a broad white smile and pulled the hammer back, clicking it into firing position.

Dropping his eyes, trembling with fear, the man cried out, "Please. I beg you."

The colt 1911, single action, .45-caliber pistol had seen better days. Though its finish was worn and pitted along its six-inch barrel, when Simon pulled the trigger, it fired as though brand new. The heavy hollow-point bullet exploded from the barrel with a deafening ring. Skimming the man's hairline, it left a perfectly shaved burn-groove to mark its path on his black wooly head.

Simon waited a long time for the man to gather his senses and realize that he was still alive. Slowly, he opened his eyes and was looking back into that same broad, white smile. The man turned pale, and his eyes began to roll up into their sockets. "Oh, no, you don't, not yet!" Simon slapped him across the face a couple of times, bringing him around.

When the man's pupils had regained their normal size, Simon asked again, "Who and where are Taveta and Petrus?" Weakly the man answered, "They are lovers. They disappeared days ago. When I heard the noise, I thought they might be returning. I was wrong."

"You were wrong, all right." Simon called his men together as he released his grip on the man. Falling over, the man buried his head in the dusty woodland floor, crying.

"There are two more, around here somewhere. If they heard any of this, they would have taken off. I want the three of you to stay here and watch the prisoners. At first light you can head back to the post and process the prisoners. Jay," Simon called to his most skilled and trusted comrade, "you will come with me. We're going after Dubois."

Chapter 20

The black shadows fused the forest to the night. Oddly-shaped midnight blue forms glowed dimly, outlining the trees and undergrowth. Dr. Mitch guessed he had run about four miles from the tented camp where he and his fellow scientists were being held captive. His lungs burned from the stress and effort, and his heart pounded so loudly he could hear each chamber pumping oxygen-starved blood.

Slowing down, he allowed his body a short break. Leaning against a tall tree, the doctor's knees buckled, and he slid down to a squat. Tilting his head back, Mitch sucked in the cold night air. Sweat rolled down the sides of his face and through his short brown hair before dripping to his sweat-drenched shirt. The dark circles under each arm merged with the wide band of wetness that ran down the center of his chest and back.

Dr. Mitch looked at his watch; the illuminated hands pointed to five minutes until five a.m. He would rest for ten minutes, just enough time to bring his pounding heart down to a quiet rhythm and to ease the stinging he felt with each breath. In a little more than an hour, the sun would be making its first appearance. Perhaps then, he thought, he would be able to get a bearing on his location.

With no idea where he was, Dr. Mitch followed a small trail down the hill that led away from camp. He was going for help. He did not know where he would find it, but he had to try. Doing something was better than doing nothing, he argued.

Slowly Mitch's breathing returned to normal. He mumbled, "I must get going. I must get help and save the others." The guards would soon awaken and realize he had slipped away in the night. They would have little trouble following him in the daylight. He needed to get as far from them as possible, and he had to stay on the trail until it was light enough to leave it. "Soon," he thought, looking at the early morning sky, "there will be enough light to open the map." He felt the folded papers still tightly wedged in his pants pocket.

The doctor remembered crossing a river and traveling alongside a line of tall bluffs. The trail was rocky, littered with large boulders. That is where the porters dropped the case carrying the radio equipment. It tumbled down the steep hill smashing into the boulders, bouncing from one large rock to the next until it splashed into the river. The porters had chased the case down the hill, but their attempts were in vain.

By the time they had reached the river's edge the big yellow case was disappearing under the muddy river. The cracked sides had taken in water, sinking the case. All of their communication equipment had been destroyed, completely cutting them off from the outside world.

"I've got to find that river crossing," Dr. Mitch thought. Traveling slowly at first, then once again quickening his pace, he pushed himself forward. Running, recklessly lost in an African forest, he followed a small animal path as it wound its way through the foothills of Mount Elgon.

The blackness of night began to lift and transform into deep shades of green and gray. The downward slope of the hill increased steeply, and it was littered with rocks and roots; each rainfall had gnawed away at the path, exposing treacherous footholds.

Stumbling over half-buried rocks, Mitch lost his balance. His momentum pushed him forward, tripping him over exposed roots in the trail. He fell hard, slamming face-first against the ground. As Dr. Mitch fell, he reached out to break his fall, scraping his bare skin against the rocks. "Damn!" he cried. His skin burned.

Twisted painfully, his ankle was trapped. Mitch cursed, "Damn it!" Reaching back into the shadows, the doctor felt the trap that caught his ankle. The warm and scaly texture moved under his touch.

Mitch jerked his hand back. "Oh, GOD!" he gasped as the snake quickly wrapped its tail around his feet. He tried to pull his legs out from the clutch, but the snake held him steady.

Reaching out to his side, Mitch grabbed onto the trunk of a small tree. Pulling with all his will, he tried to free himself from the snake's grip. As he dragged himself slowly forward, the snake tightened its coils around his ankles. Resisting, the reptile began to pull back, dragging the man toward the darkness of the underbrush.

Winning the tug-of-war, the snake began to wrap more of itself up the man's legs. Mitch's grip on the tree was no match for the powerful force that opposed him. The rough bark cut into his soft skin. His hands gripped tightly and tore loose the tree's covering.

The morning sun was just beginning to peer through the forest, lighting the darkness to a rich blue gray. Looking back over his shoulder, Mitch caught a glimpse of the natural camouflage that blended the reptile in so well, black-edged bands forming isolated gray-brown blotches along the length of the snake's body.

With a tight grip around the man's legs, the python's head began slithering over the top of his muddy leather boots. The weight and scaly texture moved up the backside of Mitch's thighs. The doctor watched over his shoulder, out of the corner of his eye, as the triangular-shaped head finally rested upon his hindquarter. The forked tongue quickly flashed out, tasting the air over the brightly colored map that protruded from his pants pocket.

Uncontrollably, Mitch's body began to tremble. He was unable to move and stared, wide-eyed, waiting for the snake to make its move. Slowly the reptile glided up onto the man's back, pausing to take in the odors of human perspiration.

The large snake rose up, swinging back and forth from left to right. Its belly was creamy white with dark speckles. Strangely beautiful, the snake leaned forward, its yellow slitted eyes glowing in the morning gloom. Mitch slowly lowered his head to the ground. Burying his face in the crook of his arm, he began to cry uncontrollably.

The sounds of his sobbing and the shaking of his body alerted the curious snake, and it moved onto the top of the man's head. At the first feel of the scales moving across his scalp, Mitch lost control. Screaming out with fear, he tried to jump up. Twisting around, he struck out frantically at the snake, flinging the pieces of bark that were still clutched in his grip. Graceful as a ballerina, the snake reared back safely, hissing its threats.

Alarmed, the snake struck in defense, slashing the man's cheek with its long, curved teeth. The doctor cried out again and lay on his back, holding his throbbing, bloody cheek, staring up at the menacing snake swaying high over his face.

The fear that had welled up inside him turned into desperate courage. The snake hovered, dominating, watching and summing up its quarry. Suddenly, without any warning, it began to tighten its coils around the man's legs. Mitch could feel tingling numbness begin in his feet as the circulation was cut off.

Dr. Mitch's trembling hand patted the ground around him, desperately searching for something, anything, to use as a weapon. His fingers gripped the crown of a partially exposed rock. Without taking his eyes off the reptile, he frantically clawed at the earth. Moist dirt and bits of stone filled and broke his fingernails. His movement spurred the snake's contractions. Screaming with pain, he felt the bones in his ankles begin to give. Gripping the rock firmly, pulling it loose, he heard his bones snap from the pressure.

Mitch screamed aloud from the pain and shot up into a sitting position. The snake, master of the unblinking stare, rose up alongside. Hissing and dancing, the large head swung back and forth. It seemed to be playing a game.

Sitting up straighter, Mitch slowly raised his left hand clenching the rock, drawing the serpent's attention off to the side by wiggling his fingers. With a fast swing of his right hand, he had the snake by the neck just below the powerful jaws. The python's strength was much greater than he had anticipated. Dropping the rock, he had to use both hands and all his energy to keep the snake from striking again.

Grunting and groaning, Mitch was able to use his body weight to wrestle the snake's head to the ground. Squeezing as tightly as he could with one hand, he reached for the rock.

An unbridled craze filled him as he wildly attacked the serpent's head. Dr. Mitch hammered away at the soft underside of the snake's jaw. Caught up in his wild fury, he missed several times, striking his own hand. Fear deadened the pain, so he never felt the life drain from the snake's deadly embrace. Even though the snake's head was soon severed from its body, the doctor, consumed by fear, continued to beat on the head until it was flattened and ripped apart.

Dizzy and panting, Dr. Mitch crawled on his elbows out of the snake's coils. He was too weak to stand, and his broken ankles were beginning to throb as the blood began to flow and swell the bruised, mangled tissue. Just a few feet away from the snake, Mitch collapsed on the ground.

❖ ❖ ❖

"Comrade! Wake up!" The rubber sole of the tire-tread sandal kicked Mitch in the shoulder. "Wake up! I have something to tell you!"

From the unconscious darkness, Dr. Mitch heard a voice calling. Slowly the pain swept up his body, and he opened his eyes. Kneeling down next to him, a black man waved the end of a rifle barrel in front of his face. "I want to tell you something. Do you understand?"

Mitch recognized Gbenya, the guard from the camp. Tears flooded his eyes, and he nodded his head.

"Good," said Gbenya. He continued in broken English, "I wanted to tell you that the snake won after all." The armed man stood. Looking at his tall skinny partner, Tshombe, he snickered, "Okay, it's your turn."

Tshombe lifted his rifle casually to his hip, pointed the muzzle at the doctor's temple and pulled the trigger. The sound of the rifle shot filled the early morning air, echoing throughout the foothills.

Chapter 21

The morning dampness was transforming into motionless dense air. Its wetness had settled on the broad-leaf, shade-loving plants, gathering as dew before rolling to the leaves' edges, then dripping into the woodland floor.

The rising sun glowed over the forest canopy. Long narrow beams of light gently descended from the lofty crown of timbers. Glistening sparks covered the foliage and ferns.

Rugged rocks lay scattered along the forest hillside. Slippery layers of moss hid the sharp edges, making movement slow and treacherous.

Having traveled continuously all day and all through the night with only brief breaks, each member struggled up the hill with the added weight of fatigue and hunger.

Songs of chanting birds high in the tree canopy infused the air. Their movements from treetop to treetop fashioned the rhythm for their choir. The occasional snapping of a limb and the sound of its falling added to the drama of the symphony. A high, slow wind drifted across the leaf-covered branches, like applause.

The hillside was alive and at peace in its own haven. "Birds are the overseers," Mhinga had said earlier. "Nothing happens in this place without their knowledge. Their songs project harmony. Cries forewarn of danger, and excited behavior may show annoyance or need."

Zawawi stopped. Something had caught his attention. He peered ahead into the shadows. He had not been concentrating as deeply as he should. His mind would not release the thoughts of the whore and her lover discussing his oldest son. That preoccupation, along with building hunger, had cost him his keen edge. Now, only his eyes moved slowly, searching across the hill's ascent. Standing several yards ahead of the others, he could feel them watching his motionless action. Scanning back across the vegetation, this time he saw it, the flicker of an ear chasing off a pestering fly.

It was a male bushbuck. Standing less than three feet tall across the back, his dark chestnut coat was flecked with a mixture of white stripes and spots. His patched tan face and short spiral horns blended into the thick stems of the underbrush. Infrequently seen, and unaccustomed to the sight of humans, he stood perfectly still, unsure if he faced friend or foe.

Just a few yards away, the animal was an easy target for the skillful hunter. But Zawawi hesitated, raising his spear seconds too late. Sensing danger, the bushbuck whirled in flight. Crashing through the deep underbrush, the animal disappeared, swallowed up by the foliage.

Instantly the forest canopy became quiet. In the echoing silence, frustration filled the Maasai. Lack of sleep and food fed his anger. He did not need to turn to see the disappointment on the others' faces; he could feel it. He knew there would be other game, and that he must concentrate in order to hunt successfully. It would not be safe to hunt with the rifle, for the sound would echo off the mountain into the valley below to the poacher's camp. Also, Dubois and the boys were out hunting for the elephant, and they could be anywhere.

From the back of the line, Mhinga broke the silence, "Look there!" Pointing high above Zawawi's head, Mhinga revealed a little bird that darted and swooped across their path from a high branch to the tops of the underbrush. Mhinga passed by the others and stood next to Zawawi, "It's a honey guide!"

Zawawi focused on the bird's movement. Concentrating on his surroundings lessened the tension in his body, filtering out his anger and disappointment with his two sons. The little bird settled on the branch looking down on them. "Mhinga!" Zawawi growled, "He would not make a suitable meal for Buster."

"I don't want you to kill it, Zawawi!" There was strength in Mhinga's voice. "I think we should follow him. He will lead us to honey."

The bird called loudly before leaving his perch. He flew ahead and landed just a short distance away. He called again, before flying back towards them. The bird repeated this action several more times.

Zawawi snapped at Mhinga, "If you want to fill your belly with honey, you follow the little bird. I want to fill mine with meat."

"I will make tea," Mhinga impatiently stood his ground. "The sweetness of the honey will curb the hunger cries in your belly while you hunt."

Jon spoke up from behind, "Hot tea and a rest does sound pretty good right now."

"Sounds good to me, too," MacKenzie dared to add.

Outnumbered, Zawawi stepped aside for Mhinga to follow the bird.

The little bird flew from tree to tree. Looking down from each perch, it called out to its followers below. It led them higher up the hillside. Not having to pick his way over the rough terrain as they did, the bird seemed annoyed that his new companions did not keep up with him. Flying on ahead, he crossed a small clearing and perched on a low tree limb. Noisily he called, directing the others towards him, impatiently waiting.

As soon as Mhinga took his first step into the clearing and made eye contact with the little bird, the bird flew off again. Mhinga crossed the edge of a clearing, staying focused on the cries of the honey guide. Fascinated, MacKenzie followed close behind.

Jon and Zawawi stopped at the edge of the clearing, looking across the opening at the flattened grasses and ferns. In the center, a large rectangle of rocks fenced a pile of white ashes. Small piles of green limbs, freshly cut, lay beside the campfire's remains.

Not hearing Jon and Zawawi following them, MacKenzie and Mhinga returned to the clearing followed by a mad little bird, squawking his disapproval. As they entered the opening, they stopped and stared dumbfounded. Zawawi walked over and squatted down next to the ring of rocks.

Jon silently walked the perimeter as if he were investigating a crime scene. By the time he made his way around to MacKenzie and Mhinga, Jon's face was etched with worry. In a low solemn voice, he said, "Mhinga, follow your bird, if it isn't too much farther. Bring the honey back here. Keep a sharp eye open for snares." Turning to MacKenzie, he said, "Leave your pack here. You will travel much easier without it." As she slid it off her shoulders, he asked her, "Where's that strange knife of yours?" His voice was deep with worry.

Reaching into her pants pocket, she produced the knife with all the tools.

"Keep it handy. You may need it." Jon called Buster to follow him as he turned and walked around the clearing again.

"Mhinga, what's going on?" MacKenzie asked. "I don't understand. What are snares?"

Mhinga glanced up at the little bird prancing across a branch over head. "Snares are animal traps, usually made with a wire noose. They could be small enough for a man to get a foot caught, or large and high enough for his neck. Please keep knife-tool handy." Mhinga turned and followed the bird into the bushes.

"Wait!" MacKenzie grabbed his arm, turning him back around, "Maybe it isn't safe to go after the honey." She glanced across at Zawawi poking around in the cold white ashes.

"Of course you do not have to go," Mhinga answered. Zawawi looked up at MacKenzie and snickered at her hesitation.

Seeing the mockery on his face, MacKenzie turned back to Mhinga. "Lead the way," she said, with just a bit of apprehension in her voice.

"Mhinga," Zawawi called.

Stopping, Mhinga turned toward him. "*Ndio?*"

Zawawi stood and tossed his spear to Mhinga. "Use this to test anything suspicious." Squatting back down by the old campfire, he looked over his shoulder again, adding, "And don't get honey all over it."

Mhinga gave a small bow of appreciation to Zawawi. Turning to MacKenzie he gave a wide smile and said, "Let's go."

Jon ignored Zawawi's chuckle; instead he focused on investigating the campsite. He carefully studied the ferns, noticing that some had been pushed over, while others seemed woven together, and then broken at the base as if something heavy had laid in the center. These plants had wilted and just started to brown along their edges as the stored nutrients depleted. Other plants had started to stand tall again after just being pushed aside. Jon called to Zawawi, "Something made a nest over here." He pointed across the clearing, "And something heavy lay over there, along side of the log, too."

Zawawi was poking in the ashes with his hands, sifting the powdery dust through his fingers. On one of the outlying rocks, he piled up heavy lead pellets from a shotgun. Nearby, he laid a pile of small bones and little curled lumps of dried roasted skin with dark scorched hair still attached. Looking up at Jon, he said, "Whoever made this fire stayed here for a couple of days. They ate the fresh meat they had killed with a shotgun."

"How long ago?" Jon asked.

"Less than a week," Zawawi guessed.

Jon kneeled down and poked around Zawawi's findings. Picking up a clump of dried skin, he studied the scorched hair. "This could be from almost anything. Too much is burned away to identify it."

Buster put his nose up to it, hoping to find a morsel to chew on. Instead he sneezed at the white ash he had sniffed up his nose. The dog let out a depressed whimper before lying down next to Jon.

Zawawi got up and wandered about the camp. Turning his back to Jon he lowered his head and said, "This is where Valli shot the *sokwe.*"

Jon tossed the curled skin back into the ashes. "How can you be sure?"

The Maasai crossed over and sat next to his friend. Drawing his knees up, he wrapped his arms around them. In a low, sad voice he answered, "You know that these are not the bones of an antelope, they are too small. And they are too big for ground rodent." He paused while Jon looked over the mixed pile of bones. "Do you remember Valli's words to the lorry driver? He said he got three big *sokwes,* and he smoked them. This fire is too large for just cooking a meal. It was made long to smoke many strips of meat. The green limbs in this pile would have provided such a curing smoke."

"Yeah, but that doesn't prove it was Valli. It could have been another hunter. Valli also said the woods were full of hunters working for the loggers."

Releasing the grip on his knees, Zawawi leaned back on the palms of his hands. Tilting his head back, he grinned at his friend's attempt to rationalize what was so clear to him. "Jon, Valli also spoke of the location of the elephants, the same spot where we found them, below the bluffs in the valley, where the river bends before the fork. This is the spot, my friend." He looked over at Jon with great sadness in his eyes. "Remember, I taught that boy how to hunt and build such a fire. This is the spot, and it was Valli." Zawawi's voice trailed off as they stared at the pile of bones. Jon thought over all that he had just heard, and he knew that Zawawi was right.

Zawawi looked up and scanned the campsite. His eyes had changed from sadness to hatred. "I would even wager," he began, "that Valli laid the limbs and heads upon that log to bleed them."

Jon looked over his shoulder at the fallen log. "Yeah, the ants and insects would have feasted on the drippings."

"Yes," Zawawi continued, "Then Valli slowly smoked the meat, preserving it for transport. Khosa was here, too. He would have helped carry it all back to that Dubois bastard and the whore." He leaned forward again, concluding, "Valli was here, and it was he who shot, skinned and smoked three chimpanzees." Jon laid his hand on Zawawi's shoulder. He had no words that could comfort his friend.

After a few minutes of silence, Zawawi tried to change the subject. "Perhaps we will cross paths with the bushbuck again."

Jon grinned, "Perhaps so. If we do, will you throw your spear this time?"

Zawawi smiled back. "Perhaps," he joked.

The grin on Jon's face faded, and he looked over the pile of bones and pellets.

Zawawi's face hardened. He was still holding a few of the buckshot in his hand. He rolled them around in his palm before tossing them back into the white powder. He then hung his head and closed his eyes.

Jon did the same. The two men and the dog rested quietly alongside the ring of white ashes, bones, and shotgun pellets, waiting for MacKenzie and Mhinga to return with the honey.

As the placid morning sun turned to the heat of high noon, the birds' choir gave way to the rising sounds of insects. Upper branches of the tall trees swayed gently. The high, slow breeze could not penetrate the thick canopy, so it offered no resistance to the tiny flying bugs or to the circulation of the rising moisture summoned by the noon sun.

The hive was nestled deep inside the base of a log, a perfect, natural housing for the bee colony. The log provided excellent shelter from rain, falling limbs, and, of course, predators. The little honey guide rested on a delicate branch of a nearby bush. Impatiently watching his new colleagues working, he frequently called out, offering encouragement. Flapping his wings about, ruffling and preening his feathers, he cheered them on.

Mhinga had built a small fire at the opening of the trunk. MacKenzie supplied him with fresh green limbs and dried leaves for fuel. Together they created a cloud of light gray smoke, gently fanning the fire with broad leaves, carefully directing the smoke into the bees' porthole. Almost immediately the bees quieted. Soothed by the smoke, they fell in clumps to the bottom of the log where they lay unharmed in a hypnotic state.

Bravely, the little bird flew from the bush to the ground, landing just a few feet away, eager for his reward.

Watching the bird's every move, MacKenzie asked, "If we hadn't come along, how would the bird get to the honey?"

Mhinga handed the big leaves to her. "Keep fanning." As he reached into his pack, he answered her question, "The bird would have found a honey badger. Their sweet tooth is just as strong. It would have followed the bird like we did."

"We have badgers in the States," MacKenzie said, looking over at the bird, "but I've never heard of anything like this. Don't you think that it is a bit odd that the bird would encourage us, not its usual partner, the honey badger, to dig out the honey? I mean, how did it know we would follow him?"

Mhinga smiled as he pulled out a large sturdy knife. "That is very observant of you, Ms. Mac." Kneeling by the opening, he said, "Keep fanning. I would guess there are people who live in these hills."

"Like the tribe your father is from, the Okiekes?"

Mhinga's hands disappeared into the smoke-filled log. He smiled at MacKenzie, "Close. But it is the Ogiekes. Hold out one of those leaves."

MacKenzie held the leaf centered over her palm while still fanning with the other one. Mhinga pulled out a small chunk of cone dripping with honey and laid it on the leaf. At the first sight of the honey cone, the little bird went wild, hopping up and down, flapping his wings, and calling out hysterically. "All right, all right," MacKenzie said to the little bird. "You get the first piece." She laid the leaf down next to the bird. "He doesn't seem timid at all. Do you think this bird may have directed some-one from the Ogiekes to this hive?"

Reaching into the hive, Mhinga said, "Possibly. The bees will start rebuilding their nest as soon as they wake up from their sleep, so there is no way of knowing if someone else has been here before." Mhinga cut out a bigger section and handed it to MacKenzie. She kept the broad leaf cupped. Mhinga said, "This piece will do us fine."

"Shouldn't we take some extra for later?" MacKenzie asked.

She could see by the look on Mhinga's face that her question irritated him. "Ms. Mac, we will take only what we need from the earth, when we need it." He handed her the honey cone. "That way when we or someone else passes this way again, their needs can be met as well. This keeps the natural resources from becoming depleted. That is one of the first things my father taught me about the ways of his tribe."

MacKenzie felt humbled at his words. "They sound like very wise and gentle people."

Mhinga ran his finger down the flat side of the knife, and then stuck his finger, dripping with honey, into his mouth, licking off the sweetness. He held the knife up to MacKenzie; she wiped clean the opposite side. As she enjoyed the freshness of the warm honey, Mhinga explained, "Many of the people of Africa are like the countryside in which they live. Some are like the mysterious quiet of the forest, some are like the aggressive wilds of the plains."

"More words of wisdom from your father?"

Smiling as he rose, he said, "No. Words of Mhinga, from observing both worlds." He stomped the smoldering fire, wiped the blade clean with a leaf and replaced it in his pack. "We must go back now. The bees will be waking up soon and will not be happy."

"What about the bird?"

"He will enjoy his honey until he gets his fill and leaves. The bees will not bother him."

"I wonder if my father has met any of the forest people?"

Mhinga stopped and looked into MacKenzie's eyes. "If he has, he is in very good company. Try not to worry about him, we will find him soon." Trying to lighten the pain that showed on her face, he smiled and said almost jokingly, "What will your father think of Jon?"

"Of Jon?" She was taken by surprise. She wondered if he had seen them in each other's arms. "What do you mean? I would think that he would be grateful towards all of you for bringing me safely." She paused, "Then he'll be mad as hell at me for coming."

Mhinga chuckled softly. Swinging his pack over his shoulder and picking up the leaf with the honey cone, he said, "You know what I mean." Reaching for Zawawi's spear he turned and walked into the thick brush.

His comment stunned her, leaving her standing by the smoldering fire. She wondered how he knew. Her mind sped back the last few days. Perhaps he had seen them embracing the other morning in the fog.

Mhinga called back, snapping her out of her thought, "Are you coming?"

When she caught up with him, he was smiling like a kid with a secret. "Well?" he said to her.

Nonchalant, she answered with a straight face, "Oh, Mhinga, you have an overactive imagination."

But her words and her eyes gave her away, and he knew he was right.

Chapter 22

The sweet, hot tea curbed their hunger; exploring and analyzing the campsite took their minds off their fatigue. Buster had gratefully licked the sticky honey from the broad leaf and then slept quietly next to Jon. For a short while, they rested. The quiet brought peace, and one by one they drifted into some much-needed sleep.

The dog's snores and mumbling growls eventually awakened everyone but himself. Wiping sleep from his eyes, Mhinga made a fresh pot of tea. Jon and MacKenzie lay on their sides, facing each other. Awakened by the snoring dog but too tired to move, they rested quietly, studying each other.

As Mhinga prepared the tea, he watched Jon and MacKenzie gaze into each other's eyes. Their silence was filled with all the unspoken words he knew they felt but had not yet spoken.

Zawawi soon awoke and nudged Jon in the back. "That dog of yours!"

Jon sat up and grinned. "He was your dog first."

"Yes," Zawawi smiled, "and I remember why I gave him to you. So I could sleep!"

Jon chuckled, as Mhinga passed out hot cups of tea. "We need to get some fresh meat. And you should try to contact Simon again." Zawawi nodded.

The two hunters gathered their weapons and headed into the bush. Mhinga began to set up camp.

MacKenzie's eyes followed Jon as he crossed the camp. Just before he reached the bush, he turned and looked over his shoulder. She rose, and her long wavy hair fell across her shoulders, exposing the leaves and twigs tangled in her dark wavy locks. Their eyes met, holding for just a flash. Jon's stomach bunched into a knot. He thought she was truly beautiful. The grime from days of hard travel, and the leafy litter in her hair actually added to her natural beauty. He chuckled. She looked like Mother Nature.

Mhinga walked over. Snickering, he said, "Tell me again what your father will think of Jon."

Embarrassed, she looked back over her shoulder where the two men had entered the forest. "Oh, Mhinga," she said, turning to him. "Can't we just look for something to eat? You are really reading too much into this."

"And what is THIS, that I'm reading too much into?" he inquired.

Softly, she replied, "I think it is nothing."

"I think you are trying to hide the truth from yourself."

She did not have a response. Dropping her eyes, she knew he was right. But this was not a time for romance; she had to find her father. She didn't care what he would think of Jon, she only wanted to know that he was all right. As she poured another cup of tea, worry clouded her face. Mhinga left her alone as he continued searching for mushrooms and edible plants.

Dropping a small handful of mushrooms and several stalks of wild celery at MacKenzie's feet, Mhinga said, "We will need a few more, and there is a large old fig tree over there." He pointed across the clearing. "Would you gather some ripe figs, while I go find some herbs?"

"Sure, Mhinga." MacKenzie set down her empty cup and wandered over to the fig tree. Scattered on the ground were hundreds of fallen figs. Small brightly-colored bugs and bees feasted on the sweet juices of the overly-ripe fruit.

Turning them over with the toe of her shoe, she looked for fresh ones, avoiding the ones claimed by the insects. She noticed some of the figs had been half eaten. She wondered what type of forest animal had casually strolled by, eating only half a fig. Some appeared to have been turned inside out, with skin still intact and the juicy innards sucked out.

The sound of leaves rustling high in the forest canopy was the only indication of a strong wind. The thick upper branches acted like a roof, allowing the sound to filter down while keeping the circulating air from ever reaching the lowest levels of the forest. MacKenzie looked up at the top of the tree swaying back and forth with the unfelt breeze. A dead branch broke loose and fell to the ground near her. She took a step back to avoid being struck, mumbling the old proverbial question, "If a tree falls in the forest and no one is around, does it still make a noise? I shall have to ask Mhinga that one." She chuckled at the thought.

The wind was starting to grow stronger, and the branches of the old tree moved wildly. Hearing a crack, she looked up again. A big branch, midway up the tree was moving. MacKenzie stepped back to get a better look. Just past a fork, a dark object stirred on the limb. As it moved, the branch dipped and cracked. She could not see it clearly, but again it moved, and again the branch dipped and cracked. Feeling uneasy, she walked backward into the clearing, not taking her eyes off the spot. Reaching down, she picked up a long, sturdy stick, in case she needed a weapon. She looked around the camp wondering which way Mhinga had gone, and if he would be close enough to hear if she screamed for help.

With the strong wind and the heavy movement, the branch gave a loud pop, followed by snapping crackles of splintering wood. The big forked branch broke loose. Swinging down, as on a hinge, it slammed against the smooth barked trunk. Through the leafy branches, MacKenzie could see part of the creature still clinging to the limb.

Bravely, with her stick in hand, MacKenzie walked slowly around the perimeter of the tree to get a clear view of the creature. With the long stick, she slowly reached high above her head into the leafy branches. A high-pitched, weak squeal filtered down. She reflexively jerked the stick back. Her heart raced. Not knowing what to expect, she blindly poked again. The animal hidden in the leaves squealed again and started to move. Startled, she jumped back. As the creature stirred, the splinters that held the branch to the tree tore loose, and it came crashing down in a blustering racket.

Wide-eyed, MacKenzie stared at the pile of leaves and broken branches that lay directly in front of her, waiting, watching for some maddened animal to jump out. "Where are those guys?" she muttered nervously. She wondered if the fall had killed the beast and what type of animal it was. Perhaps it was something that would be good to eat. She smiled at the thought of Zawawi's reaction, and the delicious prospect gave her new courage. She took a step forward and poked her stick into the branches. She could feel that she was pressing against something fleshy, but this time there was no noise. Slowly, she pushed aside the leaf-covered limbs. Without getting any closer, she could see just a small section of the animal's back. It was covered with short black wiry hair.

The leaves were thick, and the branches were laden heavily with fresh ripe fruit. She mumbled to herself as she assessed the downed limb, "At least, we will have plenty of figs to eat." Listening for another noise, she poked again with still no response. Feeling braver, she took a step closer. Reaching out, she grabbed the nearest branch at the top of the pile and pulled some of the branches away. Again she listened and watched for some indication that the creature might be alive and dangerous, but all was quiet. Stepping up to the pile with the stick held high, ready to defend herself, she leaned over and looked into the massive heap of greenery.

Inside she could see the mass of short black hair. Whatever it was, it was curled up and intertwined in the branches so she could not get a clear view of it. Swiftly she poked it again, ready to flee. There was no response. She said, "Good, I hope it's dead." She reached in and pulled away more branches, exposing a small humanlike creature clinging to the limb.

"Oh God! No!" she cried. "I've killed it! I've killed a chimpanzee!" She was glad its little face was turned away from her so she didn't have to see its lifeless expression. MacKenzie hastily started digging her way into the heap of broken limbs. Carefully, she reached out and gently stroked the narrow little back. She could feel the warmth of his skin. Tears started to fill her eyes. "Oh, I'm so sorry," she whispered.

The chimp's arms were stretched out. His hands clenched a small forked branch. With tears streaming down her face, MacKenzie loosened the tight grip. One by one she gently pried off each tiny flesh-colored finger. Holding the little hand in hers she marveled at the similarities -- each wrinkled knuckle, the long, shapely nails, and the soft cushion where the thumb attached to the palm. Leaning over, she kissed the back of the tiny hand. At that same instant, as her lips caressed the tender skin, the little hand grasped around her finger.

Startled, she squealed, "You are still alive!" Leaning over, she looked into his face. His eyes were still closed. "You are still alive!" she said again, almost laughing. "Oh God, what do I do now?" Freeing his grip from the tree, she said, "You're going to be just fine, little fellow. Jon and Mhinga will know what to do, and you will be just fine." Looking over the little creature, she worked her hands down each of his legs and arms. She could feel no broken bones.

Carefully, she lifted the little chimp from the branch, cradling him in her arms like an infant. His round head lopped lifelessly over the crook of her arm. Slowly rolling the chimp over onto his back, she looked at his tiny, precious face. Above his right eye rose a large bump that ran across his forehead into the center peak of glossy coarse hair that covered his head and body. The red and blue bruising discolored the soft tan skin of his face. A trickle of bright blood dribbled from a small cut low on his cheek, staining the fine white hairs that outlined his chin. Carrying him back to the clearing, she spoke softly to him, "There, there little guy, you will be just fine. We're going to take good care of you."

Sitting on the log, she stroked the hair that parted down the top of his head. Studying him with wonder, MacKenzie's eyes gazed into his peaceful face. Everything about him was so remarkably similar to humans: the short lashes that lined the edge of his eyelids, the creases of skin that encircled his eyes and chin, the long graceful curves and folds of his ears and the tiny nostrils of his pug nose that softly flared with each breath. The creases in his hands and feet strikingly paralleled hers.

He felt like a sleeping child in her arms, and she whispered to him, "I wish I knew what to do. But the others will be back soon." As she said this, she realized he could not understand her words. To soothe him, she hummed a children's lullaby. The chimp may not have understood, but at least she felt better. It was all she could think of. As she hummed to him and stroked his hair, his tiny grip tightened again. Perhaps, she thought, he did understand that she was going to help him.

❖ ❖ ❖

Together, Jon and Zawawi explored the hillside, watching for signs of wildlife. Occasionally, they crossed a narrow animal path and examined a spoor. Recognizing the types of animals and the age of the tracks or droppings turned into a game. Laughing and joking with each other, the two men reawakened their youth.

As young boys, they had hunted together. With each story or hoof print they encountered, another memory surfaced, beginning with "Remember when . . ." or "Whatever happened to . . ." or "I still can't believe you . . ." or "Did Simon ever find out about . . ." or "Good thing our fathers never knew that . . . ." And the years melted away as quickly.

The bond that formed in childhood had cemented them together for life. Though it had been severely damaged, repairs were slowly being made, and it was once again growing strong.

They talked about Simon, Colleen, and their parents. Eventually they talked about women. Both men tried to avoid the memories of a tall, longhaired blonde and the tragic death of Zawawi's first wife, though it weighed heavily on their minds. Neither one dared bring up the terrible memories. As they trekked up the hillside, the silence between them was so loud that each man could hear the other's pain.

Crossing a new trail, they stopped to investigate tracks. They examined a set of small, cloven-hoof prints in the soft ground. They both grinned in unison, "*Ngure!*" Wild pig! Their spirits lifted as they followed the tracks, their hunting skills took over. They worked with hand signals and body language, one entity following their prey.

A happy, grunting noise gave the pig's position away. Busy digging and rooting for some sweet-smelling morsel that lay buried beneath the forest floor, the wild hog was consumed with his work. The deeper he dug, the stronger the scent became and the more intently he dug. The moist, soft, top layer of dirt soon began to yield to a sandy, rocky layer. He loosened the small rocks with his forked toes, or pried them free using the long, curved canine tusk that grew from his lower jaw and curled up towards his flat snout. With the rock free, the pig clamped his mouth around it and backed out of the hole he had dug. Dropping the rock, the pig dived back into the hole filled with the maddening scent. So powerful was his passion that Jon and Zawawi, who sat just ten yards away, watching, were completely unnoticed.

The anticipation of fresh meat had Buster salivating with gusto. As they watched the pig working, Jon had to hold his arms tightly around the dog's chest. Zawawi helped by clamping his hands around Buster's muzzle. But still the dog anxiously danced with his front paws.

The back end of the pig was all that showed above the hole. The back legs worked furiously to keep the hole from caving in. Dirt was kicked out, spraying the air like a shower from a garden hose. Quite suddenly the movement stopped, and the pig's body trembled. Squealing with delight, the boar backed out of his hole with a large, dingy orange-colored root ball clenched in his mouth. When he crunched into it, breaking it in half, juicy slobbers ran down the edges of his lips. As he chewed, he made deep grunting noises. Biting into the other half, he closed his eyes with delight.

Seizing the moment, Zawawi stood, throwing his spear with such accuracy and strength that the boar fell instantly dead, still clenching his prized root tightly in his jaw. The aim was perfect, severing the spine just behind the skull.

Jon and Zawawi, laughed aloud at the comedy show the hog had given them. They felt like a couple of boys who had sneaked away from their parents and made their first kill.

In just a few minutes, they cleaned and quartered the hog, but the sun was dropping quickly, and the forest would soon be very dark. They traveled much faster on the return, not having to check each trail for a fresh spoor. Their keen sense of direction guided them swiftly down the hillside to the camp where Mhinga and MacKenzie waited for them.

Chapter 23

The sound of leaves rustling prompted a quick look over her shoulder. MacKenzie relaxed and flashed a bright smile at Mhinga as he entered the clearing. In his shirttail, he cradled a mixture of mushrooms, wild celery, roots, and leafy herbs. "Were you able to find any ripened figs?" he asked her.

"Yes, many. They are over there." She pointed at the pile of ash and turned away from him.

"Would you like to see the herbs that I found?"

Seemingly distracted, she sat peacefully on the log across the clearing, her hair blanketed over her shoulders. Without looking at him she answered, "No, not really."

Surprised by her answer, he said, "Very well. I thought it might interest you." He began washing the dirt off the plants.

"Well it does, but I have something else on my mind now."

With her back toward him, she could not see the big grin across Mhinga's face. "Let me guess: Jon?"

The unexpected tease sprung a surprised look his way. Quickly recovering, flashing a bright smile, she said, "Oh no. This is much more tangible."

Mhinga continued to work on his delicacies. "Tangible?" he mumbled. "Care to share your thoughts with a friend?"

Again she turned away from him, "You know, I would like your opinion on something."

"Sure. What is it?"

"Is it safe for me to assume that African mothers sing lullabies to their infants to help them go to sleep?"

Mhinga stopped what he was doing, puzzled by the question. "Yes, they do sing lullabies to their babies. Why do you ask?"

Ignoring his question, she asked, "Have you ever heard this lullaby?" She began to sing softly:

Rock-a-bye baby, in the treetop,
When the wind blows, the cradle will rock.
When the bough breaks, the cradle will fall,
And down will come baby, cradle and all.

"Ms. Mac, this is not like you. Did you eat something while I was away?"

"No, no. Just stay with me. Have you ever heard that lullaby before?"

"Not that I remember. I don't really understand it. Why would the cradle be in the treetop?"

"Oh, Mhinga!" She gave him a sour look.

"Okay, go on. What is this all about?"

"Well I rewrote some of the lyrics." She giggled. "Tell me what you think of them." Again she softly sang:

Rock-a-bye primate, in the treetop,
When the wind blows, the tree limb will rock;
When the limb breaks, the branch will then fall,
And down will come primate, tree limb and all.

"This is all very strange, Ms. Mac. But I like that you changed the word cradle to limb, because it makes more sense. Although I don't understand why you changed the word baby to primate."

"Well, that is the easy part, Mhinga. You see, I changed it because that's the way it is."

"You are talking in riddles I don't understand."

"Come here then, and I will show you."

MacKenzie watched over her shoulder as Mhinga crossed the clearing with a puzzled, look on his face. The closer he came, the more she smiled. When Mhinga was almost upon her, she twisted her shoulders toward him. Cradled in her arms, he saw a small bundle of dark, wiry hair. Mhinga stopped abruptly and his mouth dropped wide open.

He sat down on the log next to her, and peered at the child-like creature, asking, "Is it alive?"

"Yes. But I think he may have a concussion. He fell pretty hard."

"Ms. Mac, I don't think it is safe for you to be holding him. Perhaps you should lay him down in case he gets violent."

"Mhinga, I think this time you may be over-protective. Watch how he responds to my touch," she said, trying to move her finger out of the clasp of his hand. The chimp quickly responded by gripping tighter. "Now watch the movement in his eyes as we talk. See how they move back and forth. He hears us."

"Yes, he may hear us, but he doesn't understand what we are saying. And, yes, he grips his fingers around yours. That is just a reaction. But he is a wild animal and not accustomed to humans. He could be very dangerous. Please put him down and move away from him."

Firmly, she said, "As long as he is quiet in my arms, I will comfort him. When Jon gets back, he can take a look at him." Looking down at the chimp, she added, "You will see. It will be all right."

Mhinga was not sure if she spoke to him or to the chimp.

Early evening settled the day's heavy heat with cool calmness. Shadows grew longer and darker, seemingly swelling the forest, swiftly enclosing the small clearing. High above, the canopy was quiet except for an occasional lonely bird cry. There appeared to be a changing of the guard as a new set of forest noises arose and the day closed. Rising leisurely with the dimming light, thousands of insects began calling to their mates, filling the forest with a continuous hum like a smooth-running fan.

When the first mosquito made its appearance, Mhinga built up the fire. Across the clearing MacKenzie sat on the forest floor, leaning against the old log, her head tilted back and to the side. To Mhinga it looked like an uncomfortable angle, but her eyes were closed and her breathing relaxed as she slept, still holding the small unconscious chimpanzee in her arms.

A green branch on the fire created a white smoke, which warded off the molesting biting insects. Mhinga watched as the smoke rose, dancing and curling as it faded and disappeared in the darkness. The snapping and crackling of the freshly cut wood in the fire added drama to the consistent murmur of the evening.

Jon and Zawawi appeared abruptly, parting the bushes. Each carried across his shoulder a hindquarter of the wild hog. Exhausted from the long day and the hard trek, the men dropped the meat near the fire. Recognizing the meat, Mhinga smiled broadly. "With the fresh herbs I gathered today, you will eat like kings tonight!" he promised as he began preparing the food.

Zawawi dropped to the ground and stretched out his long legs. "More like hungry lions," he promised.

Looking around the dimly lit camp, Jon asked, "Where is Mac?"

Waving his hand in the air, Zawawi blurted, "With any luck, she has gone away."

The men's voices stirred MacKenzie. From across the clearing, she responded, "Sorry to disappoint you, Zawawi." With a disapproving grunt, the Maasai warrior lay back and closed his eyes.

Tossing scraps of meat to Buster, Mhinga said, "Jon, she needs to talk to you right away." Setting his rifle down, Jon slowly headed across the clearing. MacKenzie sat on the opposite side of the log.

The cooking fire glowed brightly in the nightfall, casting a golden backlight around Jon's silhouette. MacKenzie could see that Jon's stride was shorter, and his muscular shoulders slouched wearily. She was unable to see his face, and worried how he might react if he saw the chimp before she could explain.

In the shadowy outskirts of the clearing, MacKenzie sat up straighter, drawing her knees up and locking her arms around them, sandwiching the chimp in-between. As Jon neared, she flipped her long hair over her shoulder, shielding the chimp from view.

Jon let out a long yawn as he stepped over the log and sat down on top of it. Cupping his hands over his face, he rested his elbows on his knees and rubbed his eyes. "Mhinga said you needed to talk to me." His voice was tired and low.

"Yes! I have to tell you what happened this afternoon." Jon rested his head on his hands, tilting his face toward her. The warm glow of the fire lit the side of his face, enhancing the dark lines in his weathered skin. She began her story at the very beginning when Mhinga had left her to find mushrooms, and she had begun to gather fruit from the old fig tree nearby. In her excitement, she described everything in great detail. She told him of the high winds and falling limbs. Jon waited patiently while MacKenzie rattled on.

He noted the excitement in her voice and watched her eyes flickering with gold sparks when she turned to face him and the firelight lit her face. In the faint glow, the shape and movements of her lips aroused a new awakening in the pit of his stomach. He was soaking in the sound of her voice, not really listening to the long-winded story she told. When she paused, she smiled brightly at him and he smiled back, encouraging her to go on. Inside he wanted to hold her in his arms and once again feel her soft lips on his.

"Well?" her soft, soothing voice had changed, breaking him out of his spell.

"Well, what?" he answered, puzzled.

"Do you want to see what I found clinging to the fallen branch?"

"Yes, of course." He acted interested, though he hadn't a clue what she was talking about.

As she turned toward the light she reached behind her head and pulled back her long hair from across her shoulder. Jon then saw the small chimpanzee cradled in MacKenzie's lap. Instantly he became fully coherent and said, "Tell me about it again. A short version this time."

As she began, Jon scooted off the log and sat on the ground next to her. While she retold the story, he began to examine the chimp. Having a father who was a veterinarian gave Jon some experience. Shining the beam from a small pen-light into the chimp's eyes, he watched for a response, checking the pupils. He examined the large bruise and lump that ran across the chimp's forehead and parted the lips to check the gums for color.

"Well," she asked again, "what do you think?"

New energy showed in Jon's face when he turned his attention back to her. "I think he may have a concussion."

"That's what I said!"

Blown over, he did not remember most of what she had said. "I don't think he has any internal injuries," he continued.

"Do you think he will be all right?"

165

"Yeah, but the longer he is unconscious the more symptoms he may suffer when he comes out of it."

"What kind of symptoms?"

"He could experience blurred or double vision; maybe weakness or numbness in his limbs. Guessing by the size of that lump on his head, he will have a whopper of a headache."

They sat side-by-side, fussing over the little chimp in MacKenzie's arms. Leaning across her, Jon reached for the chimp's hand. At the first touch the tiny fingers gripped tightly, but barely encircled his index finger. Surprised, he flashed a smile at MacKenzie. Spontaneously, she met his smile, and their eyes locked.

"He is very special." She whispered. "Don't you think?"

Holding her stare, his face just inches from hers, he replied softly, "Yes, very special." He could feel the warmth of her skin radiating out and her voice compelling him closer.

Uncontrollably, she began to lean toward him. Anticipating his kiss, her eyes slowly closed and her soft, full lips started to part. As their lips touched, a wave of electricity sparked between them. Jon reached up, wrapping his hand around the nape of her neck, supporting her, drawing her nearer to him. Her long hair cascaded off her shoulder, caressing Jon's bare arm, awakening tingling sensations in his body. The kiss and their closeness absorbed them totally, blocking out all sense of their surroundings. They were no longer aware of the coolness of the night air, nor the heavy shadows that surrounded them. The sounds of a pestering mosquito faded, as did their hunger and fatigue. Only they existed, the two of them, with their tender passion.

They were completely oblivious to Zawawi looming over them. Disgust filled his eyes and, with a solid thrust, he kicked the log the two lovers leaned against. At the same time, his voice, filled with hatred, barked at them. "You throw yourself into a pit with a hungry lioness," Zawawi spoke in his native language. "While you stroke her coat, she will claw out your belly and feast on you alive."

Bursting up from MacKenzie's side, anger flared through Jon's body. Zawawi continued, still in his native tongue, "Now is the time to stop, while the cut is small and the infection can heal."

"You don't know what you are talking about," Jon growled back fluently in Swahili. Pointing his finger at Zawawi's face, his voice ravaged with anger, he exploded, "And you should be minding your own business. This doesn't concern you!"

MacKenzie stood, still cradling the chimp in her arms, not understanding the words that flew between the two friends. She felt the tension between them. "Jon, don't!" her voice quivered with fear. "He is your friend. He's just trying to protect you."

Taken aback by the tone of her voice and her words, Jon nearly laughed. "Protect me! From what? You?" His temper was still rising.

"No!" She tried to gain control of her shakiness. "From the evil white woman in his past." Her words brought up the turmoil of old feelings in both men. As they stared at each other, their anger erupted.

The sight of the chimpanzee in MacKenzie's arms temporarily distracted Zawawi's attention. He demanded, "Where did that come from?"

"He was hurt when a tree limb broke free." MacKenzie tried not to sound intimidated.

"You cradle the animal as if it were your own child. The stupid ways of the *mzungu.*"

Zawawi's insult was the last straw. With a sudden rush of anger, Jon took a swing at Zawawi. Still looking at the chimp, the Maasai was caught off guard and took the powerful punch squarely on the jaw. MacKenzie screamed.

Jon followed with another swing with his left. But the Maasai was quick, and his reflexes saved him from the blow.

Stepping backward, Zawawi's head and upper body twisted, avoiding Jon's flying fist. Finding his balance, he gathered himself and began fighting back with a low left jab into Jon's midriff.

The weighty jab knocked some of the air out of Jon's lungs, and he doubled over. Zawawi rushed shoulder first into Jon's waist, bringing both men to the forest floor. Rolling around, the two bodies entangled. Each was trying to get a solid swing at the other. Fists flew wildly. Grunting noises filled the campsite when a punch landed well.

"Stop it! Stop it, both of you!" MacKenzie yelled from the side. "Mhinga! Make them stop before they kill each other!"

Mhinga barely looked up from his work. "Ms. Mac," he said calmly, "let them work this out in their own way. Come here and help me with the meal. They will settle this soon."

Breaking apart, the two men rose. Bent at the waist, arms reaching out, they stared at each other, circling around, anticipating the next move. In unison they charged in. Locking arms around each other's bodies and holding close, they pounded tight, heavy punches into each other's rib cages.

"But, Mhinga!" her voice broke off into a scream as two black men ran into the camp from the forest. The woman's scream checked their speed in the shadowy light. Slowly they entered the fire's light.

Mhinga looked up from the cooking fire and smiled, "We're having wild pork with a sweet fig gravy with mushrooms and celery tonight. I hope you two are hungry. We have plenty, but we'll wait for those two to finish." He pointed at Jon and Zawawi, who were so engrossed with their fight, they hadn't noticed the two newcomers.

MacKenzie finally recognized Simon. Running toward him she begged, "Please stop them!"

Simon looked at the bundle she carried, "Where did you get that?"

Frustrated, MacKenzie's face flushed red. Stomping her foot, she screamed, "What the hell difference does it make? I'll tell you about it later. Just go over there and stop those two before they kill each other."

Simon grinned. Handing his rifle to Jay he looked down at MacKenzie and winked at the frustrated woman. "Okay, I'll break it up," he said nonchalantly.

As Simon approached the two fighting men his size grew in the dim flickering light. Reaching down, the giant man plucked both men up from their fighting embrace. As he held them at arm's length they still flung out at each other. Simon shook them and snapped, "You two still fight like boys!" They struggled to free themselves from his powerful grip. "Stop it!" Simon demanded.

Jon and Zawawi struggled against Simon's grip. The colonel body-slammed the two men together, stunning them into silence. Pushing them apart Simon grinned, "Just like old times! What are you two fighting about now?"

MacKenzie ran across to Jon and reached up, wiping the blood off his face. Simon laughed out loud, "Oh, my God! You are fighting over a woman and a chimpanzee!" Shaking his head, Simon laughed as he walked back to where Mhinga was cooking the meal. Accepting a plate of food he asked, "Am I right?"

"Yes, Simon. It is like the old times, in many ways," Mhinga replied.

Simon summoned the others to the fire as Mhinga filled the plates high. Reluctantly, the two men, breathing hard from fighting, followed Simon's orders. MacKenzie sat next to Jon, still cradling the chimp. Simon questioned her about the animal, and she retold her story.

Zawawi spoke to his brother, "The animal will not make it through the night and yet she holds it as if it was of her own blood."

Butting in, MacKenzie's voice was strong and determined, "He will make it! I know it!"

"You are a bigger fool than I thought," Zawawi snapped back.

Jon started to rise. Simon grabbed his arm pulling him back down. "Enough, Jon! Have you examined it?"

"It's unconscious, probably a concussion. It doesn't appear to have any internal bleeding. He will probably be all right."

Zawawi dropped his eyes to the ground. "You are already gone, my friend. I had hoped it wasn't too late." Shaking his head in disbelief, he sighed, "So now it all begins again."

"That is a small matter for now," Simon began. "We must find her father and the other scientists first. Plus, Dubois and the boys are still out there."

At mention of his sons, the look on Zawawi's face turned to despair. Seeing this, Jon's face softened, and he asked about the raid.

Simon and Jay had traveled all day to join Jon's group. The hard, fast trek, and the huge meal Mhinga had prepared, tested their endurance to stay awake. As they ate, Simon yawned, stretched and told his story.

When he finished his account of the raid, Zawawi asked softly, "Are you going after Dubois and the boys?"

"Yes." Simon dropped his eyes from his half brother, affirming, "It is my job. Considering our relationship and their ages, we may be able to get Khosa off fairly easy. Valli may require a bit more work. Perhaps we could work a deal and get a reduced sentence or possibly a working patrol under my guidance. I will do all that I can for him."

Zawawi nodded approval, but his words were cold, "They have done shameful things and must pay." As his voice trailed off, he stood and walked away from the group.

Jon asked Simon, "What are your plans? Dubois first, and then find the scientists?"

MacKenzie straightened and for the first time took her eyes off the chimp, still quiet in her arms. "Hey, I hired you to find the scientists, not to go off chasing some poacher. Don't you remember?"

Jon started to respond but was interrupted by Simon, "I believe we can do both." Pulling a map out of his pocket, he continued, "I found this at their camp. I believe Dubois could be using Lifi as his base camp. It is so remote, trucks and helicopters could move in and out without drawing any attention."

Zawawi turned back around. Glancing at Jon, he asked the question on both their minds, "Lifi? Where and what the hell is Lifi?"

Simon showed them the circles on the map and explained about the once-prosperous copper mining town, now nothing more than a ghost town. "It would be a perfect place -- isolated, empty buildings, easy to hide large trucks, equipment, and a helicopter." He let his words sink in while they looked over his shoulders at the map. "There is hardly a village within a hundred miles of the place. It is just a few empty buildings a couple of miles off an old two-lane road. With a good generator, he could keep the meat frozen while waiting for transport. And it's not far from here; just a few good days hike northwest. By road or air he could be across the border to Sudan, Zaire, Central African Republic, or Congo in a matter of hours. The bushmeat trade is thriving there."

Jon and Zawawi nodded their heads in agreement. MacKenzie asked, "But what about my father and the scientists?"

Jon, still studying the map, butted in before Simon could respond, "What is this other red circle?"

"I don't really know, Jon." Simon looked at the faces around the fire, and his eyes rested on MacKenzie's. Feeling his stare, she looked up at him. "It could be the location of the scientists' base camp." MacKenzie gasped. Simon continued, "Dubois could be involved with it somehow, or could have marked it on the map to avoid the area, or it could be the location of a campsite. We won't know until we check it out."

"So we are going with you?" MacKenzie asked.

"Yes. At this point," Simon concluded, "we're better off sticking together."

Chapter 24

Woody plants with long slender stems crept up the tall columns of mahogany trees. Rafting high overhead, intertwined with long branches of the hardwood, climbing vines shaped the forest roof. Around the clearing's edge, walls of greenery cascaded down, creating dark rooms scattered with shade-loving plants. The thick partitions of dense vegetation feasted on sunshine.

Resting inside this refuge, the old bull elephant poked his trunk through the greenery to sniff the warm breeze of the sunny opening. The drifting wind brought no scent of the hunters, but his long experience told him they were still near -- following, stalking, waiting until they could get close enough to point their sticks and kill.

Many times he had returned to an area where his kind had been taken. Inhaling their death and rotting flesh, he shifted their bones and mourned their loss. The humans always took their long teeth. They were never left behind in the open graveyard with the bones and decaying carcasses.

Years ago, it was his great speed and strength that carried him to safety. With each experience, he grew wiser and more perceptive. Over time, he moved from the great, grassy veld to the lush green hills and dense forest. His massive bulk made traveling more difficult among the trees, but his old age welcomed the slower pace.

He was not alone in the forest. Wandering among the rolling hills were bands of small, almost delicate, forest elephants. Because of his grand size, and long, thick ivory, the other bulls never challenged him. This allowed him to dominate over the females, and they gave birth to many of his offspring. The herds and their lives were simple. Over the years, memories of the dangerous open veld had diminished. However, a few days earlier the memories intruded from his past like a flash of lightning.

The old male had crossed paths with two adolescent bulls. They were on the threshold of adulthood, and their rising urges had become a nuisance to the herd. The matriarch had chased them away, protecting her young cows.

The three had met along the cool banks of the muddy river. They splashed and played in the stream, then fed and rested in the sweet, grassy field. They passed half the day in the sunshine, until restlessness prodded the old one to move on across the field to the quiet and solitude of the woods.

His peaceful existence was shattered by sounds and scents from the past. One of the young bulls had gone down. The other frantically tried to help him up. After years of tranquility, the dangers of the past had invaded his forest.

The gallant old bull's first instinct was to charge and bring down the human with the death stick. But experience checked his stride, for he remembered that these creatures could kill from a distance. His will to survive took control and he turned, fleeing into the safety of the dense woods. Just as he entered the forest's edge, he felt a stinging sensation high on his neck. The bullet penetrated deep into the fleshy area in front of the withers, above where the shoulder blades and the spine connect. With each step, the shoulder blade rotated forward, irritating the bullet wound.

Now, two days later, the wise old bull felt the deep throbbing pain of infection. Straddling the graceful, reaching curves of the mahoganies' roots, he leaned his shoulder against the smooth bark of the tall timber. Pushing hard, the old bull squeezed the shoulder bone against the tree, pinching the wound into a head. The deep infection was forced through hot flesh to the surface layer of thick skin. With a popping relief, pressure under the crusty covering broke loose, releasing the curdled poison of infection. His pain eased immediately.

The old bull closed his eyes with a sigh, relishing his relief from the throbbing pain. He could go on now, moving deeper into the forest, farther from the stink of man and gunpowder and the scent of death that followed him.

Once more the old bull elephant poked his trunk through the greenery, sniffing the warm breeze of the sunny clearing. Again, the slow moving breeze crossing the small field brought no scent of the hunters. Cautiously, he took his first steps into the little sunny field.

Securely hidden by the thick brush at the edge of the woods, the hunters watched as the elephant's trunk periscoped above the greenery. Unlike anything Dubois had hunted before, this old bull was proving himself worthy of his ivory prize. Valli and Khosa squatted on each side of Dubois. Silently, they watched with great anticipation for the elephant to emerge from the shady bush across the meadow.

The tip of the trunk appeared again, twisting left and then right, searching the wind for any scent of danger. Finally, protruding from the greenery, two glimmers of long, white, graceful ivory appeared. Cautiously, the massive head poked out from the bushes, still searching for any sign of danger. One step at a time, he moved out from behind his dark blind into the sunshine. With tattered ears flared wide and trunk held high, the majestic old bull scanned the area across the field, ready to flee at the first hint of evil.

Inch by inch, Dubois began to rise, halting as the elephant's trunk darted straight out, pointing towards him. Breathing long, deep, breaths, the hunter fought to calm his pounding heart. He was unsure if his movements had been seen or if a draft of air had given away his position. After several long minutes, the elephant cautiously lifted his trunk high in front of his head.

Dubois stood up and raised his .460 Weatherby Magnum rifle to his shoulder. Resting his cheek on the walnut stock, he spied the elephant down the rifle's long barrel. A wet streak of blood and puss ran out of the open wound where his first shot had pierced the old bull two days earlier. Slowly the hunter's breathing became nearly motionless, steadying the weight of the ten and a half-pound rifle. Relaxing his shoulder, he prepared for the fierce recoil. Tightening on the trigger, he was ready to fire. Soon the old bull would surrender his ivory prize.

Dubois waited until the elephant lowered his trunk, exposing the small area between his eyes that sheltered his brain. Almost as if the old bull was willed by the hunter's thoughts, his trunk lowered a few inches. A bit more. That a boy, Dubois thought. Come on, there's a good fellow. Give me a clear view of that big ugly head of yours. As if following a command, the old bull lowered his trunk some more. A crooked grin appeared on the hunter's face. "You're all mine now," he thought, and gently squeezed the trigger. The rifle delivered nearly four tons of smashing power to the five-hundred-grain bullet.

With a burst of speed like Dubois had never seen before, the old bull dashed unharmed back into the dark forest. Lowering his rifle to his side, Dubois stood there bewildered that he had missed. "Damn!" he bellowed out loud.

"How can that be?" Valli could not believe what he had just seen. "You had him!"

Dubois' face flushed with irritation. As he flexed his shoulder, working out the soreness from the recoil, he heard a noise in the underbrush behind him. Turning around quickly, he raised his rifle and prepared to shoot again. The old bull's keen sense of hearing must have heard the noise long before he had.

From the dark shadows, two people emerged. Taveta and Petrus scurried through the underbrush toward them. "What the hell!" Dubois shouted at them. Winded, they slowed their pace as they approached the hunter. Petrus fell to her knees, from the long run. In deep gasping breaths, Taveta explained the campsite had been raided, but they had escaped and feared that they might have been followed.

Valli knelt down next to Petrus. Softly, he whispered to her, "Are you all right, my Pet?"

Stressed and tired from the long run, her eyes narrowed and she snapped at him, "Don't ever call me that again. My name is Petrus!"

Valli's face went blank with confusion; she had never spoken so harshly before. "But . . . ."

Dubois snatched the girl by the arm, jerking her to her feet. He tossed his rifle to Valli. "Stay here," he ordered. "I want to talk to these two alone." Dragging Petrus away from the boys, he motioned for Taveta to follow.

At a safe distance, he released his grip on Petrus. Weakened by the hard run, she fell to the forest floor. "I'll get to you in a minute." Turning to Taveta, he demanded, "Now, tell me everything. Don't leave anything out!"

Taveta told their story, the *whole* story. Dubois snarled back and forth between the two lovers. Jerking Petrus up, he growled at her, "Valli doesn't know about you two, and it must stay that way for your own good." She tried to shake herself free. Fiercely, he lifted her up by the shoulders and pulled her close to his face. "Do you understand, Pet? I pay you to be his pet!"

Memories of a brutal street beating flooded her weary body. Dubois had saved her life that day, but now his raging expression sent chills down her spine. For the first time, she feared this man. Submissively, she nodded her head.

"Good!" Dubois put her down and released his grip. "Valli is a perceptive young man and will be asking you a lot of questions. You two better put a good story together, explaining how you escaped without a rifle. He must not find out about the two of you. I need that boy to stay focused on tracking that elephant. When this is all over, you can go off together. I don't give a damn, but not until I have that ivory! Have I made myself clear?"

They nodded. Taking a deep breath, Dubois calmed himself, "Good. Here is what we are going to do. I'll take the boys across the field, following the bull. We've lost another day because of this. You two follow behind in two hours. That should give you enough time to rest and get your story together." Dubois glanced at his watch. It was almost noon. "Travel for four more hours, then set up a camp along our trail. No big fires. If you have been followed, we don't need to show them our location. The boys and I will back-track and meet you at the campsite at dusk. I'll have Khosa leave you the gear to carry. We'll cover more ground that way." Dubois turned away. Stopping, he looked back over his shoulder. "Oh, by the way, Petrus," he added, "Plan on making up with Valli tonight. I want that boy very eager and happy tomorrow."

She dropped her eyes from him and mumbled under her breath, "Yeah, fuck you, too."

Dubois snapped back, "What did you say?"

She smiled sweetly at him, "Yes, *Bwana.* After we rest we will follow, make camp, and wait for you to return."

Dubois hesitated, then nodded his approval and went back to where Valli and Khosa waited. "Let's go, boys, and find that elephant again."

"*Bwana,* I must speak to Petrus before we go." Valli pleaded.

Dubois dismissed his request with a wave of his hand. "No. You can talk to her later tonight. She is irrational from her escape and long run. Let her rest now and clear her head." His voice became fatherly, "Tonight, my son, she can tell you of her ordeal, and you can comfort her. But now we have work to do, catching up with that old bull with the long ivory. We are short on time, and only you can lead me to him."

Glancing back over his shoulder, Valli flashed a proud smile and waved to Petrus. Sweetly she smiled and waved back to him. Quietly, she muttered, "Fuck you."

From the distance, Valli misread her lips. His heart pounded strong and lovingly for he read her words as 'Love you.' With a new spring in his step, he led Dubois and his little brother across the field, following the old elephant's trail.

Valli floated on air through the forest underbrush. The thorn bushes that snagged his clothing and the ankle-twisting rocky trail did not slow him or distract him from his loving thoughts of Petrus. The pace that he set was knowingly fast. The quicker he found *Bwana* Dubois' long ivory, the sooner he would be in Petrus' arms.

After several long hours Dubois called a halt. Sitting on large moss-covered rocks, he watched Valli fidget about with a dreamy look on his face. "What has gotten into you, Valli?"

Unable to hold it in, Valli spread his arms wide and then grandly crossed his chest as if he were hugging himself. "Oh *Bwana!* I am in love," he began, "and all the world feels so good. I can't explain it. I've never felt like this before!"

Dubois smiled at the young man's joyous zest. Khosa was shocked, "In love! With who?"

Valli dropped his hands to his hips. "With Petrus! You are too young to understand, Khosa. *Bwana* understands. See the smile on his face. He is happy for me, he understands a man's need of a good woman."

"What need is that? I don't have a need for a woman."

"When you are older you will understand and need the warmth of a woman to care for you. One you will want to marry and . . . ."

Khosa interrupted, "Marry! You are going to marry Petrus?"

"Yes," Valli, said with confidence.

"How do you know that she wants to marry you?"

"She has told me that she loves me, and we have talked of having many sons."

"When did she tell you this, Valli?" Dubois asked.

"Just a few hours ago. Before we left them to rest. I read her lips. She said, 'Love you'. "

Dubois grinned at Valli, "Well, then, there you have it." He thought grimly of what the street girl might have really said.

Khosa sat on the ground at Dubois' feet. "What about me? Who will watch over me after you are gone and married to her?"

Valli crossed over to his little brother. Kneeling down he spoke very manly, "When we left our father's *kraal,* I promised I would always be there. That has not changed. Petrus will care for you, too, until you find a woman of your own."

Khosa smiled back weakly, "But I don't want a woman."

Dubois rested his hand on the young boy's shoulder as he said, "You will feel differently in another couple of years." Turning to Valli, he asked, "When is this marriage going to take place?"

"As soon as we get those ivory teeth from that old elephant!"

"Well then," Dubois stood, "we need to get moving. Lead on, Valli!"

Chapter 25

Meaty chunks of rodent sizzled over the fire, the bright pink quickly seared brown, locking in its wild juices. Watching the meat, Petrus listened to Taveta tell their story of heroic escape.

"You see, Valli," Taveta began, "Petrus was going to the river to get water. The buckets were large and very heavy for her to carry up the steep bank. So I leaned my rifle up against the tree and went down to the river's edge to help her."

Valli's eyes flashed lovingly over to Petrus every time her name was mentioned. She played along, smiling back at the appropriate times, reassuring the young man. When Valli's attention was back on Taveta's story, she would snarl to herself and reluctantly return to the meal she was cooking.

Taveta continued, "Just as we were about to climb the embankment, I heard the footsteps of many men approaching." Khosa's eyes widened, and he leaned in towards Taveta, soaking in every word. "I grabbed Petrus and pulled her down along the steep edge near a bush. We hid there as a line of armed men passed just a few feet away from us."

"How many men were there?" Eager and excited, Khosa was taken in by the fireside story.

A natural storyteller, Taveta fed off the young man's appetite. "There were many. Maybe as many as fifty!"

"So many men and none of them saw you or your rifle?" Valli asked suspiciously.

Taveta sat back and looked Valli straight in the eyes. Waving his hands in the air dramatically, he said, "The Gods had sent in a heavy fog. It shielded them from seeing us."

Khosa jumped in, "Which Gods?"

"Don't be a fool, Khosa," Valli interrupted. "So where is the rifle now?" he asked.

Taveta made a grand sweeping motion with his hand. "In my haste to protect Petrus," he glanced over at her in time to see her roll her eyes up, "to bring her safely away from those men and back to you," he continued, dropping his eyes as if he were ashamed of himself, "I left the rifle behind. It is probably still leaning against that tree, unless the raiders searched the area later and found it."

"The important thing is," Dubois ended the storytelling, "that you both are safe now."

"But *Bwana!* The others are in jail now." Khosa was very upset.

Dubois laid his hand on the young boy's shoulder, "Don't you worry about them. I'll get them out of jail. If Taveta and Petrus hadn't gotten word to us, we wouldn't have known what had happened to them. At least now we know where they are and that they will be safe until I get back. I'll take care of everything." Khosa relaxed. He believed Dubois.

"What is most important," Valli announced in his manly voice, "is that my woman has been returned to me."

Petrus dropped the fork she was holding. Her mouth gaped, and she stared at Valli.

Valli gave a little laugh, "Do not worry, my love. I have told *Bwana* Dubois of our love and our wish to marry."

"You did!" Glancing back and forth between Dubois and Taveta, she thought about fleeing the campsite.

"Yes, and he is very happy for us." Valli was glowing with high spirits.

"Really?" she snarled at her employer.

Dubois grinned back at her, "Oh, yes. You seem to make him very happy, and I will never forget that."

Stabbing the cooked meat with the fork, Petrus stated, "Nor will I."

As she handed a plate of food to Valli, he gazed into her eyes and whispered, "I will show you my love tonight. I know of a quiet place not far from here. We will go after the meal."

Petrus tried to cover her true feelings with a smile. Turning her attention back to serving the meal, she was sickened at the thought of playing this game any longer. It had gone on long enough.

After the meal, Valli and Petrus headed off into the woods together. Petrus looked back over her shoulder and gave a little nod to Taveta. It was her way of telling him they would meet later. Winking back, he acknowledged her discreet code.

The actress and the young man walked side by side through the darkness of the forest. The moon streaked gray-blue light from the tall trees to the woodland floor. The sound of an owl haunted Petrus' dark thoughts of how to get away from this boy quickly and back to Taveta's arms. She was not going to play this game much longer. She had already saved enough money to start her own brothel. She had Taveta willing to work for her and keep her needs met. This was going to be the last time. She did not care if it broke Valli's heart or angered Dubois. She just wanted to be free.

Valli's voice startled her. "Why would you be fetching water so late at night?"

His question stopped her dead in her tracks. Her mind raced back over the story that she and Taveta had concocted.

Valli took a step forward and grabbed her tightly by the arms. "Why?" he demanded.

He was grabbing her in much the same way Dubois had earlier that day and again the memories of a beating rushed in. Her words flew out, "I couldn't sleep! I . . ." she searched for more but no other words came. She just stared frantically up at Valli and stuttered, "I . . ., I . . . ."

"You what, Petrus?" He released his grip on her arms.

She covered her face with her hands and began to weep. "I . . ." her shoulders shook uncontrollably. Then the words came to her, "I couldn't sleep because I was thinking about . . ."

Valli pulled her near, "Me?" he said softly. "You couldn't sleep because you were thinking about me?"

Through her sobs, he heard her say, "Yes, I was thinking of you." The sounds of her own voice saying those words shocked her. That was not what she wanted to say. She wanted to tell him that she did not love him and that she was with another man. That Dubois was paying her to be with him. She had her chance to escape from this boy, and now she had lost it.

Valli rocked her in his arms, comforting her. He kissed her on the forehead and rubbed her back until she quieted down. He pulled back and cradled her face in his hands. Softly he said, "I was afraid that you may have been tricked into going into the woods with Taveta. That he may have tried to harm you."

Petrus gathered herself and smiled sweetly at him, thinking, "What a stupid fool you are."

Lowering her to the ground, Valli was nearly laughing with relief, "My black viper is ready to strike out for you, my little pet." With all his youthful energy, Valli made love to Petrus several times that night. She encouraged him by clawing her nails into his back. Her deep rasping moans he mistook as fulfillment. When finally he collapsed into a stupefied sleep, Petrus quietly slipped away.

Taveta was waiting for her at the edge of the campsite. The look on her face told him all that he needed to know about her time with Valli. He pulled her in and wrapped his arms around her. Softly, he spoke, "Perhaps another night, Petrus."

She shook her head and said, "I need a real man to make me feel whole again."

With one arm around her shoulders, Taveta reached down and buckled her knees, lifting her up. He carried her deep into the woods far away from the campsite. In the last quiet hours before dawn, Taveta skillfully drove his love into Petrus, driving out the memories of the boy and his black viper toy.

As dawn edged away the night, the two lovers were sound asleep, wrapped in each other's arms. Fatigue consumed them, and they lay naked on top of their scattered clothes. Spooned against her back, Taveta wrapped his arm warmly over Petrus' shoulder, his hand still cupping the nipple of her full breast.

The bird's soft choir slowly awakened Valli. A joyous smile crossed his lips as he gently patted the ground where he lay. Opening his eyes he scanned the area, calling, "Where are you, my beautiful pet?" His search was wasted Petrus was already gone. He mumbled outloud, "She must have gone back to prepare *Bwana* Dubois' breakfast. She is so dutiful." Whistling a tune, he dressed and headed toward the campsite, his eager mind filled with the woman he loved.

Valli entered in the camp with steps as graceful and light as a dancer. His whistling stopped abruptly as Dubois set the gun-cleaning kit aside and growled at him, "Where the hell have you been? Do you know how late it is?" The angry man crossed the campsite and towered over the astonished Valli.

Khosa quietly packed the gear. Looking around the camp, Valli's grin faded. Ignoring Dubois, he asked Khosa, "Where is Petrus? And Taveta?"

Without warning, Dubois struck Valli hard across the face, knocking him to the ground. "I don't know and I don't care. I've had enough from those two. Get your gear together and let's go!"

Slowly Valli rose, rubbed his cheek. Dubois continued to bellow at him, "Your job is to track down that elephant! Now get your things together and let's get going. We've wasted a lot of time with your adolescent escapades."

Unbalanced from the blow, Valli stumbled over to his little brother. His young face was creased with worry.

Valli pleaded, "Tell me, Khosa! Where is Petrus?"

Nervously Khosa looked past Valli to Dubois who was packing his gun-cleaning kit away. Valli seized his younger brother and asked again. Khosa nodded towards the woods, "I saw Taveta carry her off. They have been gone all night." Khosa looked away from the pain that was swelling up in his brother's eyes.

Under his breath, Valli mumbled, "I'll kill that bastard!" Quickly he snatched the rifle. Reaching out, Dubois grabbed hold of the young man's arm, swinging him around.

A malicious savagery took control of Valli. Without thought, he swung hard at the man who was his mentor. His fist landed squarely on the bigger man's jaw, spinning Dubois to the ground. Without hesitating, Valli was off, clutching the high-powered rifle.

Through the underbrush he ran, frantic, without direction. Calling to Petrus as he ran, his mind raced with thoughts of her taken against her will and raped. He clicked the safety off as visions of Taveta's face, contorted with pleasure from raping his woman, filled his eyes with tears. Running blindly he stumbled over a rock. The momentum sent the maddened boy flying face first onto the trail, and his grip on the loaded rifle flew out of his hands.

Spinning out of control, the weapon landed in a thick cluster of ferns. The impact jarred the trigger, and the rifle fired. The blast echoed among the trees. Instinctively Valli covered his head for protection. Bits of rock, dirt, and forest litter showered his hands and head. When the ringing in his ears quieted, he looked out over the edge of his arm. The high-velocity bullet had penetrated into a tree near the threshold of his reach. Consumed with bloodthirsty emotions, he crawled like a wild animal to the rifle.

Trying to rise, his knees buckled underneath. He had to will his body to work. Crawling over, Valli checked the rifle. He thought, "One bullet gone, two left; that should be enough." At the top of his lungs, he shouted, "Petrus!" Wanting but not really expecting a reply, he headed across the hillside.

Ahead in the dim light of the forest he saw movement in the underbrush. Quickly he ran toward it calling out, "Petrus! I'm coming!" As he neared, a head appeared over the top of a large clump of ferns. Eyes wide with fear, Petrus stared back at him.

Valli lowered the rifle and approached her, asking, "Are you all right, my darling?"

Her body trembled, but she nodded. Holding her hand up she said, "Stop right there, Valli."

"But my pet, I've come to save you. You do not have to be afraid of me." He took a step closer.

She screamed at him, "Valli, stop!" Her voice quivered, "Right there! Don't come any closer."

"But my pet . . . ."

That name crawled under her skin, gnawing at her nerves. She tried to control her shaking and speak calmly, "Valli, just go back to camp. I will be along soon. Now, just go."

Confused, he insisted. "I love you and will not go unless you come with me. What are you afraid of?"

"Valli," she tried to sound convincing, "I'm not afraid. If you truly love me, you will do as I ask. I have never asked anything of you before. Please do this for me."

"Why do you hide behind the plants? Stand and let me see that you have not been harmed."

Hesitantly, Petrus looked around before standing up behind the greenery. She did not try to hide her nakedness from him. From the distance between them, she easily saw the fury rising in Valli.

"Where is that raping son of a bitch?" Valli's yell startled Petrus, and she began trembling. From behind her, Taveta finally showed himself.

Raising the rifle to his shoulder, Valli motioned to Petrus, "Get out of the way, my love. This rapist must pay for what he has done to you."

"Valli, don't be such a fool!" Petrus screamed.

"Move, my pet!" That name struck her like fingernails scraping across a chalkboard. Ignoring her screams, Valli continued, "Taveta is no man. A man does not take another man's woman! Nor does a man hide behind a woman for protection." He screamed wildly, "NOW MOVE!" Valli's command startled Petrus, and Valli took a step closer.

Petrus moved toward Valli. Her eyes narrowed, and her hands clenched at her sides. The dark ebony tone of her skin flushed with the strength of a storm. Gritting through her teeth, her words tore into him, "Valli, you are such a childish fool."

"Step aside, my Pet. I don't want you to get hurt." Valli hadn't taken his eyes off Taveta.

"Valli, look at me!" she demanded.

Valli's eyes shifted briefly from Taveta to Petrus.

"I am not hurt! Taveta did not rape me. We have been lovers for a long time, before you came along."

"What?" Valli's attention flew back to Petrus. "But you said that I was your first and that you loved me. You said we were going to be married and have many children."

"No, Valli! Those are all your words. Dubois pays me to sleep with you. To keep you happy so you will remain loyal and continue to track for him." Over Valli's shoulder she could see Dubois and Khosa coming fast. "If you don't believe me, ask him for yourself!" She pointed behind him.

Valli could hear them thrashing through the underbrush. His eyes flickered back and forth, not wanting to believe her.

Dubois stood by Valli's side and placed his hand on his shoulder.

"Put down the rifle, son," he said in a soothing voice.

"She is telling me that you pay her to love me. Is that true?"

"It is true that I pay her to do many things for me. But I cannot control whom she loves." Dubois' voice was clear and calm.

"You swine!" Petrus barked. "I should have known that you would turn on me this way. All for your precious ivory."

"It is true, my dear, that our business affairs are now over," Dubois began. "With the raid of the workers, I will have to lay low for awhile and regroup. I will go back to France with my ivory and logging contracts. I no longer need an assistant who causes trouble by not keeping her knees together, and tells lies to impressionable young men." Turning to Valli, he saw a raging madness in his eyes. "It's your decision what to do with this liar and thief."

Petrus' words caused rage to boil up inside Valli. His love for her was equally as strong. "Move away, Petrus." The feel of the cold strength in the rifle's steel and polished wood surged through his body. Centering in his groin, it deviled his soul. "Move away from him, and I will end this darkness. Then we can go together as we planned."

"Those are not my wishes," Petrus stepped back next to Taveta.

Hatred clouded Valli's eyes. "Move away," he said it again.

A small familiar voice broke from behind. "Valli," Khosa's soft voice pleaded, "Let's just go, you and me, and forget about them. We have each other. You don't need a woman. I will care for you." Desperately, he begged, "You can't just kill them. They are not like the animals we hunt." Khosa's words released the demon in Valli's soul.

"No, Khosa," Valli's voice was calm now. "They are just like the animals we hunt. See how they make a nest in the tall ferns? Just like the chimpanzees. Only these two are not as valuable."

Transferring his anger to the rushing sensation of the hunt caused Valli's body to throb. His breathing became rapid and shallow. A hot pressure flowed across his midriff, and the growing need of powerful orgasmic satisfaction filled his trembling body. "You were not there, little brother. You do not see the similarities between these two and the chimps that I hunted. I will explain it to you and show you how they are the same."

Raising his rifle, Valli aimed at Taveta's chest. Looking down the barrel, Valli explained to Khosa, "Of course when I took the male chimp, I was right over him, not at this distance." His words were slow and precise. Taveta turned to take cover, but he was too late.

The recoil knocked Valli off balance. The blast obliterated all other sound, including the thump Taveta's body made slamming to the ground. The bullet went cleanly through the man's chest, and slammed deeply into a tree several feet behind him.

Petrus screamed wildly. Uncontrollably, her body trembled with shock. Her hands covered her face. Distraught, she looked through her fingers at the bloody lifeless body of her lover. Unable to move, she just stood there, screaming hysterically.

Khosa fell to his knees, not fully grasping that his brother had just killed a man. Valli grinned and snickered. Watching how Petrus was responding, he said, "See Khosa, just like the chimps." His voice was cold and steady. "She is screaming and carrying on just like the chimps did."

Dubois laid his hand on Valli's shoulder, "Let's go, son. Your work is done here."

"No, wait. I must show Khosa what happened to the screaming chimp." Wildness flooded Valli's face as he raised the rifle to his shoulder. Looking down the barrel, he centered the bead directly on Petrus' temple. "Whore," he whispered under his breath and squeezed the trigger. Her head popped back, bursting open from the impact, and her naked body flew backwards like a rag doll, landing next to her lover.

Lowering the rifle, he handed it back to Dubois. Though his eyes moved rapidly, his voice was calm, "Let's go find your ivory." Walking over to Khosa kneeling in the weeds, Valli looked down at his little brother. "Just like the animals. Just like them."

Chapter 26

The small bristly head flopped over the girl's slender shoulder, and it bobbed and rocked gently in rhythm with her walk. His peaceful expression, together with a long, clear slobber dribbling from his parted lips, looked rather comical. Occasionally, his muscles tensed and the chimp's face twitched and contorted before easing back into tranquil unconsciousness. Following behind MacKenzie, Mhinga could see the young creature's eyes scanning beneath its eyelids. The chimp's left arm draped across MacKenzie's neck and hooked the elbow over her right shoulder. His flesh-colored fingers dangled beside her long braid. The chimp's other arm swung freely, hanging along the young woman's bent arm that supported his weight by his bandanna-covered bottom.

Several stops were made to allow MacKenzie to modify her home-made protection from the chimp's uncontrollable wetting. With each short break, her gear was gradually divided among Jon, Simon, and Jay. She now had only the chimp's ten pounds to carry.

As MacKenzie stepped over a fallen log, her long braid swung like a clock's pendulum across her back. The chimp's fingers grabbed a tight hold. Not feeling the return swing, MacKenzie stopped. Softly she asked, "Mhinga, what is he doing?"

Jon and Simon, walking ahead, stopped to look back. The chimp raised his dangling right arm, gripping onto MacKenzie's short-sleeved tee shirt. Standing perfectly still, her eyes widened and her eyebrows rose, questioning at Jon. The chimp then lifted his knees and wrapped his legs around her narrow waist. "Mhinga?" she whispered.

Very quietly Mhinga described the view from behind her, "He seems to be gripping on to you. His face is still peaceful. His eyes are closed . . . he is starting to close his lips together."

MacKenzie looked up at Jon, the smile on her face fading fast, and worry took over. "Is he waking up?"

Jon shrugged his shoulders, "He could be."

"What do I do now?" MacKenzie whispered.

"I don't know. Let's just see what he does. Don't resist him if he wakes up and wants down. Don't fight him or try to hold him."

MacKenzie's eyes softened as she felt the chimp turn his head. She felt his delicate breath on the nape of her neck, and she felt his body relaxing slightly. She smiled as the chimp adjusted himself to a more comfortable position in her arms.

After a few minutes, Jon stepped up behind her. Lifting each eyelid, he checked the chimp's pupils.

"What do you think?" MacKenzie asked.

"His pupils are still a bit off. I guess he could come out of it at any time."

MacKenzie reached up and stroked the chimp's hairy back. He responded by tightening his grip and locking his feet together behind her back. With renewed energy she took an easy step forward, careful not to jar the sleeping chimp cradled in her arms.

Surprisingly, Zawawi remained very quiet today, only offering a snide look towards MacKenzie when the group halted for her to make adjustments. His thoughts still dwelt on his sons. They had disgraced him and their Maasai heritage when they left to work for the logging concession. He should have been stricter with Valli, knowing that Khosa would follow him. Valli was a strong-willed young man. Zawawi still felt a lot of pride in his first-born, though he could not shake the disappointment he also felt, nor get over the words of the whore and her lover about playing his son for a fool. Zawawi worried what effect this affair was having on his younger son.

Khosa did not have a mean bone in his body. He was so much like his mother -- kind, gentle, and fair. Still so young, his older brother was his hero. He always trusted Valli would watch out for him.

Zawawi's mind raced. Soon, he thought. We will find the scientist and go after Dubois and the boys. Perhaps I can convince them to come back with me . . . .

❖ ❖ ❖

Trailing the old pachyderm across the soft forest floor was an easy task. He was traveling slowly, weaving in and out of the tall trees. The dinner-plate size tracks showed that the elephant was favoring his right front leg. Valli took pleasure in knowing the old bull was in pain they had inflicted. Though the old giant traveled slowly, his pace was steady. Each mound of dung was carefully checked, and consistent temperatures indicated that they had not closed the distance to their prey. The old bull was smart, pushing himself onwards, not stopping to rest or feed. Circling and backtracking, he moved from the soft forest to the rocky cliffs, traveling up and down streams trying to shake and wear down his pursuers.

Rage filled every cell in Valli's anatomy. He fueled himself on it, burning away any remorse he might have felt after killing Petrus and Taveta. Adrenaline surged through his body, heightening his natural instincts of some primitive intuition. Unlike any orgasmic experience he had felt before, Valli believed he had transformed himself into a God, completely absorbed into the environment. Every sound he recognized instantaneously, whether it was animal, bird or insect. He immediately noticed the smallest movement of leaf or the tiny blink of an eye that gave away the hiding place of some elusive forest animal. As if on drugs, his senses heightened. He noticed the smallest change in direction of the lightest breeze and instantly analyzed it. Reveling in his new abilities, he felt, somehow, that by taking human life, he had merged with nature. Each new awareness lifted him higher and deeper into the complex whole. The old bull elephant was his for the taking, and the excitement of the kill grew in his soul and in his loins. The only weight he felt was the old white man and his little brother tagging along, slowing him down.

Dubois followed a few paces behind Valli. He saw the change in the young man since the shooting. Valli was no longer a youth searching for his own way into adulthood. He had crossed that line in a most horrifying manner. The Frenchman had not tried to stop the shooting, but rather had encouraged it. He had tested his own persuasive capabilities on the young man, and he had won.

But now a more delicate test was coming, one that Valli would win or lose on his own. The taking of another human's life weaves a powerful and angry vine through one's mind and soul. Would the strength or the weakness of the young man's personality win out? He would have to wait and see how Valli reacted to the vine's growth. If he could manage this weed in Valli, then the young man would be a valuable asset. If the vine grew too strong, it would take over, binding its roots, tearing its host apart.

Traveling behind Valli, Dubois carefully watched his body language. He had never seen the young man so in tune with his work before. He moved with the grace and silence of a leopard stalking its prey. The only sounds were his own footsteps and those of the younger boy lugging himself lethargically behind him.

Slumped shoulders bore the weight of the supply pack. With arms folded across his chest, Khosa carried a second bundle. His eyes drained of energy, he stared at the forest floor. He walked carelessly, stepping on piles of dried leaves and snapping sticks under foot. He did not care where he was or what he was doing. The weight that he carried seemed to be no burden for his young frame. He moved mechanically, following behind like an abused pack animal. He had just witnessed his brother, his hero, do the unspeakable. One day he had watched Valli spinning with his arms outstretched, declaring his love for Petrus. The next he witnessed his brother murdering her and another. He did not fully understand what had brought the anger in Valli. What had she done to him? Was he getting sick? Khosa could not figure it out, but he knew who had encouraged his brother to pull the trigger.

Khosa thought, "If I had only kept my mouth shut. If I hadn't compared the people to the animals, to the chimpanzees that they had taken, Valli would not have lost his temper. He would not have killed those two people. It is my fault that my brother is a murderer." He felt the guilt, so it had to be so. It was not what he wanted. He wanted his brother to put down the gun and not to fire. Instead, his words, his pleading words, encouraged Valli to do it, to kill. A single tear formed. Then his eyes flooded and tears rolled down his cheeks. Lifting his shoulder, the young boy tilted his head and wiped them away on his tattered sleeve. Filled with emptiness, he followed in the white man's footsteps, feeling as lifeless and cold as Petrus and Taveta.

❖ ❖ ❖

The narrow animal trail wound through the forest, in and out of bright clearings, scaling the rugged hillsides. Twisting down the face of some bluffs, the trail ended at a rocky river bank. Sun-baked boulders and rocks created a blazing bright bar, free of shade. Only knee-high alfalfa-like river plants with tiny purple flowers grew here. Their delicate roots took hold in the tiny mud-filled crevasses between the rocks and the running water. Dragonflies fluttered among the rocks and plants. Their long abdomens, sparkling with iridescent greens, blues, and reds, appeared too heavy for their nearly translucent wings. Still they flew and danced easily, unbothered by these visitors to their world.

Buster waded past the river plants into the stream, his long pink tongue scooping up gulps of cool water. Mhinga gathered driftwood to begin the noon tea. MacKenzie selected a large flat rock at the river's edge. There she laid her little bundle, then sat to soak her aching feet.

Zawawi had acquired a student. Jay, although a trained soldier, had limited tracking skills, and the Maasai's natural tracking abilities amazed him. The tiny details that Mother Earth provided showed them the direction, speed, and time of another's passing. Zawawi relished his new role as teacher. The white woman had her chimp. Jon and Simon had new toys -- the GPS receiver and the detailed topographical map. Zawawi now had Jay, eager to learn the art of tracking. This boosted the Maasai's ego and took his mind off his sons.

MacKenzie was kept busy caring for the little chimp, who fidgeted more but had not yet fully awakened. Gladly, she had handed the GPS receiver over to Jon and Simon. The coordinates helped them locate the first campsite of the scientists. The men's careful examination of the area showed no signs of a struggle. The scientists and porters had made no attempts to hide their existence or the direction in which they had left. The wide trail hacked through the underbrush had nearly grown back. It had been over two months since the line of heavily burdened porters and the four scientists had slashed away the foliage. Their spoor was not difficult to follow until they reached the rocky path that led down the steep hillside to the river's edge. There Zawawi and Jay separated, one traveling upstream and the other down, looking for clues as to where the porters may have crossed the muddy river.

Jon and Simon unfolded the map and marked their location. They then projected an easy route that the group with the scientists might have taken to reach the coordinates of their proposed second campsite. MacKenzie was to meet the scientists there, deliver the fresh supplies, and collect their findings.

MacKenzie's dreadful fears for her father had lessened with the finding of the first campsite. Soon she would know that her father was safe. As she removed her sore feet from the cool stream, she turned and looked at Jon hovering over the map. Although deeply tanned, his skin was still light next to Simon's, and his broad shoulders and muscular arms looked small compared to those of his friend.

She had trouble comprehending just how large and powerful Simon was. And the contrast between Simon and his half brother Zawawi was even more striking. They looked to be no more closely related than a fine American Thoroughbred and a hefty Percheron workhorse. It was not just the differences between the tones of their skin or body mass. The bone structure in their faces reflected their personalities. Simon had a square, strong jaw-line, where his younger brother's was long and narrow.

A light breeze rolled across the river's surface, flickering as it caressed. The dark curls that fluffed out from beneath Jon's ball-cap danced in the gentle wind. The sun sparked highlights of sterling, giving a clue to Jon's age. Along the edge of his cheeks, silver showed in the soft growth of beard that partially concealed his tender lips.

MacKenzie's eyes followed the line of his back down to his well-defined, brawny legs. She remembered the feel of his skin and its soft hair against her legs when he held her close in the cave, and again that misty morning at the river crossing. The memory made every fiber in her body tingle. Passionately, her eyes strayed up Jon's frame to the long arm that rested on the rock, holding the edge of the map down with weight from his upper body. Perhaps, she thought, perhaps I should stay on here in Africa. My dad will need my help. This trip must have taken a lot out of him, and I should be here to care for him. He will need me. Her eyes continued to drift up Jon's arm, then, like a magnet, to his eyes. He had been watching her.

A blush flooded her face. She realized then that she had been grinning, too. She felt foolish because the man she had been daydreaming about had caught her. Embarrassed, her eyes dropped.

The small chimp lay next to her. Engrossed in her daydream, she had not seen the furry bundle move. He had rolled over onto his side and had covered his face with his arm, shielding his eyes from the bright sun. Relieved at the distraction, she dared not look back at Jon, though she still felt his stare.

She rolled the chimp over onto his back and checked his bandanna bottom. One neatly tied knot held the folded triangular diaper in place. Once untied, she could easily see the yellow wetness that had soaked into the sanitary napkin. Replacing the wet napkin with a dry one, she continued her duties, suppressing her guilt.

As she fussed over the chimp, she leaned forward, shading his face with her shadow. Her long braid of hair slid from her shoulder and gently swept across the chimp's nose. His reaction came so swiftly that it ended before MacKenzie realized it had happened.

The chimp snatched the tasseled end of her hair in his tiny pale fingers. Gripping tightly, his wide eyes stared up at her. He moved the tassel across his nose. Breathing deeply, he tried to sort the strange smell of human intertwining with his own scent in the lock of hair. Holding the tied end very close to his eyes, he studied the bright-colored elastic band. He moved it back and forth from one eye to the other as if trying to get a clear view. His little fingers worked up the long braided lock. Brushing it across his face, he felt the texture and smelled the hair. Parting his lips, he put the tasseled end into his mouth and tasted it.

MacKenzie stared with wonder as she watched the chimp examine her hair, his nose twitching from the tickles and the unfamiliar scent. His lips, previously so loose and placid, now curled at the taste and soft texture of her braid, so unlike his own coarse hair. She watched him squint as he held the item so close that she feared he would stick himself with the tassel end.

He examined her for several long minutes, and then the little fellow displayed strength beyond MacKenzie's belief. Having worked his hand midway up the length of her braid, he jerked hard, twisting her head and pulling her face down to his.

With their noses nearly touching the little chimp squinted his eyes, staring up into MacKenzie's. Her breathing had nearly stopped. Her heart pounded as their eyes studied each other. The depth of his chocolate brown eyes and the tiny red veins that zagged across the creamy whites captivated her. Fine lashes and tiny creases marked his skin. She was so close she could nearly watch the muscles underneath contract with movement. Then his brows relaxed, and the chimp released his grip. With an open palm he laid his hand on her cheek. Pursing his lips, he hoarsely tried to utter something. At first only a small breath of air escaped from his dry throat. Licking his lips he tried again. The little voice was low and frail as he puffed out, *"Huu."*

MacKenzie backed away a few inches from the chimp's face. Tilting her head slightly, she could see from the corner of her eye that Jon and Simon were watching her. They had not moved from their earlier positions over the map, hovering there like two stone statues, mouths open, wide-eyed in amazement. MacKenzie beamed and turned her attention back to the chimp. Once more he wet his lips and breathed in a big breath, puffing out more strongly, *"Huu."*

Unsure of what to do, MacKenzie tried mimicking the chimp. She breathed in and pursed her lips, in a soft deep breath she puffed out, *"Huu."* The little chimp touched her face again and dropped his lower jaw, showing a row of sharp canine-like teeth across his jaw. He held that grimace for several seconds, then grabbed MacKenzie's hair again and pulled her face down to his. Repeating the movements several more times, he huffed out *"Huu"* and dropped his lower lip showing his small white teeth. MacKenzie finally realized he was trying to communicate, and she mirrored his actions. He seemed pleased and released her hair. He smacked his lips together again, then placed his tiny thumb in his mouth and sucked on it.

MacKenzie rose. "Mhinga," she called softly across the gravel bar. The sound of her voice and word startled the young chimp. He tried to sit up. Unbalanced, he fell over, arms waving in the air. MacKenzie tried to soothe him, but her voice and unfamiliar sounds frightened him more.

Jon called as he crossed to her, "Don't try to restrain him, remember he doesn't know what you are." MacKenzie backed off a little bit. Her shadow no longer shaded his face and the chimp reacted badly to the bright sunshine. Screaming loudly, covering his eyes with his hands, he thrashed about the rock trying to turn over. MacKenzie leaned forward, casting her shadow over his face. Immediately, he quieted down and stopped struggling. Reaching up, the little chimp waved his hand in the air, searching the empty space until it found the long braid of hair. While clinging to it and smelling it, he puffed out, "*Huu*." Once again he put the tasseled end in his mouth and began chewing the hair.

Mhinga hurried to MacKenzie's side, followed by Simon and Jon. Feeling their presence, the chimp waved his free hand in their direction, searching the air where the men leaned over. They each ducked out of reach. Very softly, MacKenzie whispered, "I think he is hungry." The sound of her voice halted the chimp's wild search. Jerking her braid, again he pulled her face close to his and again breathed in deeply and puffed out, "*Huu*." As she mimicked the chimp, he brought down his lower lip, baring his teeth at her. Tilting her head to the side she mouthed the word 'figs' to Mhinga. With a nod, Mhinga reached into his pocket and pulled out a plump ripe fruit.

Carefully, MacKenzie peeled off a section and held the soft juicy innards up to the chimp's nose. With a weak squeal, the chimp puckered up his lips and greedily snatched the fig from her fingers. His eyes closed with delight while he chewed. Then, wide-eyed again, he smacked his lips together and puckered up for another bite of the sweet morsel. They fed the chimp six more figs before he slowed down. His eyes grew heavy and he soon fell into a deep slumber, still clutching the long braid of hair.

Very gently, MacKenzie pried the tiny fingers from her hair. Rolling the chimp onto his side, she laid his arm over his face, as he had done himself, shielding his eyes from the bright noon sun.

Chapter 27

Nature kills so that she may give and inspire new life. Time, disease, and predators are her workers. When weakened and aging root systems can no longer supply the nutrients needed by towering branches, majestic old trees die. Tumbling, their wide-spread limbs knock down neighboring growth. The length and mass of fallen trees create buttonholes in the woven cloth of the green canopy. When the sun first reaches the delicate moist layer of earth, shade-loving plants are burned away. The warming of the ground awakens tiny seeds that have lain dormant, some waiting patiently for years until their time arrives to sprout and flourish.

Tender new shoots spring to life and fill the void. Bright, colorful flowers lure insects and birds to spread their pollen and seeds. Forest herbivores feast on the new growth, and use the open area for birthing and sunbathing after damp cool nights. The mighty tree that once stood tall, protecting the forest from above, now supports and nourishes it from below.

On this new day, bright stars sparkled together in a wide band, hugging the sky of black velvet. Musty smells of fungus perfumed the mist that bathed tall mahogany trees. The day's first glow of light slowly broke over the woodland, illuminating the sea of green leaves. Treetops filtered the sun's glow, dividing the delicate mist into translucent emerald sheers that sprinkled across the forest floor. Emerging from the darkness, heavy shadows formed once again into tall forest trees.

The awakening and stirring of brightly colored birds praised the splendor of each new day. Choirs sang in mixed harmonies, calling to their chicks and mates. Fluttering wings stretched and flapped away the morning dew. Piercing eyes watched for unsuspecting insects crawling from underneath broad leaves to warm their cold and stiffened bodies. Snatching up bugs, the birds returned to their nests, feeding their young.

The gray-green morning brightened to gold as the full, exposed sun raced across the cloudless African sky. The buttonhole clearing with its rotting wood and thick new bottom growth awakened with all the small wonders of the forest. The sleeping giant stirred last of all.

Cradled in a bed of soft greenery, the old bull elephant opened his eyes. Blinking fast, his long, wiry lashes filtered the harsh morning sun. His broad head rested upon his long ivory tusks. Draping the tip of his trunk over the curved ivory, he fingered tall blades of dew-moistened grass.

On stiffened joints, he drew each leg out from under his bulky mass. Hindered by the week-old bullet wound in his shoulder, the bull wobbled as he pushed his body up and above the flattened plants. Slowly stretching each leg, he looked more like a trained circus animal than a wild creature awakening from a long night's sleep. With his trunk held high, he searched for an air current. Finding only stillness, he inhaled deep breaths, and then, inserting the tip of his trunk into his mouth, he released the captured air, testing for any faint scent of danger. Basking in the warm sunshine, he examined air samples from a full three hundred and sixty-degree radius. The stillness in the air brought no indication of the hunters being near. For several days, he had not slept a full night nor taken the usual long naps at noon. Being pursued by the humans was wearing him down. He had been in need of this long rest. Peacefully, he now gorged himself on the fresh green shoots that sprouted across the small sunny clearing.

The hunters had been traveling most of the night. Valli's restlessness to hunt and Khosa's despondent spirit left Dubois no choice but to keep moving. They took a short rest during the darkest part of the night, but Valli awakened them long before the break of day to continue the hunt for the old bull. By torchlight they followed the trail of broken limbs, piles of dung, and huge footprints. As the day broke into its first light, Valli skillfully led Dubois to a small clearing where the old bull elephant peacefully slept.

Hiding near the edge in a pile of dying limbs, the hunters waited for the morning light to appear. As the day brightened, the old bull stirred and finally rose to his feet and stretched. Dubois looked in awe at the long curved tusks. The shafts of creamy gold bore tips stained with streaks of red and black. Years of fresh berries and digging in the clay soil had left their marks. Dubois imagined stroking the pure white section, as big around as his thigh, which lay protected under the tough hide of the old elephants' cheek. Today, he thought, would be the first time the delicate rooted end would ever know the warmth of the sunshine. He imagined running his hands down the length of the ivory curves, caressing them like a virgin child. His mind began to piece together how and where he would smuggle these large beauties.

Anxiously, Valli fidgeted behind Dubois, bringing him back from his daydreams. The young man, full of anticipation, rocked uneasily from foot to foot, glancing back and forth between the elephant and his employer. As they watched the bull sniff the air in all directions, Valli tried to will the man holding the big .460 rifle. His mind raced, "Shoot him! Shoot him!" Determined and eager to take his prize, he unwittingly spoke the words under his breath.

Dubois glared back at the young man, thinking, Valli is getting out of control. Smartly, Dubois winked at the young man and smiled. Valli settled down when the big rifle was lifted to the man's shoulder.

The still morning air kept the old bull from catching their scent. Rushing excitement fevered Valli's body and soul. Pride straightened his back and squared his shoulders because he had tracked the elephant at night. He had gotten the hunter so close they could clearly make out the wiry lashes that shaded the elephant's eyes from the bright sun. It was he, he prided himself, the greatest tracker of all time. His father would have to bow down at his story, a story that Khosa witnessed, and would tell truthfully. Glancing over his shoulder, Valli looked at his little brother sitting quietly on a rock. He had not spoken a word since the shooting of Petrus and Taveta. Valli grinned at his little brother and pointed to the old bull. Khosa's eyes followed the point, but the blank expression did not change. Without wasting another thought about his brother, Valli turned his attention back to the task at hand. Though he did not hold the rifle in his hands, nor feel the curve of the trigger against his finger, Valli's heart raced. Warmth settled in his waist, and he felt himself harden, his breathing deepen and slow, and he clearly heard each pounding beat of his heart.

Dubois stood in the classic stance, his feet apart, weight slightly forward, shoulders squared, the rear foot turned out, giving support without restricting the hefty recoil. The rifle's dark American walnut stock was securely wedged into the fleshy part of his shoulder. His left hand supported the rifle's ten and a half pounds and almost four-foot length. His right hand softly cupped below the trigger guard. Dubois tilted his head onto the ridge of the rifle's stock. Closing one eye, he lined up the v-notch with the bead, centering it between the elephant's eyes. Slowly, he positioned his forefinger over the trigger and pulled back until he felt the tension resist his touch. Slow, deep breaths steadied his aim.

The old bull shook his head, ridding his face of pesky insects. A light breeze rustled in the high branches, and the elephant's trunk shot up to catch it. Deeply inhaling obscured bits of odors, the fingered tip periscoped around. When pointing over his back, directly behind him the old bull stopped chewing. Spinning around on his hind leg, his tattered ears flung out in an alert stance, focusing in on distant sounds. The only movement was his trunk held high in the air, reaching out, drawing in the air to sample.

Dubois held his stance, waiting for the elephant to relax and turn back towards him. He could feel Valli's presence lurking over him. He knew he had missed his window for a clean shot but had not given up. Soon, Dubois thought, soon he will lower his trunk and turn back around. The weight of the rifle began to take its toll on his left arm. His strength started to lessen; he must rest his arm while the elephant was out of position. As he lowered the rifle, a distant gunshot rang out, echoing across the hills, followed closely by another.

The old bull spun around faster than Dubois could react. Out of position, with his rifle lowered and a tired arm, he was unable to get his aim quickly enough. The elephant charged towards the thick underbrush that lined the edges of the clearing. He charged directly toward where the hunters stood, concealed in the shadows.

The earth vibrated with each heavy step, though the only sound was that of the tall grasses being pushed aside by the bulk of the elephant's body. Reacting quickly, Valli rushed forward, grabbing the rifle from

Dubois' grip. Raising it into position, he ran from the shadowy depth of the bushes into the sunshine of the clearing. He charged the frightened bull.

At first sight of movement in the bushes in front of him, the old bull checked his stride. Panic-stricken he turned, changing direction.

Valli fired the rifle in haste. Recklessly, wild shots flew in the general direction of the fleeing elephant. One of the shots hit high in the fleshy part of the hip. The old bull squealed with the new burning sensation from the penetrating bullet. Very quickly all three shots were spent before Dubois could grab the rifle from Valli's grip. The elephant disappeared through the dense wall of foliage at the clearing's edge.

With one quick motion, Dubois jabbed the butt end of the rifle into Valli's stomach. Folding over, the young man gasped for air. "What the hell do you think you are doing?" Dubois struck him again, sending him to the ground. "That little stunt of yours has cost us another week in the damn forest!"

Still trying to catch his breath, Valli crawled onto his knees. "I thought . . . ," he began.

"NO!" Dubois jumped in, "You don't think. I do the thinking here. Your job is to track. You don't decide anything. Do you understand me, boy? I do the thinking, not you! Got it?"

Unbalanced, bent at the waist, heaving in large gulps of air, Valli's voice broke, "But the bull was charging us."

"The bull would have run right past us, and he would have stopped a few feet inside the tree line to smell the air again. I could have made the shot then. But now he is really scared and will run hard. It will take us a week to catch up with him now."

Stumbling backwards, Valli tried to stand fully upright, "But . . . ."

"But nothing!" Dubois snapped back. Crossing over to him, pointing his finger in Valli's face, he gritted through his teeth, "Don't you ever pull another stunt like that again, or I will stuff and mount your head on my wall. Do you understand me, boy?"

The white man's cruel words burned hatred into Valli. Standing tall, he stared steadily at Dubois. Face to face the men stood their ground, sizing each other's strengths and weaknesses with new interest.

Although he stood a full six inches taller, and his chest out-spanned the younger man's, Dubois knew that Valli would not be an easy opponent to fight. He had youth and speed on his side, as well as that fierce Maasai blood running through his veins. Dubois, on the other hand, had military training and experience on his side. For the first time he was not seeing an eager-to-please teenager. In front of him now stood a man holding his ground and willing to fight for it. Valli had leaped into manhood. Realizing that he may have gone too far, Dubois tried to defuse the tension. Cracking a little grin, he tried to cover what he saw and felt. Valli did not back down nor return the grin. H was ready for a fight.

Dubois backed away, turning his back to Valli, giving him several seconds to spring his attack and be caught in a well-thought-out trap. Tensed and charged-up Dubois was ready for the assault that did not come. He still had the upper hand. Taking his hat off, running his fingers through his graying hair, bringing his temper under control, he stretched out the moments. "Look, Valli." He used his fatherly charms, turning toward the angry young man and placing his hand upon Valli's shoulder. "I think we should let the old bull run out his fright. Let's go see who fired those two shots. I need you, Valli." His voice was humble. "I need you to track for me. You are the best, remarkable, really. Will you use your natural gifts and lead me to the other hunters?"

Dubois' words caught Valli offguard. The Frenchman sounded sincere. Still a bit uncertain, Valli hesitated before reaching out, offering his hand to shake. Without faltering, Dubois' shook in the traditional Maasai fashion, palm to wrist. Tightly, the men grasped onto each other and grinned uneasily. In the moment of release Valli grabbed Dubois' loose wrist tightly. Pulling him up close, chest-to-chest, looking the white man straight in the eyes. He spoke in a firm, manly voice, "You will never strike me again, or I will feed you to the loggers steak by steak." Releasing the wrist with a shove, Valli turned away. He did not need to see Dubois' reaction. He knew that the unexpected words and action cut deeply into the white man. As he crossed the sunny clearing, Khosa rose from the shadows and followed his older brother.

We shall see, Dubois thought, as he followed in line. We shall see.

Around noon, Valli crossed a small creek bed, formed by rain water as it gathered speed and cascaded down the steep hill. Very narrow, the runoff twisted and eroded the soft earth, half-exposing embedded rocks. Animals used it as a trail, and not just ones with cloven hooves: up and down the trail, human footprints stood out in the dirt. Valli squatted beside the trail. He smiled up at Dubois and pointed to the tracks. "These are a few days old." Bending down at the waist, Valli skirted the edge of the trail, careful not to disturb the prints as he studied them. "There were three men. One white and two black." Valli passed up and down the trail for many yards. "The three of them traveled very fast down the hill. The white man was weak and very tired. Then later the same two black men traveled very slowly up the hill, carrying a heavy weight."

Dubois was truly amazed. "How do you tell these things?"

Valli shrugged his shoulders indifferently, and motioned for Dubois to kneel alongside. Valli pointed to the dim prints in the soil. "See how these four treaded prints are different from those two? Those are factory made shoes worn by a white man. These others are made by hand from a worn tire," Valli explained in a firm voice. Although Dubois already knew many of these things, he let the Maasai continue on with his expert commentary. "See the spacing between the steps? They are different lengths apart and carelessly placed. The white man stumbles over the uneven ground. The black men are strong and careful where they put their feet. They know the forest well. They chase the white man and will have caught him soon. See how their return tracks are deeper and closer together? They carry a load, perhaps the white man."

Dubois ignored the sly comparisons of the black men's superiority over the white man, and the implication Valli was making about himself and Dubois. Instead, he encouraged the young man to continue. "You are quite the detective, Valli!" he said, patting him on the back.

Valli smiled. Feeling a bit cocky, he added, "These are the things that I do best."

"Yes, and I'm lucky to have such a skillful man working for me." Dubois' flattery encouraged the young man's superior attitude. "Can you lead me to where they caught the white man?"

Valli snickered as he rose and headed down the trail. Dubois looked back at Khosa, still depressed, following quietly behind.

The hill became steeper. Exposed rocks and roots also increased, as each rainfall gnawed away at the path, unmasking dangerous footholds. The rank smell of rotting flesh filled the air. Finally, Valli stopped alongside the rotting python carcass. Small ripples moved about under the thin layer of the long scaly body. The severed head lay a few feet further down the trail, reduced to a flattened, shattered skull. The birds and insects had already picked it clean. Curiosity and cockiness overwhelmed Valli. Kneeling alongside the snake's body, he probed his fingers at the rippling movements just under the skin.

Dubois stood back, covering his nose and mouth with the collar of his shirt, trying to filter out the stench.

Khosa stood behind Dubois, staring silently and wide-eyed at the grotesque animal stretched out along the trail. His arms went weak, dropping the packs as he watched his brother poke at the dead animal with his bare hands.

The dry thin layer of skin, stretched tight from the bloating, burst open at the first light touch, splitting the length of the body. Thousands of shiny fat white maggots fell out in waves, and pungent gas filled the air.

As the snake burst open, Khosa spun away. Dropping to his knees, he vomited uncontrollably. Dubois had to turn away, too. To take his mind off the sight, he tried to help Khosa. Holding the young boy's forehead, he supported the slim shoulders as the youth heaved and heaved. As the boy gained control, Dubois finally dared to look back at Valli.

Engrossed in his work, the tracker had turned his attention to the other side of the trail, inspecting the ground and a torn strip of bark from a nearby tree. Unaffected by the stench or scene, Valli called back to Dubois, "The white man was killed here."

Dubois nodded, trying to control his voice and breathing. After swallowing hard, he said, "The snake?"

Valli rose up from his squat. Straightening his back, he stretched and yawned. "No," he answered coldly. "Rifle shot to the head."

Releasing Khosa, Dubois nearly dropped the weakened boy into a pool of his own vomit. "Do the tracks continue on?" he asked.

"No. The heavy tracks of the black men begin here." Valli's voice was cool and unaffected, as it had been a few days earlier when he had put bullets into the heads of his girlfriend, Petrus, and her lover, Taveta. Standing in the center of the stench, the young Maasai seemed to absorb the violence that had happened here just a few days earlier. Dubois watched with horrified thoughts as Valli's shoulders straightened and his muscles tightened with tension. Kneeling down by the barked tree, his caressing fingers crossed the scars made by a dying man. He studied bits of bone chips. A rock covered with dried blood may have been used to fight off the snake. With his clasp knife, he dug into the trail for the bullet that had ended the man's life. He sniffed it for any remaining traces of gunpowder. Finding none, he rolled the brass shank with his fingers. Once again Valli's eyes glazed wildly. Smiling at Dubois as he rose, he asked, "Shall we follow the trail and see where they took the white man's body?"

Appeasing the young man, Dubois returned the grin. Picking up one of the packs, he tossed it to Valli. "Khosa is too weak to carry these now."

Valli looked past the Frenchman to Khosa, trembling with weakness. Coldly, he spoke, "You will be better by tomorrow. Won't you, little brother?" Unbalanced, the lad grabbed onto a sapling for support and nodded. Dubois picked up the other pack, tossing it over his shoulder as Valli passed by. Khosa fell into line, bent over at the waist, barely able to walk.

Chapter 28

Well, I'll be damned!" Dubois was perched on a rocky outcrop atop a small hill. Through his field glasses, he watched two black men in a clearing at the bottom of a hollow. They worked over their kill. Hanging by the hocks from a low branch, the leopard's paws had been removed, and a long slit had been made down the animal's belly to its breastbone. The men worked carefully pulling the skin away from the body a little piece at a time and cutting it free with a sharp knife. "I didn't realize we had traveled so far northwest."

Fidgeting alongside, Valli asked, "What do you see?" From this distance he could only make out dark objects moving among the tall green saplings.

Lowering the field glasses, Dubois shook his head. "Would you believe there are two men down there who work for me?"

Tensing his eyebrows together, Valli questioned, "We are a long way from the logging concessions. Why would you have men so far away?"

Dubois handed the field glasses to him. "Valli," he began in a fatherly tone, "I have a lot more going on here than just hunting to feed a bunch of hungry loggers."

As Dubois spoke, Valli tried to look through the magnifying lenses for the first time. Brown streaks of tree bark filled his blurred view. Moving the glasses away, he looked at Dubois mystified. "I think that the shade of the forest has darkened your mind. I don't see any men. These must be broken." He handed the glasses back to Dubois.

"Keep trying," Dubois said pushing them back to him. "You'll figure it out." After a short while Valli closed one eye, focusing and adjusting to see very large objects from far away in the tiny circle of the lens. Panning the binoculars around, Valli was amazed at all the details he now saw.

Dubois smiled and watched patiently as Valli played with the field glasses and became familiar with their use. The demon that had overtaken Valli was now suppressed. The curious teenager was back. When the two men came into focus, Valli smiled, "Ah, I see them now. But I do not know these men."

Dubois winked and grinned at Valli. "I have a long list of clients who are hungry for the spotted pelt of that animal," he said, pointing to the sunny hollow, "as well as that exotic meat. Those men are part of a special team I formed just to do this."

"All these men do is hunt for you? That's what I do for you. What's so special about that?"

"The difference, Valli, is that you hunt mostly for a large number of kills and the meat is consumed immediately. We have the licenses to hunt food for the loggers. These men hunt for the rarest types of animals. These are labeled 'endangered animals', hunting licenses are not given or very rarely. These men are the cream of the crop, the very best. They work hard and keep their mouths shut about their work. They are very well paid for their loyalties." Dubois could see the wheels turning in Valli's head. The young man's curiosity had been piqued.

"How much money?" Valli glanced out of the corner of his eye. Khosa was sitting apart, alone, with his eyes closed.

Dubois' smile faded, and he leaned toward Valli. In almost a whisper, he said, "Many times more."

Lowering the glasses, Valli looked Dubois straight in the eyes and said, his voice confident, "I could do such work."

Dubois let his words hang in the air. Studying the stony face, he waited for Valli to back down, even a little. But no. Finally, Dubois gave a little nod, saying in a soft voice, "Perhaps. You have the makings to join my special group. But your temper worries me."

Looking through the glasses again, Valli tried to hide his disappointment. He considered Dubois' statement without protest. As he studied the men working below, he asked, "Where are these men from? They have strange markings on their faces."

"Those two are from the Congo. The skinny one is Tshombe and the other fellow is Gbenya. They are of the Madi tribe."

Lowering the glasses again, Valli repeated, "I could do this work very well."

"Yes, Valli, I believe you could. That is why we are following the old bull together. This is the test to see if you will fit into my elite group."

"Have I not proven to you my ability to track?" Valli pleaded his case.

"You are a most impressive tracker, Valli. That is why I have told you all this. But you are quite a bit younger than the others and have not yet learned to control your temper." He tried to provoke him, saying, "These men are hardened soldiers and will not tolerate such childishness."

"Childishness! It was not a child who judged and took care of

Petrus and Taveta. It was a man, and that man was me. I will prove to you that I can be worthy of being in your elite group."

A crooked smile cracked Dubois' face. "Very well, Valli, we shall see. Now let's go down and say hello."

The sunny hollow nestled between two hills. Tshombe and Gbenya worked together carefully, removing the spotted pelt from the leopard's carcass. These poachers were part of the two four-man teams. Each team member was a highly skilled tracker and soldier, trained in the Congolese Army. Tough and professional, they now worked efficiently in independent groups. Their loyalties of fighting for Congo independence quickly ended when Dubois made his pitch. He invited them to join his elite group of poachers offering unbelievably high wages.

Each group had eight members, divided into two teams. One group hunted, and the other group handled the transport. The poaching team rotated weekly. Using the American scientists' campsite as a front, one team hunted, and the other team worked as guards.

The transport team included four runners and four drivers. The four foot-runners traveled back and forth over the same ground, relaying the meat and pelts from the poachers' rendezvous to the main base camp set up in the deserted mining town of Lifi. The other four members maintained the mechanical equipment, driving the refrigerated transport trucks or flying the group's only helicopter.

There had been a fifth team of four men who guarded the Lifi base camp, but they had perished in a cave-in while searching for the witnesses to the elephant kill.

The area the hunters worked was dense with animals, but largely uninhabited by people. A few small family groups of the Okiekes tribe lived peacefully, scattered among the hills. As harvesters of wild fruit, nuts, and honey, they provoked no quarrels with a few hunters in their forest.

The woodlands spanned the invisible borders of neighboring countries, allowing easy access for transferring the goods. Fresh exotic meats of primates, elephants, and large cats were delivered on foot to Lifi. There the meat was further processed and packaged, then transported to either a presidential palace or to a large, refrigerated warehouse in the Congolese city of Ouesso, the heart of the bushmeat industry. There, false labels were put on the packaged meats, and they were shipped out to several European countries for distribution to restaurants. Pelts were also flown into Europe, but in the safe hands of corrupt diplomats.

Six years earlier, Dubois had a much larger organization. But last summer some employees' loyalties gave way to lump-sum bribery and Dubois found himself in a war with the trained soldiers of Kenya's Wildlife Service Anti-Poaching Unit. The leader, Colonel Simon Kuldip, cost Dubois his large-scale operation, but paid for it with his own blood.

Quietly, several central African governments offered support to Dubois. Equipment, weapons, transport, a few highly skilled guerrilla soldiers, and inspection immunity at the airports and roadblocks put Dubois back in business. Allowing the American scientists into the remote area provided cover, and headed off awkward questions. Within a few weeks, the palaces once again had fresh exotic meats. In return, Dubois' family business, Camino Timber Enterprise, received exclusive timber-cutting rights in the old-growth forest.

As Dubois descended the hillside, he called out, alerting the men, "Hello! Tshombe, Gbenya." His voice broke the peaceful silence of the meadow, startling the two poachers. The two men reached for their weapons. "It's me, Dubois. Put down your rifles." Recognizing the thick French accent, the armed men lowered their rifles, but kept them ready, just in case. When Dubois broke through the thick undergrowth into the sunny clearing, the men relaxed and set them down. Greeting them with handshakes, Dubois introduced Valli to the men. Khosa had stopped at the clearing's edge. At the sight of the bloody red torso slowly spinning in the breeze, he dropped the packs. Lying down, he closed his eyes, ignoring the others squatting and chatting near the hanging carcass of the leopard.

"Nice find," Dubois nodded toward the leopard. "Where are the other two?"

Tshombe thumbed the air over his shoulder, pointing to the leopard. "She has cubs around here; they are out looking for them."

A few feet away, Khosa lay listening. The mention of cubs caught his attention. Opening his eyes, he rolled over onto his side and listened more closely. Once he had raised a cheetah kitten. As it grew older, it developed a taste for calves and goats. One night his father, Zawawi, threw his spear and ended its life, saving his precious herd.

The men spoke mostly of the kills they had made recently, and of the news of the transported goods. Business was going well for Dubois. The transport team had put a discreet word out to a few selected people that they needed replacement guards for Lifi. When Dubois was ready, he could select from tough, trustworthy men.

The small talk bored Valli. Silently, he watched the faces of the Madi tribesmen. Tattooed scars of straight lines ran from each nose, across cheeks to jaw lines. It looked like a large cat had raked its claws to mark its territory.

Across the meadow, the bobbing heads of the other two poachers became visible over the tops of the tall grasses. As they got closer, high-pitched squeals could be heard. They had found three kittens and were bringing them back. Surprised to see Dubois, they set the kittens down to wander about. Around seven weeks old, they had bright eyes and moved quite strongly. Their sense of smell led them to the small pile of four paws. The kittens crawled over the bloody feet, purring at the familiar scent of their mother.

The tiny cries draw Khosa from his resting spot, and he moved closer to the kittens. Playfully, he petted and rolled them onto their backs, rubbing the velvety fur covering their plump bellies. The kittens clinched needle-like claws around Khosa's fingers and attacked him with sharp tiny teeth. Absorbing himself in the playful jesters, he laughed out loud and tried to tune out the men's conversation.

Dubois asked about the scientists. The change of subject caught Valli's attention. He remembered, when he met Jon at the logging road, that he had spoke about searching for four lost American scientists. Jon was traveling with his father, Zawawi, and his sister-in-law's brother, Mhinga. Also a white woman was with them. He did not know that Dubois knew about the scientists. Until now, he had forgotten about them himself.

Tshombe and Gbenya spoke eagerly in turn, each butting in to tell the next part of the story. The more they spoke, the faster the words flew out. It was the most excitement they had had in a long time. They told

Dubois about the one scientist who had tried to escape. In great detail, they explained how easily they tracked him. They laughed at the white man's stupidity -- not trying, nor knowing how, to cover his own tracks.

Valli listened closely, hanging on every word. The poachers caught on quickly and played up to their attentive audience. Dubois wondered how much of the story was fabricated for the young man eagerly waiting for the next part of the story.

The gunmen told how they found the white man with broken ankles from a large python. They laughed, and Valli laughed with them, as they explained how they woke the man before they blew his brains out.

Valli's eyes grew wild, and he slapped Dubois on the shoulder, exclaiming, "Did I not tell you it was a bullet to the head?"

The men's laughter stopped, and they looked quizzically at Dubois. "We found the spot where this happened," Dubois offered. "We were following the tracks when we ran across you."

Full of excitement, Valli told his story of the maggot-filled snake and how he dug the bullet from the ground. He pulled it from his pocket to prove his story. While Valli talked, Dubois paced around the leopard.

Childish giggles were coming from Khosa. The sight of the young boy playing with the leopard cubs made Dubois smile. Rolling around in the tall grass, the spotted kittens pounced on the young boy; they bit into his clothing and nibbled his ear.

Dubois looked over his shoulder at Valli. The wild craze had filled him again. His eyes narrowed like a hawk's, and his shoulders straightened and squared. Muscles seemed to materialize, defining themselves under his black skin. When Valli finished telling his story, Dubois strolled back to the group. Squatting down, he asked, "What did you do with the body?"

Gbenya spoke, "We took it back to their camp as an example to the others."

"They buried him and have been very well-behaved since," Tshombe answered with a smirk. The other followed with laughter, agreeing with him, then added, "The old one has slim's. He will be dead soon too."

Valli questioned the men for more details about the hunt and the scientist they shot. Happily, the gunmen retold their story, enlarging many details, spurring Valli into a flushing fury. Dubois watched as Valli quickly became absorbed by the moment. He realized then that he would not be able to control Valli much longer. He must rid himself of Valli and Khosa. They had become a liability, and he didn't want to lose his elite group. Dubois stood and inspected the beautiful spotted coat on the leopard's hanging corpse.

Tshombe called across to Dubois, "What do you want done with the cubs?"

Dubois glanced down at Khosa playing with the little fluff balls. Sensing he was being watched, Khosa looked up. Dubois stared directly at the young upturned face and said coldly, "Skin them. There's enough hide there to make a handbag."

The smile and laughter drained from Khosa. He held Dubois' stare as Gbenya grabbed one of the kittens by the loose hair on the back of its neck. The familiar feel of being carried this way quieted the kitten's cries as it hung in mid air, moving slowly away from the other kitten still playing on Khosa's chest. The flickering sound of the folded knifeblade opening did not alter the blank empty expression on Khosa's face. A tiny half squeal was cut short as the sharp blade slit open the kitten's neck, nearly severing the head completely. Gbenya tossed the small lifeless body over to one of the others to skin and reached down for the next kitten. As he pulled it out of Khosa's hands, a single tear rolled down the boy's cheeks. Dubois still hovered over the boy and said to him, "It's my business, boy. They are only animals." Khosa turned over and closed his eyes.

One of the poachers showed Valli the art of skinning such a small animal while the other three turned their attention to the female leopard. Dubois began cleaning his rifle and mentally mapping out his future plans. Now that one of the scientists has been killed, he thought, they will all have to be disposed of. It will be months before a search party will come looking for them and even longer before they can be found, if at all. We'll go back to the campsite. I'll leave Valli and Khosa at the scientists' camp and dispose of them as well. Tshombe and Gbenya will be able to pick up the elephant's trail. Once I collect the ivory, we can finish up in this part of the forest and move on to a new location. I won't risk losing it all again.

Chapter 29

Did you see him? Wasn't he just precious?" MacKenzie glowed with excitement. "His eyes are so big and dark." The more she talked, the faster the words flew from her mouth. "He was so gentle when he ate the figs from my fingers. Oh Mhinga . . . ," her voice whirled without restraint, "he is just so wonderful! So sweet and gentle!"

"Ms. Mac, please, calm down," Mhinga prodded.

"Yeah Mac," Jon cut in, "I don't want to rain on your sunny day, but . . . ."

"But nothing," she cut in. Then snickering, "Too bad Zawawi wasn't here to see it for himself."

"You can tell him all about it," Simon began, "when he and Jay return from scouting the river bank."

"Oh, you better believe I will," MacKenzie said, turning her attention back to the chimpanzee.

Simon, unaware of the tension between his brother, Zawawi, and MacKenzie, looked at Mhinga, raising an eyebrow.

Mhinga shrugged him off, "It's a long story."

"Mac," Jon continued, "remember, it is a wild animal." Laying his hand on her shoulder, he leaned over and whispered in her ear, "Don't get your hopes up for a new pet. As soon as he comes to his senses, he'll be up the nearest tree. You'll be lucky if he doesn't take a bite out of you on his way up."

"Ms. Mac," Mhinga glanced around uneasily, then continued, "perhaps it would be best if you leave him here. Now that you know that he is going to be all right."

Flashing a wicked look from the corner of her eye, she commanded, "Oh, you two, just stop it." Turning back to the chimp laying on the flat rock, she said, "It's too soon to tell if he will be all right or not. If I were to leave him here," she argued as she straightened up, "some hungry meat-eating animal could come along and make a meal out of him." Waving her hand toward the stream, she added, "Or he could stumble into the river and drown. No, it's too soon to leave him." Jon and Mhinga glanced at each other. "Besides," MacKenzie went on dramatically, "not only does he need me now, but he trusts me, too. I know it."

Taking a deep breath, Jon said, "Mac," then stopped as, out of the corner of his eye, he caught Simon shaking his head. But it was too late, he had already begun. "Just how do you know that? And please don't say it is woman's intuition."

MacKenzie glared at Mhinga and Simon who were beginning to chuckle. Crossing her arms over her chest, she sputtered, "Mhinga, I thought you of all people would understand." Then turning to Simon, she continued, "And you, since I've met your wife, Colleen, I thought that you might understand, too. But I see I was wrong."

The two men could contain themselves no longer. Laughing out loud, Simon tried to recover, "Oh, but I do understand. Colleen tells me the same thing quite often."

"Yeah, me, too," Mhinga added.

Tossing her hands up in the air, MacKenzie declared, "Oh what's the use? Never mind. You'll never understand."

"You're kidding?" Jon's words slipped out.

"Jon, you're just digging yourself into a deeper hole." Walking away from the group, Simon called back over his shoulder, "You should just shut up while she is still speaking to you." Then he whistled and slapped his thigh. "Come on, Buster. Let's go find Zawawi and Jay."

With hands on her hips, MacKenzie hissed through her teeth, "No, I'm not kidding!"

"It is true, Jon." Mhinga said, "I don't know how, but women often know these sorts of things."

Dropping her hands from her hips, MacKenzie questioned, "If you understand, Mhinga, then why are you laughing at me?"

As Mhinga walked away, he began, "Ms. Mac," then he paused to gather his thoughts. He laid his hand on Jon's shoulder and continued, "It is not you that we were laughing at."

Jon shook his head in disbelief. "Mhinga, you don't really believe in that nonsense, do you?"

"Not only do I believe it, Jon, but . . . ."

"Hey, Jon!" Simon interrupted. "Come look at this."

"But what?" Still talking to Mhinga, Jon turned toward Simon who knelt at the river's edge. "What makes you an expert on women anyway? You're only nineteen years old."

Mhinga followed Jon down the riverbank toward Simon. "Well, if you must know, I have learned a great deal about women from watching you with them."

As the two men walked, carrying on their conversation, MacKenzie picked up the little chimp. "Don't you worry, little fellow, I won't leave you behind." At the sound of her voice, two dark brown eyes slowly opened. MacKenzie leaned very close to his face and softly puffed out, "*Huu.*" Slowly the chimp raised his hand to her face, extending his forefinger. Gently he pushed the tip of his dark-skinned pointer between her lips and felt around the inside of her gums. MacKenzie smiled and again puffed out, "*Huu.*" In response the little chimp happily smacked his lips together. She whispered, "I can't wait to show you to my dad." As she spoke, he reached for her long braid of hair. Catching her scent, he smacked his lips together again and puffed out, "*Huu.*"

Simon held up a small, cup-sized fragment of thick plastic for Jon to see, "What do you make of this?" One side of the curved form had dense foam rubber glued to it. Mhinga picked up several pieces of the splintered yellow pieces that lay scattered among the rocks at the river's edge.

"I have no idea. It could be from almost anything." Jon exchanged the piece with those Mhinga had picked up. Wiping the dried mud off with his thumb, Jon uncovered the small trademark stamped in the plastic. MADE IN THE U.S.A. was clearly legible over the long patent number. "Well, it's from her world, not ours." Jon handed it to Simon.

"It could be from a piece of their equipment or from a carrying case," Simon stood thinking out loud.

"But how did it get all busted up?" Jon asked.

At the sound of approaching footsteps on the gravel bar, they turned. Jay was returning from exploring downstream.

"Did you find where they might have crossed?" Simon asked.

"No, the river gets very swift and deep." Jay leveled his hand about chest high.

Holding out a handful of the plastic pieces, Jon asked, "Did you find anything like this?"

Jay looked at the yellow splinters. "Yeah, but the pieces that I found were a lot smaller. Just little chips, nothing as big as this. I didn't know what it was." Reaching into his pocket he pulled out a small fist full of the pebble-sized plastic. "What do you think they're from?"

"They may be part of the scientists' equipment or a case." Simon tossed the tiny fragments into the river.

"At least it shows we're on their trail," Mhinga offered.

"Maybe, or we could be just following the route the equipment took," Simon's voice dropped off.

"Do you suspect someone could have raided them?"

"Mhinga," Simon began, "think about it this way. If this is part of a carrying case the scientists used, then why and how did it get all busted up into tiny pieces? Also, remember we have this Dubois chap running around out here with a poaching operation, and we don't have any idea how big it is. If it's anything like what I ran into last year, we could get into a mess of trouble. So, yes, I think it's possible MacKenzie's father and the others could have run into trouble."

"Let me have that big piece," Jon said to Simon. Turning it over, he looked at both sides. "I'll ask Mac if she recognizes it."

Perched on a flat rock near the river's edge, MacKenzie held the young chimp on her lap. In one hand, the chimp held tight to MacKenzie's braid, pulling her face close to his. The long, dark-skinned fingers on his free hand worked their way across her hairline, clothing, and skin. As he explored, he uttered soft grunts, pants, and hoots. MacKenzie mimicked his sounds and actions. As the little chimp fingered her hairline, she too ran her fingers through the coarse hair on his chest and arms. When the chimp tugged and pulled on her clothing, she did the same to the diaper she had placed on him. The chimp smiled, showing only the bottom row of teeth, MacKenzie mirrored the action.

The men watched from a distance, hardly believing what they saw, but not wanting to interfere with the woman and the chimp. "Well, I'll be damned!" Jon was the first to break the silence that had fallen over them.

"He does seem to trust her!" Simon added.

Even Jay was amazed at the sight. "I've never seen anything like it."

"I'd say her intuition is quite good," Mhinga said smiling.

Jon slapped Mhinga fondly on the shoulder, grumbling, "Did you have to bring that up again?"

"You know," Jay spoke from behind, "I almost hate to disturb them."

"Yeah, me too. But here comes Zawawi and look what he's carrying," Jon said, pointing upstream past MacKenzie. "Her peace is going to be shattered soon enough."

As the four men approached the woman and chimpanzee, Simon leaned over and asked, "Mhinga, what is going on between Mac and Zawawi?"

"They got off to a bad start." Mhinga nodded his head towards Zawawi. "He blames all white women for Moyo's death."

"Has he been tough on her?"

"Not so bad. Not since he learned that Khosa and Valli are involved with Dubois."

Approaching from the other direction, Zawawi carried his long spear in one hand and a large piece of yellow plastic tucked up under his arm. Reaching MacKenzie just before the other men, he tossed the broken section, startling the unsuspecting pair.

The sound of the plastic banging up against the rocks frightened the chimp into a frenzy of loud screams. MacKenzie instinctively held tightly to the hysterical chimp trying to calm him down. Brisk black hair rose high over wildly swinging arms and legs as the little chimp tried to free himself from the embrace and get away from the loud noise. Twisting and corkscrewing around in her arms, he broke free of her grip. Unable to gain his balance, he fell headfirst, several feet onto the sharp rocks. He lay motionless and quiet.

"Oh God. No!" MacKenzie cried as she fell to her knees and slowly rolled the chimp over. Jon and Mhinga rushed to her side. Tears instantly flooded her eyes as she slowly picked up the limp little chimp. Cradling him to her chest, she rocked back and forth. Jon placed his arms around her trembling shoulders, pulling her close, trying to soothe her.

Mhinga stood up, shook his head in dismay at Zawawi and turned

216

away. "Let's gather some firewood," he said to Jay. Looking back over his shoulder at the still body of the chimp clutched in MacKenzie's arms, he said, "We should get this over with quickly." Silently the two men walked away to gather driftwood.

Unabashed, Zawawi stood tall and square-shouldered, looking down at his friend comforting the white woman as she mourned an animal. Turning his back to them, in a restrained low voice he muttered, "Stupid white woman."

Simon heard the comment. Shaking his head he stared in disbelief at his brother's cruel hatred. Kneeling down, Simon took the motionless chimp out of MacKenzie's arms. Blood dribbled in a steady stream down his forehead. She melted into Jon's embrace as Simon carried the small, silent body to where Mhinga and Jay had built a fire.

Through her tears, she said over Jon's shoulder, "See what you caused, Zawawi?" Her words broke with sobs.

Ignoring her, Zawawi calmly pointed to the large piece of yellow plastic he had carried back, "When you are done with your suffering, tell me if you recognize this."

MacKenzie glanced at the big piece of yellow plastic. Painted across the flat surface was a stylized 'S' in the shape of a chemistry bottle, the logo of Sperry Pharmaceutical Company, and the company that employed her father. Her body convulsed with anguish. Pulling her in close, Jon wrapped his arms tightly around her. Out of the corner of his eye, he watched as Zawawi again turned his back to them.

Mhinga took the little limp body from Simon. He spoke a native prayer and, as the fire blazed high and hot, gray smoke danced around the three men. As Mhinga knelt alongside and started to place the body in the flames, the chimp's eyes flickered. Quickly Mhinga jumped back, taking the chimp into fresh air. Placing his cheek near the chimp's nose, he checked for exhalation, while Simon grabbed the tiny, dark-skinned wrist and searched for a pulse. Astonished, they cried out in unison, "He's alive!"

Chapter 30

Glittering sparks danced across the ripples where the clear stream narrowed before a bend. Lined with smooth stones, the riverbed gave the illusion of being only inches deep. Growing between the rocks, a band of knee-high, delicate weeds fused the edge of the gravel bar. Each frail, column hosted a tiny, single, blue flower as a crown, attracting a procession of buzzing insects.

Across the river, overhanging trees cast long shadows, draping the bank in a curtain of dark coolness. Sitting alone on the shady edge, Zawawi waited for the others to catch up. He had scouted the river crossing and found an entrance to a trail. New growth hid the path that had been widened with machetes just a few months earlier. His keen eyes looked past the dense greenery, spying dried leaves clinging to sharply cut limbs littering the trail. The height and width of the cut limbs and the sprouting new growth gave a clue to the size of the bundles the porters heaved upon their shoulders.

It had been over three hours since Simon and Mhinga cried out, "He's alive!" Their joyous announcement that the chimpanzee had survived its fall was still echoing in Zawawi's mind. Wrapping his arms around drawn-up knees, the Maasai bowed his head, shaking it slowly in anger and confusion. In frustration, he spoke out loud, "It's just an animal. Why are they all so upset? She treats it like her own child."

The mention of children brought up feelings of concern for his two sons. Valli had changed; a dark oppressed badness clouded his young spirit. Zawawi had seen it on his son's face when they met at the logging road. He wondered, has it always been there? Where did this hatred come from? What is it doing to Khosa?

Khosa, the gentle one, the younger son, followed Valli around like a shadow. He could still hope for Khosa. Khosa's eyes had not hardened, though his voice failed him, and Valli spoke in his place. Striking the ground with his fist, Zawawi snarled, "Damn you, Valli, for turning Khosa against me!"

Deep in his thoughts, Zawawi had not realized the others had caught up with him. Simon and Jay walked ahead of the others. As they neared the weedy bank, Zawawi waded into the swift water. "Over here," he shouted.

Waving an acknowledgment, the two men took their first steps into the river. As they crossed, Jay asked Simon, "How does he do it?"

"Do what?"

"How does he know what's what? Where to look? How does he look at a piece of land or," Jay waved an out-stretched hand around, "a river and tell where someone had crossed several months ago? How does he do it?"

Simon chuckled, "Yeah, I used to wonder about that myself. It must be something born in him, like a sixth sense. He has always been like that, even when we were kids. He's got sharp eyes and can tune into his environment. He also has an uncanny way with animals."

"I wouldn't have guessed that with his attitude toward the chimp."

"That took me by surprise, too. I think it has to do with MacKenzie. Zawawi may be amazing with nature, but he has always had problems dealing with people. His oldest son, Valli, is the same way."

"The poacher kid? He's Zawawi's son?"

Simon nodded his head, "It's not just one son. His oldest two are mixed up with this Dubois character. I think that is the only reason he has stayed with the group for this long. He is going to try to bring them home." As the two men reached the shady side of the stream, Simon added, "A word of advice, Jay. Don't bring the subject up." Jay nodded as they ducked below the hanging limbs where Zawawi waited for them.

The three men inspected the trail as Jon, Mhinga and MacKenzie, still carrying the chimp, reached the stream and crossed. Keeping his distance from the white woman, Zawawi moved ahead of the others. Jay set off with him. Together they would scout for clues to keep them on the trail the scientists had taken several months earlier. Simon stayed behind to guide the others to the trail's entrance.

Working on Simon's hunch that the scientists had run into trouble, they followed behind at some distance from the scouts. If Zawawi smelled danger, he and Jay could backtrack and warn the others. Simon, alone in the middle, stayed some distance between both groups, enabling him to reach either party quickly if help were needed. As well, their new travel line-up served a purpose other than safety: it kept Zawawi and MacKenzie far apart from each other.

Parting the branches to make MacKenzie's traveling easier, Jon and Buster led. Mhinga followed behind MacKenzie, closely watching the little chimp who faded in and out of consciousness. His head rocked and bobbed with the uneven gait of her stride. Long, wiry arms swung freely across her back, occasionally reaching out to grab her long braid or the back of her tee-shirt, as if it were his safety blanket. Moments later, he would slip back into a deep slumber and release his grip.

It was late in the afternoon when Jon's group caught up with the others. Simon, Zawawi, and Jay were huddled in a tight circle. With a stick, Zawawi was drawing an outline in the dust. "Wait here," Jon halted his group several yards away. Approaching the men, he asked, "What's going on?"

The look on Simon's face told him that it was important. "They have found the scientists' camp."

"How far?"

"About one mile."

Turning to Zawawi, Jon asked, "What did you find?"

"We saw only three white men; one of them is very old and sick looking. There are four armed black men. One of them walks the perimeter of the camp. The other three were just lounging around, but their rifles were at their sides."

"Guards, not porters?" Jon questioned.

"Could be. Kind of hard to tell." Zawawi pointed to the square drawn in the dirt. "The scientists were working at the tables under an open tent, here in the center of their camp. We watched them for an hour or so. It seemed quiet."

"What's your gut-feeling, Zawawi?"

"Hard to say," he answered, rocking back on his heels. "It was very quiet."

"Too quiet?"

Shrugging his shoulders, Zawawi said, "Yes, possibly."

As the four men talked in private, MacKenzie turned to Mhinga.

"What do you think they are talking about?"

"It could be almost anything, Ms. Mac."

Turning her back towards Mhinga, MacKenzie watched as the men drew lines in the dirt. "I wonder if they have found some more clues! Let's go see what they are talking about."

As she took her first step, Mhinga grabbed her shoulder, brushing up against the black hairy arm dangling over her shoulder. "Ms. Mac, wait. Jon will call to you." As he spoke, the chimp's eyelids flickered and sprang wide open.

The tight grip on her shoulder alarmed MacKenzie. "Really Mhinga, I don't think that it will be a big deal. I just want to know . . . ."

"He's awake!" Mhinga's low voice stopped her in midsentence.

"What's he doing?"

Mhinga whispered, "He's just staring at me."

Slowly MacKenzie started rubbing her fingers along the chimp's spine. In response the chimp grabbed her long braided lock. Slowly with the other hand he reached out, palm down, towards Mhinga.

Feeling the movement MacKenzie asked in a whisper, "What's he doing now?"

Mhinga whispered back, "He's reaching his hand out to me."

"Do whatever he does," she encouraged.

Slowly Mhinga lifted his hand, palm down, touching the chimp's hand. Mhinga held his hand still and relaxed while the chimp explored the similar dark skin. Grabbing hold of Mhinga's thumb, the chimp pulled the man forward. Holding the strange hand close to his face, he smelled and inspected each finger.

Very slowly MacKenzie pulled back, turning her face toward the little chimp. Feeling the movement, the chimp turned his attention to her. With curious eyes, he gazed closely, studying the pale skin of her face. Softly the chimp gave a gentle breathy, "*Huu.*" MacKenzie mimicked the chimp's sound.

Still clinging to Mhinga's thumb, the chimp pulled, bringing the young man even closer. Again, gazing hard into his strange face, he breathed out, "*Huu.*" Following MacKenzie's example, Mhinga imitated the sound.

"Figs!" she whispered ever so quietly. The sound of her voice snapped the chimp's attention back to her.

With his free hand, Mhinga reached deep into his pocket for three ripe figs. "*Huu,*" Mhinga softly huffed, attracting the chimp's attention. He held a fig close to the chimp's tiny face. Releasing the lock of hair, the chimp snatched the fig from Mhinga's outstretched hand. "Boy! He's hungry."

"What did he do?"

"He grabbed it out of my hand," Mhinga said, almost laughing.

"Give him another one!"

Before Mhinga had a chance to offer one of the two remaining figs, the chimp snatched them both from his palm. "That's the last of them."

"Quick, go find some more!" The chimp's head snapped back and forth following the strange sounds of their voices.

"I can't!" Mhinga chuckled out loud. "He's got my thumb."

"Well, can you reach anything? A plant? Chimps eat plants, you know."

"Yes, I know they eat plants." The chimp finished off the figs and yanked Mhinga's hand for more. Snapping off long green branches, Mhinga offered one to the chimp. Accepting the branch, the chimp picked off each green leaf with his lips, them held out his hand for another. MacKenzie closed her eyes and listened to the sounds of the young chimp eating his first real meal in days.

"Jon," Simon asked, "What are you going to tell her?"

"Very little. If this is going to work, the less she knows, the more convincing it will be. It's the only way to be sure."

The soft laughter of MacKenzie and Mhinga caught the men's attention. Seeing Mhinga feeding the chimp, Simon was amazed. "Will you look at that!"

"That is really something!" Jay added.

"Yeah, she sure is," Jon was smiling from ear to ear as he watched MacKenzie cradling the small chimp.

Hearing Jon and Jay switch from planning the invasion of the scientists' camp, to discussing the white woman and the chimp, infuriated Zawawi. Rocking from foot to foot, Zawawi exclaimed, "You have to tell her, Jon."

The smile faded from Jon's face. "Yeah, you're right. You guys go on ahead and get into position around the camp. We'll be about two hours behind you. That will give her an hour before dusk to see her father. And it should give us enough time to figure out what is going on."

As Simon, Zawawi, and Jay disappeared into the dense foliage, Jon turned to MacKenzie. Their eyes locked. The warmth of her voice and her bright smile beckoned him. He couldn't resist, and found himself immersed in her joy. He wanted to wrap his arms around her and hold her. He wanted to feel her soft skin and tender lips against his. He wanted her. "MacKenzie," his voice was velvety soft. The new sound attracted the chimp's attention, breaking the spell between them. The smile faded from Jon's face.

Feeling anxious, MacKenzie asked, "What's wrong, Jon?"

"Zawawi has found your father's campsite."

Silence flooded the air. Her eyes searched Jon's face, looking for more information, yet unsure she wanted to know. Her breathing deepened and slowed as her eyes lowered, pondering the possibilities. After several moments of silence, Mhinga took the chimp gently from her arms. Carefully Jon took a step toward her, asking, "Mac? Are you okay?"

Slowly she nodded her head. "Did they see him?" her voice quivered.

Reaching out, he placed both hands on her shoulders. Very softly, he said, "Yes, and he doesn't look good, very frail."

Looking up at Jon, she fought back the tears as she said, "Thank you for telling me that." She rocked her head back, working out the tension in her neck. Then she took a deep breath, and her voice was strong again. "How far?"

"A little over a mile." Jon searched her eyes wanting to help her with her pain.

"Well, then, we had better get going. My dad needs me."

"Mac, wait." Jon squeezed her shoulders. "We have to wait a while. At least two hours."

"Two hours! But why?" Pulling away from his gentle grip, she asked, "Where are the others?"

"They have gone on ahead to set up."

"Set up? What are you talking about?"

Taking her hands, he explained, "Simon is worried there could be trouble in the camp."

"Why? What did they see?"

"Not much. It was all very quiet, maybe too quiet. Zawawi had a bad feeling about it."

"A bad feeling?" MacKenzie jerked her hands from Jon's. "Zawawi had a bad feeling? Well if that doesn't . . . !" Taking a step back, her face flushed red. "You mean to tell me that . . . that good-for-nothing, selfish ass had a bad feeling, and you guys are all worried about it?"

Jon shook his head.

"*Amazing!* Simply amazing! Did you hear that, Mhinga?"

"Yes. Ms. Mac, please try to put your personal feelings aside. Zawawi has . . . has instincts. I can only explain it as the same as when you felt the chimp trusted you."

"I don't believe this! You two are siding with him!" She felt the tears coming and turned away. "So what are they doing now?"

Jon approached her. "They are going to hide near the edge of the camp, in case there is trouble."

"This is just nonsense, Jon! Think how crazy this all sounds. Here we are in the middle of a forest, an African forest. We are hundreds of miles from any type of civilization. And you think four hippy-like scientists," she held up fingers as she counted, "one botanist, one biologist, and two primatologists, are being held captive! That's just crazy! What on earth would anyone out here, if there *was* anyone out here, want with four wimpy lab guys?"

"I don't know Mac. But there has to be some reason they haven't been communicating with you." He placed his hands on her shoulders. "Zawawi counted only three white men, not four, and the porters were acting suspicious."

"Oh, really?" she sighed. "I doubt Zawawi can even count to four! One of them could have been out gathering plant specimens. And the communication equipment could be broken." Her lower lip was starting to tremble. "Did you think of that? No, of course not." Tears filled her eyes. "Nothing bad has happened to them!" her voice raged. "Except that my dad is very ill and he needs me. I must get him home to a doctor. Nothing is wrong, it just can't be."

Jon pulled MacKenzie into his embrace, "Shh, now, quiet down. I will take care of it, I promise you. We don't know that anything is wrong. We hope it isn't, but we have to be sure. We're just being careful, that's all. Remember that the poacher fellow is out here, too." He stroked her hair, murmuring, "Do you trust me?"

She nodded her head.

"Good. Now listen to me," still cradling the sobbing woman in his arms, "you need to pull yourself together." Glancing at his watch, he said, "In an hour or so, we are going to head out. You, Mhinga, the chimp, and I are going to march right into that camp like we don't suspect a thing. Got it?"

MacKenzie choked back the tears, "No. I don't understand. If you think there is trouble . . . ."

Jon interrupted, "Just trust me, Mac. I thought you trusted me."

With a slow nod, MacKenzie replied, "I do trust you."

Jon wiped away her tears. Looking down at her upturned face, her bright-hazel green eyes were dim, and they were puffy and surrounded with red streaks from crying. Trying to distract her, he smiled. "Don't you think you should help Mhinga feed your chimp? I'm sure your father will be interested in hearing all about him."

"Yes, I should look after him," she agreed.

Jon pulled her in close for a reassuring hug. She lingered in his arms, folding into his embrace, not wanting to leave the comfort and security. He held her tightly until he felt the muscles in her shoulders and back relax a little.

As she started to pull away, Jon stopped her from leaving. Passionately he pulled her slender frame up against his. She tilted her face, her eyes closed naturally, and their lips softly met.

Mhinga politely turned his back to them and carefully carried the eager chimp into the dense underbrush to feed. As he left the trail, he glanced back over his shoulder smiling, stealing a glimpse at two people lost in each other.

Gently and slowly their kiss deepened. As her body slackened, no longer needing to be strong, she folded into his arms. Slowly he carefully lowered her to the earthy floor, never breaking the connection of their bond. All sounds of the forest disappeared. Their awareness narrowed and all else vanished. It was just the two of them, floating together in the abyss of their embrace, in the warmth of their kiss, lost for a time from the physical world.

Chapter 31

At the first glimpse of the green tents, MacKenzie lost control of her emotions and broke out of line. Running hard and fast, passing Jon, she bolted recklessly into the scientists' camp. With outstretched arms, she ran across the small clearing. Buster dashed out of line, too, and ran protectively by her side. Rushing toward an old white-bearded man seated at a metal folding table, she called out as she ran, "Dad! Oh, Daddy!" The bold unexpectedness of the girl's presence snapped everyone to attention. Her cries caught the unsuspecting guards by surprise. Grabbing their rifles, they quickly came to a firing stance as she ran past them still calling, "Daddy!"

The old man, half asleep, slowly lifted his head hearing a familiar voice. Running towards him was his only child. "MacKenzie? Is that really you?" he muttered softly.

The hollow, sunken eyes looking back at MacKenzie stopped her dead in her tracks. From a few feet away, she stared at the old man sitting limp and still on a canvas folding chair. "Daddy?" she whispered. Buster moved on ahead and greeted the old man.

Carefully and slowly, Dr. Blankenship rose. The scraggly, unkempt silver beard could not hide the old man's pain. The arms, once strong and athletic, reached out to her, looking like empty sleeves of material draped across old broomsticks on a farmer's scarecrow. His eyes softened and filled with tears. His voice trembled, "MacKenzie."

The sound of his voice saying her name propelled her into his embrace. Wrapping her arms around his skeleton frame felt more like grasping thin air than the once-active man she remembered her father to be. Without words, they held onto each other crying tears of joy and sorrow.

Following close behind her, a white man and a shorter young black man carrying a chimpanzee entered the camp. Cautiously, one of the guards approached the white man. Ignoring the frantic young woman, he asked, "Who are you?"

Showing no sign of concern, Jon carried his rifle low and relaxed. He avoided a direct answer. "I was hired to help this young lady find her father."

"Well, now that you have found him, you can take her back," the guard snapped. The rake of scars across his cheeks and his deep French accent carried the bold authority of an unexpected thunderstorm, and betrayed both his Congolese heritage and military training.

Jon knew instantly that these men were more than just hired porters. Yielding to the guard's authority, Jon avoided a confrontation, asking, "The old man will be dead soon. What do you say about letting him have one hour with his daughter? Then we'll go."

The guard glanced past Jon at the frail old man with tears running down his ghostly face. Then he turned his attention to the semi-conscious chimpanzee in Mhinga's arms. "Where did that come from?"

Jon answered for Mhinga, "Four or five days north of here," he lied.

"He's not very big, skin and bones," Mhinga added. "It hardly weighs anything at all. So light, she has been carrying it."

Glancing over at the thin white woman, the guard agreed, "It's not worth anything."

"No, it's not." Mhinga went along, flattering the guard, "You've got a good eye for value."

The guard snickered at the compliment. "All right, one hour." Then returning his attention to Jon, he said, "Then you go, back to the south like you came."

"We came from the north." Jon realized the guard tested him.

"To the north, then."

Dr. Blankenship pulled away from his daughter, saying, "You're a sight for sore eyes."

Choking back the tears, she said, "So are you." She looked at his tattered, dirty clothes and felt his scruffy beard.

"MacKenzie, I must sit down," Dr. Blankenship pulled away from his daughter's embrace. "I can hardly believe it's you!" His voice began to shake. "How on earth did you find us?"

MacKenzie steadied her father back to the canvas chair, then she glanced back over her shoulder at Jon. Mixed emotions contorted her tear-streaked face as she tried to bring herself under control. "Well, I don't really know where to begin. It's such a long story." Buster butted his head under the frail hand, forcing the old man to pet him. The dog's friendly action lifted a smile above the scruffy white beard.

Looking lovingly into her eyes, he could see it pained her that he was so ill. He broke a smile, "Well why don't you just start by introducing me to your friends over there."

"Oh yes! Daddy, this is Jon." She reached for his hand. Drawing him near, she continued, "Jon Corbett. It was his expert tracking that brought us here." Jon squeezed MacKenzie's hand and rolled his eyes, motioning towards the guards, reminding her to be careful what she said.

Dr. Blankenship noticed a change in her voice when she introduced Jon, and the subtle exchange between them. "My daughter obviously thinks a great deal of you. I am grateful you brought her here safely."

As the men shook hands, Jon downplayed his role. "It was more luck than skill. Your daughter flatters me. We had the coordinates of your first campsite, and we just happened to cut a trail with human footprints. We followed them here."

"Well, none the less, it does this old man good to see his daughter again. I didn't think . . . ." His voice trailed off.

Not wanting to hear the words, MacKenzie jumped in. She motioned for Mhinga to come forward. "And, Daddy, this is Mhinga." She took the chimp out of his arms, explaining, "Mhinga is very knowledgeable about the native plants and medicines. I'm sure you two will have lots to talk about."

"Yes, I'm sure we could learn many things from the local people."

As the old man shook Mhinga's hand, his eyes never left the semi-awake chimpanzee in the girl's arm. "But there must be a good story about him!"

"Yes sir," Mhinga responded, "Ms. Mac has a very long story about him."

"I'd like to hear all of it." Turning around, the professor motioned to Henry. "Bring our guests something to sit on."

Buster laid his head on the bony lap of Dr. Blankenship, begging for more attention. MacKenzie added, "And Buster here is your new best friend!"

As Henry and Don carried a large yellow plastic container around, MacKenzie's mouth dropped open, and she pointed at it. "That's how we found you. We found pieces of a broken crate along a stream. Then we cut across a trail and followed it here." The men crossed over and shook hands, introducing themselves.

"The case you found contained our radio and satellite equipment," Dr. Blankenship explained. Slowly shaking his head, he said, "It was a terrible misfortune. It was all destroyed falling down that rocky hillside. It broke into little pieces. So we were cut off from the outside world, but we decided to continue anyway and work on the study." Jon noted the hate-filled glance the old man threw at the guards.

As Henry put the case down, MacKenzie ran to his arms, "Are you guys all right?" She whispered in his ear.

"Yes," he whispered back. Pulling back, she saw a different answer in his eyes.

Hugging the other man, she said, "Oh Don. It's so good to see you!" Looking round the camp she asked, "Where's Mitchell?"

"MacKenzie, come here and sit down." Her father motioned to a stump next to his chair.

"Daddy, where's Mitchell?" She searched his eyes and found deep sadness. She turned to Don and Henry, but they dropped their eyes and looked over their shoulders. Taking a step backwards, they opened a view of a long narrow mound of high dirt below a crudely made cross. MacKenzie's eyes widened, and she exclaimed, "Oh God no! Mitchell's dead? But how? How could that have happened?"

Don and Henry were at a loss for words. Jon noticed them looking around uneasily at the camp and the guards. Handing the chimp back to Mhinga, MacKenzie turned back to her father. Taking his frail bony hands in hers, she knelt in front of him. "How daddy? How did Mitchell die?" Dr. Blankenship looked down at his daughter's soft hands and dirt-encrusted fingernails. His eyes followed her youthful strong arms to her beautiful face that he had thought he would never see again. "How?" her voice whispered softly, but her eyes were demanding. Choking up, unable to speak, he looked over her head to the camp guard for the answer.

The guard's voice bellowed unexpectedly, startling her, "Big snake. Your friend wandered away from camp, and a big snake got him."

MacKenzie turned back to her father. "But Daddy, how? You have anti-venom."

His hand reached up and wiped away the tears. "We were too late. We were just too late." His sad voice trailed off.

MacKenzie rose from her father's side and looked hard at the guard who had answered. The scarred lines that ran across his face gave him a sinister look, and it made the hairs on the back of her neck stand. She crossed over to the grave and stared at the sight, still unbelieving. "His wife and children, they have no idea that he's . . . gone. I can hardly believe it myself. Oh, his poor family."

Dr. Blankenship watched uneasily as the guards paced around them. Buster began to growl, and Jon bumped the dog with his foot to quiet him. Looking Jon squarely in the eyes, he said, "She should not have come. You must take her away. Take her back and put her on the next flight home. It is dangerous here." The scar-faced guard stopped nearby, listening. Buster growled low, and the old man squeezed the hair on the back of his neck, silencing the dog. "It is dangerous here in the wilds of Africa. This is no place for her." He laid his finger alongside his nose.

Jon mimicked the motion, nodding his head, "I understand."

"Don, why don't you prepare the unidentified pressed-plant speci-mens for MacKenzie to take with her. Henry, write a letter for me explain-ing how Mitchell died from the big snake." There was a trace of sarcasm in the old voice, and he glanced at the guard who reluctantly nodded his approval. "Copy all of our electronic notes on a disk for her to take, too."

Again the frail old man with the gleaming, wise eyes laid his finger alongside his nose and looked for Jon to recognize his signal.

Again Jon mimicked the subtle sign before he crossed over to MacKenzie. Wrapping his arms around her, he held her to his chest as she grieved the loss of her friend. "Mac," he whispered in her ear, "Go to your father before we have to leave." She pulled back and looked up at him.

"I'm not sure I can leave him."

Wiping the tear from her cheek, he said, "It's going to be all right." He forced a little smile. "You've got to be strong for me," he said, glancing over his shoulder, "and for him."

A nod was all she could manage. Following Jon's gaze she went to her father's side. Holding his frail hand, she told him of how she had found the chimpanzee. She carefully told the story of the buffalo she had shot, leaving out all mention of Zawawi, the helicopter gunmen, being lost in the cave, the elephants that were poached, and Simon and his men raiding the poacher's camp. As she talked, her tears dried up, and she felt tired and weak. She could see that her dad was tiring. He looked so different, so old and frail. His illness was winning. When she finished her story, they sat in silence, gazing at one another, imprinting tiny details into their memories, until it became too painful and together they looked away. Unable to find the words, unable to express what their hearts felt, they just sat silently holding hands, touching souls with deep unspoken expressions of love.

The choir of birds had faded with the coming of darkness in the mountain forest. All that broke the silence was the annoying, tiny high-pitched drone of mosquitoes. Dampness rose as the temperature fell, and the bright warmth of the small fire did not lighten the dim mood.

Trying to move about on his own, the young chimpanzee could only take a few steps without falling. Feeding quietly on the plants that bordered the tiny clearing, he stayed at the far edge of the burning hot light, keeping his distance from the strangeness of the fire. Mhinga allowed the chimp to move about freely, but kept a close eye on him.

Impatiently, the group awaited the return of Simon, Zawawi, and Jay. The three had scouted ahead of them and hidden in the dense foliage that surrounded the scientists' camp, ready to spring into action if the scientists' guards tried to harm the unexpected guests. The three scouts then stayed behind after Jon, MacKenzie, Mhinga, and the chimp left the campsite. Watching the guards' reactions, they tried to gauge the situation. Now, several hours later, the forest slipped into still blackness.

"Mac," Jon's voice slipped across the flickering fire light. The woman's face was heavy with worry. Slowly she lifted her swollen eyes. "Mac, why don't you open your computer and have a look at the disk your father prepared for you." Jon chose his words carefully. He was not certain they had not been followed by any of the scar-faced guards.

"No, it's just plant data and a letter to Mitchell's family. I don't want to read that. I can hardly believe he's gone."

Jon crossed over to her. Wrapping his arm around her shoulder, he pulled her in with a hug. "Come on, Mac." He tried to sound cheerful. "Show me how the computer works." He kissed her on the forehead and she gave in. While she set up the laptop, Jon glanced at his watch. It was nearly nine o'clock. The others should have been back by now, unless they had run into trouble. He was beginning to worry. Jon wanted to know what was on the disk, recalling how Dr. Blankenship had laid his finger alongside his nose each time he mentioned it. There must be something important on the disk the scientists wanted him to know.

Finally the colorful screen lit up and MacKenzie moved the cursor, typing on the keyboard to open the first file. Explaining as she worked, she read down the list of file names. MacKenzie disappointedly shook her head, "Look, just names of plants, mostly digital pictures of them and field notes. There's nothing interesting here."

"You can put pictures in that thing?"

MacKenzie giggled, "Jon, you've got to get into civilization more often. Here, I'll show you." Clicking the icon, MacKenzie opened a picture of a large, succulent green, leaf lying on a white sheet of paper surrounded by hand written notes. Mhinga peered around trying to see the computer screen and still keep close contact with the chimp. She turned the laptop around for him to see the picture. "Do you know this plant,

Mhinga?"

"Yes, it is what we call *Mlama.* I believe it is used to help with an upset stomach."

"What else is there?" Jon asked.

Closing the file, she went back to the list. "Just more of the same. More pictures of plants, and descriptions. Not very interesting for you."

Jon read down the list of names. "What is this one?" He pointed to a file at the bottom of the screen. "Your dad mentioned it to me."

"Hmm, a *helpersevildoerours,* I don't know. Sounds like something he made up . . ." her voice trailed off in a quiver. *"Helpersevildoerours?"* Though Jon winked at her, his voice was somber. "We'd better open it and see what is in there."

The computer screen changed, showing a large jagged-edged leaf surrounded by notes. Dr. Blankenship's shaky lettering was quickly recognized by MacKenzie, "See, it's just more of the same mumbo jumbo as the other plants."

Jon squinted to read the text on the small screen. "I can't read it. The lettering is so small."

"Wait, I can zoom in on it." With a move of the cursor and a click on the keypad the text area filled the screen. Together they read the few lines of text:

> *'Eight guards, four in camp,*
> *changing every four or five days,*
> *again very soon. Mitchell no accident.*
> *MacKenzie, I love you. Dad.'*

MacKenzie's shoulders drooped as she reread the words. Jon wrapped his arms around her shoulders and pulled her in close. With flooded eyes she tilted her face towards Jon's. "How did you know there would be a message?" she whispered to him.

"Your father kept mentioning the disk and the plants. Each time he signaled to me by placing his finger alongside of his nose. It was only a hunch that he would try and communicate this way. He must have put this together while you were at the grave."

"Well," her voice was hoarse, "Zawawi was right." Pulling away from Jon's embrace, she closed down her computer. "What do we do now?"

"We must wait for the others," he whispered back. "They should have been back by now. We may have been followed by those scar-faced guys."

MacKenzie nodded her head and gazed into the fire.

"Are you okay?" he asked.

"Yeah, I'm just . . ." she choked back the tears.

Jon hugged her and kissed her forehead. "I need to tell Mhinga, but I'll be right back."

"I could use a little time alone to think," she said. Nodding his head, Jon rose slowly, trying not to spook the chimp. He made his way over and talked quietly to Mhinga for a few minutes. Pouring a cup of tea, he sat down across the fire from MacKenzie. Beside him, Buster's snores rumbled in harmony with his deep breathing.

Bending over clumps of greenery, the chimp attempted to build a nest. MacKenzie watched him with little enthusiasm. Her mind was heavy with thoughts of her frail father and the danger he and the other scientists faced.

Her eyes left the chimp and gazed instead across the bright flickering colors of the flames. Jon sat quietly holding his tea, his eyes closed. He looked so peaceful and handsome in the dancing light that fluttered across his face. Instantly, her thoughts of her father and her longing for the comfort of Jon's arms became a confusing mix.

As if her thoughts reached across and gently caressed Jon's mind, his eyes opened to her. Heavy dark lines draped below his cobalt blue eyes that matched so perfectly the wild African sky. Feeling the woman's pain, Jon moved to her side. Without a word, he lay near the crackling fire. His strong muscular hand guided her weary frame down to his side, spooning her back against his chest. She pillowed her head on his arm. He protectively wrapped his other arm around her shoulder, needing no words. He kissed her softly on the back of her head as she closed her eyes and fell into a deep sleep, wrapped in the comfort of his warm embrace.

❖ ❖ ❖

Well past midnight the scouting party entered the camp. Jon quietly rose from MacKenzie's side, meeting the others on the opposite side of the campfire. Mhinga awoke, too, and started a fresh pot of tea while the men discussed their findings. "One of the guards followed you back here," Simon began. "I followed and kept an eye on him until he left an hour or so after you settled in. I thought he might bring the other guards, so I waited until Zawawi and Jay came back."

"Zawawi, you were right," Jon began. "The scientists have trouble. Dr. Blankenship gave Mac a couple of computer disks. One of them had a message. Mitchell's death was no accident. There are eight guards that rotate every four, or five days and will do so again soon."

"After you left, the guards questioned the scientists and spoke among themselves." Zawawi sipped his tea as he spoke. "They were edgy and very irritable."

"So we really took them by surprise," Jon added.

"Yes. After they talked, one of them took off in the same direction as you. Simon followed him back here." Zawawi continued, "The scientists seemed uncomfortable, too. The old one went to his tent and stayed in. The others looked in on him at times, but one of the guards stayed close."

Jon shook his head humbly. "Sounds like we might have wound them up pretty tight with our unexpected visit."

"They appeared that way, yes," Zawawi replied.

"Were you still there when the guard returned from following us?" Jon asked.

"Yes, but they spoke in French." Zawawi nodded to Jay. "He understood some of what they were saying."

"I'm afraid not very much," Jay replied. "Just a few words here and there. They were very surprised by your visit. They were worried about Dubois finding out or how to let him know. I wasn't clear on that part."

Hearing the name Dubois snapped Jon and Simon's attention. "How is that poacher mixed up in this?" Simon asked.

The group fell silent; they had no answer for the question. Jon broke in, "Jay, was there anything else?"

Jay continued, "I think they believed your story because you had the woman, the chimp, and a dog with you. Also, I couldn't hear them clearly, but I heard the word *'mort,'* which I think means death and *'en masse'* meaning all together. I don't know if that means they are planning on killing all of the scientists or all of us." Jay's voice trailed off.

"When we left," Zawawi added, "they were setting themselves up, loading and checking their weapons, expecting some kind of trouble tonight. Two of them bedded down, and the other two were walking the perimeter."

"Bad night for an attack," Simon added quietly. "Especially when you're outgunned. Better to wait 'til they aren't expecting trouble."

"Yes, but remember what Jay heard about killing the group," Zawawi interrupted. "We can't wait too long."

"What's your gut feeling?" Simon asked his brother.

"I think that if tonight is tranquil, they will send a scout back here in the morning to check on you." Zawawi nodded toward Jon.

"If they see us leaving casually, without any signs of suspicion," Jon followed the line of thought, "they might ease up on their defense."

"Opening a window for us to get at the scientists a bit easier," Simon thought out loud.

Mhinga had been listening in. "So, what's the plan?"

Jon looked to Simon to begin. "Well, you and Jon get to sleep tonight, and in the morning you slowly head north. Jay, Zawawi, and I will cut back to the other campsite and hide out, keeping an eye on them. If it looks like they are going to kill the scientists, we can jump in and try to stop them."

"Or if it looks like they are coming after you, Jon," Zawawi added, "we can intercept them along the trail."

"Good." Jon joined the brainstorming, "We will travel slow, so I won't have far to backtrack in the evening to meet with you."

"Jon, if one of the guards leaves their camp in the morning," Zawawi remarked, "I will trail him while he is following you. Simon and Jay will watch over the others. When I am sure the guard is not a threat and is going to return to his camp, I will stay behind and make contact with you. We can return together and prepare for the rescue tomorrow night."

Jon nodded his head, "Yes. Mhinga, tomorrow when I take off with Zawawi, you and Mac continue on alone. Cut back to the east. Stay off the game trails. When you find the river, follow it downstream to where we crossed. Wait for us there on the opposite side. Find a place to hide, but where you can see the river-crossing. Wait for us there."

"Mhinga, when you get there," Simon began, handing his brother-in-law his two-way radio, "set the dial to this." He pointed to a number on the frequency dial, and continued, "Click the push-button twice. That will signal us that you are safe. If we don't respond within an hour, get the hell out of there. Head back to the bluff overlooking the field where the poachers took the two elephants. My men should be on their way back there now. You can communicate with them on this frequency," Simon pointed to another spot on the numbered dial.

"Got it," Mhinga said, and then he began packing small bundles of meat for the men to take with them. Over a second cup of tea, they went back over their plan, working out the details and back-up plans.

With guns loaded, the men gathered their equipment and took one last drink of the strong tea. The three then quickly disappeared into the darkness of the forest. Mhinga tossed another limb on the fire and rolled up in his blanket near the chimpanzee. Soon his breathing was deep and slow, and he fell into a deep sleep.

Jon crossed over to MacKenzie. Lying down, he spooned up against her back. As he wrapped his arm around her, she spoke quietly, "So you guys are really going to do this." It was more of a statement. Her voice was raspy from the damp night air.

"Did I wake you?" he whispered.

"No, I heard it all. The whole plan."

"We didn't know you were awake."

"They are taking such a big risk. All of them, even Zawawi." Rolling over she pressed her face against his chest. "None of this seems real. It's like a movie or a television show, where the authorities get called in to do the rescue, not your friends."

Jon pulled her close and kissed her sweetly on the forehead,

"Simon is the authority," he said.

"Yes, but Zawawi. He had no real reason to put his life on the line. We don't even know why my father is being held captive."

"Oh, Mac," Jon sighed. "No, we don't know why, but we do know that Dubois is tied up in this, so Zawawi has the best reason of all to help. He is here because he doesn't have a choice. His boys could be in danger, too."

"I just don't understand him at all."

"A lot of times I don't either." Jon chuckled. "But he is a good person, and I respect him."

"What about you? You're not the authority, and you don't have any emotional ties. Why are you risking your life?"

"You think I don't have any emotional ties?" he asked gently. "Well then, my sweetheart, it is because I never break my promises."

Pulling back from him, MacKenzie stared at him. "Make me one more promise. Promise me you will come back to me."

"Oh, MacKenzie." He kissed her lightly on the lips. "I promise you that I will do everything I can to make that happen." He kissed her fully, not allowing her to speak.

Gripping him across his shoulders, she rolled over onto her back, guiding his body on top of hers. Feverishly, their kiss deepened. His husky beard whisked across her cheeks, tingling her sensations. Her fingers floated along the solid ridge of muscles mounding over his shoulders. Locks of black hair fluffed out from the rim of Jon's cap, tickling the backs of her hands. Knocking the cap off, she gripped a handful of long soft curls combing them with her fingers.

Moans rose from within her as his kiss moved down to the nape of her neck. Lifting up and breathing hard, he waited for her eyes to open. Slowly her lids raised, and her bright hazel eyes sparkled flecks of gold at him. As he started to speak, MacKenzie placed her hand over his mouth lightly and smiled. Her fingers moved through his beard, following his cheeks up the fullness of his sideburns to the top of his head. She pulled Jon's face closer to her, their lips parted, and once again they found the momentum of their kiss.

Gently, Jon gripped MacKenzie's breast, rubbing the nipple with his thumb until he felt it harden and raise through her clothing. Her soft moans of pleasure encouraged him. Tracing the edge of her ribs, Jon searched for the tail of her shirt, and pulled it from its neatly tucked position. He reached under the material to feel the satin texture of her skin. The smooth curvy softness of her body sent rolling waves of desire drifting through him. The smell of her, natural and wild, washed his mind free of any other thoughts.

Her fingers raked down his spine and tugged at his clothing. Their breathing quickened, as they explored each other's bodies. Under the blanket of darkness, they expressed their yearning for each other.

Chapter 32

A cold dreary mist filtered down the hillside and settled over the campsite. The gloomy grayness prevented the sun's light from awakening the forest. The birds had not begun their morning choir, and the usual buzzing of insects was strangely absent. The heavy dampness blanketed the lovers, encouraging them to stay warmly wrapped in each other's embrace.

Sleeping peacefully, MacKenzie lay on her side using Jon's shoulder as a pillow. Though they had been asleep for only a couple of hours, their internal clocks were quietly nudging them. With limbs entangled, the lovers slowly became aware of their surroundings. Each listened to the subtle rise and fall of the other's breathing, not daring to move. Awakening the other would spoil the quiet solitude of their private sanctuary.

Lying on his back, Jon unconsciously twitched away an annoying tickling on his forehead. A few seconds later, his ear became the attention of another soft tickle. Again, a small twitch of his head sent it away. Once more the tickling swept across his forehead, just above his brow. Coming out of his relaxed state, Jon raised his free hand and waved it quickly over his face. Soon after, he felt MacKenzie twitching and shooing.

Other sounds began to draw them awake. Their ears tuned into the sounds of Buster scratching, and Mhinga's deep, slow breathing. The feel of their naked bodies linked together under the scratchy wool blanket opened their eyes. Gazing with warm smiles, they kissed.

When their lips parted, the sense of being watched fell over them. As they tilted their heads up, a small tan leathery face framed with short black wiry hair lurched forward hovering closely over them. A grimace of yellowed spiked teeth soon appeared as the chimpanzee drew back his lower lip and opened his mouth wide. With large dark eyes, he held his playful look for several long seconds, dashing his eyes back and forth between the man and the woman.

MacKenzie mimicked his expression. Dropping her lower lip, and covering her top teeth, she grimaced back at the chimp and prodded Jon to do the same.

The chimp lowered his face a few inches closer and moved his head back and forth to see clearly that both people were grinning back at him. In a flash, his happy grin changed, and the chimp began stomping his feet and shaking the handful of short leafy branches he clutched. Whirling away, dropping the limbs, the chimp dived into the bushes, stirring up as much noise as he possibly could. His rampage of noisemaking filled the campsite, spurring Mhinga and Buster from their sleep.

Buster immediately joined in the ruckus. Barking, he chased the little chimp, who was swinging from low branches, around the perimeter. When the riotous pair circled back to Jon and MacKenzie, the chimp dropped to the ground and dashed towards them. As he passed by their feet, the little primate grabbed at the blanket, pulling it off the lovers. With Buster hot on his tail, the chimp released the blanket before scaling the nearest tree. Jon sprang up to retrieve the blanket.

The sight of the two naked bodies took Mhinga by surprise. Quickly recovering his composure, he called across the campsite as he rolled over facing away from the others, "Jon, get a hold of that dog of yours! And, Ms. Mac, please control your chimp. I'm trying to sleep!"

From the limbs above, the chimp laughed in a gasping, snickering, high-pitched way, *"Hee huu, hee huu, hee huu!"* Buster bounced around on the ground, jumping up at the low limb that was out of his reach. Jon tossed the blanket to MacKenzie who quickly covered herself and looked over her shoulder to see if Mhinga was watching. He was not. Jon grabbed Buster by the loose hair on the back of his neck and pulled the dog away from the tree. Settling the dog down, Jon began to dress. "I guess that is our wake-up service," he said, laughing.

MacKenzie reached out from her blanket and stroked Buster's back. He was beginning to whine as his eyes continued to follow the chimp moving about in the tree. "Gosh, I hope it isn't like this every morning." Dark circles draped under her green eyes, and her hair was loose, wildly tossed and mixed with leaves and debris.

Kneeling beside her, Jon gathered her clothing. "Mac, I think your chimp-raising days may be over." A small pout graced her face. He began picking out the small dried crumbs of leaves from her hair, as he continued, "You knew this would come someday."

As they spoke the little chimp moved down from the tree. Giving Buster a wide berth, the primate picked his way closer to the couple. Sitting a few feet away, he watched as Jon removed bits and pieces from MacKenzie's long, thick hair.

"What's he doing?" she whispered to Jon.

"Right now, he's just sitting watching us."

With slow movements, MacKenzie quietly dressed. When she finished, the chimp moved a bit closer. Reaching out, the chimp held his hand out to them and smacked his lips together.

MacKenzie looked back over her shoulder to see the chimp stick one arm up in the air and wrap it over the top of his head. With his other hand he began enthusiastically scratching his raised armpit while clacking his teeth together.

"What do you think that means?" She asked.

"I have no idea. Why don't you do the same and see how he reacts?" Jon leaned back to give her some space.

"What did he do first?"

MacKenzie followed Jon's instructions. Smacking her lips she reached out, palm down, towards the chimp. The little chimp lowered his arms and on all four limbs slowly strolled forward. He sat down very close and reached up, removing a crumble-dried leaf from MacKenzie's hair.

"Well, if that doesn't beat all!" Jon kept his voice low, but his amazement was unchecked. "He wanted to groom you!"

"I guess it would be rude of me not to groom him back," MacKenzie said as she slowly turned side ways and began picking at his hair. The chimp scooted around, turning his back to MacKenzie, and looked over his shoulder at her. Lost as to what to do, her hands fell silent. Encouragingly, the chimp reached behind his back and scratched. Immediately she understood and started parting his hair and looking for tiny objects to remove.

As Jon rose from her side, he kissed her sweetly on the forehead. He whispered in her ear, "Looks like you have a new friend."

Under cover of the morning's heavy dampness, Jon left the camp to hunt for fresh meat. Mhinga went about his work tending to the camp's other needs while MacKenzie and the chimp spent hours grooming each other and learning how to read body language. Buster, left behind by Jon, wandered around the camp looking for some attention.

Mhinga would shoo the dog away, and he would stroll over to MacKenzie. After stroking the dog's back a time or two, she would return to grooming the chimp. Buster persisted by shoving his nose into her face. Unaccustomed to having wet, cold noses rubbing her face, she pushed the dog away. Buster returned several times, only to be pushed away again and again.

After a short time, MacKenzie and the chimp traded positions and the chimp now groomed through her hair. Buster approached the chimp cautiously and nosed the chimp's face. As casually and gently as MacKenzie had done, the chimp pushed the annoying dog away.

Buster stood back and whimpered a sad, lonesome sound. The whining stopped the chimpanzee from his work, and MacKenzie looked over her shoulder at the chimp. After a brief moment of looking into each other's eyes, they simultaneously turned towards Buster.

Patting the ground beside her leg, MacKenzie invited Buster over. The dog raised his eyes in question, one after the other, while looking back and forth between the girl and the chimp. As she patted the ground again, his tail lowered and wagged happily. Submissively, he lowered his head and approached. MacKenzie pushed his rear end down and rolled him over on his back. Trying not to arouse Buster too much, she gently started to scratch the dog's belly. The chimp followed MacKenzie's example and began rubbing the dog's soft belly. Buster reacted with ecstasy. His hind leg began to pedal in the air, and his foot lopped up and down uncontrollably.

Squirming about, his head rested against MacKenzie's knee. Joyfully, he licked her skin to return the good feeling. Then stretching his nose higher, Buster smelt the bare foot of the chimpanzee. At first the chimp pulled away but eventually allowed the dog's cold wet nose to sniff about and lick his skin as he had done to his pale-skinned grooming partner.

Late in the morning as the mist dried away, Jon returned to camp carrying the meaty hindquarter of a bushbuck. Dropping the meat, he asked Mhinga, "How long has that been going on?" He pointed over to the grooming party.

"Since you left. Buster joined them almost an hour ago," Mhinga replied. Then changing the subject, he said, "I didn't hear your rifle being fired."

"No, I found this bush buck, hanging in a snare. It had been there for a few days. I was surprised to see it was still alive. The wire was tangled all around his belly, up between its front legs and looped round his neck a few times. It was a real mess."

Mhinga hung his head. "Do you think the snare was set by the guards from the scientists' camp?"

"I don't know who else it could be, unless that Dubois chap has set up an operation around here. This was a big trap, set for a bigger animal. There was enough high-gauge wire to tangle an elephant."

Mhinga studied Jon's worried face for a few seconds as he watched the girl and the animals. "Are you thinking that somehow the scientists got tangled up with the poachers?"

Jon turned back to his young friend. The small nod of his head was barely seen. "See what you can do with this. The meat will be pretty tough, but we'll need it for tonight and tomorrow. We need to get moving soon and get her out of the area. Give you a head start to keep her safe."

By noon, the damp coolness of the morning was turning into sweltering humidity. The grooming party had long since stopped, and Mhinga had made all the necessary arrangements to move on. Gathering their gear, Jon led the group into the forest, following a narrow game trail to the north.

Hesitantly, the chimp followed. Occasionally the group waited for him to catch up. He was not allowed to climb onto MacKenzie's back, as she now had to carry her own pack as well as some of the others.

The extra weight that they all carried and the chimpanzee traveling on his own slowed them down considerably. Breaking every hour or so for a ten-minute rest also slowed their pace, making it easier for Jon to backtrack later and meet Zawawi. Leisurely, they traveled up and down the steep rock hillsides. As they walked, Jon pondered different ways to free the scientists. He did not worry whether or not they were being followed. Jon knew Zawawi would guard his back.

The afternoon fell away more quickly than the number of miles that passed below their feet. At the top of a ridge, the group stopped in a pleasant little shady area where the native grasses grew sparingly in the shadowy light under a large mugumo tree. Dropping their heavy packs, they rested for a short while before setting up camp for the evening. Here they would wait for Zawawi.

The scar-faced man was good at his job. Leaving the camp long before dawn, he had slowly and carefully made his way through the forest in the darkness with the quiet delicacy of a leopard. A hundred yards away he began crawling on his hands and knees. When the scent of the fire drifted to him, the man dropped to his belly and snaked along the forest floor. Careful not to make a sound, he moved slowly, searching the ground in front of him for any sticks or piles of dried leaves. He avoided anything that could make a noise and give his position away. He was well trained and experienced, but he was unaware of the man following him. This second man was very good.

How well the scar-face man tracked and prowled impressed Zawawi. It was obvious he had a good military background. But he lacked the one vital element that would have made him excellent, his lack of hunting instinct that allowed the Maasai to follow like a shadow, unde-tected.

The tracker took an hour to move the last twenty feet. Each move was carefully calculated until he had found a thick clump of fallen limbs and underbrush. There the man was well hidden and would have a fair view of the campsite. Preparing his rifle, he waited for nature to raise the curtain of fog and light the stage.

Making nearly the same moves, Zawawi followed the man towards the greenery at the edge of the camp. Carrying only his spear, the Maasai climbed a near-by tree. From his lofty outpost he would be able to get a clear view of the campers and of the tracker who lay perfectly still in the bush below him.

The mist hovered over the campsite and all remained quiet. The heavy morning dampness suppressed the voices of songbirds and insects. All was eerily quiet, until the sounds of limbs being violently shaken and a barking dog broke the gray tranquility.

Through the denseness of the gray mist, the silhouettes of a dog chasing a chimpanzee materialized and disappeared within a few feet of where the tracker hid. The party was waking up. Their muffled voices mumbled through the gloominess, then quieted again. After a short while the stirring movements of people were heard and their shadowy outlines seen.

From his hiding place, the tracker could see only two. There should have been three. The young man worked around the camp while the girl, chimpanzee, and dog sat huddled closely together. The tall white man who had the rifle had slipped out under the cover of the morning fog. Not knowing when he had left or where he was, the scar-faced gunman held his position quietly and waited. The white man would have to be the first one to go.

Three hours had passed, and the misty morning had brightened into a balmy day. The tall white man finally returned with a hindquarter of an antelope draped across his shoulder. The tracker took aim and waited patiently for the movement in the camp to quiet before taking his first shot.

The campers stirred about, packing their gear and soon heading out, following a narrow game trail north. The perfect shot never presented itself, and the tracker lowered his rifle and quickly left his hiding place. He knew this forest well because he had been hunting it for months. He cut his own trail, skirting his quarry's path to an area where he was sure they would pass and he could wait to ambush them. All the while, Zawawi followed closely and silently.

The tracker moved fast. Cutting across country he ran recklessly through the forest and arrived on the hill's crest with plenty of time to pick his spot. He would then spring out from behind the boulder at the edge of the trail and finish his work. It was a simple plan. Positioning himself, his breathing slowed from the hard run and he waited, listening for the careless footsteps of his prey.

Within the hour, he heard them echoing across the forest valleys. They were coming. The tracker was a sharpshooter. Though his FN FAL was flecked with rust, the clip was full and the safety off. Motionless, he lay as still as the rock he hid behind. Only his eyes moved to the far corners searching for the first glimpse of them. He didn't have to wait long before the tall muscular white man appeared over the ridge, followed by the dog, the girl, the chimp, and the young black man. The white man carried his rifle casually over his shoulder, showing no suspicions that death could be hiding nearby.

As they passed, the tracker thought, this is too easy. The fun will be over too soon. So he waited. They traveled down a short, steep grade, crossed a dry creek bed at the bottom of the hill and continued up the opposite hillside. This narrow hollow and hillside lacked ground-covering foliage because a wild fire had swept the area a few months earlier. The trees, tall columns, slender and spacious, left few places to take cover. The tracker still had easy targets as they slowly climbed the hill.

Rising from behind the boulder, the scar-faced gunman raised the rifle stock to his shoulder. Resting the rifle on a thick limb, he steadied his aim. Slowly tilting his head, he sighted onto the back of the white man's head. The front sight centered on the point where black curls fluffed out from under a tan-billed cap.

Cupping his right hand around the trigger guard, he positioned his forefinger over the gentle sweeping curve of the trigger. At first, the feel of the cold hard steel seemed to resist the mild squeeze. Thousands of hours in training and the intimate knowledge of his firearm had increased the scar-faced gunman's sensitivity. Gently he tightened his grip. He sensed the microscopic movement taking place within the mechanical core of the weapon. He felt the ever-so-slight release of the spring tightening mechanism as the weapon dutifully gave into his action. The trained-assassin-turned-poacher, took pride in his expertise. With one last soft exhalation he steadied his heartbeat and secured his aim.

Suddenly a force slammed into his back and knocked him forward. The surprise thrust him off balance, breaking his grip on the rifle. In slow motion he watched as it twirled out of his hands. In a surreal focus, his eyes followed its fall and turbulent landing at his feet. As he looked down, he observed a strange deformity protruding from his chest. His mind struggled to grasp and recognize the shape of the spearhead. Bits of fleshy tissue draped along the top edge and dripped the red sap of life. A numbness swept throughout his unsteady body. With his head lowered, he watched his olive-colored shirt soak up his blood and change to brown. Weak and trembling, his fingers traced the edge of the bloody metal point. As his eyes grew dim with death, his knees buckled, and he quietly collapsed face down onto the ground.

Now unarmed, Zawawi waited until the gunman lay unmoving before approaching the body. Cautiously, he picked up the rifle from under the man's ankles. It was unharmed and fully loaded. The Maasai moved alongside the torso. With the rifle in one hand ready to fire, he gripped the shaft of his spear with the other, pulling upwards.

The bones and wet tissue clung tightly to the crudely made metal surface, resisting release. Slinging the rifle over his shoulder, Zawawi placed his sandaled foot squarely on the dead man's back and bore with all his weight. With both hands gripping the spear, he pulled hard. As the spearhead was plucked free, a strong sucking drag came from within the wound. Blood streaked the sides of the blade. A snarl of uneasiness veiled Zawawi's face as he wiped the bloodied blade over the pant leg of the man he had just killed, a man who had been sent to kill his unsuspecting friends.

❖ ❖ ❖

As the evening shadows grew long and dark, each member of the group found his place in the camp. Mhinga began preparing the fresh meat that Jon had brought earlier that day. Buster and the chimp pestered each other playfully around the fire. MacKenzie wandered about picking up sticks for kindling while Jon dragged in larger logs that would burn throughout the night.

Mhinga looked up from carving the hindquarter into steaks and strips of meat. "I think that will be plenty of wood, Jon."

Dropping the end of the log he was dragging, Jon stretched his back as MacKenzie came up alongside him and dropped her armload of smaller sticks. "What about kindling?" she asked.

"Yes that is plenty, Ms. Mac. Thank you," Mhinga said, as he tossed the scraps of meat and bones off to the side for Buster.

The dog took off for the scraps, and the chimp followed him. In starving gulps Buster quickly began devouring the meat and cheerfully chewing on the bones. The chimp moved in closer to see what the dog was eating. Carefully, he circled around until he was standing right in front of Buster as the dog snatched up the last bit of the meaty morsel.

As the last bits were devoured, the chimp sank to the ground and watched the dog with the bones. The little tan face grew long as his lower lip dropped and his eyebrow raised. With a tiny whimper, the chimp cried out a sobbing sound, *"Hoo,"* then gulping in air he followed with *"Wha."* Again he sobbed out, *"Hoo-hoo."* He repeated these cries several times. His tiny sad voice whimpered out a string of chants, *"Hoo-wha-hoo-hoo."* Realizing that he now had everyone's attention, the little chimp moved closer to Mhinga and whimpered out his chant to him.

Dumbfounded, everyone stared at the chimp unsure of his meaning. The small black head of bristly hair looked back and forth searching the faces of those around him, the people and then the dog. After a moment of silence, the expression on the chimp's face changed dramatically. His eyes softened and he pursed his lips, and then energetically began a series of deep grunts. Starting off soft and gentle, they grew stronger and louder. "Ough, ough, ough, ough." The chimp began to point at the dog with one hand and reached out with the other, palm-side up.

Mhinga looked at MacKenzie and Jon, then asked, "What do you think he is trying to tell us?"

Shaking her head skeptically, MacKenzie said, "It looks like he is begging for some meat scraps." Then she turned to Jon, "Do chimps eat meat?"

A bit baffled, Jon said, "Well, I don't know about chimpanzees, but I've seen baboons eating meat. Hell, I've seen those nasty creatures kill their own young."

As they talked, the chimpanzee grew impatient. Looking over at Buster enjoying his meal and back at the people who were no longer paying attention to him, the chimp became furious. Again his lips pouted and with low grunts that grew louder and louder he soon was screaming at the top of his lungs, *"Eee, eee, eee, aah, aah, aah, AAH, AAH!"* By the time the chimp had hit his high notes, he was rolling around on the ground waving his feet in the air and pulling at the hair on his head. What began as a quiet little pout had now turned into a full-fledged temper tantrum.

Caught in the frenzy, MacKenzie jumped up and down screaming, "Mhinga! Give him some meat! Give him some meat!"

Mhinga was caught in the middle. Instinctively, he tossed a couple of strips of meat at the chimp. Flustered, he was not careful with his aim. The strips slapped the little chimp across the face. Instantly the chimp quieted down, as did MacKenzie.

Gathering his two strips of meat, one in each hand, the chimp sat up and looked at his prizes for several long seconds before biting into one. As he ate his first bite of the raw meat, his eyes closed and he tilted his head back, chewing slowly, truly enjoying his meal. He chewed on his second bite for a long time. Then with a happy look on his face, he grunted three times, *"Her, humm, her."* Sticking out his lower lip and looking down his nose, the chimp took a good look at the mushy red meat he was chewing.

As the camp became quiet again, they noticed that, in all the commotion, Buster had taken his bone away to enjoy it in peace. Mhinga shook his head in exasperation and returned to his cooking, mumbling under his breath something about three-year-olds.

Jon wrapped his arms around MacKenzie's waist pulling her close. Standing there with her back to his chest, he whispered in her ear, "Well, my darling, I guess that clears up that mystery. Chimpanzee's eat meat and know how to beg for it." She melted back in his hold and closed her eyes. He kissed the nape of her neck. Tilting her head, she encouraged the soothing feel of his lips.

The tranquility was short-lived as Zawawi came running into camp at top speed. He reached the shade of the big tree wide-eyed and breathing hard. He was carrying his long spear streaked with blood in one hand and a rust-spotted FN FAL rifle in the other, his finger positioned around the trigger, ready to fire. Stopping dead still he looked around the quiet camp. Gradually he lowered the weapon. His unexpected arrival surprised them all. Shoulders hunched tight with tension, he crossed over to where Jon held MacKenzie. The look in Zawawi's eyes was wild and sharp.

Releasing the girl, Jon met Zawawi half way. "What's wrong?"

Zawawi glared around the camp. "I heard screaming," he gasped, breathing hard.

"Oh, that." Jon looked at MacKenzie uneasily. "Yeah, that was the chimp having a temper tantrum over some meat."

"The chimp? All that noise was made by the chimp? I heard that racket two miles away." Zawawi glared at MacKenzie, who hung her head and looked away. He knew the chimp had some help with the screaming. Hatred filled him. His breathing slowed, and he rolled his eyes in dismay. "Stupid white woman," he mumbled. "We don't have time for such nonsense." Tossing his spear over to Mhinga, he exclaimed, "Jon, you were followed. I had to kill him. Those people are more than just poachers. They are very seasoned and serious. We've got to get back there."

Chapter 33

The tents that once had housed the sleeping quarters of the scientists had been taken down. The cots now nestled together under the large open-sided tent in the center of the small compound. The scientists lay there quietly. Unable to sleep, they were acutely aware of the tension among the guards and the uncertainty of their own future. They had been forced to work hard that day closing the campsite. The folding table had been collapsed, and all the scientific equipment had been stored in its bright yellow crates.

Filling their cups with freshly brewed coffee, the three scar-faced guards squatted around a ring of hot coals that glowed with bright hues of red and orange. They had let their fire die down, blanketing their campsite with the darkness of the setting sun. With the tents down and the equipment all stored away, they had an open view of the perimeter bordering the campground. Chatting in French, their voices were low and hard to follow from the bush where Jay lay in wait.

Jay cupped his hand over his digital wristwatch masking its face as he illuminated the timepiece. Two hours until midnight. It was time to return to the others and report what he had heard and seen. Moving very slowly from his concealed place in the bushes, he was careful not to make a sound. The snapping noise of the tiniest twig could betray him and cost him and the others their lives. Having lain completely motionless since the night before, his limbs had stiffened and cramped. The crescent moon offered no light, and he had to feel his way inch by inch. Jay took the better part of an hour to back himself away from his post.

Hearing the carefully-placed footsteps, Jon, waiting nearby, whistled softly the cry of a brown-throated martin. Jay recognized the signal and called back the same way. Together they cut through the underbrush, making their way to where the other two men rested.

At the first sounds of their approach, Zawawi jerked awake and nudged his brother Simon.

Stretching and yawning, Jay tried to stir up the last bit of his energy to recount the guard's actions. His voice was frazzled and weak, and he could not hide his exhaustion as he told the others about the breaking down of the camp. "Things were all quiet until around midday. Then, when the guy that had been following Jon's group did not return, the others became edgy and started ordering the scientists to pack up their gear and take down the tents."

Jon shot a glance over at Zawawi, who shrugged a shoulder in dismissal. "It had to be done and now the guards had a day to prepare for a raid."

"Yes," Jay said weakly, "they have a clear view of the entire compound. There is nothing to conceal us once we get inside the perimeter."

"We'll be in the open like sitting ducks," Simon mumbled.

"Could you hear any of their conversation?" Zawawi asked.

"Very little. They believe their man must have failed with the assassination when he didn't return, but they'll wait until morning before continuing with their plan."

"Their plan?" Jon questioned.

Letting out a big yawn, Jay explained, "From the bits and pieces I was able to pick up, I think they plan to kill the Americans in the morning and then return to their base camp."

Staring at Jon, Simon stated, "So it must be tonight."

"We'd better get a plan together," Jon replied. "Got any ideas?"

"Well," Simon began, "We outgun them four to three."

"Yeah, but we've lost our element of surprise. They are expecting something to happen," Jon added.

Zawawi began chuckling, "We do have one other advantage." Capturing Simon and Jon's attention, he pointed across the fire they huddled around. In the dim light of the dying glow of embers, Jay's head slowly bobbed to his chest as his body shut down, demanding sleep. "Those three scar-faced gunmen have been awake nearly as long as Jay. In a few more hours they are going to be in the same condition he is. Struggling to stay awake." Jay's body slowly fell over in a deep coma-like sleep.

Simon grinned at Zawawi and slapped him cheerfully on the shoulder. "You're right, little brother! In the wee hours before dawn, we'll make our move. That way Jay will get a few hours sleep to recharge, and we will have time to work out the details."

❖ ❖ ❖

As evening began its descent, MacKenzie rested her chin on her drawn-up knees, staring blankly into the crackling fire. Buster lay next to her with his crossed paws supporting his muzzle. Having climbed up the Mugumo tree, the little chimp gathered leafy branches, creating a nest in the fork of a thick gnarly limb. Across the fire, Mhinga lay on his back, hands pillowing the back of his head, watching as the chimp worked overhead. The last three hours had been very quiet in their camp.

Jon had left with Zawawi so swiftly that MacKenzie had not had a chance to wrap her arms around him and wish him luck with a longing kiss that would bring him back safely to her. She worried about the rescuers' safety, as well as for her father and friends held captive by the poachers. Closing her eyes, she was able to visualize the layout of the scientists' camp, the location of the tents, the workstations, and Mitchell's grave. Again, she saw her father, frail and weak from the illness, yet presenting a strong front for her. With a gentle sigh, she tilted her head and watched Buster's sides gently rise and fall with each breath.

The start of evening began with the cricket chatter slowly rising. The warm air cooled, accruing heavy moisture. The chimp had finished his nest and was barely visible from the fireside. Mhinga's breathing was slow and shallow as he fell asleep.

MacKenzie too, closed her eyes. Her trust in Jon and the others brought her some comfort, though she could not turn off the worry or the visions that clouded her mind. While she sat near the warmth of the fire with her eyes closed, she started to relax, unaware that Buster had raised and cocked his head, tuning into a strange sound coming towards them.

Half raising his body, Buster began a soft whimper, stirring MacKenzie from her solitude. With a gentle stroke she ran her hand down the length of the dog's body. "Hey, Buster," she whispered trying to soothe him. Distracted, the dog glanced back at her and fondly licked her hand before his keen hearing picked up the sound again.

Snapping his head back, ears raised, standing at full attention, Buster peered into the darkness of the surrounding forest. Then he began growling. Summoned from his sleep, Mhinga rolled over and propped himself up on his elbow. Tilting his head, Mhinga tuned into what was alarming the dog. Buster took a step forward and growled louder.

"What do you think it is?" MacKenzie whispered.

"It could be most any kind of animal," Mhinga replied as he rose and picked up Zawawi's spear, the only weapon they had. "Move closer to the tree and be prepared to . . . ." His voice dropped off as he saw a dim spot of light moving through the forest towards them.

MacKenzie started moving towards the tree, ready to climb, when she saw the glowing light too. Excitedly, she said, "Maybe it's them! Jon and my father! They are coming back!"

Mhinga grabbed her by the arm tightly and pulled her protectively behind him. "No. It couldn't possibly be them. Not enough time has passed."

Buster's attention was drawn to the side, and he growled again, taking a step forward.

"MacKenzie, use your belt as a leash on him. Keep a tight hold on him." Working quickly, MacKenzie followed Mhinga's instructions, looping her belt around the dog's neck as she pulled him back safely behind Mhinga.

The light danced, zigzagging around the trees, illuminating a winding tunnel in the forest. As the strangers grew near, the fused light focused into the flames of a torch held high above a tall man's hatted head. Behind him two smaller figures followed closely.

Buster pulled in the opposite direction than before.

Within a few seconds Mhinga could clearly see them. Buster barked loudly and pulled strong against MacKenzie's hold. The strangers stopped and Mhinga called out to them, "Who goes there?"

They could see his features clearly, he was a broad-shouldered middle-aged white man; he carried the flaming torch in one hand and a heavy big-bore rifle swung casually over his shoulder. He wore oval, wire-framed glasses and a long handlebar mustache that curled up on the ends like the horns of a cape buffalo. The man was dressed in dirty pocket-covered khaki hunting clothing. Mhinga could not clearly see the two smaller people who followed behind the white man, but judging by their size and stance, he believed them to be young natives.

The white man answered back, "We are lost and saw your fire's light from a hilltop. May we approach?" Though he answered in English, his accent was clearly French.

"How many are you?" Mhinga called back.

"We are just three, myself and my two young native guides. May we approach?"

Mhinga glanced uncertainly at MacKenzie. She shrugged her shoulders and said, "We can't just send them away if they are lost."

Mhinga agreed and called back to the white man, "You may come." Buster was sitting quietly next to MacKenzie, and she removed her belted collar from the dog. Within minutes the Frenchman was breaking out of the underbrush into the bright firelit camp. As the two younger people emerged from behind him, Mhinga was taken by surprise. "Valli! Khosa! What are you two boys doing out here? I thought you were working near the logging concession."

Khosa broke out from behind the Frenchman and knelt by Buster's side, stroking and hugging the liver-colored Ridgeback. Affectionately, the dog's pink tongue licked the youth's face until he was rolling around on the ground laughing.

Dubois held out his hand to Mhinga, asking, "You know my guides? Your dog surely does."

"Yes, by marriage they are my cousins." Mhinga shook the man's hand. "And you are?"

"Let me introduce myself. I am Francois Dubois."

Upon hearing his name, MacKenzie spontaneously gasped. Realizing what she had done, she tried to cover her mistake by turning away and politely coughing a few times. Her mind raced. This is the man. This is the poaching bastard who shot those beautiful peaceful elephants and who had gunmen chase us into that cave. Fury started to build inside her. This is the same son-of-a-bitch who may be responsible for my father being held captive and for Mitchell's death. She could feel her face flushing with redness and knew that she had to get herself under control. She coughed a few more times before turning to face him.

Dubois recognized the blunder but continued as if he hadn't. "I own the logging concession these two young men work for. We were out hunting and lost our way in the heat of the hunt, you might say. Fortunately, we saw your fire. What did you say your name was?"

"His name is Mhinga," Valli's voice broke in rude and sharp. "They," he pointed at Mhinga and MacKenzie, "were with Zawawi and Jon Corbett a few weeks ago. They were starting a search for four lost American scientists." Buster had stopped playing with Khosa and began to eye the bush around the camp's edge, growling as the men spoke.

"Really?" Dubois acted surprised. Ignoring the dog, he continued, "My family's company, Camino Timber Enterprises, gave permission to an American laboratory to send researchers onto our leased land. They were going to study the forest's plant life. We co-sponsored that group. Why, we even supplied them with the porters. But I thought they were to be camped miles south of here. Perhaps we are not talking about the same group?" He lowered his rifle from his shoulder. "What was the name of that company? Sperry something, a medical research group?" Dubois handed the torch over to Valli and scratched his head. "No, that name isn't it, but it was something like that."

Playing along with the Frenchman, Mhinga continued with the small talk, "Why, yes it is. But it is Sperry Pharmaceutical Research Laboratories."

Mhinga was paying attention to Buster's peculiar behavior. The dog was turned around, watching the bushes behind him, a clear warning of a growing danger at his back. But there was a dangerous man standing just a few feet in front of him. Their only hope was that Dubois would not pick up on their fears and would leave as quietly as he had come. Mhinga also hoped that MacKenzie would pick up on the danger too and keep her mouth closed.

"Ah yes! That is the name! And so this pretty young lady is a part of their search party?"

Still growling, Buster's attention stayed focused on the perimeter of the camp. Khosa's attempt to distract the dog with play was failing.

"May I introduce, Ms. Mac." Mhinga responded politely.

"It's a pleasure to meet you, Ms. Mac." Dubois offered her his hand. "Is Mac your last name?" He questioned.

Having regained some of her composure, she followed Mhinga's lead and kept cool. Reluctantly she broke a smile and accepted his hand to shake. "Blankenship. MacKenzie Blankenship."

"That is an unusual last name. Blankenship. It seems like I have heard it recently." Dubois grasped her hand firmly. Turning it over, he kissed the back. "It's always a pleasure to meet such a beautiful and courageous woman. There are very few women who would venture out into the wilds of the African bush to look for . . ." he hesitated changing to a question, ". . . strangers?"

The hairs on the back of her neck perked up. She knew he was fishing for information. Accepting the compliment gracefully without a verbal response, MacKenzie forced another smile while withdrawing her hand from his.

Dubois turned his attention back to Mhinga. "Valli has just said that there were two others with you. Are they now among the missing, too?" Dubois chuckled at his own joke.

Mhinga played along with the Frenchman, trying to convince him that he held no suspicions. Shaking his head slightly, he relaxed his stance before answering, "No, no. They are nearby doing a little scouting. They should be back any minute now."

Buster pulled hard against Khosa's grip trying to free himself from the restrictive hold.

"Is that dog of yours always so jittery?" Dubois asked, then returned to his original line of questions. "What about the scientists? This is the first time I've heard about them being missing. You are searching a long way from where we gave them permission to conduct their studies. What made you travel so far away from the concession's leased land? Have you located signs of them?"

"You know, Mr. Dubois," Mhinga leaned leisurely against the tall Maasai spear, "we have hardly seen a trace of them. We thought that we had found their old campsite by a river crossing. But we could not find any trail of them since. So we followed the river upstream and found a well-worn path. We took it, and it led us here."

Buster pulled again and let out a bark. This time Mhinga scolded the dog, and Buster sat down dutifully, though he looked around whimpering. Khosa looked up at Mhinga and said hatefully, "I can handle him!"

"Have you been searching this area long?" Dubois gathered Mhinga's attention again.

"Just a couple of days. We have ended our search. Ms. Mac must catch a flight back to the United States."

"What a shame, Ms. Blankenship. A real shame, having to leave empty-handed. I do wish to help you find your scientists. Some of our workers may still be with them."

She had been watching the conversation between the two men closely. She did not doubt that this Frenchman was dangerous. Suppressing her true feelings was becoming harder to do. MacKenzie's temper was beginning to boil, and she wanted to lash out at Dubois. Instead, she was able to smile and ask sweetly, "How could you help us with the search?"

"Oh, my dear," Dubois began with charm, "my company leases several helicopters and small prop planes. We would gladly do a thorough search by air. We'll find your missing father and friends." Her sudden wide-eyed surprised look gave Dubois all the answers he had been fishing for.

When he referred to her father, the woman lost control. Flinging herself at Dubois, her clinched fists flying wildly at him, she shouted, "You lying bastard! You already know! You're the son-of-a-bitch who poaches animals and kidnaps innocent people and gets them killed. You had Mitchell killed. I'll kill you, you murdering French bastard." Although Dubois out-weighed MacKenzie two to one, that didn't deter her fearless, reckless attack.

Instantly, Mhinga reached out, trying to pull the wild woman away from the Frenchman. Valli jumped in front of him and pointed the rifle muzzle in Mhinga's stomach, "Step away, cousin, and drop the spear!"

Buster finally broke away from Khosa's grip and darted into the bush surrounding the clearing.

Just as the spear touched the ground, Mhinga was seized from behind. The surprise attacker was Tshombe, one of Dubois' elite poachers. He caught Mhinga off balance and easily threw him to the ground. "Good work, Valli. You did exactly as I told you." Tshombe praised his young protégé as he tied Mhinga's hands together behind his back.

Dubois was laughing at the woman, who was swinging mad, vigorous punches at him. He toyed with her, letting her have some easy open shots, safely blocking, and diverting any lucky shots. When Mhinga was held securely, Dubois stopped the play-fighting with the woman. Grabbing her hands tightly, he pulled her forward. Wrapping his leg behind her knees he pushed back, breaking her stance, knocking her to the ground. In one swift motion he rolled her over face down. Binding her hands behind her back, he growled at his men, "Where is Gbenya?"

Buster's barking had changed into angry growls coming from just beyond the edge of the clearing. Khosa ran to the dog and stroked his back, "Good boy, Buster! Good boy. You got him! Now get off the man and let him up." The leafy branches hid the others' view, but they could clearly hear what the young boy was saying to the dog. "Come on, Buster. Come on and let the man get up. That's a good boy, let him get up."

"Khosa! What's going on over there?" Valli called out.

Khosa's head appeared over the top of the bushes as he answered, "Buster has Gbenya pinned down. His jaws are clamped around the man's neck. He's okay, there's not very much blood yet."

"Son-of-a-bitch!" Dubois stomped over to the edge of the clearing. Buster stood at a right angle to the man's motionless body. When he did move, Buster would clamp down a little tighter. A tiny trickle of blood ran down each side of Gbenya's neck. Wide-eyed, he looked back and forth between Buster and Khosa. Dubois laid his hand on the young boy's shoulder, "Son, I'll take care of this from here. You go on back and wait next to your brother."

"What are you going to do?" Khosa was petting the dog's back. "You've not going to kill him are you?" Dark round eyes looked up at Dubois. "It's not like the leopard kittens. This isn't your job." Tears streamed down the youthful face. "Buster is a dog, he was mine as a puppy. You can't kill him."

The young boy's pleas were hard to ignore. "Khosa, go on back over there next to your brother. I'm just going to scare Buster real good so he will let go of Gbenya's neck. You don't want Gbenya to be hurt by Buster, do you?"

Khosa looked down at the man whose neck was locked in Buster's gripping jaws. Slowly, he shook his head. Dropping down on his knees, he wrapped his arms around the dog's shoulder and cried, "Oh Buster, please let go, come on, boy . . . ."

Buster responded by wagging his tail and growling. Dubois reached down and squeezed the youth's narrow shoulder, "Go on back over there and wait with your brother."

Reluctantly Khosa rose and, as he walked back towards Valli, his youthful ears picked up the sound of the rifle's safety being clicked off. He spun around just as the blast from the high-powered rifle thundered out from the bushes. Khosa dropped to his knees in painful agony. Seconds later, Dubois and Gbenya, rubbing his neck, emerged. Walking past Khosa, Gbenya knelt down beside the young boy. There was laughter in his voice as he said, "The big man scared your dog real good."

Khosa jumped up as Gbenya's words soaked into his youthful soul. With his small fists squeezed tight, he ran towards the big Frenchman and began pounding away on the white man's back. "You killed him! You killed him!" he cried. Dubois spun around and with one easy back swing of his powerful arm, knocked the little boy back ten feet. Valli ran to Khosa's side. Tears streamed down the boy's dark cheeks, and his chest pumped heavily, gasping for air. "I hate you! I know you killed him." The little voice was loud, rapid and strong, "I'll get you for this! Someday you are going to pay for killing Buster!"

Dubois' shoulders squared up tight as he walked over to where the two boys clung to each other. Standing over the pair, he growled angrily down at them, "Grow up, Khosa. Go on over there and look for yourself. I scared your dog, and he took off."

Valli stood and looked at Dubois directly and solidly. In a manly voice he asked straight out, "Did you shoot the dog?"

Dubois rolled his eyes and swung his rifle up on his shoulder saying, "I don't believe this." He mumbled spitefully under his breath. "Son of a bitch, Valli, you're acting like Khosa."

Valli glanced down at his little brother. His face was contorted with anguish and hate, flushed red with streams of tears pouring from painful eyes. His shoulders trembled, and he was gasping for air. Again Valli squared up to Dubois and asked, "Did you shoot the dog?"

With tense shoulders and clinched fists, Dubois' voice thundered down over the boys and struck them as a bolt of lightening, "I did not kill the dog!"

Trying to distract the raging man, MacKenzie began screaming at Dubois. "What the hell is wrong with you? You just killed a dog!" Calling his attention away from the boys, she continued her badgering, "Oh, big white hunter, killer of the domestic dogs of Africa, now picks on little boys."

With long strides, the big Frenchman straddled the woman's small, tethered body. Bending over at the waist he lifted her torso up with one hand by the neckline of her dingy white tee shirt. Holding her just inches from his face he stared into her angry green eyes. In a deeply rich voice and heavy accent he gritted through his teeth, "You'd better shut the hell up!"

MacKenzie stared back at him, her rage boiling out of control. She cursed him with every evil word she had ever heard. Mhinga pleaded with her to control her tongue. She could not respond to anything but her own anger.

Open-handed, Dubois struck her hard across the face. Her head spun so fast it jarred her teeth and left her dazed. "I told you, wretch, to shut the hell up! Not another word out of you." When he released his grip she fell hard to the ground.

Dubois, glancing over at the boys, spoke in his native language, "We're going to have to get rid of the boys soon. They are too much trouble." In English, he yelled to the boys, "I didn't kill the dog," but his words fell on deaf ears.

Tshombe asked in fluent French, "What are we going to do with these two?"

"Let's find out how much they know about our operation first."

Stepping over the woman, Dubois headed towards Mhinga. With both hands he grabbed the young man and propped him up into a sitting position. Kneeling in front of him, Dubois spoke authoritatively, "We can do this two ways. One way is that you can cooperate and tell me all that I want to know, or the other way is that I can beat it out of you and your lady friend. Which do you prefer?"

"What do you want to know?" Mhinga inquired.

Grinning, Dubois glanced over his shoulder at Gbenya and Tshombe. "Now this is a cooperative young man." Turning his attention back to Mhinga, he said, "Tell me where the other two men are."

Mhinga held a straight emotionless expression, "They are, as I said earlier, scouting the area. As you can see, we have not carried any provisions with us. They should be returning very soon."

Once more Dubois looked over his shoulder at his two elite scouts. "I guess I was wrong about this one cooperating. You see," he turned to face Mhinga again, "if they were in the area, they would have heard the shot I fired and would have been back here by now. So now I understand that you would rather not be very cooperative." The big Frenchman stood back and made way for the two scar-faced Madi tribesmen to approach.

The smaller of the two guards, Tshombe, moved behind Mhinga. Grabbing his tied hands, he roughly lifted Mhinga to his feet. Gbenya stood directly in front with a wide snicker across his face. Pulling back, he slammed a hard right into Mhinga's midriff.

The air exploded out of his lungs, and he doubled over as far as Tshombe's hold would allow. After a few seconds to allow Mhinga to recover slightly, Dubois repeated the question. Mhinga shook his head. "I told you the truth, all that I know."

"No, no. In this situation, young man, bravery will leave you dead." Dubois' voice was smooth and controlled. He gestured over his shoulder at MacKenzie, who was still in a daze. "And I'm sure that you are old and wise enough to know what I and my men are capable of doing to your Ms. Mac lying over there. Now, are you sure you don't want to change your story?"

Mhinga looked past the big, mustachioed man at his friend lying on the ground. Her cheek was starting to show bruising, and she was beginning to come out of her daze. There was no way that he could help her. These men were going to kill him and the boys; he saw it in Dubois' eyes. The most Mhinga could possibly do was stall them from finding out about the raid to save the scientists. Once more Mhinga shook his head, repeating, "I told you all that I know. You will kill me anyway, and I am powerless to help her. So begin what you must."

Dubois studied Mhinga, looking for any signs of weakness. He saw none. Nodding his head, he stood back allowing Gbenya and Tshombe to do their work. For nearly fifteen minutes, Gbenya laid hard solid punches to Mhinga's body and face. Stubbornly, Mhinga absorbed the beating with small muffled cries of pain. Dubois stepped in and grabbed Mhinga by his short cropped curly black hair. Pulling his face up he saw that the young man's eyes were nearly swollen shut, blood flowed evenly from both nostrils, and his lips had pillowed out, bruised as blue and red as his cheeks. Forcing his eyelids open, Dubois searched for some sign of awareness. Ever so slowly, the blood-bruised whites of Mhinga's eyes lowered, and his dark brown pupils stared back, revealing that a struggling life still existed inside. "Still sticking to your story? I can see that it's not too late for you. But you are getting close to your limit."

Mhinga coughed and gagged on the rising blood from his lungs. Staggering on his feet, he tried to gain some sense of balance. He would have collapsed if Tshombe had released his grip. Swinging his head loose, he willed up his last bit of energy and looked into Dubois' evil blue eyes.

"Do you want to talk now?" Dubois was speaking as gently as a loving parent to a small child.

Mhinga nodded his head and whispered so softly the big Frenchman could not hear him. Dubois leaned in closer to the bloody and swollen face to hear the tiny voice. Unexpectedly Mhinga spit a huge wad of blood into Dubois' pale face. Long slobbers of bloody saliva clung to his mustache and splattered over the lenses of his wire-framed glasses.

Stepping back, Dubois calmly wiped the bloody spit from his face and cleaned his lenses with a handkerchief. Composing himself, the Frenchman seemed to grow into a mountain of strength and control. With a huge, tightly clenched fist, he sent a powerful blow across the young man's already badly beaten face. The power in the punch knocked

Mhinga free from Tshombe's grip, sending the tattered body tumbling across the ground near to where Valli embraced Khosa. The boys, still clinging to each other, vaulted out of the way of the tumbling, rumpled body.

Consumed with rage, Dubois followed the rolling body across the clearing. With the body's momentum slowed, the towering man kicked it into motion again. After several brutal kicks, the white man left the limp and motionless body and hovered over the woman.

MacKenzie was shaking with fear. She had silently watched the entire beating. With one hand he reached down and jerked her to her feet. Holding her body up to his, he grabbed her chin. Gritting through his teeth, he said angrily, "You are going to be more cooperative, aren't you?"

Unable to speak, she could only stare up at the tense, hardened man. Then everything went blank. Her body collapsed from fear.

"They were up to something," Dubois growled in his native language. Tossing the woman's limp body at Tshombe, he commanded, "Here, carry this one, we might need her." He barked at Gbenya, "How far are we from the scientists' base camp?"

Breathing hard and sweating from the pounding he had given the young man, Gbenya pointed south, "Less than ten miles. We can be there just after sunrise."

"Good, let's get going." Dubois picked up his rifle and the torch.

Tshombe untied the unconscious woman. Tossing her over his shoulder, he asked, "What about that one?" Pointing where Mhinga's tumbled and broken body lay.

"Leave him. If he isn't dead by now, he will be soon." Then scowling an evil look at the boys, he ordered, "Get your packs together, we're moving out." Without hesitating, the boys obeyed.

Gbenya spoke in French, "Dubois, why don't we just finish these two off here?"

Dubois glanced at the boys. "They know who the other two men are. They may be useful. We'll take care of them soon enough."

The line of men filed out of the campsite and was quickly swallowed up in the darkness of the forest. Only the glow of a hand-held torch zigzagging around the trees showed their position. The sound of crickets was once again the only noise filling the clearing under a large old mugumo tree. High in its branches, a small wiry black-haired chimpanzee stared down at the crumbled body of his human friend.

It was not until well after the first light of day brightened the forest that the little chimp ventured from the safety of his high nest. Climbing down, he slowly made his way over to Mhinga. With utmost care he began comforting the motionless body the only way he knew. He began picking out the leaves, dirt and twigs that were glued with dried blood to his skin, hair and clothing.

Alone they remained in an eerie silence.

Chapter 34

The little fire had burned down to nothing but a tiny spinal smoke. The orange and red glow had cooled and transformed into a covering of black ash. Only the tiny crevices deep below the outer surface radiated the bright glowing colors, suggesting a hint of life in the dying embers.

Simon stirred the man's shoulders with an easy shake. "Come on, Jay, wake up. We need you on this one." The few short hours of sleep were barely enough for a quick recharge, but within a few minutes, Jay was fully awake and diligently gathering his gear. In the darkest hours of the new morning they checked their rifles. The crescent moon could do little to brighten through the dense fog that hovered in the high branches.

Through the gloomy hues of blue, black and charcoal grays of the awakening forest, Zawawi led the group by instinct. Following a dry creek bed down a deep hollow, they neared the scientists' campsite. They had used this as a path before, because the flat rocks lining the creek left no trace of their comings and goings.

With the coming of dawn, ghostly outlines appeared in the leafy branches above. A natural water runoff created a stony path that twisted and turned as it wound its way to the bottom of the incline. Once on the flat, the hollow opened up, widening into a softened path of moist, decaying leaves.

A light breeze whisked up from the valley, following the hillside, bringing with it a strangely familiar scent. Zawawi stopped in mid stride. Sniffing in deep breaths of air, he focused on the faint foul scent. Separating the odors, he identified two barely familiar ones. One had the hint of moist old wood burning, while the other smelled like the bitter reek of chemicals. Unable to put the pieces of the puzzle together, Zawawi continued on. His stride lengthened, for dawn was approaching quickly. They had no time to spare, because they needed the cover of darkness to conceal their arrival.

They quickened their steps to a light jog, landing each foot quietly on the soft moist ground. Rounding a curve in the hollow, the foul scent became stronger, and a strange glow materialized ahead of them. The woodland flickered with movement and light. Cautiously, Zawawi slowed his pace. Simon came alongside his brother, and Jon approached his other side. They stared into the back-lit trees that silhouetted the tall columns in front of them.

"Rubbish," Jon broke the silence and muttered the answer to the question on all of their minds. "It smells like rubber and plastic burning."

Jay brought up the rear. Clicking off the safety of his M-16, he looped the rifle's sling around his left wrist. "That doesn't look good," he whispered.

Nudging his brother on the shoulder, Simon motioned for the others to follow him. Hunched over at the waist, he left the trail, slowly blazing a path skirting the bright burning glow.

Coiling inwards, the group of four made their way closer to the flickering light. As they approached the edge of the clearing, a loud banging noise popped out at them.

Instinctively the men dived to the ground, covering their heads. In a flash there was another explosion. Jon turned to Simon and whispered, "That one sounded like a spray can exploding. You wait here."

Jon crawled through the thick greenery and halted ten yards from the edge of the clearing. Directly in front of him was a wide horseshoe-shaped band of flames, crackling sharply. The yellow plastic and fiber-glass cases that housed the scientists' research materials and equipment melted and sagged in grotesque shapes over the pile of limbs and logs that formed the foundation of the fire ring. The blaze burst and popped in the turbulent uproar, transforming the campsite into raging heat as bright as a desert at midday. Nestled in the center of the fire ring, the three American scientists sat bound together. With deep hacking coughs, they struggled to rid their lungs of the choking smoke and chemical-filled air.

The heat and smoke rose in a towering cyclone, scorching the leafy branches high in the trees. A few feet over the scientists' heads hung a yellow-gray cloud of poisonous gas from the burning man-made materials. Suspended between the dew-heavy air and the rising heat of the flames, the ghostly apparition circled and danced.

Crouched low, several yards from the break in the trees that edged the burning campsite, Jon scanned the area for the three scar-faced guards. He knew they would be well-hidden, waiting for his return, for they had purposely left a gap in the fire ring to lure him. As quietly as he had come, the others moved up to Jon's side, one by one.

Well-hidden in the undergrowth, Jay mumbled under his breath, "Sweet mother! What a welcoming surprise."

Zawawi whispered back, "As the spider said to the fly, welcome to my home."

"Looks like they were pretty sure someone was coming," Simon added.

"We didn't plan for this," Jon replied. The open trap the guardsmen had presented stunned them. There was only one way to reach the scientists, and only one way to get them out, through the open gap in the fire ring.

From the edge of the forest, it was twenty yards to where the scientists struggled. There was no cover anywhere. Even an amateur with an old rifle could pick off his quarry in this setting, and Zawawi had discovered that these men were no amateurs.

"Got any ideas?" Jon asked.

"Yeah, I got one. But you're not going to like it." Simon's expression was less than exuberant. Looking around the area, he put the final pieces of his plan together and started giving directions. "Remember, the guards saw only Jon, Mhinga, and MacKenzie, so they think there are only two men with one rifle. They don't know about the rest of us." Simon quickly began going over his plan.

"You're right, I don't like it," Jon said, "but it's all we've got."

"Yes," Simon added, "If we don't risk it now and get them out of there, the guards will finish them off as soon as the fire dies down and dawn breaks."

"Hell," Jon nodded towards the three scientists, "see that yellow gray cloud lingering over their heads? My guess is that it's made up of toxic fumes from the meltdown of their equipment. The guards wouldn't have to fire a shot."

"You don't think they have already gone, do you?" Zawawi asked hopefully.

"No way," Simon responded, "These guys know what they are doing. They are here, hiding very close, fishing for someone to take their bait and swallow the hook, line, and sinker, too. These guys want to take everybody out of the boat."

Zawawi mumbled quietly, "Revenge for their friend." He recalled the assassin he had stopped with his spear the day before.

Jon gave his friend a pat on the shoulder. "Let's get this started. Simon, you take the FN and go off to the left." Jon handed his old .375 Holland & Holland to Zawawi and said, "And you, my friend, are on the right. Jay, you've got the center. I'll wait three minutes for you to get into position before I take off."

The darkness of the undergrowth seemed to swallow the black men as they headed in opposite directions to take their positions. Jon and Jay waited in silence, listening as the three Americans coughed and hacked. "They are getting weak," Jay finally broke the quiet.

"Yeah." Jon pulled out his knife and flicked opened the blade. "I guess I had better get going." Together the men crawled to a nearby tree and stood in the shadowy light.

Sporting a grin and giving a nod of luck, Jay patted Jon on the shoulder and watched as the tall white man crept carefully to the edge of the brush. Twenty yards ahead of him was a raging ring of smoke and fire with three bound men struggling for their lives. With a deep breath, Jon sprang from the greenery, breaking into a full run towards the open passageway, into the unconcealed trap.

As his fifth stride spanned the open ground, a loud burst of gunfire erupted from behind. *Rat-a-tat-tat, rat-a-tat-tat.* Kicking up balls of earth, the bullets of the AK-47 gnawed the ground at Jon's heels.

The flash of the rifle gave away the location of one of the guards. Jay had a clear, view of the man's outline against the bright burning circle. With a careful aim and a squeeze of the M-16 trigger, Jay brought the man down.

The slug struck the gunman solidly between the shoulder blades. The shove drove the man's arms into the air, flinging the rifle loose. It cartwheeled through the air and bounced hard on the ground a few feet away. The force of the jar jammed the trigger back, and a wild array of bullets scattered in an unbridled storm. Jon heard them whiz past his head. Instinctively, he dropped his head and shoulders and curled his torso, rolling to the ground. The loose rifle fell with a thud and abruptly went silent as it spun alongside Jon. As the momentum of his roll slowed, Jon sprang to his feet and started to sprint.

Jay stood to the side of the tree, watching for one of the other guards to reveal his position. He scanned the area where the poacher had fallen. The area was quiet, but he wanted to make sure the man was dead. Jay glanced up and noted that Jon had risen to his feet again and was nearly a third of the way across the clearing. Simon and Zawawi would be covering him from there on.

Slowly, Jay emerged from behind the tree. Bent at the knees and waist, he held his rifle up in a ready firing position. Surveying the area in front of him, he slowly waved the rifle's muzzle back and forth as he crept towards the body of the fallen man.

A few feet in front of him, the body lay face down, spread-eagled in the dense greenery. The heavy shadows from the fire seemed to have dissipated with the coming of the morning sun. The light was bright enough that Jay could clearly see the pool of blood that flowed from the man's spine. As he knelt alongside the body, checking for a pulse at the man's neck, Jay felt the cold steel of a barrel being pressed against his back.

With nerves already heightened and blood pulsing with adrenaline, Jay's subconscious took control. Springing back, he twisted his upper body to the left just as the gunman pulled the trigger. As he spun away from the deadly burst of the AK-47, Jay swung his fist into the man's groin. The bullet sliced through his right shoulder. The bullet slamming into his shoulder knocked Jay's rifle from his grip and flung him spinning on top of the dead man. Rolling off the body, Jay looked up at the gunman looming over him. The man was doubled over with pain holding his crotch and stumbling a few steps backwards, trying to regain his balance. With his good hand, Jay patted the ground around him, searching for his own weapon.

Just above his head, Jay felt the leather sling of his rifle. Clawing at the ground, he got his fingers hooked over the strap and began pulling it to him. Glancing up, Jay saw that the man was recovering.

Bent at the waist, struggling for balance, the man aimed at Jay. Stripped of most of his strength, Jay struggled to raise his M-16 towards the gunman. Just then he heard the crash of a single rifle shot and, at nearly the same instance, the thumping noise of a bullet striking solid flesh. The gunman wobbled backwards, and his grip tightened on the trigger, splattering bullets up into the trees.

The sound of running footsteps grew louder as they approached. Another single shot rang out, quickly followed by another solid thump of the bullet striking a solid mass. The scar-faced man spun around, dropping his rifle. His mouth dropped open as his eyes rolled up into his head. When his knees finally gave way, the gunman dropped dead to the ground.

The footsteps were closer. Though the wound in his shoulder left his right arm numb and useless, Jay managed to grip his rifle. Lying on his back, he tilted the barrel upward, rotating the stock against the ground, supporting the balanced weight with his left hand cupped over the trigger. In the growing light, he could see the silhouette of a tall broad-shouldered man running towards him. As the figure dodged around the trees, his pace slowed, and Jay could see that it was Simon. The relief slackened the tension in his body, and the rifle fell away from his hand.

The massive man knelt alongside of Jay, looked at the wound and asked, "Are you all right? I thought I was going to lose you. I didn't have a clear shot."

"They were great shots and, yeah, I'm going to be all right. I think it went all the way through. What about Jon? Did he make it? Is he okay?" Simon looked up. Jon was just entering the opening of the fire ring. "Yeah, he's fine and just getting to them now. Do you know where the third man is? Have you seen him?"

"No. But I bet he's close." Their conversation was interrupted by the sounds of an automatic rifle and single shots coming from Zawawi's area. Jay pushed Simon's hand away, "I'll be all right. Go help Zawawi and Jon."

Looking around, Simon nodded. Ripping a piece of cloth from the back of the shirt worn by the guards, Simon bandaged Jay's open wound the best he could. "Try and keep pressure on it." Placing the heavy Colt 1911 pistol on Jay's chest, Simon said, "This will be easier for you to use." Jay nodded, and Simon, carrying Jay's M-16, headed off towards the sounds of the individual gunshots.

As he moved through the thick greenery, his vision limited by the smoke-filled morning haze, Simon followed the sound of the .375 H&H rifle Zawawi was carrying. Simon knew his brother had only four shots before he must reload -- not very good odds against a semi-automatic rifle.

Simon had counted two. Zawawi had used two of the four Winchester shells and yet he could still hear the constant clatter of the AK-47. *Rat-a-tat-tat, rat-a-tat-tat,* then a few minutes of silence before the loud ring of the single shot of the .375. Zawawi was choosing his aim carefully. Then again, *rat-a-tat-tat, rat-a-tat-tat, rat-a-tat-tat, rat-a-tat-tat.* Zawawi had one shot left before he would need to reload. Simon changed course and followed the consistent burst of the AK-47, as it hammered out mercilessly. *Rat-a-tat-tat, rat-a-tat-tat.*

The muzzle flash gave away the scar-faced man's position. He was in the fork of a big old tree limb, perfectly protected by the arms of the fork and well camouflaged by the leafy branches. From his vantage point twenty feet in the air, he had a clear view over the slight incline that dropped away. Below the gunman, behind a rocky outcrop, Zawawi was pinned.

Zawawi poked his head over the top of the rock, and the man in the tree opened fire again. *Rat-a-tat-tat, rat-a-tat-tat.* Splinters of flint, moss, and earth kicked high off the big rock outcrop. Zawawi was teasing the gunman, getting him to use up his ammunition and keeping him busy while Jon freed the scientists.

Simon circled around to the side of the tree where he had a clear shot at the last of the three guards. Simon wanted information from this man, so he needed to take him alive. Playing Zawawi's game, he waited and listened.

And it came soon enough. *Rat-a-tat-tat, rat-a-tat-tat, rat-a-CLICK!* The man's rifle was empty. Zawawi heard it too. As the man quickly released the empty clip and reached to his belt for a full one, Simon stepped to the side of the tree he was behind, aimed his rifle and bellowed, "Drop it!"

The sudden voice from behind startled the man. Quickly turning to see who was behind him, he twisted himself up from the thick limb he was lying against. It was all one swift continuous movement, while he continued loading the fresh clip and took aim.

In the full morning light, it was easy to pick out Simon's bulk alongside the tree. As he zeroed in on this new menace, Zawawi zeroed in on him. The squeeze of the trigger rang out with the last of the three-inch long .375 caliber cartridges.

The bullet struck the man to the left of his spine. The exit wound opened up his chest cavity, splattering blood and flesh all over the white-barked tree that had protected him. The body fell from the tree, striking the ground with a hard thump.

Simon was kneeling over the body by the time Zawawi had made it up the hill from the rocky outcrop he had been hiding behind. "I didn't know you were close by," Zawawi said to his brother.

"I just got up here when he was changing clips. I had hoped to take this one alive for information."

Zawawi kicked the body, rolling him over onto his back. "Sorry, big brother, but I don't think you're going to get much out of him now."

"No I guess not . . ." His comment was stopped short by a woman's scream and heavy shots being fired from the vicinity of the scientists' camp.

Chapter 35

The narrow stony path twisted and turned, winding its way to the bottom of the steep incline. Hazy morning air grew dense and smoky gray near the bottom of the dry creek bed. Stair-stepping down on the flat rocks, Tshombe led Dubois and the others through the hollow near the area of the scientists' campsite. The poachers had used this path often, as the rocks lining the bed left no traces of their comings and goings. Once on the flat, the hollow opened up, widening into a softened path of moist decaying leaves. In the dampness of morning, a heavy stench of burning plastic hovered in the air between the hillsides.

Dubois stopped the group. "What the hell . . . ?" His words were cut short by the distant echo of a single rifle shot followed closely by a burst of semiautomatic gunfire. Gbenya dropped his shoulder, letting the girl roll off.

She landed face down in the moist ground. The wet leaves and mud covered the side of her face. The muddy coolness started to bring her back from unconsciousness.

Gbenya and Tshombe looked at Dubois with eager eyes. Their trained military minds had quickly put the pieces together. Readying his rifle, Gbenya spoke first. "Now we know."

"Now we know what?" Dubois demanded.

"What the girl and her friends were up to. Remember you gave us instructions to kill the scientists and burn the campsite if there were any problems? Well, that is the smell of burning canvas and melting plastic."

MacKenzie slowly pushed herself up from the ground. Her head ached, and the side of her face was badly bruised and swollen. There was an odd taste of dried blood in her mouth. Her lips were dried and scabbed over. Raising up on her knees, she scraped the cool mud from her face with trembling hands. Her mind fuzzy, she tried to piece together what had happened and where she was. Men's voices were nearby. Forcing herself, she swung her head drunkenly towards the voices. She could hear them, but not make out the words. One voice stood out, strong as a commander. Calling out weakly, her voice was low and raw, "Simon? Is that you?"

Spinning around, Dubois saw that the woman had risen to her knees. His voice lowered to a whisper, "Simon?" The hairs on the back of his neck stood erect as that name struck him, scratching every nerve in his body. His mind raced over the name, over and over again it stabbed through his soul. He thought Simon was dead. How could he have lived? It was well over a year ago when he saw the bullets strike the beefy body. He was the one who had fired the weapon. No man could have survived that or the fall. Dubois dismissed the thought that the girl was calling to the same man who had ended his very profitable poaching operation. It was the same name, but it couldn't be the same person. Though he tried to console himself and tried to rid his mind of Colonel Simon Kuldip, he could not shake the feel of the past that haunted him now. The Colonel was dead. He had killed him, regrouped, and reorganized. No one was going to stop him this time. Now, he had the backing of government officials of several central African countries behind him. "Perhaps," Dubois spoke quietly to his men, "she will be more willing to give us the details now."

Slowly, the vague shape of a tall white man came forward. Blurred vision kept MacKenzie from clearly seeing the details of his face, but his skin was pale. "Jon?" Her hoarse voice was hopeful.

Dubois knelt down close to her and at the short distance his long handlebar mustache and wire-framed glasses came into focus. She covered her mouth and gasped, pulling away from him as she recognized him. Dubois grabbed her hand and jerked her to her feet. Wrapping her arm behind her back, he clenched her wrist with one hand and grabbed her chin tightly with the other. "Ms. Mac, isn't it?" She tried to pull her face from his grip, but he squeezed tighter.

"Who is this Simon and Jon that you call to?" His eyes were bloodshot and his breath sour.

MacKenzie's mind cleared. She remembered the beating this man had given Mhinga, and the heavy blow he had given her. She stared wide-eyed and frightened, unsure how to answer. He shook her head so violently she thought her neck was going to snap.

"Answer me!" Dubois demanded.

MacKenzie's mouth opened, but no sound emerged. Frightened and trembling, she could barely manage to nod her head.

Impatiently, Dubois pulled sharply against her twisted arm wrapped around her back, lifting her off her feet. The weight of her body hung from straining muscles of her shoulders and arms. Flexing backwards with the unnatural pull, her cry of pain was cut off as Dubois squeezed his powerful hand over her neck. "Tell me! What is Simon's last name!"

"Kuldip!" Khosa yelled at the top of his lungs. "His name is Kuldip! Now, let her go!" The young black boy was standing with his hands on his hips just a few feet from where Dubois held the woman. There was a wildness in the child's eyes that Dubois had seen before in Valli, but not in this child. His narrow frame stood tensed and squared.

Looking down at him, red-faced with anger, Dubois growled, "What?" He pushed the girl away. The sight of the little boy challenging the towering white man made MacKenzie's heart skip a beat.

The small boy stood his ground and answered again, "Kuldip. Simon Kuldip."

"Simon Kuldip?"

Khosa nodded his head.

"Colonel Simon Kuldip is dead! You lying little flea!" Dubois towered over the boy, ready to squash him. Quickly, Valli jumped between the white man and his brother. "He is alive! He had a long medical leave."

Dubois turned his attention to Valli. "You know this man, Simon Kuldip?"

"Yes."

"How? How do you know this man?"

"He is our uncle. My father's brother."

Dubois' face flushed bright red. He wanted to reach down the boy's throat and rip out his heart. "Why didn't . . ." his voice was cut off by the sound of rifle fire echoing up the valley. Dubois spun around. "How far are we from the campsite?"

"Half an hour," Tshombe answered.

Dubois pulled himself together, suppressing his anger, and drew upon his military training. His nerves jumped but he appeared calm when he turned back to face Valli. "Son," he said unruffled, "that is the sort of thing you should have told me." The redness was draining from his face. "Who else is traveling with your Colonel uncle? And who is this Jon person?"

Valli tilted his head, puzzled at the change in Dubois. His eyebrows narrowed, and he hesitated.

Speaking in a fatherly tone, Dubois said, "Valli, you said you wanted to join my elite group of hunters. Well, right now, son, we might have to fight to keep our jobs. If you really want to join us," he continued as he motioned over to Gbenya and Tshombe, "we need your help. What can you tell me about this man, Jon? You still want to join us, don't you?"

Valli looked at the two hardened men and at his little brother. Khosa was shaking his head no. The sound of gunfire filled the smoky air and filled him with excitement. "Jon Corbett is a white man, a family friend."

"Valli, don't!" Khosa cried out. "Let's just go away from here. Let's find our father and go home. I want to go home."

"Valli, is your father with them?" Dubois asked firmly.

Valli looked at his little brother, who was starting to cry. "Yes, he was traveling with Jon, Mhinga, and the woman. We last saw them at the logging concession road after we killed the chimpanzees, a few days before we left to hunt the tuskers in the valley."

With eyes flooding with tears, Khosa jerked on Valli's arm. "Come on, let's go. Let's go home. I want to go home, Valli."

"Valli," Dubois began, "you told me you wanted to get away from your father, to be your own man. I'm offering that to you now. Are you with us now?"

"Yes. I'm with you."

"Valli, no!" Khosa cried out, as his shoulders shook and tears streamed down his cheeks. "I want to go home." MacKenzie ran to the little boy, kneeling down beside him, she reached out to the small trembling frame. The little boy jumped into her warm embrace. Wrapping his arms around her neck, he buried his tearful face against her chest. His shoulders shook with grief, and his muffled voice kept repeating, "I want to go home. I just want to go home."

MacKenzie whispered softly, "That's right, go on and cry it out, we'll get through this."

Dubois placed his hand on Valli's shoulders, and nodded his approval at the young man. "Valli, do you think your Colonel uncle is with Jon and your father?"

Valli's shoulders squared and his muscles tensed under Dubois' grip. "I don't know. I don't know when he was going to come back to work."

Another echoing sound rang up the valley. Dubois stood back. Removing his hat, he ran his fingers through his greasy hair. His mind raced, putting the pieces together. He realized that this group must be the people on the bluff that he thought had perished in the cave-in along with his sentries. The helicopter pilot had said two blacks and two whites, and one of them was a woman. They must have radioed Simon. It was the Colonel who had raided his campsite, the raid that Petrus and her lover had warned him about.

So the Colonel was not dead after all. That thought gnawed at Dubois the worst. His reflections were interrupted by a series of bursts from a semiautomatic weapon followed by the single shot of a rifle. Quickly Dubois started shouting orders. He pointed at MacKenzie, "Take your belt off!" Shaken and scared, still holding the small crying child in her arms, she hesitated. "Do it now or I'll have Tshombe do it for you!"

A wide grimace of rotting teeth snickered across the tattooed face. Slowly MacKenzie released the little boy. She cupped his face in her hands and wiped the tears away with her thumbs, then forced a little smile and stood. With trembling hands she removed her braided leather belt and handed it to Dubois.

Dubois snatched the belt from the woman's hand. "Valli, tie her hands behind her back. Make sure it is good and tight."

Grabbing her wrists, Valli twisted her hands behind her back like he had seen Dubois do earlier. She cried out with pain.

Khosa stomped up to his brother and demanded, "Don't you hurt her!"

Valli glared down at his little brother with malice and hate. "Shut up, you baby!"

277

Khosa, sobbing, stepped back, astonished that his brother had spoken to him so harshly. "But Valli . . . " he whimpered softly.

"Just shut up, Khosa, and do what *Bwana* Dubois tells you." Valli looked at Dubois for approval.

A fatherly half-grin lifted the side of his handlebar mustache as Dubois winked at Valli. "Now use your own belt as a leash for the bitch. I'm giving you the responsibility of watching over our prisoner." As Dubois continued, Valli looped his belt around MacKenzie's neck and jerked hard. "Gbenya and Tshombe and I are going to find out what all the shooting is about. You are in charge of the prisoner and Khosa. I want you to stay back and stay out of the way. Do you understand?"

Valli beamed with pride. The hate he had been building against Dubois vanished, transformed into pride. He was now part of the elite group of hunters. In an instant, he was a man. The multiple blast of gunfire continued, swelling up a new surge of loyalty and excitement inside him. It was the same as the rush he felt during a hunt. The growing sensation of a kill flooded his body. He watched as Dubois and his two thugs dashed off into the smoky haze towards the sound of gunfire. He desperately wanted to go with them. A gush of warmth centered in his loin. The feel of the rifle caressed the inside of his palm, and his heart beat rapid and strong. He turned to his little brother and smiled an evil grin, wildness contorting his eyes. "Let's get going." He pulled on the leather leash that tightened against MacKenzie's neck, jerking her forward. "We don't want to be too far behind."

Within minutes the boys, leading MacKenzie, had caught up with Dubois. He and the two men were crouched low in the smoky haze intensely watching a blazing fire. Twenty-five feet behind them, Valli could not see clearly what they were watching. He could see Dubois lean over and whisper something. Then the men stood back, giving Dubois room to shoulder his rifle.

Curiosity filled the young Maasai, and he glanced back at his little brother and the white woman at the end of the leash. He held his index finger up to his puckered lips and breathed, "Shhhh," as he jerked on the leash. Quietly they crept closer, until they were only a few feet behind Dubois.

Ahead of them a bright fire blazed, and the silhouettes of men moved about in the center of the fiery ring. Through the smoke and heat vapors the motions were unclear. Then one man crawled out on his elbows. Inch by inch he dragged himself forward. A few seconds later a second man followed. And a few minutes after that two other men appeared in the opening of the burning ring, one dragging the other.

From the shadows, MacKenzie watched as the tall man rose, gently picked up the smaller, weaker man, and carried him across. Her eyes switched from them to the others crawling on the ground. The smoke distorted her vision, and it was several seconds before she realized who she was watching. The two men crawling on the ground were her father's colleagues, Henry and Don. Straining hard, she was able to focus on the tall man carrying the other. She gasped when she realized that it was Jon carrying her father.

The unexpected sound from behind startled Dubois, and he fired the high-powered .460 caliber rifle prematurely. MacKenzie screamed. Quickly spinning around, Dubois jabbed the butt of his rifle into her stomach.

MacKenzie doubled with pain and fell to the ground. With her hands still tied behind her back, she lay on the damp ground gasping for air.

Khosa dropped to his knees beside her and tried to help her sit up. As his hands gripped her shoulders, he felt her body trembling with fear and watched as tears streamed down her grubby cheeks.

Dubois' swing continued toward Valli, but the young man ducked away from the blow. Turning back to the fire-ring, Dubois started firing at Jon, who was zigzagging across the open area carrying the frail old man. Dubois shot and reloaded and shot again until the tall white man was out of sight.

Fuming, Dubois reached back and grabbed Valli by the shirt. Pulling him up to his face, he growled, "What the fuck are you doing? I told you to stay the hell out of the way!" He pushed Valli back. Losing his balance, Valli stumbled and fell next to MacKenzie. Turning to Tshombe, Dubois said, "We've got to get the hell out of here -- get back to Lifi and clean house." Stepping over to Valli, Dubois put his muddy boot on his chest and pushed him back down. "Not another word out of you!"

Tshombe spoke in French, "Let's just shoot them now."

Dubois glanced back at the fire, and answered in French, "We need them alive now more than ever." He continued in English, "We don't have any time to waste. Let's go." Then he motioned for Gbenya to lead the way. Reaching down, Dubois picked Valli up with one hand and pushed him forward, growling, "I want you in front of me so I can keep an eye on you." A hateful glance at Khosa and MacKenzie quickly brought them to their feet. "Grab hold of that leash, boy, and bring the woman along." Turning to Tshombe, he ordered, "If you hear one peep out of her, put a bullet in her head." Tshombe nodded with a grin.

Gently, Khosa reached for the leather belt that looped around MacKenzie's neck. The boy looked into her eyes, and she forced a tearful smile, seeing the same fear she felt, reflected in his face. With a tiny nod, Khosa led her behind the big Frenchman, while Tshombe brought up the rear.

Chapter 36

Jon had made his way through the dense smoke into the ring of fire. A solid mass of heat engulfed his body. Sweat seeped from every pore only to be evaporated by the sweltering heat. Though he held his breath, trying to protect his lungs from the smoke and fumes, the flavor of melting plastics and sap-filled wood had coated his mouth. His eyes attempted to rinse away the smoke that blurred his vision, without success.

Once in the center of the ring, Jon positioned himself between two of the scientists. They were all bound together at the elbows. Their hands were crossed and tied behind their backs. Stretched out in front of them, their feet were fastened together by their shoestrings and tied to a stake, preventing them from rising. The heat from the fire had scorched their hair and blistered their skin. Their heads drooped lifelessly on their chests. Occasional feeble coughs were the only indication that life still existed in their blistered bodies.

Jon could no longer hold his breath. The fast run across the open area and the falling roll had robbed his blood of its oxygen. The scorching air entered his lungs like a searing weight. Coughing and hacking, he fought the urge to dash out for cool, fresh air. He squinted up with tear-filled eyes, monitoring the closeness of the yellowish cloud of toxic fumes that hung just a foot or two above their heads. As the fire raged, gobbling the plastic, the toxic yellow cloud dropped lower and lower.

Moving swiftly, he tried to work the point of his knife between the strips of animal hide that bound the scientists together. The thin narrow straps had been wrapped and tied while the hide was still fresh, letting the heat shrink and cure the leather into tough bands that resisted the sharp edge of the blade. Adding to the difficulty, blood was damming up at the banded elbows and wrists, causing massive swelling and bruising around the joints.

As Jon worked, Don felt the tugging sensation on his arm. Rolling his head to the side, his eyes struggled to focus through the smoke. As the knife sawed through the strips, blood flooded his arms with a shocking wave of pain. Don tried to cry out, but the heat and smoke had robbed his body of moisture, swelling his tongue and taking his voice.

Ignoring Don's movements, Jon turned his attention to the man's swollen hands, crossed and tied behind his back. His fingers were as plump and purple as concord grapes, the swelling nearly hiding the binding straps. Carefully, Jon worked the knife blade between the wrists and with a strong, quick pull snapped the leather straps.

A wave of pain shot up both arms and Don fell back dragging Henry and Dr. Blankenship down on top of Jon. The scorching heat and smoke had drained Jon of much of his strength. From the bottom of the pile, he struggled and squirmed, finally wriggling out. Avoiding the toxic cloud, he quickly began crawling about, cutting the bindings at the scientists' elbows and wrists.

The fire was dying down now. Heavy morning dampness contained the suffocating heat. Spinning, the thick silo of gray vapors swirled over the yellowish toxic murk, rippling in its dance toward the ground. As the flames shortened, the gases lowered, suspended just three feet above where the men's heads had been minutes before.

Avoiding breathing the gases by keeping his face as close to the ground as possible, Jon crawled on his elbows to the stakes. Cutting the scientists' feet free, he then rolled each one over onto his stomach. Jon lay on the ground next to Don, searching his face for some sign of life. Weakly, Don's lips parted, forcing a smile across his soot-covered face. Jon patted him on the back and pointed to the opening in the fire ring and motioned for him to go. Nodding his head, Don tried to rise onto his knees and elbows. He did not have the strength and fell back to the ground. Jon grabbed the man by the shirt collar, intending to drag him across. Don violently shook his head, and Jon released him. Flashing the okay sign, Don pointed back to the others and motioned for Jon to help them. Again patting the man, Jon crawled over to Henry. Reaching out both arms, Don slowly pulled himself forward a few inches, then reached out again. Pushing with his legs, he wormed his way across the inner circle towards the break in the fire ring.

Henry had been watching as Don dragged himself off. He tried to rise by pulling his knees up to his chest and lifting his upper body, unaware of the toxic vapors that hovered just a few feet over his head. Jon sprang from his elbows and knees to push the scientist to the ground. Henry's face contorted with anguish, then he looked up and saw the poisonous cloud. He smiled gratefully. Then rolling over, keeping his head down, Henry dragged himself in Don's wake.

Jon wormed his way to where Dr. Blankenship's crumpled body lay. As Jon gently rolled the frail man onto his back, his head flopped over to the side. With his mouth open and his eyes closed, there was a peaceful, quiet expression beneath the dirt and grime. Jon pressed his fingers against his neck, feeling a weak pulse. Grabbing the man by the collar, Jon dragged the professor to the opening of the ring of fire.

A few feet outside the gap in the fire ring, the cool dampness struck Jon's heat-stricken body. Shocked by the temperature difference, he shivered uncontrollably, pausing for a moment. The morning light had brightened the forest, but smoky haze still flooded the air, defusing images and reducing visibility. Looking ahead, Jon could see that Don and Henry were still dragging themselves slowly. Too weak to stand, they were just a few feet ahead of him. The loud roar of the fiercest flames had quieted to soothing sears and tiny pops. Glancing over his shoulder, Jon could see the flames dying over the heaping mound of glowing black ash. Trapped in the center by the surrounding heavy damp morning air, the yellow cloud of toxic gases waved like a ghostly mirage. Narrow wisps of steam escaped, funneling like miniature cyclones, entwining and dissipating into the bright cool smoky haze.

Rising to his knees, Jon picked up the frail body of the old man, carrying him like a sleeping child in his arms. The smoke hung low and thick. The green of the bush filtered through the haze, creating an eerie feel to the area. Jon wondered where Simon and Zawawi were. Jay lay wounded a few dozen yards ahead in the bushes. There was silence all around him. Don and Henry had risen to their hands and knees, still weak, but bravely crawling towards the bushes.

Breaking the eerie stillness, a thundering clang echoed across the clearing. Jon recognized it as a big-bore rifle. Don and Henry had stopped crawling and looked back at Jon in panic. A woman's scream was followed by a second shot from deep in the woods. MacKenzie? He wondered. No, it couldn't be. She is miles from here, safe with Mhinga. A third shot whizzed by Jon's shoulder. "Run!" he yelled to the others as another shot flew past.

Don and Henry struggled to their feet. Supporting each other, they stumbled and staggered towards the blurry green bushes ahead of them. Taking his first running step, Jon altered his stride to the side. He zig-zagged back and forth as he ran. Taking two strides to the right, then two strides to the left, he created a much tougher target. More shots rang out, seconds apart. Carrying MacKenzie's father in his arms, Jon could feel the old man's frail body jerking and bobbing with each step. The shots followed him as he dodged. One sped past his head. He felt another bullet tug at the loose material of his shirttail. The gunman was experienced and accurate.

As Jon made it to the bush behind Don and Henry, the shooting stopped. The gunman had lost view of his target. In the diffused brightness of the smoky haze, the scientists leaned up against trees, panting hard, trying to regain some strength. Jon continued on, leading the scientists towards the area where Jay waited. Straggling behind, Don and Henry followed.

The smoke dirtied the crisp morning air, filtering the bright greenery into a drab olive. Jon approached the big tree with caution. Jay should have been covering him as he led the scientists across the openness, but no return shots had been fired. Jon wondered if the gunmen had found Jay.

Jon scanned the area for any sign of movement. The little clearing under the tree was quiet. As he entered, Jon stumbled over the lifeless body of one of the gunmen. Ahead of him lay two other men. As Jon laid down Dr. Blankenship, he could easily see that the two gunmen were dead. One had a large hole in his back and the other had two gaping wounds in the chest. Jay lay on his back, teetering on the edge of unconsciousness. His pulse was weak, but steady. Checking the wound in Jay's shoulder, Jon could tell that his friend had lost a lot of blood. The wound was beginning to clot and jell, forming a light scab. If he didn't lose any more blood, he would probably be all right.

Picking up Jay's rifle, Jon glanced at the two scientists. Both men were kneeling over Dr. Blankenship. Jon said, "Can you take care of these two men?"

Don looked over his shoulder. Tears streaked his ash-covered face.

"What's wrong?" Jon asked.

The two scientists parted, giving Jon a clear view of the old man he had been carrying. Dr. Blankenship's face was peaceful as blood pooled beneath his head. He had been struck in the neck with a .460 caliber bullet.

Jon felt his heart stop. "No!" he said, under his breath. Hardly believing what he saw, Jon darted to the old man's side. "That can't be!" Reaching out towards the wound, Jon's hand was suddenly slapped away by Don.

"Don't touch him!" Bewildered, Jon's face went blank. "You could get infected," Don snapped.

"Infected? What are you talking about?"

Don's voice cracked, "He was dying of AIDS."

Jon rocked back on his heels and stared silently at the old man's face. "MacKenzie. What about MacKenzie? She told me her father was sick, but . . ." Jon was nearly whispering.

"She knew he had the disease," Henry told him. "He didn't want her to see him die. That is why he insisted on coming to Africa. He wanted to die here, while trying to find what plants the chimpanzees ate that kept them from developing AIDS. Then the porters . . . " His words were smothered by his sobs. Covering his eyes, he cried.

Jay rolled his head to the side and whispered hoarsely, "Simon?"

Jon turned his attention back to Jay, whose face and body were breaking into a sweat. His wound was infected. "Don, can you watch over Jay? I've got to find what happened to Simon and Zawawi." As Don nodded, the sound of people running towards them in the bushes grew louder. Jon grabbed Simon's Colt 1911 and motioned for the scientists to take cover behind the large tree. Jon stood by the tree, handgun ready. Through the smoky haze, the outline of two men approached, a tall bulky man followed closely by a tall slender figure. Jon recognized Simon and Zawawi, and stepped from behind the tree.

"You made it!" Simon called, as he entered the area and knelt beside Jay, checking his wound.

"Not all of us," Don said quietly.

Simon looked over at the still body of MacKenzie's father, "Oh no! We heard the shots and came as quickly as we could." He knelt down to check Jay's condition. "Who was firing at you?"

Jon shrugged his shoulders, "I was hoping you would know."

Zawawi said, "We got all three of the remaining guards." He pointed to the two who lay next to Jay. "These two and one on the other side of the campsite."

Don stood up next to Zawawi. "There were eight guards altogether. They rotated in shifts of four every week or so."

Jon glanced at Zawawi, "The guards were carrying AK-47's, except for the assassin, and we've got his FN. That was a bigger rifle shooting at us."

"Maybe an elephant gun?"

" It was a .460 that was being used on the elephants in the valley."

"Dubois? The poacher?"

"Could be." Zawawi's face drained of all expression as he remembered that his two sons were scouts for the poacher.

"Well," Jon added, "if it is Dubois, he is traveling with a small mixed group. We heard a woman scream. That might slow him down some."

"Perhaps it was Valli's whore," Zawawi suggested.

Listening to the conversation, Simon interrupted, "Well, Dubois will have to wait awhile longer. We've got to get Jay back to Mhinga as quickly as possible. He's lost a lot of blood and that wound is becoming infected. Mhinga can mix up some herbs to stabilize him until we can get him to a hospital." Simon looked around the area and started giving orders. "Zawawi, take the pants off the three dead men. Jon, find two long sturdy limbs. We'll run the limbs down the pant legs and make a stretcher to carry Jay."

Don turned to Simon, asking, "What about Dr. Blankenship? We can't just leave him here. And without rubber gloves, we shouldn't handle the body."

Simon looked to Jon in question. "Rubber gloves?"

"Simon," Jon said softly, "Dr. Blankenship was dying of AIDS."

"Oh, I see." Simon looked at the distraught faces of the two remaining scientists. "We don't have any tools to dig a grave . . . ."

Henry spoke up quietly, "Let's lay him next to Mitchell's grave. We could cover his body with the fire debris and rocks."

"Yes," Don answered, "that is what we need to do. We'll drag him by his boots to avoid the blood."

"I'll help you," Simon spoke softly.

"No," Henry said gently. "We would like to do it alone. You have a man who needs your attention."

Simon nodded and watched as the two scientists began their work, then turned his attention back to Jay. As he held pressure on the open wound, his mind focused on the sound of the woman's voice. His instincts told him something was terribly wrong. He was torn between the urges to return quickly to Mhinga and MacKenzie, and to go after Dubois. That name, Dubois, sent a chill down his spine.

Chapter 37

A high, gentle breeze ruffled the trees, casting speckles of moonlight across the forest floor. An owl, perched on a branch, watched the movement of the flickering lights. Gliding over the soil, the pale beams revealed the little rodents that quietly fed and moved about in the darkness. A large rock outcrop flanked a muddy pool at the bottom of a steep natural watershed. Grazing quietly at the edge of the bog, two small, light-brown duikers tolerated the insects that swarmed out of the wetness. The feasting pests, fighting against the breeze to land on the antelope's warm backs, were in no danger from the short tails that flapped about in vain. Delicate sticklike legs probed deep into the mud-thickened pool as the animals moved toward the tender shoots of greenery in the water.

A noise drew the owl's attention away from his hunt for rodents. Flapping his wings, he screeched a warning. The duikers snapped to attention, standing still as statues, their tails quiet, forgetting the biting insects. With ears forward, they tuned into the approaching noise of an animal running frantically through the darkness. Their noses rose high into the air, trying to catch a scent on the breeze.

From the top of the hill, a crash and a whimpering cry startled the duikers into full flight and scattered the small rodents underfoot. Scampering sounds rustled across the leaves as the small nocturnal forest creatures ran for shelter from the bellowing racket that was bearing down upon them.

Buster was panic-stricken, taunted by a demon that echoed and pounded in his head. The frightened dog had bolted when the elephant rifle was fired next to his ear. From the edge of the small clearing, down the hillside and along a dry creek bed, he ran without any direction, trying to escape the maddening confusion. After the first hour of the hard run, Buster's legs failed.

Tripping and stumbling, the dog lost his footing and nose-dived down a long rocky slope that had been carved into ravines by heavy rains. Rolling and bouncing from rock to rock cracked his ribs, and he whimpered with pain. Gravity and momentum accelerated his fall. Tumbling out of control, his body catapulted off a large outcrop of rock at the bottom, and he landed in a soft pool of muddy ooze.

Though shocked and dazed, Buster's first instinct was to get up. With trembling legs, he lifted his upper body. His paws searched and fought furiously for a hold in the slime. Losing the battle, he slid onto his side, raking his rib cage. He lay in the cold wetness, whimpering as the pain slowly subsided.

Raising his head and straining hard against the hurt, Buster rolled onto his belly. With his legs curled beneath him and his eyes closed, he rested, panting. Finally, he pulled his front legs out and braced himself. The soft mud seemed bottomless as the dog's paws sunk deeper and deeper until his spread toes finally found a solid footing against the intertwining roots.

Rocking back and forth, the dog struggled against the sticky mud that cemented his rear end. A throbbing pain shot along his side as he pulled. Determined to break free, Buster growled and with a sucking smack, pulled his butt loose. His back legs squirmed and found solid footing. Steadily, he gained his balance.

Water seeped into the tunnels around the dog's sunken legs and the depression his body had made. He shivered from the cold and, reacting naturally, shook his body hard to throw off the clinging muck. His slippery footing gave way, and Buster splashed into the pool. With a throbbing pain across his side and a heavy heart, he glanced around the surrounding dark forest.

The owl, watching from above, called out woefully. Suddenly Buster felt vulnerable. Despite the pain, he raised half up and shook his head, ridding his face of the clinging ooze.

Again the dog fought the muck and his pain as he slowly and carefully stepped forward. He inched his way across the muddy pool until the ground became firm and dry under his feet.

Passing through the dense underbrush, Buster scraped off clumps of mud that clung to his short, liver-colored coat. Excess water dripped steadily from his belly, and trembling, his back steamed in the cool night air. With his head down, panting hard, Buster painfully moved forward, wandering aimlessly in the night, along narrow hollows and over hills.

The moon passed its zenith, and the darkest hour of the new dawn blanketed the rolling forest hillsides. Buster moved in short tired steps, his tail hanging low and his nose nearly dragging the ground. The hours and the miles passed as slowly as his footsteps.

Soon the darkness of night began to change into tones of light gray and hues of deep blue with the coming of morning. The ringing in Buster's head had turned to deafness. With stiff and aching muscles, he strained from the long, frightful run and the bouncing tumble down the rocky slope. Lethargically, Buster labored on. Chilled and dehydrated, his mouth grew dry, and his tongue began to swell.

Gathering on the greenery, the drops of dew filled the morning air with a sweet scent of freshness. As he passed near a large leafy bush, several drops of moisture dripped onto Buster's nose. The heavy drops ignited his thirst, stopping him in his tracks. Yielding to his need for water, the dog's tongue lapped against the dew-covered leaves.

The droplets spurred his desire to survive, and a cool breeze brought the scent of a nearby river. Buster pushed on towards the smell of water. The drive for moisture powered him slowly over the hill's crest and down a long slope to another hill. The rising sun brightened the forest and warmed the cool air, taking with it the drops of dew and leaving Buster an even greater desire for water. He wandered on, following the scent. His hearing shattered from the rifle blast, he had to rely upon his keen sense of smell to guide him.

Buster walked out of the thick bush into a large, sunny clearing. The brightness momentarily blinded him, and he blinked rapidly, adjusting to the light. The scent of water, sun-dried mud, fish, and algae filled the air, and led the dog to the edge of a high embankment.

Six feet below, Buster could see a swift flowing river, though he could not hear the white caps splashing over the large boulders. The dog looked upstream and then downstream. From where he was, he could see no easy way to the water. Heavy-hearted and exhausted, Buster's legs gave out, and he collapsed onto his side.

❖ ❖ ❖

"Look, *Babu!*" the young boy exclaimed to his grandfather as he pointed across the river.

The old man placed his hand on his grandson's shoulder and pulled him back into the shadowy bank. "Lower your voice, Tiwas. Elephants have very keen hearing. You will scare him away."

The eight-year-old boy settled onto the log next to his grandfather, Teresit. In a lowered voice the child's enthusiasm continued. "Have you ever seen him before? He is so big! Just look how his tusks touch the ground!" The young boy's words flew from his mouth so fast the old man chuckled and waited patiently for him to finish.

"Yes, I have seen him before," the old man said, steadily, slowly, "but not for quite some time. It is good to see the poachers have not taken him."

The elephant was feeding peacefully. Turning sideways, he stretched his long trunk high into the trees. "What's that mark on his shoulder?"

The old man strained to see what the youth was pointing at. "My eyesight is not as sharp as yours. Where are you looking?"

"There," he pointed, "high on his neck, just in front of his shoulder." A long wet streak dribbled out of a small round wound.

Teresit leaned his long *panga* against the log and nodded. Sadly, he said, "I see it now. I was wrong. The poachers *have* found our grand king."

The child laid his arm across the old man's shoulders and said, "Don't be sad, *Babu.* If he escaped the poachers, he will be safe here in our forest."

"Oh, my sweet *toto,*" Teresit used his native word meaning little child. "The white man's greed for those long curved teeth will drive him to follow this great beast. It is only a matter of time now."

"Are all white men hunters? You have met some, are they all so . . ." the boy thought hard for the correct word, "are they all so mean?"

Teresit grinned at his grandson, "No, my *toto,* not all white men are hunters or mean, and, yes, I have met some, when my younger brother moved away many years ago. I went to the white man's world to bring him home to the forest, but I was too late."

"What happened to him? Did he die?"

"No, no." The old man chuckled, "Well, yes, in a way he did. He had fallen in love and decided to marry. He stayed in the white man's world."

"Why did he not bring his wife to our forest?"

"She was of another culture and . . . ."

Tiwas butted in, "Is she a white person?"

"Not really. She has lighter skin than you and I, but she is from a country called India. Very peaceful and quiet, but not of the forest."

"Why did your brother leave the forest?"

Teresit sighed deeply. "It is a very complicated story. You see, Tiwas, for many years the government has been trying to deny our people claim to our ancestral lands, our forest. Many promises were made and broken. We Okieks are a peaceful tribe who tried to get along with the government people. At one time some of our people were moved onto reserves with other tribes that raised cattle and goats. The rest of us moved further into the forest to escape the government. Then they cut down our trees and tried to make us farmers. Eventually most of those who moved to the plains grew lonely for the trees and moved back to the forest."

Tiwas interrupted, "They cut down the trees?"

"Yes and they replanted the forest with useless unproductive trees that the bees would not go near."

"What did they do for honey?"

The old man laid his hand on the child's short woolly head, "Oh, you are still so very young. You see the white man does not value honey like we do."

"Sounds like the white man does not value much at all -- not honey, or trees or the animals. I do not think much of them. I hope they never come to our forest."

"I wish that too, Tiwas. But remember, not all white men are bad, and many black men are just as greedy."

"What happened to your brother and his wife?"

Sadly, Teresit gazed across the river at the big bull elephant, then murmured, "I do not know. He was one of the few who never returned to the forest, so I have not seen him since then. That was a long time before you were born." He smiled down at his grandson, adding, "But I hope that he is happy."

Tiwas watched as the sadness draped the wrinkled face of his grandfather. His gaze followed the old man's across the river to the feeding elephant. He looked at the canopy of green leaves swaying overhead. They sat in the solitude of the forest absorbing and listening to the sounds of the birds singing, the insects' clatter, and the rushing water streaming over the boulders. In a wistful whisper the boy finally spoke, "How could anyone not be happiest here in the forest?"

Proudly Teresit smiled and winked at his *toto* and whispered back, "I do not know."

The elephant lingered in the clearing across the river on the high embankment, casually feeding on the many plants and leaves that densely flourished in the sunlight. Steadily, he made his way near the edge of the embankment, and then he stopped feeding. His finger-tipped trunk waved back and forth across a small area in front of his big-toed feet.

"What's he doing over there? It looks like he is playing with something on the ground," Tiwas asked.

"Yes it does. Let's watch him until he goes away, then we shall cross the river and have a look." Teresit smiled a toothless grin at Tiwas' beaming face.

After some time the big bull moved off to the side. Kneeling down at the edge of the embankment, he leaned over the edge. Teresit and Tiwas watched in amazement as the elephant stretched out his long trunk. Reaching down, he siphoned up the water, filling his trunk. He then leaned back, rose up, and moved back to where he had been. Very slowly the old bull released the water in his trunk and splattered it on the ground. He dallied in that spot for a long time, probing something on the ground at his feet.

The pair sat and watched the old elephant for more than an hour before the giant moved back into the darkness of the forest. As he disappeared from sight, the old man rose and waved, "Travel far, great one.

May our God Tororo watch over you and keep you peaceful."

Tiwas mimicked his *babu.* Raising his hand and waving, he called, "Travel far from the poachers, great beast." Lowering his hand, he beamed up at his wrinkle-faced grandfather. "Can we go see what the elephant was playing with now?"

It took some time to traverse the riverbank, find a shallow crossing, and then make their way back upstream. They cut across the path of the old bull and followed it to the small clearing on the high embankment. Young Tiwas ran a few feet in front of his grandfather and stopped abruptly in the center of the clearing. Pointing at the ground he called back, "Look, *Babu!* A dog! It's a big red dog!"

Buster could barely hear the boy's cries, but raised his wet head, whimpering. Tiwas and Teresit ran to his side. The dog was lying down, licking at the shallow puddle dug and filled by the elephant.

Teresit reached down and stroked the red coat. Grabbing a handful of skin over the dog's shoulders, he pulled up gently. The skin held the shape, indicating dehydration. Unsheathing his *panga,* the old man began to dig a slightly deeper hole under Buster's nose and gave instructions to Tiwas. "Find four or five big leaves to line this hole. The dog must drink clean water."

Tiwas quickly followed the instructions, lining the hole with the leaves before his grandfather swung his long *kabash* from his shoulder and poured water into the hole. Greedily, Buster lapped up the clean water.

"Will he be all right, *Babu?*" Tiwas asked.

"Yes, I think so. He has been without water for a long time, but he should be feeling better soon."

"How did the elephant know the dog needed water?"

"I do not know. Elephants are very wise. There is much we can learn from them."

"*Babu,* give him some more water."

"Not too much, it may make him sick in other ways. Just a little bit at a time."

"Can we keep him? I've never had a dog."

Teresit rocked back on his heels and looked carefully at the mud-spotted dog. After a few minutes of study, he glanced at his grandson and said, "This dog belongs to someone who cares very much for him. See how this old wound down his hip has been carefully healed." He traced his finger down Buster's long scarred thigh. "Those are marks from a white man's stitches. This was a very bad wound that took a great deal of time to heal."

"Oh." Tiwas' voice faded as he watched his grandfather refill the hole. The dog drank from it gratefully. "Do you think that he could be the poacher's dog? The poacher who shot at the great one that gave him water?"

Teresit considered his grandson's question before answering. He had seen the signs of poaching in his forest. "Yes, I suppose that could be true."

The young boy scooted closer to the dog and stroked his cowlicked, ridged back. Buster stopped drinking and licked the boy's knee. "He seems like such a nice dog to have such a mean owner."

"Remember, we do not know who owns this dog. But if you would like to care for him until his owner is found, I think that would be fine."

"Oh thank you, *Babu!*" the boy flew with open arms, nearly knocking the old man over with a hug. Buster whimpered and tried to stand. "See, even he thinks that is a good idea!"

"Yes, it seems he understands we will care for him. Fetch me another leaf; let's see how this dog feels about a sweet treat." The old man removed the leather pouch that hung around his shoulder. Gently cupping it in one hand, he untied with the other hand the long thin leather straps that tethered the ends. Slowly the sides fell apart, and a fist-sized piece of creamy white cone stood dripping with golden sweet honey pooling in the cup. Tiwas grinned up at his grandfather, watching his *babu* delicately scoop up two fingers full of the sweetness. Smearing it on the leaf, he then wiped the excess on the edge and held his fingers up for the boy to lick clean. "See if this animal understands the sweet value of the forest gift."

Tiwas held the leaf up for Buster to sniff and immediately he began to lick at the golden sweetness. "He is truly a smart dog, *Babu!*"

"Yes, indeed!" Teresit agreed. The morning sun rose warmly as the pair, young and old, stayed with the dog until he arose on his own and seemed strong on his legs. They continued to water the dog slowly until he was more interested in playing with his new friends than drinking. Teresit finally rose, "We must go on and check the hives; the day is nearly half over. Let's see if this dog chooses to follow us."

As they began to walk away, following the path along which they had come, Buster waited in the center of the clearing. The dog looked over his shoulder in the opposite direction, then back at his new-found friends. Buster gave a little bark, and they stopped. He turned and walked a few feet in the opposite direction, then stopped and looked back at the pair. When they turned and started walking away, the dog barked again. Once more they stopped and looked at the dog. He took one step towards them, and then glanced back over his shoulder in the opposite direction.

Tiwas tried to coax the dog to join them, but Buster stood his ground and began to whimper, continuing to glance over his shoulder. The young boy looked up at his grandfather who said, "Perhaps we should see what it is the dog wants to show us."

When they took their first steps towards the dog, Buster's tail began to wag. With his nose to the ground, following his own path, the dog led Teresit and Tiwas across the hills and down the slope to the muddy bog at the bottom of the watershed. They followed the dog up the next hill and across two others to a small clearing, under a big *mugumo* tree.

As Buster entered the clearing he trotted towards the tattered body of a young black man and the small chimpanzee beside him. At first sight of the dog, the chimp hesitantly knuckle-walked halfway to the big tree and sat down to watch as the dog licked Mhinga's badly bruised face.

Moments later, when Teresit and Tiwas emerged into the clearing, the chimp let out a piercing scream and quickly scampered up the big tree. From the safety of a high limb he watched as the strangers approached the motionless body and the dog.

"*Babu!*" Tiwas shouted out. "Did you see it? Did you see the chimp?" The boy was nearly jumping up and down.

"Tiwas, wait here." Teresit's voice was strong and firm. Glancing from the chimp high in the tree to the battered young man, the old man carefully made his way across the clearing. Kneeling down, he pushed

Buster aside. His calloused, bony fingers gently felt Mhinga's neck, searching for a pulse. It was stronger than he had imagined. Glancing around the tattered campsite, he motioned to Tiwas to approach.

With soft steps, the boy carefully moved forward and knelt next to his grandfather. "What happened to him?" His voice was tiny and frail, all enthusiasm gone. "Is he dead?"

"No, but he is badly hurt," Teresit said low and serious. "Tiwas, see if you can get that fire started and here . . . ." Off his shoulder he took his gourd *kabash* filled with water and handed it to the boy. "Boil half of this. When you go for firewood, take the dog with you." The boy rose without question and began working on the fire.

Teresit gently rolled Mhinga onto his back and looked for any signs of open wounds. He found none. Beside Mhinga, he noticed long skinny strips of light brown bark curled on top of slender fuzzy leaves. Curiously, he fingered through the pile. The scraps of bark had been carefully peeled off a freshly picked stem. The old gentleman poked around for the stem's pith. It was not in the pile. Glancing out of the corner of his eye, he gave a knowing smile to the little chimp peering down at him. In a soft voice Teresit spoke, "Did you do this?"

Tiwas looked over his shoulder at his grandfather. The fire was crackling brightly, and he was pouring water into the small aluminum pot. "Do what?"

"Oh, I was talking to the chimp. He has been trying to help this man."

"How was he doing that?" the boy asked.

Teresit winked at his grandson. "Come look at this pile." Tiwas moved closer as his grandfather continued, "See how the chimp picked off the leaves and peeled back the bark from the stem?"

"Yes. But where is the stem?"

A slow grin revealed a toothless proud smile. "Do you recognize this leaf?" he quizzed his grandson.

The boy took the leaf and studied both sides carefully. "Yes, I remember it." Making a sour face, he said, "You took the leaves and the bark off and gave me the stem to chew on when you thought I had worms. It tasted awful." He dropped the leaf. "But I cannot think of its name."

Teresit smiled and nodded, "It is called *Lwago.* You were very sick. Remember? Diarrhea, and very weak, and, oh, you had lost so much weight. You had the worms all right, and you were much better soon after you chewed on the stem."

The boy picked through the pile of leaves and bark. "But where is the stem? Did the chimp eat it?"

Teresit let the question hang in the air for just a few seconds. Patiently, Tiwas watched his skilled *babu* examine the unconscious man. Soon he leaned over and opened Mhinga's swollen mouth. White pieces of bark wedged between his lips and gums. The boy's eyes widened as he watched his grandfather pull the morsels out of the man's mouth. As he worked, Teresit said, "The chimp knows of this plant, too."

Chapter 38

Mhinga's head rolled to the side and his eyelids flickered, responding to Teresit's gentle touch. Kneeling beside the tattered body, the old Okiek tribesman dabbed a warm wet rag over the battered face, washing away the dirt and the dried blood. Slowly Mhinga's eyes began to open, and Teresit rocked back on his heels, giving him room to move. Young Tiwas sat cross-legged on the opposite side with Buster's head in his lap. Slowly Mhinga's eyes opened, they were badly bruised. One just a narrow slit, showing barely any white; the other was nearly normal in size, but the creamy white was red with blood.

Teresit smiled warmly at the young man and said, "You are going to be all right." He pointed, and Mhinga's eyes followed his direction to the young boy. "My grandson and I will stay with you until you are. You took quite a beating and are badly bruised. You may have a couple of broken ribs, but that is all I could find. Would you like some water?"

Slowly Mhinga nodded and tried to force a grateful smile. The old man cradled Mhinga's neck and shoulders with his arm, gently raising his

297

torso so he could drink from the *kabash*. Mhinga's face contorted with pain, until the lukewarm water eased his dry, parched mouth. "Not too fast," the old man coached, as Mhinga gulped down the much-needed fluid. "You don't want to overdo it. Just a little bit at a time." Removing the long gourd from Mhinga's lips, the old man lowered him back to the ground.

Buster inched over and, whining concern, licked Mhinga's face. Very weakly Mhinga reached up and stroked the dog's back. Moving closer, Buster curled up beside his friend and rested his long muzzle on Mhinga's shoulder. Tiwas' shoulders slumped as he asked, "Is this your dog?" Mhinga slowly nodded his head. The child asked, "Are you a poacher?"

"Tiwas!" the old man snapped. "This is not the time for such questions. Go and gather some greens, so I can make a tea for our patient."

Bowing his head, Tiwas began to rise, and Mhinga's hand reached up and squeezed the youth's arm. Looking shamefully at the battered face, Tiwas said, "I'm sorry, I shouldn't have asked you that question."

Mhinga rocked his head back and forth and pulled the young boy closer. In a rough, scratchy voice, he said, "No. I am not a poacher," and released the boy's arm.

A broad smile spread across Tiwas' face, "See, *Babu!* I knew this dog was too nice to belong to a poacher!" The boy rattled on, "*Babu* said I could care for the dog. We found him this morning far away by the river. We took care of him, like we are taking care of you."

"Yes," the old man smiled as he interrupted. "Now go on and fetch me the greens."

"One more question, please, Grandfather," the boy begged. Teresit looked at Mhinga, who nodded his head. Tiwas leaned over and asked, "What's his name?"

The boy's pure innocence and the kindness these two strangers were showing him overwhelmed Mhinga. A tear welled in the corner of his eye and rolled down his cheek. The small smile split his bruised and swollen lips as he softly said, "Buster. His name is Buster. Thank you for caring for him so well."

The boy continued excitedly, "Oh you are a kind man. I can see it now . . . ."

"Tiwas!" Teresit's voice was soft but firm. "Go fetch the greens. When this man is feeling stronger, you can tell him all about how we found the dog."

"Can Buster go with me?" Tiwas looked to his grandfather, who looked to Mhinga. Nodding, Mhinga stopped stroking the dog's coat. As Tiwas rose, he called to the dog, "Come on, Buster," using the name proudly. "Come on, let's go pick some greens so that . . . ." His voice trailed off and he looked down at Mhinga, "What is your name?"

"Mhinga," the weak voice broke through tears.

"Come on, Buster, let's get some greens for grandfather to make a tea for Mhinga." Buster got up and wagged his tail happily. He followed the boy around the clearing and into the forest.

"He is a fine child," Mhinga choked out and pointed to the *kabash* of water.

"Yes," the old man agreed, as he raised Mhinga up for another drink, "and so full of energy."

"He reminds me of my nephew Khosa. They are about the same age. He loves Buster, too." The fluid nourished Mhinga, and his voice became stronger.

The old man opened his pouch and offered some honey to Mhinga. "I am sorry that he asked you such a question."

Dipping his finger into the sweetness, Mhinga nodded his head in thanks and said, "He meant no harm."

The sound of Mhinga's voice provoked movement high in the big tree. The little chimp moved down to the lower branches. Now, he could easily watch what was happening below.

The two men shared the honey pouch and the water kabash. "We have seen signs of poachers in the area, and it is not often that others come this deeply into the forest."

"Have the poachers been here long?" Mhinga asked.

Teresit thought for a few seconds, "Several months."

Mhinga looked around the campsite, before asking, "Is there anyone else here?"

The old man just shook his head. Then a bright smile broke across his face revealing a dark hole from two missing front teeth. "Well, there was a chimpanzee watching over you when we arrived." Teresit pointed into the tree overhead. "He scampered up there when we entered the campsite."

Mhinga smiled and glanced up at the tree. He could see the chimp sitting quietly at the base of a thick limb. His smile faded as he asked, "But no other people?"

"No, just the chimp. He was taking care of you."

Raising an eyebrow, Mhinga questioned, "What do you mean?"

Teresit raised a leaf and a white stem, peeled of its bark, for Mhinga to see. "Do you know what this plant is?"

Mhinga shook his head.

"This is *Lwago*. Its stem, when peeled and chewed, helps rid the body of worms. That little chimp had stuffed some of it in your mouth. You are lucky he only got it in between your gums and cheek or you might have choked to death on it."

Mhinga's chuckling was cut short by the riveting pain in his ribs. "So he thought I had worms!"

"He probably saw you as weak and lifeless. He gave you what he might have once eaten to make him feel better."

The smile on Mhinga's face faded, and he looked seriously at the old man. "There was a woman here, a white woman. Did you see any sign of her?"

"No. I searched the area when we first arrived, a few hours ago. There was just you and the chimp. Do you want to tell me what happened here?"

Mhinga nodded his head sadly. "It is a long story. But in short, there are four American scientists here studying plants, searching for a cure for slims. They have somehow gotten tangled up with the poachers and were being held hostage. One of the scientists was killed. Another one is the father of the woman who came here looking for them. When we started out, we didn't know they were being held by the poachers."

"How many are in your group?" the old man asked.

"We started out as four -- myself, the woman, Ms. Mac, *Bwana* Jon Corbett and a Maasai friend, Zawawi. We spotted the poachers taking two young bull elephants and pursuing a huge old bull."

The old man interrupted, "Does this bull have tusks as big around as a young girl's waist, and so long they almost touch the ground?"

"Yes!" Mhinga exclaimed. "You know of this elephant?"

Teresit nodded his head. "He came to the forest when I was a young man. I have seen him many times. He must be of the plains because he is so much bigger than our forest elephants. I have not seen him for many months. I thought the poachers had gotten him until this morning when we saw him with your Buster." Mhinga's good eye widened. "I will let my *toto* tell you the story. Please go on with yours."

"When we saw the poachers taking the elephants, we radioed my brother-in-law, Simon Kuldip. He is an army colonel serving in Kenya's Wildlife Service Anti-poaching Unit. The poachers spotted us and sent gunmen after us. We hid in a cave and eventually we escaped. While all that was happening, Simon and his men raided the poachers campsite and captured most of them, but the leader and a few of the trackers were already gone."

Teresit finished Mhinga's thought, "They were trailing the big elephant."

"Yes. Eventually Simon and one of his men caught up with us and we found the scientists' camp. We made friendly contact with them. Ms. Mac's father is very frail and ill, but he was able to slip her a message about being held hostage. So yesterday, Jon, Zawawi, Simon, and Jay went off to rescue the scientists."

"Leaving you and the white woman here for safety." Teresit was following along perfectly.

From the tree a soft little chant began calling out, *"Hooo!her-hoo!her-hoo!her."* Then the chimp smacked his lips together several times and grunted, *"Hu-hu-hu."*

The old man listened carefully to the chimp saying his piece. "I think the sound of your voice has stirred up some bravery in your little friend. When does he come into your story?"

"Ah, yes," Mhinga smiled, "I will wait for your grandson to return for that story."

Teresit offered the water *kabash* to Mhinga and said, "Yes he will like hearing that. Please go on."

Mhinga swallowed the water and shifted, trying to get comfortable. His body ached, and he moved slowly. "So the other men had gone to rescue the scientists, and early last evening strangers came into our camp. They claimed they had been hunting and gotten lost, then saw our fire."

"The poacher and his trackers?" Teresit asked.

Nodding his head, Mhinga continued, "And two other men. Soldiers, I think. They had tattooed scars across their cheeks. I didn't recognize the markings as local tribes. There were also the two trackers, Zawawi's sons, Valli and Khosa."

"Khosa? The nephew you said reminded you of my *toto*?" Teresit sat back in surprise.

"Yes. In many ways," Mhinga explained, "they are about the same age and size. Khosa has a gentleness about him like your *toto*. But his mother died when he was quite young, and his older brother, Valli, looked after him. Zawawi did not handle the death of his wife very well and unfortunately didn't pay much attention to his sons. Valli left his father's *kraal* almost a year ago, and Khosa followed him. They are not bad kids. Really. But they have gotten tangled up in a bad situation."

Teresit listened patiently and nodded his head. "I understand. I have seen similar things happen within my tribe. Let me guess what happened last night. Many loose ends came together, and the poacher's scar-faced men did this to you. The boys knew you and easily figured that you and this woman were not traveling alone. So this leader, who is he?"

"He is a Frenchman. He introduced himself as Dubois. His family owns one of the logging companies. It is the same company that gave the scientists permission to go onto the leased land for their study."

The chimp moved to the lowest branch and began his soft chant again. *"Hooo!her-hooo!her-hoo!her."* Then he smacked his lips together several times and grunted, *"Hu-hu-hu."*

Ignoring the chimp, the old man nodded his head at Mhinga. "It sounds like he has quite an operation. His men tried to get information out of you. They beat you up and left you for dead, then they took the woman as a hostage in case they ran across the other members of your group."

Lying back down, Mhinga said weakly, "Yes, that is how it looks." Then rolling back onto his side, he tried to rise, saying, "I must go after her. She is in great danger."

Teresit gently pushed Mhinga back down. "You are in no shape to help her, and I am much too old, and Tiwas is just a little child. When are your men coming back?"

Mhinga did not have the strength to resist the old man's push. "If all went well with the rescue, they should be back this afternoon."

Teresit shook his head, "We will have to wait." The old man stood and stretched. "When Tiwas returns, I will brew you a tea to help with the bruising and swelling. Soon the pain will go away." As he walked away from Mhinga, he spoke over his shoulder, "You rest quietly to regain your strength, and I will search for something to eat."

Mhinga raised his arm and pointed in another direction. "I found some wild ndole growing just beyond the bush line, and a few feet further on the other side of a fallen tree were some young shoots of mushrooms."

Teresit stopped in mid-stride. Turning quickly, he hurried back to Mhinga's side. Kneeling down, the old man looked closely at the bruised face. "How do you know about wild spinach and edible mushrooms?"

"My father works as a master gardener for the Uganda Presidential Palace. He is from a forest tribe. My mother is from India and works there too as the chef. I learned about cooking and using many native plants from them." As Mhinga spoke he watched the old black man's face turn gray. "Are you all right?"

"What tribe is your father from?" the old man asked, starting to tremble.

Mhinga rolled over onto his side, and propped himself on his elbow. Looking deeply at the gentle face, he could not see past the confusion and anxiety that clouded the old man's eyes. "My father is a descendant of the Okiek tribe. Do you know of them?"

Slowly the old man toppled back until he was sitting on the ground. Drawing his knees up to his chest, he locked his arms around them for support. Trembling, he lowered his head into the crook of his elbow. Mhinga watched quietly as the man gathered his wits and gained control of his shakiness. Slowly he lifted his gray head and asked, "Is your father's name Sururu Kusak? And is he a bit younger than me?"

Mhinga stared out of his one good eye for only a second. Hearing this old man, a stranger, speak his father's name filled him with something he could not identify.

His voice came as if someone else were speaking. "Yes." The softness in his voice sounded more like a question than an answer.

"Sururu Kusak is my younger brother. He left the forest nearly thirty years ago. How old are you?"

"I am nearly twenty. My sister, Colleen, is twenty-eight, and has three children of her own. Her husband is the colonel I told you about, Simon."

"It was just this morning, before we saw your dog, that I told Tiwas about my brother who left the forest. He is not yet old enough to understand the powerful hold a woman's love may have on a man. How are they? Do they have many children?"

For several long minutes Mhinga and Teresit talked of Sururu and his life away from the forest, and together they shed tears of joy. When Tiwas returned with his hands full of greens, the men shared their news. The boy was full of questions, and Mhinga answered them all, even recounting the events up to the beating and how the chimp came into their group.

As they talked, they did not notice that the little chimp had climbed down from the security of the tree and sat hunched, watching from a safe distance. Buster walked around the camp and approached the little chimp. Lying by the chimp's side, the dog rolled onto his back, encouraging the chimp to groom his belly.

When Teresit finally rose to search for edible plants, they all noticed the dog and the chimp together. Tiwas started to jump up, but was restrained by his grandfather. "Just wait, my little *toto*. When the chimp is ready, he will approach you. Do not rush or you will scare him back up the tree." Tiwas sat down next to where Mhinga lay; from there he could watch Buster and the chimp together while he talked to his new-found cousin. Teresit moved quietly to the other side of the camp and slipped into the forest to forage for food.

As the afternoon shadows grew longer, Mhinga was able to sit with less pain. The swelling around his eye and on his face had gone down a great deal thanks to the herbal tea that Teresit had brewed. The men conversed comfortably as if they had always known each other.

Tiwas had moved a little closer to Buster and the chimp. Every few minutes the boy slowly eased his way a few inches closer to the chimp. Buster moved freely back and forth between the boy and the chimp, enjoying the dual attention.

Teresit reached over and stirred the hot coals and tossed on another log to brighten the flames in the dimming light. As the limb landed in the smoldering ash, he heard sounds of men coming up the hillside. He turned to Mhinga and said, "I believe your friends are returning."

Jon ran ahead of the others and burst into the campsite at full stride. The sight of the old man stopped him. The stranger standing in front of him was not who he had expected to see. Teresit saw the flash of confusion on Jon's face and stepped aside so that he had a clear view of Mhinga sitting by the fire. Buster ran across the campsite and landed his front paws onto Jon's chest. Bewildered, Jon stood frozen, unable to tear his eyes away from Mhinga's battered body. With one hand he automatically stroked the dog's back, then pushed Buster aside and glanced at the old gray-haired man. Jon then crossed over and knelt beside Mhinga. "My God, what happened to you? Are you all right?"

Mhinga nodded, then his blood-bruised eyes flooded with tears, and he gave in to his emotions. Jon tore his eyes away from the battered face and pulled Mhinga close, comforting his young friend.

The chimpanzee moved closer. Squatting next to Mhinga's back, the chimp reached out to touch the trembling shoulders.

Glancing over his shoulder, Jon saw the old man standing back several yards, holding the hand of a young boy. "Who are you? What happened here?" Jon asked.

Simon, Zawawi, and the two scientists, carrying Jay on a crudely made stretcher, entered the campsite as the old man introduced himself and his grandson. Setting the stretcher down, Simon ran over to Jon and Mhinga. He lifted his nephew's face and gasped at the bruising. Tears ran down the young man's cheeks. "Mhinga," Simon's voice was velvety smooth, "tell me who did this to you." Mhinga tried to form the words but he could only weep and shake his head in shame.

Jon looked around the camp, then asked, "Where's MacKenzie? Mhinga you must get hold of yourself. Where is MacKenzie?" Mhinga just shook his head; he could not form the words.

Teresit spoke up, "Mhinga told me that a Frenchman named Dubois came into the camp last night."

Both Jon's and Simon's attention snapped to the old man. Mhinga mumbled, "Listen to him, he can tell you."

As Jon stood, the little chimp bounced over Mhinga and climbed up Jon's body, clinging to the man's broad shoulders.

Teresit continued, "There were five of them altogether -- the Frenchman, two fighting men with scars across their cheeks, and two young boys." Teresit looked at Zawawi with compassion and said slowly, "Their names were Valli and Khosa." Zawawi dropped his eyes momentarily, and the old man went on, "They beat Mhinga when he wouldn't tell them where you were. They took the woman with them."

"What!" Jon bellowed. "Dubois has MacKenzie?"

"I tried." Mhinga's words were finally released. "I tried to stop them. Dubois struck Khosa, and Ms. Mac went wild, screaming and yelling at Dubois. I was being held and could not help. I pleaded with her to be quiet, but her temper was hot. Dubois struck her and knocked her out. That is when they started on me. I don't remember anything else until this afternoon, when Buster led Teresit and Tiwas to me."

"Stupid white woman doesn't know when to keep her mouth shut," Zawawi mumbled to himself. Jon looked over at Simon, and then together they looked disgustedly at Zawawi. Pounding his spear on the ground, the Maasai stood tall and straight as he spoke loudly, "We are wasting time here. They have a good head start on us."

Jay moaned from his delirious fever. Simon left Mhinga's side and crossed to where Jay lay. Feeling his scalding forehead, Simon said, "We must get him to a hospital first."

"You get Jay to a clearing and radio for a helicopter," said Jon, his face flushed with rage. "I'm going after MacKenzie. You two can catch up with me later."

"Wait a minute, Jon." Simon stood and faced his friend. "We've got to work together on this. If you go off alone, you're just going to get yourself killed."

Teresit pushed Jon and Simon apart. "Perhaps I can help." Kneeling beside the stretcher, the old man gently lifted the bandage from Jay's shoulder. As the scab tore off, the hot pink flesh surrounding the wound stank of infection and blood oozed out. Carefully, Teresit poked his finger into the hole. "Tiwas, get that water boiling again," the old man said, as he dug deeper into the hole.

"Can you help him?" Simon asked.

"Yes, I think so. I'll know in a second," Teresit murmured as he probed deeply into the wound. Then a hollow thud popped from inside Jay's shoulder, and curdled pus gushed out of the wound. Don and Henry stood back watching with amazement. Looking up at Simon, Teresit said, "You men go and find the Frenchman and your white woman. My grandson and I will stay here and care for your friends." Tiwas had the pot of water started, "*Toto,* do you remember what the *Mkungumwelu* plant looks like?" The youth nodded his head. "Good. Go get as much as you can find, roots and all. Also, look for *Kamnyowanyowa* leaves. Pick off only the young small leaves, get all that you can carry and hurry back. We must break this fever and stop the infection from spreading."

Don elbowed Henry in the ribs, "Let's go help the kid and see what he's getting."

"Yes! Bring back as much as you can carry. Go quickly now. *Haraka, haraka,*" Teresit exclaimed. Then turning to Simon, he said, "You must go quickly, too."

As Simon turned to leave, he smiled gratefully at Teresit. Jon lowered the little chimp to the ground. "You stay here with Mhinga," he said, shrugging the creature off his shoulder. But as Jon rose, the chimp dashed back up the man's muscular frame. Gently, he tried to remove the chimp again, but the little creature hung on with unexpected strength.

"Carry him a little way," Zawawi suggested. "He will soon grow tired or hungry and want down. Perhaps we can rid ourselves of it."

Jon fought a few more minutes with the chimp. Screaming and clawing now, the chimp refused to leave Jon's shoulders. "Come on, Jon." Simon was growing impatient. "He'll jump off in an hour or so. We're losing ground on Dubois and Mac every minute." With a shrug of his shoulders, Jon gave in to his passenger, and the men took off, backtracking to the scientists' campsite to pick up Dubois' trail.

Chapter 39

Heading west, Gbenya led a strung-out line of people towards Lifi. Located just ten miles beyond the Kenya border, the abandoned Uganda mining town was a small cluster of empty buildings, used as the base for Dubois' poaching operation. From there, the meats and pelts of exotic and endangered animals were processed, packaged, and stored until the freezer-trucks had a full load. The poached goods were then trucked to either a presidential palace or to the large rented freezer warehouse located in the Congo Republique city of Ouesso. From this Congolese city, the commercial heart of the bushmeat industry, the meat would be packaged for sale in the markets or smuggled by air into Europe for restaurants.

In the early morning, they maintained a fast pace, putting many miles between them and the team that had rescued the scientists. By mid-afternoon, lack of sleep and food had slowed the group to a lingering saunter. Avoiding Dubois, Valli kept close to Gbenya. Together, they trekked ahead, blazing a trail for the others to follow.

Cresting a hill, they saw the forest opened into a wide clearing that continued down the far slope. Gbenya stopped at the edge and waited for Dubois to catch up. Lagging far behind the big Frenchman were Khosa, MacKenzie, and Tshombe. Dubois labored up the hillside, his rifle hung carelessly over his slumped shoulder, perspiration marking his armpits and streaking down the front of his shirt. Dubois was breathing hard when he caught up with Gbenya and Valli. Dropping his rifle, the Frenchman stretched his aching back. The scar-faced poacher spoke first. "There is a good resting spot just across the field, into the woods a little ways. We have snares nearby. With luck we will have good meat."

Dubois nodded his approval. "You two go on and check the snares. Tshombe and Khosa will set up a cooking fire." The young Maasai and the scar-faced Madi tribesman cut across the field, weaving a crooked path through the tall yellow grass. Shouldering his rifle, once more the white man glanced back at the others. They were slowly coming up the shady hillside. Not waiting to wait for them to catch up, Dubois stepped into the bright sunshine and crossed the field. The hot sun sucked the moisture from his soaked shirt, drying it completely by the time he reached the other side. A few dozen yards inside the bush, Dubois found the area Gbenya had described. Obviously, his men used this spot regularly.

Centered in a small clearing was an oblong ring of rocks filled with a mound of gray ash. Propped on four high rocks, one on each corner, an iron grate spanned the campfire. A small, dented aluminum pot hung from a nail in a nearby tree. A few feet away, on both sides of the campfire, two logs were positioned for sitting. Dubois was making himself comfortable as Tshombe led Khosa and the woman into the compound.

"Where are Gbenya and Valli?" Tshombe asked Dubois.

"They went to check the snares." Then waving his arm around in the air, Dubois asked, "Do you always leave such obvious campsites when you're out hunting?"

Tshombe hung his rifle on a tree limb stub, as he had done many times before. Shrugging the stiffness out of his shoulders and pointing to the east, he said, "There is a small tribe that lives three or four hilltops over. This is their campsite. They use it when they harvest their honey." Nodding to the treetops, he continued, "They have many beehives in the trees around this field. They don't bother our snares, and we don't bother their hives."

Dubois leaned back against the log. "You and Khosa get that fire going. They'll be back with some meat soon. We'll rest for a few hours then get going again." Khosa dutifully dropped the end of the leash around MacKenzie's neck and began picking up small twigs and bark for kindling, while Tshombe dragged in a larger log and set up the cooking fire. Looking at MacKenzie, the Frenchman patted the ground next to him. "You might as well come over here and sit down. We can talk while the men work."

Through puffy, blood-shot eyes, MacKenzie stared expressionlessly at the white man with the wire-framed glasses. He patted the ground again and smiled. Her stomach twisted and turned. The beating, the long hard trek, the heat, and the trauma of seeing her father being carried out of the blazing fire in Jon's arms and shot at by this depraved, white man was too much for her. Turning to one side, she dropped to her knees and vomited.

Turning his head in disgust, Dubois barked, "Ugh! You vulgar American!" His words had no effect; MacKenzie was numb and near exhaustion. Khosa dropped his twigs and ran to help her. "Get away from her!" Dubois snapped at the youth. "You little black flea! She doesn't need your help. Get back to building the fire."

Khosa hesitated for a second. Forcing a little smile, MacKenzie, gave a nod for him to go on. Reluctantly the child left. With her hands tied securely behind her back, she wobbled weakly trying not to fall face first into the pool of foul-smelling vomit. Regaining her balance, she rocked back and wiped her mouth across her dirty shirtsleeve. Squirming backwards, she managed to wiggle her back up against a tree. Closing her eyes and leaning her head back, she gulped in deep breaths of fresh air, ridding her mouth of the vile taste of vomit and calming her shaky nerves.

Watching her closely, Dubois scowled again, and demanded, "Clean it up!"

Without moving her head, MacKenzie cracked open her eyes and gazed at him with malice.

"Clean it up, you bitch, or I'll hold your face in it and make you eat it." He yelled in his French accent. Khosa stopped his work and glanced between the two white people. Without changing his pose, Dubois snapped at Khosa, "I told you to get back to work!"

Glaring at Dubois, MacKenzie edged forward and kicked some dirt and leaves over her vomit. She tilted her head, waiting for his approval.

Leaning back against the log, Dubois snickered at the woman, "Now there's a good bitch, doing as she's told and burying her waste." He laughed aloud. "How about that, Tshombe? She was easier to housebreak than a puppy."

"Yes," Tshombe laughed with him, "but a good dog is more useful than a white woman. What will we do with her when we get back to Lifi?"

Dubois was still snickering, "I think I have that figured out." He took his wide-brimmed hat off and ran his fingers across his greasy scalp.

"I do some business with an Arab fellow. He has a taste for white women. I think he would be very interested in this feisty one."

Tshombe flashed a glance at MacKenzie. She had scooted back to the tree and closed her eyes. He knew she was still listening and not asleep. Turning back to Dubois, he asked rather coldly, "Does this man want the hide or just the meat? There is not much of either on her."

"I believe he takes them whole and keeps them alive until he tires of them. After that . . . ." Dubois' voice faded as he leaned his head back and closed his eyes. "After I'm paid, I don't really care. Wake me when the meat is cooked."

Within minutes Dubois, had fallen into a deep, noisy sleep. His head bobbed forward onto his chest, and his eyes closed.

Quietly, Khosa sat next to MacKenzie, laying his head upon her shoulder. In his soft child's voice he whispered to her, "Are you afraid?"

Nodding her head, MacKenzie kissed the top of the boy's head, and whispered back, "Yes. Are you?"

"Some," the little voice answered back. "I have Valli to protect me. But you have no one."

"Oh, Khosa." MacKenzie fought back the tears welling up.

"I tried. But I'm afraid of him."

"I know you did, Khosa. He is a very dangerous man."

Pulling back, Khosa looked into MacKenzie's tearful eyes. "Maybe I can get Valli to protect you, so the *Bwana* won't sell you to the Arab man."

"You love your brother very much, don't you?" Tears rolled down her dirty cheeks.

"Yes." Khosa cuddled up close again. "After our mom died, he took care of me. He taught me many things while our father mourned."

MacKenzie started to compose herself. "Your father was very sad for a long time?"

"Yes. I think he is still sad. But he has other wives and children now."

"Does he spend more time with them?"

Khosa thought hard. "Not really. That's why I think he is still sad."

"You are a wise little boy." MacKenzie did not know what else to say. He did not respond, so they sat quietly together, lost in their own minds. She thought he had fallen asleep until he spoke again.

The boy's voice was very soft, "Why are you so sad? Is it because *Bwana* Dubois hit you and beat up Mhinga? And what he did to Buster? All of that makes me very sad."

"It makes me sad, too. But you see," MacKenzie explained, "my father is very sick, and I'm worried about him."

Twisting around to look at MacKenzie's face, Khosa said, "Sometimes I think Valli is very sick. His eyes aren't always clear."

"What do you mean?" she asked the young boy.

"Well, when we go hunting he gets really quiet, and his eyes get real big and spooky-looking. Sometimes I can hear his heart pumping like thunder, trying to get out of his chest. And not too long ago, he thought Petrus and Taveta were big chimpanzees."

"Who are they?"

"Oh, they worked for *Bwana* Dubois. Petrus was his cook and Taveta helped with the skinning, and he guarded the campsites at night."

"What happened to them?"

"Valli got all spooky-looking and thought they were big chimpanzees, and he shot them with *Bwana* Dubois' gun. But I don't think he is sick anymore. I haven't heard his heart trying to get out of his chest for a long, long time. So he must be better. I will ask Valli to protect you. You should have someone to protect you from the *bwana.*"

"You know, Khosa, I don't think that is a good idea. I do have someone to protect me, and I'm sure it won't be long until they come here and get me."

"Really? Who?"

"Your friend Jon and your uncle Simon, and I bet your father Zawawi will come, too, and if you want, you could leave with us."

The young boy responded quickly, "Oh, no," he shook his head. "I bet my father won't come. He hates white women. I don't know why, but he does."

"Well, let's just wait and see, shall we?" She kissed him again on top of his head. "And let's not mention this to anyone, okay? It will be like a secret game between you and me. What do you think about that?"

"Okay. We'll see if my father comes or not. But I'm sure that he won't."

"Khosa, I want you to know that I think you are a really nice boy, and I'm glad you are my friend. I need a good friend, and here you are."

"I like you, too, Ms. Mac. You are not what I thought a white woman would be like." The boy let out a big yawn. "My father doesn't like white women. But I'll bet if he got to know you, he'd like you just as much as I do."

"Thank you, Khosa." MacKenzie yawned too. "Why don't we see if we can take a little nap while we're waiting for your brother and the other men to come back with the meat?"

Khosa lay on the ground resting his head on MacKenzie's lap. Within a few seconds the little boy was sound asleep. Tilting her head back against the tree, MacKenzie closed her eyes. Her body slumped and relaxed, but her mind raced over Khosa's words about his brother. Had he really killed two people? How long would it be before Jon and Simon caught up with them? Were Mhinga and her father alive? What was going to happen to her and this child? She could not sleep as her mind spun wildly. Long minutes later, she heard Valli and Gbenya stomping through the underbrush. As they entered the camp, she pretended to be asleep.

The men began preparations to cook the meat. When it was done, they woke everyone and ate in silence. Khosa tore off small pieces of meat and hand-fed MacKenzie.

Tossing a rib into the fire, Dubois licked his finger. Turning to Gbenya, he asked, "How much farther to Lifi?"

Pulling off another piece of the roasted wild pork, Gbenya replied, "Hmm, I guess four and a half to five days without a good rest, or three to three and a half days with a good rest. We were moving very slowly today and will move more slowly each day without a good rest."

Dubois nodded. They were all near the point of exhaustion. With a good, long rest they could travel much faster.

Valli chuckled as he chewed the meat off a bone. "Six days with a rest and carrying beautiful ivory."

Raising an eyebrow, Dubois asked, "What are you talking about, Valli?"

Chewing very slowly, Valli eyed the big Frenchman out of the corner of his eye and smiled. When he finished his bite, the young Maasai leaned forward and cocked his head. "Remember that big bull we've been chasing around?"

Dubois sat back and crossed his arms over his chest. "How do you know it is the same elephant?"

Shaking his head in disbelief, Valli asked, "You still have doubts about my tracking abilities? That is a shame. You will lose out on those long ivory teeth. I tell you he is here, and he is close by. He could be yours in less than two days. Ask Gbenya. I showed him the spoor."

Dubois raised his eyebrow at Gbenya. With a mouth full of food, he could only nod his head. The poacher swallowed hard and spit out, "Yes, it is true. The old bull is servicing a pod of cows. He will not be leaving the area any time soon."

Slapping Valli on the shoulder, Dubois said, "Well, then, my son, it looks like you are about to earn your keep and collect a real pay pouch. Tshombe, you are going to get your long rest."

When talk of the elephant hunt died down and they had all eaten their fill, everyone but Dubois and Tshombe lay down and slept. It was the first food and sleep they had had in nearly forty-eight hours. Tshombe went to the edge of the clearing. He would take the first watch. After a few hours, Valli would take his place, and then Gbenya would relieve Valli. In the early morning, Dubois, Valli, and Gbenya would head out in search of the elephant. Once the ivory was collected, they would hurry on to Lifi and wrap things up. It was a simple plan and would be completed easily if no snags appeared.

Looking across the campsite at the white woman, Dubois wondered how long it would be until her people came for her. He had at least one full day's head start, possibly two. If he could bag that old bull elephant tomorrow or early the next day, they could be out of the area before Colonel Simon Kuldip caught up with them. It was a risk, but one worth taking. He had lost one whole operation to the Colonel, and he had lost a big portion of this one, but he would not lose it all. With those two long, beautiful, curved tusks, he could easily restock and re-establish himself. There was no doubt in his mind that he would soon be caressing those long ivory teeth.

Chapter 40

Sleeping in a coma-like state, MacKenzie was awakened by the tingling sensation of pins and needles. Electrifying jolts wiggled tiny pricks of pain down her tethered arms. The stinging developed into a throbbing pain as the cold wet dampness penetrated deep into her stiffened muscles. Lying on her side, pillowed on woody debris, she inhaled the earth's musty odors, fighting back the urge to sneeze. Opening her crust-filled eyes, her fogged mind struggled to evaluate the pain and sort out her plight. With her hands still tied behind her back, she rolled onto her knees and rested her forehead on the ground. Sitting up, she looked around the area. Grumbling noises seized her attention. Rolling her head slightly to the side, she saw Tshombe curled up in a fetal position. Cradling his rifle like a teddy bear, he was snoring.

MacKenzie tried to rise to her feet, but her body ached and resisted the movement. Slowly, on weak and wobbly legs she stood and looked around the quiet campsite. Remembering that Dubois, Gbenya, and Valli were leaving early to track an elephant, she scanned the area for Khosa. He was gone too. There was only her and Tshombe.

MacKenzie's mind whirled. *Run! Run!* Her weary consciousness demanded. Here was her chance to escape. Attempting to focus on the opportunity, she shook her head hard, thinking, if I can just cross the campsite without awakening him. She glared through bruised and swollen eyes at Tshombe sleeping like a baby. Just for a moment she had second thoughts about escaping without Khosa. I'll find Jon and the others, she consoled herself, and they will come back for him.

She studied the campsite before taking the first step. Glancing over at Tshombe, she took a deep breath and stepped out. From the corner of her eye, she saw that the gunman was still soundly asleep. Bravely she took another step and then another, always watching over her shoulder for any movement from Tshombe.

At the outer edge of the campsite, she let out a little sigh and stepped into the bushes. The underbrush rustled as her legs pushed past the broad leaves. Cringing at the swishing noise, she hesitated and listened. Goosebumps rose over her skin, and butterflies frolicked in her stomach. She fought back the urge to break into a wild run. Taking in a deep breath and holding it, she slowly looked over her shoulder at Tshombe. He was still sleeping. Quietly exhaling, she turned her back to the campsite and timidly took one quiet step at a time until she had made her way further from the sleeping gunman. With each step a rush of adrenaline pounded her heart fiercely against her chest.

In a few moments, she arrived at the edge of the treeline surrounding the hillside. Hesitating only a second, she listened for any sounds of Tshombe following her, but she heard only the hammering in her chest. The sight of the open field rattled her. Her stomach muscles tightened. Breaking into a savage run, she followed the wake in the tall grass where the group had crossed the day before. The long blades of golden grass were angled against her and tugged at her feet. Using high stepping, horse-like strides up the hillside, she quickly became weary. Her wrists, tied tightly at the small of her back, hindered her movement. Losing her balance, she staggered. The long, tough grasses got tangled around her feet. She stumbled and fell face first into the high grassy field. Unable to reach out and break the fall, her chest slammed onto the ground with a rigid thump, jarring her teeth and knocking the air from her lungs.

Lying on the ground, gasping, MacKenzie's body trembled uncontrollably. "Oh God, oh God," she pleaded softly. A cool dampness hung low in the deep grass and filled her lungs with a mild, chilling pain. As she coughed and wheezed, tears streamed down her cheeks. Trembling, she rolled onto her knees and vomited. Rolling onto her heels, she flung her head back and looked up at the cloudless African sky. Breathing in deep breaths of fresh air helped clear the vile taste from her mouth. "Stupid," she mumbled softly to herself with a shaky voice. "Zawawi is right. I am a stupid white woman, and I have no business here." Her shoulders shook, and she welcomed the tears. Salty drops rolled down her cheeks. She closed her eyes but was unable to shut out the brightness of the warm African sun. Soothed in the sunlight, MacKenzie's nerves quieted, and her mind slowly cleared. Taking in deep warm breaths of the summery air gave her new strength. She shook her head and said aloud, "NO! I won't give up that easily." MacKenzie listened carefully for any sounds of Tshombe. She chuckled to herself and thought, "He doesn't know I'm gone. I still have a chance." Slowly she rose and looked around. She was nearly across the field. Besides the wind rustling the tops of the tall, golden grass, there were no signs of movement. She felt alone and abandoned, but stronger. I'm not stupid, she thought to herself, I'm just learning as I go, and Zawawi will not be proven right.

Carefully and slowly, Mackenzie started following the golden wake up the hill. Once into the woods, she picked up her stride. Continuing her unbalanced gait, and watching the ground, she carefully avoided fallen limbs, hidden rocks, and other traps that might cause her to stumble and fall again. Jogging easily, she picked out landmarks from the day before, following the route that would take her back to the scientists' camp, and from there to where she last saw Mhinga. She was certain that somewhere along the way she would meet Jon and Simon.

After a few hours of following the ridge, MacKenzie's unsteady run slowed to a wobbly jog. She needed a rest, but fear pushed her on. Fatigue crept over her, and the landscape began to all look the same. Slowing to a walk, she continued down the slope where she crossed a narrow game trail. Pausing to gather her bearings and her breath, she rotated her shoulders and stretched her neck, working out the stiffness. Glancing at the trail in front of her, she saw from the day before the treaded prints of her hiking shoes embedded between the stones. She had found the path that led back to the scientists' burnt camp. Relief swept over her and soothed her aching body. Leaning against a large rock, she dropped her head, closed her eyes, and smiled.

Her dirty tee shirt was wet from sweat, and her leg muscles tingled from the long exertion. The tingling numbness in her fingers had gone nearly dead. She could feel nothing of her swollen hands, and trying to move them brought burning pain and stinging hot pins and needles. Opening her eyes, she tilted her head back and rotated her shoulders, working out the stiffness and preparing to move on. Absurd thoughts tempted her not to go on, but to wait instead for Jon and the others to find her. However, her tethered hands were a constant reminder of the dangers she had escaped. Soon, she thought, soon I'll run into Jon. I must keep going. Looking up into the tree's canopy, MacKenzie listened as the birds chirped and sang freely. Their music was all around her, and she relished its beauty.

She pushed off the rock, but her legs were weak, she continued at a slower pace. As she crested the next hill, the sound of the birds left her, and an eerie silence fell over the forest, stopping MacKenzie in her tracks. Something was wrong. What was it Mhinga had said? Her mind traced back. There was something he said about the birds being the overseers of the forest. She stood in the shady, silent forest listening for what might have alarmed the birds. Then she heard something running towards her. Turning around slowly, she saw him coming up the hill. Tshombe was running fast and strong.

MacKenzie's heart jumped with renewed energy. Taking off, she ran, looking for some place in the forest to hide. As she ran, she heard him shout, "Stop, bitch!" He had seen her.

Her heart pounded hard against her chest. Tingling sparks jumped deep within her weakened muscles. Hearing his footsteps closing in on her, she pushed herself harder. Running wildly down the slope from the scar-faced man, her stride lengthened and became clumsy.

Tshombe was well-rested and running fast. The hammering beat from each of his footsteps stabbed at MacKenzie's pounding heart. The thumping in her chest rose and battled the booming sounds filling her head. The unbalanced rhythms hindered her. Her long braid of hair bounced and swung around, adding to the madness. Adrenaline pumped wildly, seizing control of her body, and quickening her stride. Her long sloppy steps propelled her, although she was losing ground and could feel him closing in.

Sounds of his deep steady breaths turned her fear into frenzy. He had finally caught up with her. Reaching out, Tshombe grabbed MacKenzie's braid. As her head jerked back, she cried out in pain. Tshombe pulled MacKenzie to the ground. With her last bit of energy, MacKenzie struggled and screamed, but Tshombe overpowered the small woman and pinned her to the ground. With her hands tied behind her back she had no means of defense.

Rolling around on the ground, she screamed, "Get off of me!"

Tshombe laughed at the struggling woman. "You were not such a good chase. But I must get you back to camp before Dubois finds us gone."

"No!" she gritted through her teeth.

"No?" Tshombe laughed aloud. "No?" His voice turned cold and deep, "Missy, you do not have a say in the matter." Straddling her waist the scar-faced man leaned over her. When his face was only inches from hers, his expression changed. The exhileration from the game of chase had melted away. The streaks of tattooed scars across his cheeks took on an evil seriousness. His eyes flickered back and forth across hers. As he studied her face, his foul-smelling breath grew shallow and swift.

MacKenzie's chest heaved for air after the long chase. The sound of her heart pumping filled the narrow space between her and her tormentor. MacKenzie watched in horror as the man's expression hardened. She followed his eyes as they outlined her face, followed her neckline and gawked at her heaving chest. The pounding of her heart increased, and beads of sweat soaked through her dirty white tee shirt. She watched as his eyes slowly traced back up to her face, then widened as a devilish half-grin emerged.

MacKenzie screamed at the top of her lungs, "NO!" She screamed again, "Get off of me!"

Tshombe laughed as she struggled to sit up. Grabbing her by the shoulders, he shoved her back to the ground. Still screaming, MacKenzie kicked and bucked her hips trying to get rid of the man. Seizing her neck Tshombe's face drained of all expression and he growled, "You like to buck, Missy? Hmm? I've got something for you to buck on." With one hand clutched tightly around her neck, he reached down and pulled her tee shirt up to her neck. He hooked one finger under her bra between her breasts and pulled quickly. With a snap, the material gave way, and he roughly squeezed one of her breasts.

MacKenzie struggled and tried to scream, but Tshombe's grip was tight, and only a muffled cry wheezed out. She rocked her head and arched her back straining to open her air passageway.

The poacher leaned forward, supporting his upper body weight on her neck. With his free hand, he grabbed the top edge of her shorts and pulled hard. The button separated, and the zipper pulled opened.

Blood pulsated against the inside of MacKenzie's skull. She could feel it pooling, dammed against the large hand squeezing around her neck. Her body temperature rose, sweat oozed from every pore, and vessels of blood swelled and popped in her eyes.

Tshombe shifted his weight to tug at the leg openings of her shorts. The heaviness squeezing against her neck released. MacKenzie's restricted blood flowed freely again. The blood rushed into the nearly crushed veins, bringing with it a strangely warm, numbing sensation. Her airways opened, too, and she drifted into the numbness. Closing her eyes, she felt her shorts being pulled over her knees. Subdued by the numbness, she no longer struggled and felt strangely relaxed. She could breathe, and that was more important than what Tshombe was about to do to her. MacKenzie slipped into unconsciousness.

The man concentrated on working her shorts down her long legs. She no longer fought him. She had given in to him. Sitting up, Tshombe leered at the woman's pale flesh while he unbuckled his pants. He found the tan lines around her thighs, waist, and breasts repugnant. Ignoring his distaste, he spread her knees apart. On his knees, he wedged himself between MacKenzie's legs. As he lifted her legs, Tshombe heard a high-pitched noise whisk over his head.

His head snapped around, and he saw a small clump of earth kick up just to his left. In a flash, a second whizzing noise flew by his other side. As he quickly rose from the woman's body, pulling up his pants and grabbing for his rifle, a third shot sprayed up more dirt. Tshombe's military training took over. Crouching low, he started to run towards a tree, his eyes searching the wooded hillside for the source of the shots. He saw the white man running down the hill, a few hundred yards away. A fourth shot rang out, striking the black man in the left shoulder, shattering the bone and tearing away most of the flesh.

The first sounds of the old .375 Holland & Holland rifle still echoed between the hills as Tshombe's half-naked body bounced back onto the ground at MacKenzie's feet. The poacher's weapon was flung out of his hand and twirled through the air. Stunned, Tshombe slowly rolled onto his side, trying to support his wasted arm.

The white man still ran towards him. Tshombe saw the man was reloading. Clutching his arm, Tshombe slowly struggled to his feet. Dazed by the throbbing pain, he reached out to a tree for support. His left arm dangled from a shredded piece of skin over the shoulder. The natural weight of the arm pulled against the wound, stretching the skin until it tore loose from his body. Tshombe spun and dropped to his knees as waves of pain engulfed him and blood poured out of his body.

The white man fired another round. The bullet ripped open Tshombe's stomach. He hung his head drunkenly and watched as his red and gray insides slid through his fingers and oozed over the ground. A second hefty thump smashed into Tshombe's chest, flinging his torso backwards and sending his arm flying. The third shot snapped his head back, dribbling a tiny stream of blood from a small round hole in his forehead. The back of his head exploded, sending blood, bone and flesh splattering in every direction.

Jon was reloading a second time as he ran toward the lifeless body of the guard. He glanced down at MacKenzie, but passed by to double-check the bleeding man. He was very dead. Spinning around, Jon looked down at MacKenzie's naked body. Dropping to his knees he leaned over and cupped her cheek with the palm of his hand. "MacKenzie," he spoke softly, "Mac?" His thumb gently massaged her cheek. "Sweetheart, can you hear me?" With his other hand, Jon pulled down the woman's tee shirt covering her breasts. "Come on Mac, wake up." Slowly, her head rolled toward the feel of his hand, and her eyes opened. "You are all right. He didn't hurt you."

MacKenzie's lips trembled, and her face contorted, releasing all the terror she held. Tears flooded her eyes and streamed down her grubby cheeks. Pulling her close, Jon held her tightly. "Shh, you're all right. You are safe now. He didn't . . . ." His voice broke as he felt her whole body tremble. She buried her head in his neck. "He didn't . . . ." Jon kissed the side of her face. "He didn't hurt you. I got here in time. Do you understand?" He felt her nod. "Oh, Mac. You are all right, I'm here now." He closed his eyes and whispered it over and over. Holding her close, trying to absorb her pain, Jon did not notice Simon and Zawawi had approached.

Kneeling behind the woman, Simon looked at Jon. "Is she all right?" He spoke with a velvety whisper. Jon nodded. Untying

MacKenzie's hands, Simon continued, "There's no sign of the others. They must have been alone."

MacKenzie recognized Simon's voice and nodded. "Mac," Simon said softly, "When I release the pressure from around your wrists, it is going to really hurt. I need to massage the area to help get the circulation going. This is going to hurt, but we have to do it. All right?" She nodded and he continued. As the last wrap of the binding was released, a throbbing heat thrashed down her arms and centered in her hands. She screamed and bit her lip but did not pull away from Simon's massaging grip.

Zawawi chuckled. "Jon, you did a great job on this one." He was examining Tshombe's body, "You blew his whole arm off!"

"Never mind that," Simon snapped. "Does he have any papers on him?"

"No, nothing. Looks like he's clean," Zawawi's voice dropped. Tumbled up near the dead man's feet lay MacKenzie's shorts. Sympathetically, he picked them up and tapped Jon on the shoulder, "Here, she's going to need these." Simon moved over to Zawawi. They studied the poacher's body, turning their backs to MacKenzie.

With a nod, Jon took the shorts and held them for MacKenzie to slip her feet through. The soreness continued to pulsate up and down her arms, and her hands were almost useless. Shyly, she whispered, "Thank you," to Zawawi and Simon. While Jon zipped up her shorts, she asked, "Jon, what happened to Mhinga? Is he all right? Where's Jay?"

A loud ruckus interrupted her. The noise came toward them from deep in the underbrush. Simon and Zawawi leveled their rifles, and Jon jumped to his feet, dashing behind the tree for protection, with MacKenzie in his arms. Out from the bush, the little chimp emerged on all fours, dragging two very large leaf-covered branches as he charged. Stopping a few feet away, he stood up and screamed, waving and thrashing the branches around. Jon put MacKenzie down, and the others lowered their rifles. Wobbling on two feet and showing his full set of vicious teeth, the little chimp made his way past Simon and Zawawi to Tshombe's body. The primate looked back at MacKenzie and screamed. Raising the limbs high above his head, the primate began to beat the scarred face of the dead man. With ferocious rage, the chimp pummeled the lifeless body. His powerful blows crushed the skull, and the man's face collapsed into a bloody mass. Tossing down the branches, the chimp turned his attention to the severed arm. Picking it up, the chimp screamed and climbed high into a tree.

The four people watched in silent astonishment, unsure what they had just witnessed. Zawawi broke the silence with an uproarious laugh. Slapping Simon on the shoulder, he said, "You need to put that little hairy fellow on your payroll. He could take Jay's place while he's recovering."

MacKenzie turned to Jon, "Where is Jay? And where's Mhinga? What happened to them?"

"Mhinga is fine. Badly bruised, but he will be okay. Jay took a shot in the shoulder but it looks like he will be all right, too. An old man and his grandson found Buster . . . ."

"Buster!" MacKenzie interrupted, "Oh my gosh, I forgot all about him. He's still alive? I thought Dubois killed him."

"No, he is all right. We left them all behind with the old man. He seems to be a medicine man."

"What happened at the camp? I was there. I saw the fire. I saw men crawling out of the flames, and I saw you carrying one of them. Are they all right? Is my father with Mhinga and the medicine man? There were shots. Jon, what happened?"

Jon searched her face, stalling, buying time to find the words that would gently explain what happened to her father. Horror stole over her face. She was reading him, feeling his thoughts. She gasped and choked back the tears, then looked down at the rugged hands that tenderly held hers. "My dad. He's dead? Isn't he?"

Jon squeezed her hands gently. "I'm sorry. I tried my best." His voice was barely a whisper. He held her close.

She nodded her head. "I know you did." She pulled back, "It was Dubois, wasn't it? I saw him aiming." Her voice broke as she lost control. Bursting into tears, she cried, "I tried to stop him, to make him miss . . . . I thought he was going to kill you."

"Shh, Mac. He did miss. You saved my life, and now you are safe. So are the other two scientists. Mhinga and Jay are going to be all right.

Think of all that." Jon held her to his chest and rocked her.

"Yes. You are right. And Daddy was so sick, he was in so much pain." She choked back the tears. MacKenzie tore away from Jon, and wiped her face. Her eyes widened, and she gasped, "Oh my God! We've got to go after Khosa!" She crossed over to Zawawi, speaking rapidly. "He's such a nice little boy. He thinks you are still mourning for his mother, and he is afraid of Dubois. He thinks Valli will protect him, but I don't think Valli is completely stable."

Looking down at the white woman, Zawawi's stomach sank. "What happened? What make you think that about Valli?" he asked.

"Khosa said Valli believed that a couple of people who worked for Dubois, a cook and a guard . . . I can't remember their names . . . ."

Simon interrupted, "Petrus and Taveta?"

"Yes!" MacKenzie exclaimed. "That's them. Khosa said that Valli got all spooky-looking and thought they were chimpanzees and killed them. Khosa is not safe, and he is with them now."

Grimness covered Zawawi's face. "Where are they now?"

"Yesterday, Valli saw elephant tracks." MacKenzie looked back at Jon. "I think it must be the same old bull we saw from the bluff." Turning back to Zawawi, she said, "They were talking about his really long tusks."

"That will make them easy to follow," Simon offered.

"Yes, they'll be traveling slow, tracking him. We can catch up with them pretty quickly," Jon added.

"How many are there?" Simon asked MacKenzie.

"Four: Dubois, Valli, Gbenya, and Khosa," she replied.

"Take us back to their campsite. We'll have to start from there." As the four started down the trail, the little chimp climbed down from the tree and followed behind dragging the severed arm.

Chapter 41

The ridge straddling two hills was a long field of tall grass, devoid of trees. Surrounding the grassland, thick green bushes formed a dense hedge. The elephants stood huddled closely together near the hedge, and their gray backs rose above the golden blades like misplaced boulders. Perching on the sun-warmed backs, small birds hopped around, ridding the beasts of annoying insects. From across the field, it was impossible to distinguish one cow from another, but the back of the old bull stood out clearly above the others.

Dubois patted Valli on the shoulder and smiled. Leaning over, he whispered in the young man's ear, "Well done, Valli!" Then grinning at Gbenya, the big Frenchman whispered, "The boy has promise, don't you think?"

Gbenya smiled and whispered back, "Yes, he brought you in close, down-wind and well hidden. The ivory is yours to take."

The three men stood close together. Khosa wandered nearby, finding a comfortable spot to sit down and lean against a tree. Yes, Dubois thought as soon as their siesta is over, and the cows move off to feed, the old fellow will be all mine. Once again, he daydreamed about the length and girth of the berry-stained teeth. Dubois pictured the pure white root of the ivory as thick as his leg. He imagined its feel, smooth, protected under the tough hide of the old elephant's cheek. Silently lusting for the kill, his hand caressed the length of his .460 Weatherby Magnum rifle as if it were the inner thigh of a lovely young woman.

Valli watched the way Dubois caressed his rifle. His senses were heightened from the thrill of stalking and tracking. He could almost feel the shape of Dubois' dark walnut rifle stock in his own hand, not the battered double-barrel shotgun he used for shooting chimps. The young man's anticipation grew with each gliding stroke. A familiar warmth settled below his waist, and he felt himself harden as his breathing deepened and slowed.

Sitting several feet away from his big brother, Khosa noticed the change in Valli. The young boy watched as the transformation took place. As Valli's eyes darted back and forth from the elephants to Dubois' rifle, his back tightened and his breathing became rapid and shallow. The young boy heard the deep thumping in his brother's chest. It was all happening again. Valli was getting sick.

Dubois felt Valli fidget next to him and noticed the glazed look veiling the young man's eyes. He had seen that look before, three times. The first time they had been in a similar situation. The old bull was close and then became spooked by the distant gunfire of Tshombe and Gbenya as they hunted the leopard. Valli had lost control of himself and grabbed the rifle, firing wildly, striking the old bull high in the fleshy part of the hip. That same day it happened again, when Valli found the tracks of two black men chasing a white man. The last incident was with Petrus and Taveta. The young man had lost all control of himself and killed them both. He had shown no remorse, no sorrow -- just pure primitive savagery.

The bloodthirstiness in Valli was like nothing Dubois had ever seen before. It seemed to rise up from somewhere deep inside the young man and take control, forcing him to kill. His ancestral people, the Maasai, as a whole, although small in numbers compared to other African tribes, were fierce opponents in war. If Dubois could not find a way to dominate and harness this wildness, Valli would be a liability he could not afford to have around.

Gently Dubois nudged Valli in the side, distracting him momentarily. Removing his field glasses from his pocket, he handed them to the young man and grinned. "Do you think there is anything else out there worth taking?" he whispered.

Carefully Valli adjusted the glass and studied the pod of sleeping elephants. Scanning back and forth, he could see only the tops of their heads. Their ivory was well hidden in the grass. Shrugging his shoulders, he whispered, "Can't tell." As he made one last pass, he centered the lenses on the large bull. With the aid of the binoculars he could clearly see the old wound high in the left shoulder. It was put there by Dubois' bad shot. Valli snickered to himself at the memory. Dubois had taken one young bull down fast and clean, but had only wounded the second because Khosa saw this big bull and tried to warn him.

Valli glassed the length of the old bull's back until he came across another wound, high in the fleshy part of the elephant's hip. This one he had made with a hasty wild shot after Dubois missed. He had taken the rifle away from the big white man and fired as the animal spun away into the darkness of the forest. Seeing the results of being outsmarted by the old bull made him angry. Things are going to be different this time, Valli promised. He will not escape again.

Lowering the field glasses, Valli looked out over the open field. Except for an occasional flicker of an ear, the humps clustered tightly together did indeed look like big rocks. As he watched, one trunk periscoped up and swiveled about, searching. Within a few seconds a second trunk rose, quickly followed by others. Heads rose and bodies turned to face the same direction.

Dubois whispered, "They've sensed something."

Raising the binoculars, Valli looked over the area. "Shit!" he whispered.

"What do you see, Valli?" Dubois asked.

"You won't believe it!" Valli said.

Dubois snatched the glasses. "It's that colonel! And that bitch MacKenzie is with them." His voice was loud, and some of the elephants turned towards the new sound. Seeing Simon alive raised the hairs on the back of Dubois' neck and twisted his gut painfully. Coming toward them was the man who had ruined his poaching operations. The Frenchman was not going to let Colonel Simon Kuldip escape alive this time. He would finish the job he had started more than a year ago.

"Ms. Mac?" Khosa said quietly. "But I thought we left her with...."

Gbenya interrupted, "Tshombe must be dead if she is with them. And this hunt is over for now."

"Wait a minute. No, it isn't," Dubois said with a half grimace. Turning to Valli, he continued, "Is it, Son? We've been chasing that old bull for weeks now. I'd say we don't let anyone get in our way. What do you think?" He handed the field glasses to Gbenya. Turning back to Valli, he said, "Ready for a little more sport of the two-legged kind? These won't be as easy as the last pair. Are you up for it?"

Valli smiled knowingly. He was primed and pumped, desperately

327

wanting to feel the cold curving steel of a trigger against his finger, to feel the fear of the hunted and the sight of fresh blood.

Gbenya spoke as he looked through the lenses, "What kind of score are you trying to settle with this one?"

Dubois answered with a chuckle, "A big one. That man and his friends with him are responsible for the raid on our operation. He is an army colonel assigned to the special division of the Kenya Wildlife Anti-poaching Team." The Frenchman took the field glasses from Gbenya, adding, "He's our biggest thorn. But if we eliminate him, there's no rush getting back to Lifi."

Looking at the men standing around him, Gbenya snickered. "We're even, gun-wise, three to three. We overpower them a bit with my AK-47, your .460, and Valli's shotgun. But what about . . . ." Nodding towards Khosa, he raised an eyebrow, his voice trailing off.

Dubois glanced toward the little boy staring at his older brother, and not paying any attention to the older men's conversation. With a devilish grin, he leaned towards Valli and whispered loud enough for Gbenya to hear, "What's the easiest way to hunt leopard?"

Valli flashed a look between the two men, confused by the change in the conversation.

Dubois asked again, "What's the easiest way to hunt leopard?"

Valli answered this time, "Bait a tree and wait."

Dubois nodded his head and smiled proudly at Gbenya. "Isn't that right, Gbenya? Bait a tree and wait." The big Frenchman turned slightly, clearing Gbenya's view of the little boy seated on the ground drinking from the canteen. Whispering more to himself than the others, Dubois quietly said, "The bait." He pointed across the field, "Over there comes a father and a white woman who has made a close friendship with . . . ." He nodded towards Khosa. "That's the only reason they are coming. Colonel Kuldip is coming after me, and he is all mine." The Frenchman raised his eyebrows at both Gbenya and Valli. In unison they nodded. "Gbenya, you take out the white man. Valli, if you really want to leave your childhood behind, here's your chance. You kill your father."

Valli's shoulders squared, and he looked Dubois straight in the eyes, "Yes. It is past time for that."

Dubois patted the young Maasai on the shoulder and nodded his head.

Snatching Dubois' hand, Valli squeezed hard and in a low voice grunted, nodding towards his little brother, "But he will not be hurt in any way. Do you both understand?" Valli flashed an evil glance at Gbenya.

"Valli, my son," Dubois said in a fatherly voice, "there's no reason to harm a boy like that." Ignoring the painful grip, he continued, "He will be quite safe, I give you my word as a gentleman. I've never lied to you or cheated you. I've no reason to start now. I just want the Colonel and that ivory."

"Okay," Valli said, releasing his grip. "So what's the plan?"

Dubois raised an eyebrow at Gbenya and then scanned the golden field. The elephants were still staring off in the opposite direction, evaluating the new scent that wafted towards them on the gentle breeze. They were not moving. Dubois calculated that the other group was not moving either. "Valli, you know those men well. What do you think they are doing now?"

Valli thought the question over carefully before answering, "It looks like they followed our spoor from the campsite, which has gotten them into trouble. The wind has changed and the elephants know where they are. They know we are hunting the old bull and are around here close by. The elephants are showing us their position, and they see that as well. It was a stupid mistake, one my father would not likely make."

Dubois interrupted, "Unless he was angry. Unless he was worried about his young son."

Valli shook his head and snickered, "Not likely. He does not think of us as his sons."

"Come on, Valli. Maybe he has realized his error. What would he do next? What would you do?"

"Wait and let the elephants settle down, or for the wind to change. Then back-track around, staying down wind."

Gbenya added his opinion, "They would glass the area and look for a vantage point we might use to get a clean shot at the old bull. They might . . . ."

Dubois cut him off, "Yes! And that is where our little friend will be sitting. They move in, thinking they will be finding us, instead finding . . . ." He nodded towards Khosa. "As they approach, we take them." Looking Valli straight in the eyes, he finished, "Leaving the lad safe and unharmed."

Valli smiled, acknowledging Dubois' plan. "Okay," the Frenchman began, "while they are pinned down by the elephants, let's find a good spot to set up. Valli, you lead the way. Find us a spot that would give us a clean shot at that old bull." As Valli started to turn away, Dubois laid his hand on the young man's shoulder, "Valli, don't mention this to your little brother. We don't want him to seem nervous or to call out a warning to them as they approach. It's for his safety, too. Understand?"

Valli nodded his head and called to Khosa. Picking up the water canteens, the young boy approached his older brother. "Are you going to go shoot the old bull now?" he asked Valli.

"Yes," Valli whispered to Khosa. "We're going to move closer and find a safe place for you to wait while we finish the hunt. *Bwana* is concerned that when we start firing some of the cows might charge wildly, and you might get hurt. You will be all right by yourself for a little while, won't you?"

"Yes. But what about Ms. Mac and the others? Where are they?" Khosa asked.

Dubois heard the little boy's question, "Khosa, we saw them turn the other way. They must be going to take Ms. Mac back to the city."

"Oh," the youth said sadly, "I didn't get to say goodbye to her." "Don't worry about it, Khosa. Perhaps they will hear our gunshots and come back to see the old bull up close. You could talk to her then." Dubois' voice was smooth and fatherly.

The youth looked up at the big Frenchman with a puzzled expression. "If she comes back to see the elephant, will you try to keep her to sell to that man?"

"Oh, Khosa!" Dubois laughed. "That was just a little joke. No one is selling anyone. Now go along and follow your brother. The elephants will be done with their nap soon, and we need to get into position."

With a friendly smile, Khosa fell in behind his brother. As the two boys moved through the bushes, Gbenya closed up next to Dubois and whispered in French, "Those two are becoming more trouble than they are worth."

Dubois nodded in agreement. "*Oui.* As soon as the Colonel and the other two men are down, go ahead and get rid of them. I'm tired of baby-sitting Khosa, and Valli is too unstable."

"What about the woman?" Gbenya asked.

"Like I told the boy, no one is getting sold. Take her out, too." Dubois moved off, following the wake of the boys. "She's too damn much trouble."

Valli carefully picked his way down the ridge, parallel to the golden field where the elephants were. His excitement heightened with each carefully-placed step. From this location midway down the hillside, Valli could not see the position of the elephants, yet he could feel them. His entire soul united with the simplest elements of the wilderness. In this deep state of concentration, Valli did not understand this rare ability that possessed his body; he could only follow its primitive orders to hunt. Mystically, his acute hearing allowed him to follow the low-frequency rumbling communication between the elephants. When he was directly below the elephants' position, Valli cautiously began to move up the hillside. Attuned to any change in the breeze, he led the group closer to the elephants' location.

Khosa followed several yards behind his brother. They had hunted this way many times. The younger boy had noticed that with each stalk the hunt grew more intense for his brother. Sounds from Valli's heart amplified, pumping, pounding and trying to escape. The boy did not need to see his brother's face to visualize the wildness in his eyes. That look would remain until he fired his shotgun. Then a sudden calmness would replace the savagery that had seized control and caused his illness.

Dubois and Gbenya followed closely behind Khosa. This was the first time the scar-faced Madi tribesman had seen Valli work. He thought he moved more like a hungry leopard approaching an unsuspecting antelope than a young Maasai man. What a pity, he thought. This talented young man could not be controlled. Dubois is right; Valli is just too unstable.

Silently making his way up the hillside, and staying down wind,

Valli led the others to within twenty yards of the elephants. Stopping a few yards from the clearing, Valli rested against the root buttress of a thick old mahogany tree. When the others caught up with him, he pointed at the elephant herd and smiled. The large gray animals had settled down and were no longer studying the bush surrounding the clearing. Most of the cows were peacefully eating berries from thorny bushes. The majestic bull was standing next to an old cow, touching his trunk to a pool of her urine, tasting for hormones that would indicate she was ready to mate.

Pointing to a thick branch ten feet up the tree, Valli motioned for Khosa to climb up. Ducking through the shoulder straps of the canteens, Khosa hung one on each side with the straps crisscrossing his chest. Valli squatted down, and the youth quietly climbed onto his shoulders. As the boys worked on their balancing act, Dubois stepped closer to the edge of the field. Still concealed behind the thorny edging, he glassed the area for any sign of the Colonel and his party. Gbenya came alongside and scanned the area too. The elephants had quieted down, and were no longer concerned with the scent of humans. Dubois whispered, "They must have pulled back and moved downwind, but where?"

Sitting on Valli's shoulders, Khosa was still too short to reach the branch. Valli took a step onto the thick root that ridged gracefully to the ground. Reaching up, Khosa was able to touch the underside of the branch, but he was still several inches too short to pull himself up. He would have to stand on Valli's shoulders.

Leaning slightly to one side and using the tree trunk as a support, Khosa lifted his foot, placing it on his brother's shoulder. Shifting his weight as he stood, the metal water canteens hanging around his neck slid around his back and knocked together with a loud double clink.

Dubois and Gbenya spun around and glared at the boys. The elephants had heard the noise too and had turned to look in their direction. Dubois mouthed the words, 'Don't move!'

Ever so slightly Valli nodded that he understood and hoped that his little brother would know to do the same.

Out of the corner of his eye, Dubois could see the trunks shooting up and reaching out trying to identify what had startled them.

Khosa began to waver, losing his balance. Squinting, Valli strained to stay still. The young man could feel the thin layer of damp moss covering the ridge of the root buttress pulling off. He was slipping and losing control. In an instant, Valli's foothold gave way, and the boys tumbled to the ground.

The loud crash spooked the elephants into a run. Across the field they crashed through the thorny line of bush. Dubois growled loudly, "You black son of a bitch!"

The big Frenchman was reaching for his rifle when Gbenya grabbed his arm and pulled him around. "Look! There they are!" The poacher pointed into the woods between them and the elephants. "The elephants flushed one of them out of his hiding place."

"I don't see a damn thing!" Dubois snarled.

"Keep looking. I saw one of them run from that log toward that big rock." After a few minutes, a head poked up over the top of the rock looking in the direction of the log he had just left. This time Dubois saw the hiding place. The Frenchman reached down and grabbed Valli by the shirt, pulling him close to his face and snarled, "This is your last chance to prove to me you are a man! They are hiding over there, scattered behind the rocks and logs. They must have a good idea where we are. I want you to lead Gbenya and me around behind them. We'll leave Khosa here just as we planned, got it?"

Valli nodded and returned to Khosa's side. Shaken from the fall the young boy leaned up against the tall curving buttress in tears, holding his arm. "Valli, my arm is hurt. I think it's broken."

"Stop crying, Khosa. I've got to take the *Bwana* scouting. You stay here. I'll be back in just a little bit."

"But, Valli!" Khosa cried.

"Stop it! Stop acting like a baby." Valli's voice was cold and hard. "I've got work to do. Now you just stay here. Keep your head down and your mouth shut." Glaring at Dubois as he passed, Valli motioned for them to follow him.

On hands and knees, Valli crawled and snaked his way under the thorny hedges. Once Dubois and Gbenya were through, they all ran hunched at the waist along the edge of the tall grassy field, screened by the thorny shrubs.

Chapter 42

Do you see anything?" Jon whispered to Simon, a few feet away. Hunching his shoulders, Simon looked to his brother for an answer. As silently as a big cat, Zawawi moved closer. Huddling together behind a log, the men whispered back and forth. Zawawi said, "I know they are up there, but I can't see them. That would be a perfect place for a clean shot at the herd. I'm sure they are behind that big mahogany tree, a few yards from the edge."

"Yes, that's an ideal position," Jon said. "Big tree. High spot to shoot from. It's overlooking the herd and it's downwind."

A hollow sound of metal cans bouncing together echoed through the forest.

Zawawi pointed towards the elephants. "Look! They heard it."

Through a small window in the thorny hedges, they could see that the elephants had stopped eating and were peering intently down the field toward the big mahogany tree.

Jon looked back at where MacKenzie and the chimp were hiding. Sitting behind a large outcrop of rock, she peeked her head around. She had heard the noise too. Jon snarled a look at her, and she flashed him the 'Okay' sign and ducked back out of sight.

"Maybe we should swing a bit downhill and come up from behind . . . ." Simon's words were cut short by a crashing noise from the direction of the big mahogany tree.

As Zawawi whispered, "What . . . ?" the elephants took off in fright. They crashed through the thorny hedge only twenty yards away. In their panic, they stampeded around the bigger trees and knocked over the smaller ones. The cracking of limbs being torn from the tree trunks and the snapping of the younger trees echoed down the hillside as the fleeing elephants disappeared from sight.

Without hesitating, Jon jumped to his feet and ran towards the out-crop where MacKenzie and the chimpanzee were hiding.

The ruckus of the charging elephants unnerved both the woman and the chimpanzee. Twisting and struggling, the chimpanzee tore loose from MacKenzie's arms and scurried up the nearest tree.

Jon dived behind the large rock just as the chimp disappeared into the leafy branches. Wrapping his arm around MacKenzie, Jon asked, "Are you okay?" and kissed her on the lips.

"Yes. Whatever spooked the elephants sent Huffy up the tree."

Jon raised his eyebrow in question. "You named him?"

"That's the safest place for him." Peering over the rock, Jon glanced up at Simon and Zawawi. "I think we're going to swing down the hill a little way and try and circle back behind them. Ready?"

"What about Huffy?" MacKenzie glanced up in the tree.

"Mac, he's a wild animal. He knows how to take care of himself. Come on, let's go." Taking MacKenzie's hand, Jon led her down the hill a little way to another large rock. Scurrying closely behind was the little chimp.

Jumping into her arms, Huffy wrapped his long hairy arms around her neck and locked his feet together behind her back. "I guess he's not so wild anymore," she smiled.

"Mac, just don't get too attached. Okay?" Glancing over the rock as he spoke, Jon scanned the area where Zawawi suspected Dubois and the boys to be. Quietly, Simon moved down the hill and then Zawawi followed. The men alternated down the hillside, covering each other.

As they started back up the hill, a strange feeling swept over Zawawi. He stopped and listened. The forest was quiet except for the consistent buzzing and humming of insects. Zawawi looked behind them, and the hairs on his neck rose, though he could see nothing moving. The feeling of being followed was strong. He motioned for the others to continue on for a short distance, while he stayed behind. For ten minutes the tall Maasai waited, turning over the uneasy feeling that tugged at his nerves. He could see nothing unusual. Though something was certainly puzzling, he finally moved on to join the others.

Zawawi found Jon, MacKenzie, Simon, and Huffy waiting for him behind a tall hollowed-out tree trunk. As he approached, Simon read his brother's face. Worry and uneasiness showed in his eyes. "What's wrong?" he asked.

Zawawi shrugged his shoulders and glanced around. "I don't know." His voice was low and dry, "I can't shake this feeling of being watched and followed."

"Your feelings are usually pretty accurate," Simon said as he looked around the area. "We're getting close to where we think Dubois was. We could be heading into a trap."

"Could be." Zawawi took his rifle from his shoulder and checked to see that it was fully loaded. "There's only one way to find out."

Simon looked at Jon and flicked a glance towards MacKenzie and the chimp. Acknowledging the look, Jon wrapped his arm around the woman's shoulder, "Mac, I want you and Huffy to stay here, in this hollow tree. We might not find anything when we get up there, or we might run into trouble. Odds are that Dubois is already gone, tracking the ivory."

"Oh, God, Jon, I don't want to stay here alone. Remember what happened the last time you left me alone." Her eyes filled with tears.

Pulling her close, he said, "Yes, I remember." His voice was deep and soothing. "But this time we're only going to the top of the hill. We'll be close by." He kissed her forehead. "If something should happen, you just scream really loud, and we'll be right back for you." MacKenzie took a deep breath and sighed. Jon cupped her face in his palm. "I need you to be strong and brave." Wiping the tears away with his thumb, he chuckled, "And I'm sure Huffy will help you scream, too."

Swallowing hard, MacKenzie choked back the tears and smiled, "I did promise you that, didn't I?"

He kissed her softly and whispered, "Yes." Searching her eyes he saw her strength and hugged her tightly. "Now crawl into that opening. I want to see how you fit before we leave."

MacKenzie, with the chimp clinging to her side, squatted and backed into the dark open split in the hollow tree. Peering out the opening she waved at Jon, and Huffy raised his hand too, copying her every motion.

❖ ❖ ❖

Valli had stopped. Listening and looking about he studied the land-scape, picking up subtle clues left behind by his prey. Ghost-like, he fol-lowed his quarry down the hill and back along the slope. They were close now, so close that they occasionally caught glimpses of them slipping behind a rock or large tree. Stimulated by the stalking, Valli's passion glowed with violent energy. He lusted in his power, and reveled in instructing Dubois and Gbenya where to hide and how to get there quiet-ly. Following the young man's instructions, the Frenchman and the scar-faced poacher were able to close in on Colonel Kuldip, Jon, and the young tracker's father, Zawawi.

Gbenya moved up next to Dubois. Valli flashed a disapproving glance. He had not instructed Gbenya to move from his position. Leaning very close to Dubois' ear, Gbenya whispered very softly, "They're loop-ing back to the old mahogany tree where we left the boy."

Dubois peeked up and glanced around at the landscape. It was true. Completely tuned into playing cat and mouse, Valli had not been watch-ing where he had led. "Psst," Dubois captured Valli's attention. Valli silently backtracked to Dubois. The young man was rigid. His shoulders were square and tight, defining every muscle and enhancing the throbbing veins running down the length of his arms. The Frenchman could easily hear the chambers of his heart pounding, and yet, except for the wild look in his eyes, the young man appeared calm. He did not speak, but rather seemed to perceive Dubois' thoughts. With a flick of his eyes and a small nod of his head, Valli led them directly up the hill to the mahogany tree.

When Valli was several yards ahead, Gbenya grabbed Dubois by the arm and whispered ever so lightly in his ear, "That kid is going to explode." Dubois silently agreed. Valli glanced over his shoulder and flashed Gbenya an evil look, sending chills down the poacher's spine. Dubois nodded for him to continue leading the way.

When they reached the old tree, Khosa was exactly where they had left him, sitting between the buttresses holding his arm. As Valli approached him, Khosa saw the wild look in his eyes and slowly stood up. Reaching out, Valli offered his embrace and led his younger brother to the back of the tree. "Stay down and this will be over with."

Nodding, Khosa squatted down and watched his brother and the other two men take cover behind other trees. Readying their rifles, they aimed down the hill. Peeking over the other side of the buttress root, Khosa saw movement midway down the slope. He watched as three men slowly made their way up the hill. His youthful eyes picked out his uncle Kuldip, Jon, and his father. His young heart raced. Ms. Mac was right. His father was coming to take him home. Valli, too, he was sure of it. Rising up, the boy began stepping over the gracefully curving roots. He wanted to tell his brother the good news. They could go home; their father had finally come for them.

Valli had quickly tuned out everything but the task at hand. He focused totally on proving to Dubois that he was a man by taking the life of his father. He centered all his energy on the men carefully creeping up the hillside. His mind willed his father's every step and, as if following instruction, Zawawi took each step exactly. Valli's breathing was steady and deep. A hot pressure flowed across his midriff, pulsating his masculinity. Feeling the cold steel of the trigger against his finger and sighting the bead dead center on his father's chest, he anticipated the orgasmic rush of the kill.

Khosa stepped out from behind the tree. His face glowed with delight until he saw the alarming wildness in Valli's eyes. The young boy followed his brother's stare and saw that it was directed at their father, the man who had come to take them home. Khosa looked closely at his brother. The sickness was worse than he had ever seen it, and it was affecting Valli's eyes again. Valli was very ill and needed help.

He looked around for Dubois and saw him several yards away to Valli's left. The Frenchman was kneeling behind a log, aiming his rifle at his father and the others coming up the hill. The sickness must have gotten him, too.

Gbenya! If he had not become infected too, he could help. The eight-year-old scanned the area. Leaning against a tree several yards behind Valli, Gbenya readied his rifle. Khosa watched as Gbenya switched his aim from the men coming up the hill to the back of Valli's head, then back to the men coming up the hill. 'The infection has gotten them all,' Khosa thought, 'Gbenya has it the worst. He thinks Valli is a chimp too.' The young boy felt his temperature rise as his heart pumped fast and furious. He had to do something.

Gbenya felt Khosa looking at him. Slowly rotating his head, the guard made eye contact with the boy. With a slanted half-grin, Gbenya slowly swung his AK-47 around, pointing directly at the young boy.

The little boy's eyes widened and his mouth dropped open in surprise. When Gbenya mouthed the word 'BANG!' Khosa felt his knees start to buckle and his head start to spin. "LOOK OUT!" he screamed at the top of his lungs.

The unexpected scream startled Valli. He lost his concentration and fired prematurely. Dubois reacted with the same shock and began firing, too. Gbenya turned his attention back to the men sneaking up the hill.

Instantly, Jon and the others ducked for cover. For the next few seconds, total insanity reigned. A series of rifle blasts was followed by more firing, both single shots and the steady rumbling of an automatic rifle, *rat-a-tat-tat, rat-a-tat-tat*. Solid thumping tones bellowed as high-powered bullets smashed into trees and rocks that the men hid behind.

Khosa's knees gave way, and he dropped in-between the tall buttresses' roots and covered his head with his hands. The barrage of gunfire drowned his sobs and cries. After a few long seconds, the firing ended. Khosa remained in his fetal position, too afraid to look up. Then his hearing cleared and he could hear voices. It was Dubois' French accent booming orders, "They're getting away! Reload! After them." Khosa looked up just in time to see the men taking off at a run down the hill. They were still firing at his father and uncle. The illness had turned them all into madmen.

MacKenzie could barely make out the sound of their footsteps creeping up the hill when she heard a tiny voice scream, "Look out!" Then came a series of rifle blasts. Her heart leapt. Breaking from her arms, the chimp scrambled for the nearest tree. There was more firing, both single shots and the consistent rumbling of an automatic rifle, *rat-a-*

tat-tat, rat-a-tat-tat. Solid thumping tones bellowed as high-powered bullets smashed into trees. Fear paralyzed her body, but her mind raced. Should she stay hidden or run?

As quickly as the gunfire started, it ended. Alone in the hollow tree with her knees drawn up to her chest, MacKenzie hugged her knees and trembled. Her mind tortured her with images of Jon, Simon and Zawawi dead, their bodies riddled with bullet holes, their blood pooling on the forest floor. She knew Dubois would search for her, and she knew what he would do when he found her. MacKenzie's mind raced off into the most horrid places, spiraling out of control.

MacKenzie snapped back to reality when a lone shot was fired, striking the trunk high above her head. She could hear the men running down the hill. Jon called to her, "MAC!" Crawling out of the tree she jumped to her feet. "RUN!" Jon yelled, and she began to run with him.

They dodged to the left with one stride and to the right with the next, letting the trees absorb the bullets. A lone round was fired, and then it was quiet while the men reloaded. Simon and Zawawi worked as a pair, covering each other as they made their way down the hillside, buying time for Jon to escape with MacKenzie.

At the bottom of the hill, MacKenzie ducked behind a large rock protruding over a deep creek bed. Following close behind her, Jon fell in next to her. Pulling back the bolt, he quickly reloaded the Model 70 Winchester .375 Holland & Holland. Four in the magazine and one in the chamber was not going to buy a lot of cover, but it was all he had to offer. Tucking two fingers in his mouth, Jon blew a loud piercing whistle and took aim. He had a limited view through the trees, but he knew Simon and Zawawi would not be long. "Mac, crawl down the embankment and keep your head down," Jon ordered. Peeking around the side of the rock, Jon saw a small, hairy figure running wildly down the hill. Glancing over at MacKenzie, Jon said, "Guess who just won't be left behind?"

MacKenzie scurried out of the creek bed and peeked cautiously over the boulder. The chimp was chasing after them. "Huffy!" she screamed. The little chimp heard her voice and checked his stride, not sure where the voice had come from. Again, MacKenzie called out, "Huffy!" This time the chimp zeroed in on her location and ran towards her. Rounding the side of the boulder, he jumped into her arms and hugged her tight.

"Get back down in that creek and stay there," Jon growled as he looked over the top of the rock. Within a few seconds, Jon could see Simon and Zawawi working their way down the hillside. Gaining ground, they crisscrossed back and forth, taking turns running down, and then firing back up the hill at the men chasing them. Jon whistled again, giving them his location.

The poachers fired another round, splintering woody debris all around. Simon was leading and was just a few yards away from the dry creek bed when Zawawi cried out. He had felt a hot stab in his thigh. Grabbing his leg, the tall Maasai lost his rifle and fell hard. At the same time, Simon heard his brother's cry of pain.

Jon yelled, "Zawawi's hit! Stay down, Mac!" He jumped up from behind the safety of the big rock protruding over the creek bed. Jon carefully lined up the rear v-notch with the front blade sight, patiently watching for Dubois or one of the others to emerge from behind a tree. He had only five shots, and he intended to make each one count.

Curled up, Zawawi squeezed both hands over the fresh wound in his thigh. Trickles of blood dribbled between his fingers. Simon wasted no time getting to his brother's side. Grabbing Zawawi by the shirt, Simon dragged his brother behind the nearest tree. "How bad is it? Can you make it?" Simon asked.

Zawawi shook his head; his face was twisted with pain. Releasing the pressure slightly allowed a large amount of blood to escape. Quickly he clamped down on the wound again. "It's pretty bad," he said, looking up at his older brother.

Gbenya stepped out from behind a tree and Jon caught him out of the corner of his eye. Swinging quickly, he sighted on the black man and shot. The bullet struck the tree, missing the black man's shoulder by inches.

The poacher ducked back as Jon dashed to a nearby tree. Seeing the white man break cover, Dubois opened fired, and just missed Jon.

From behind the tree trunk, Jon caught a glimpse of Valli. He was moving down the hill, closing in with Dubois. Firing as he ran, the young man advanced quickly. Jon fired a shot at the ground a few feet in front of Valli, as a warning. Jumping behind a tree, Valli glanced around, looking for the source of the firing.

Jon had three shots left before he had to reload. Looking over his other shoulder, he saw Simon kneeling over Zawawi. The blood ran between his fingers and dripped to the ground. Simon nodded, and Jon stepped out from behind the tree. Gbenya and Dubois were ready for him and opened fire as Jon raced towards Simon and Zawawi. Concealed by another tree, Jon asked, "How is he?"

The beefy black man shook his head and said, "Not good. It's in or near the artery. Here . . ." Simon tossed Jon the FN FAL military rifle, "It's got a fresh clip."

Jon pointed over his shoulder. "There's a deep creek just on the other side of that rock. Mac is there." Jon glanced around the tree and Valli took a shot at him. Shaking his head in disbelief, Jon looked at Simon, "Ready?"

Simon picked up his brother and nodded his head. Jon slung his old H&H over his shoulder and stepped from behind the tree and began firing the FN. Running as he went, Jon continued firing until Simon and Zawawi were safely behind the rock. The military rifle, set on full auto fire, discharged its bullets smoothly. The sound of the high-powered rifle, *rat-a-tat-tat, rat-a-tat-tat, rat-a-tat-tat,* kept the poachers down behind their trees. As Jon approached the big rock that shielded his friends, the FN went silent. Its clip was empty. Jon swung the military rifle over his shoulder as he drew down his H&H. It took only a couple of seconds before the poachers realized the white man was out of ammunition.

Valli was the first to step out from behind his tree. Jon was ready and took a wild shot at him, sending the young man back into hiding. As Jon reached the big rock, Simon stood up to help his friend down quickly. Looking past Jon, Simon saw Gbenya step from the tree. "Behind you!" Simon yelled. Just as the black man opened fired, Jon leaped, falling into the creek. Both rifles jarred loose from his grip. Quickly, Simon grabbed his weapon and slammed in a fresh clip. Jon rolled up on his feet and recovered the H&H.

As Jon reloaded, he looked over at Zawawi and then to Simon, saying, "They've got us pinned. Any ideas?"

After taking a few wild shots over the embankment, Simon looked up and down the creek, "Yeah, you move down the creek a couple hundred yards and I'll go up. We'll circle back behind them. Mac stays here with Zawawi. She can make the occasional wild shot to keep them on the hill."

As Jon and Simon took off, the chimp pulled out of MacKenzie's arms. She turned to reach for the chimp, but Zawawi released one of his hands and grabbed her arm. As the blood poured from the wound, he said weakly, "Let it go. He is better off in a tree."

"Oh God! The bleeding." MacKenzie quickly turned her attention to Zawawi. Leaning over she applied pressure to the bloody hole, slowing down the outpour. "We've got to get some kind of tourniquet on this," she mumbled. Shots came overhead from high on the hill. "Can you hold this tight for a few seconds?" she asked Zawawi. He nodded his head and, as she removed her hand, he applied pressure. MacKenzie grabbed the well cared-for FN, which Zawawi had taken off the sniper. The ten-pound weapon felt heavy. She looked it over briefly and held it up for Zawawi to see. "Is this thing ready to fire?"

Slowly Zawawi turned his head and looked at the weapon. Nodding, he said, "Point and shoot. It's on automatic." He looked at her skeptically, and asked, "Are you sure you can handle it?"

MacKenzie smiled and nodded, "Jon taught me. Remember, I shot a buffalo."

Zawawi smiled weakly. "I'll tell you when to fire."

With a nod of thanks, MacKenzie leaned against the embankment and waited for Zawawi to give her the okay.

As the sound of the firing lessoned Zawawi growled out, "Now!" Jumping up and raising the high-powered rifle, MacKenzie fired. The weapon hammered against her shoulder, the bullets streaming out as she gently pulled the trigger. Waving the rifle back and forth, she was amazed at the ease and power she controlled. Zawawi yelled at her, "That's enough!" and MacKenzie retreated behind the embankment.

"Wow!" she muttered.

Zawawi looked up at the woman staring at the gun. "Don't get too carried away. We're limited on ammo."

"That was easier than I thought. How are you doing?" she asked.

"Still bleeding." Zawawi's voice was harsh and dry.

Setting the FN down, MacKenzie quickly unbuckled the nylon webbing that made up the rifle's sling. "Here this should help," she said as she wrapped the sling around Zawawi's leg. Grabbing a sturdy stick, she put it under the webbing and twisted. Before it got tight, she stopped. Wedging the end of the stick between her knees, she pulled off her dirty white tee shirt. Using Zawawi's knife, MacKenzie cut off the bottom portion, folding it up into a small tight bundle and placing it over the wound. The sound of gunfire burst over their heads. As she twisted the stick, the nylon strap tightened down, holding the bandage and applying a consistent pressure to the bleeding artery. With the long loose end of the nylon strap, MacKenzie secured the stick from unwinding. As Zawawi lay back, he sighed, "Thank you. Perhaps you are not as stupid as I thought. For a white woman."

Smiling, MacKenzie put her cropped top back on and grabbed the rifle. Leaning up against the embankment she asked, "How much longer until Jon and Simon get into position?"

"Soon," Zawawi was sounding stronger.

The firing from the hillside had stopped. MacKenzie could hear the men's footsteps as they made their way closer. Rising up, she let off another round. The approaching men jumped behind trees for protection and held their fire.

MacKenzie ducked down below the embankment and listened. She could hear them talking, but couldn't clearly understand what they were saying. Looking down at Zawawi, she whispered, "What do you think they are they doing?" He shook his head. The silence was shattering. MacKenzie slowly peeked over the bank. All remained silent; she could see no movement on the hillside. Her eyes scanned slowly back and forth. The men were well-hidden.

In the strange silence, she heard a rustling high in a tree over her head. Looking up, she could see Huffy looking down at her. When they made eye contact, the little chimp started to move. He was climbing down the tree.

"Oh God, no!" MacKenzie whispered.

"What? What's happening?" Zawawi's voice was worried.

"It's Huffy. He's coming down the tree."

"Forget that stupid animal. What's Dubois doing?"

"Nothing, I can't see them. I don't know . . . ."

A deep French voice interrupted her, "Shoot that damn thing!" It was Dubois. He was ordering Valli to shoot the little chimp as he came down the tree.

As Valli stepped to the side of the tree and raised his shotgun, MacKenzie screamed, "NO!" With rifle in hand, she jumped up the embankment and ran towards the tree trunk. As she ran, Valli fired, grazing MacKenzie's arm. The burning sensation spun her around, and she dropped the rifle as she fell to her knees.

"Hold your fire, Valli," Dubois barked out. The little chimp jumped from the tree into MacKenzie's lap. Instinctively, she reached for the rifle and Dubois fired a shot that kicked up debris in front of her hand. Uncontrollably, she screamed. "Hold it right there, Missy," he yelled. MacKenzie froze; the chimp was wrapped around her, clinging tightly.

"But I can get them both!" Valli cried out.

"Do what I say, Valli! Hold your fire," Dubois roared out.

Zawawi rolled onto his good side and pulled himself up to the edge of the embankment. He mumbled, "Stupid white woman!" and growled against the pain as he lifted his head over the embankment. He could see MacKenzie kneeling just a few feet to his left, holding the chimp. Their only weapon lay a few feet away. Dubois and his men were hiding behind the trees. He could see only their gun barrels pointed towards MacKenzie.

Dubois barked out, "I've no reason to shoot you, Missy, but I will. Right now I'm only interested in the Colonel." Dubois raised his voice and yelled, "Colonel, come on up here and save the nice American girl."

Running down the hill just as fast as his short legs would carry him, Khosa cried out, "NO! NO!" The young boy ran past Gbenya, Valli, and Dubois. Panting, he stood between the poachers and MacKenzie and cried out, "You can't kill her and she isn't a chimp. You are all sick."

The sound of the young boy's voice stabbed at Zawawi's soul.

"Get out of the way, Khosa!" Valli yelled. "I don't want you to get hurt."

"No! Valli, you don't understand. You can't understand, you're sick!" Khosa pleaded.

Ignoring all the pain, Zawawi peeked over the creek's edge and called out to his youngest son, "Khosa! Come here." The child spun around and looked at his father. "Come over here, son, where you will be safe."

As Khosa took his first step toward his father, Dubois barked out, "Khosa, no! Go on back over there next to your brother." The young boy turned and looked both ways.

Valli called out again, "Khosa, come here! We must stick together like we promised. Remember?"

Khosa turned and looked hard at his brother. "Khosa," his father called softly, "Valli is sick, and you can't help him." Holding out his arms, Zawawi said, "Come home with me where you can be safe. Come here, son."

As Khosa took another step towards his father, Valli stepped from behind his tree. "You son-of-a-bitch!" his voice bellowed, "Leave him alone! You don't love him; you don't love anyone!" Valli raised his rifle and aimed at his father. The young man's eyes narrowed, and his body pulsated with a hot raving madness. "I'm going to kill you, you son of a bitch!"

Khosa glanced over his shoulder. The illness had taken complete control of his brother. "Valli, no!" the young boy screamed, and darted towards his father. Valli could no longer control his anger and squeezed the front trigger on his double barrel shotgun.

The nine lead balls of the Cheverotine cartridge struck the young boy squarely in the back. The heavy buckshot flung Khosa's small frame forward, directly toward his father. The eight-year-old's arms and legs spread-eagled as his wound splattered his blood over the lush green foliage and on his father's face.

"NO!" Zawawi screamed and struggled to climb up the embankment.

The little chimp bolted from MacKenzie's arms and darted up the nearest tree. MacKenzie reached for the rifle again, and once more, Dubois fired a shot at her hand.

Rage totally consumed Valli, and without thinking he quickly pulled the second trigger, firing the second barrel. Striking Khosa high in the shoulder, it flung his arms over his head and spun his little frame around like a ballerina. Twirling to the ground, the young boy's body rolled and came to rest face up at MacKenzie's feet.

Valli lowered his shotgun and stared in horror as his little brother's body rolled, leaving a bloody streak across the ground. A numbing sensation swept over his body as he watched his father crawling, dragging his wounded leg toward his young son. The sight of Zawawi cradling Khosa's limp body infuriated Valli. MacKenzie covered her face with her hands and screamed. The anguished ringing echoed in Valli's ears, and a ravishing heat quickly replaced the cool numbness. Bursting into a sweat, the young man trembled and raised his gun. "YOU!" he screamed out, pointing the weapon at Zawawi, "You killed him! Just like you killed our mother!"

In the madness of Valli's fury, Gbenya had made his way near Dubois. Speaking softly, the scar-faced man said, "The colonel and the white man must be circling around us. If they had been with the others, they would have prevented Valli from shooting the boy. I'm getting the hell out . . . ." Gbenya's words were cut off by the sound of a rifle shot. His eyes rolled back into his head, and his mouth dropped open, blood spewing out. He had been hit high in the back. As Gbenya's knees buckled and he collapsed, Dubois saw the brawny frame of Colonel Kuldip charging towards him. Hearing more footsteps behind him, Dubois glanced over his shoulder. The white man was approaching from the opposite direction. Gbenya had been right; they had circled around.

Reloading the double-barreled shotgun, Valli screamed, "And you! Stupid white woman, you're the reason all of this happened. You will pay, too!" Bringing the butt of the shotgun to his shoulder, the trembling young man took a step forward, screaming as he walked, "I'll kill you both for what you've done to Khosa!"

Hearing Valli's words, Simon checked his stride and looked away from the big Frenchman. Jon was also distracted, and was now running towards Valli. Seizing the moment, Dubois turned and ran up the hill. It was his only chance to escape.

Valli was just a few feet away from Zawawi when both Simon and Jon stopped. Both men were astonished to see Valli reloading his shotgun and pointing it directly at his father's head. Simultaneously, Jon and Simon raised their rifles and fired. The .375 Holland & Holland that Jon carried and Simon's FN crashed together. In unison the high-powered bullets slammed into the tense young man. Zawawi looked up as his oldest son's chest exploded. Valli's face transformed from savage wildness to muddled confusion. The shotgun dropped from his hands, and his body collapsed on top of it. Lying with his eyes wide open, he stared toward the body of his little brother.

Tears streamed down Zawawi's anguished face. Very gently he picked up his young son's bloody body and held it tightly to his chest. The Maasai trembled and cried, "Oh Khosa, my sweet little Khosa." He repeated over and over, "I'm so sorry, I'm so sorry."

MacKenzie knelt nearby, her hands covering her mouth in shock. Tears streamed down her cheeks. Reaching out, she wrapped her arms around the mourning man's shoulders and cried with him. She did not know what else to do. Jon and Simon slowly walked toward them. Kneeling down next to Zawawi, Simon was speechless. Jon knelt alongside MacKenzie and pulled her close.

With trembling hands, Zawawi closed Khosa's eyes and laid him down peacefully in front of him. Gaining control, Zawawi wiped away his tears, smearing his son's blood across his cheeks. Ignoring his own pain, Zawawi struggled and stood. Jon rose with him, helping his friend with his balance. Hopping a few steps over to where his oldest son lay, Zawawi reached down and grabbed the young man's ankle. With Jon's help, they dragged the body over to the ditch and rolled him over the embankment. Turning back to his brother, Zawawi said, "Get that ivory poaching bastard."

Without a word, Simon and Jon picked up their rifles and reloaded. Zawawi wobbled on one leg and leaned on MacKenzie for support. Bowing his head, he said, "We will tend to my son." Then looking to his brother and his friend, he said, "Don't come back until that bastard is bushmeat."

Chapter 43

Dubois had made it to the top of the hill when the two shots were fired simultaneously. The noise caused him to pause for just a second. They took Valli down, he thought. Then ducking low, he crawled through the thorny hedge that outlined the golden field where they had found the elephants earlier. Emerging into the sunny field, Dubois ran along the same trail that Valli had led him and Gbenya down a few hours earlier. The tall razor-sharp blades of grass had been matted down as the elephants fed on the berries, making his run awkward and slow. The big Frenchman ran the length of the long field. He was nearly at the spot where the elephants had stampeded into the forest when a booming voice bellowed his name.

Dubois stopped dead in his tracks and turned around. Standing at the far end of the wide, matted path were the white man and the unmistakable form of Colonel Simon Kuldip.

Winded, Dubois stood and quietly measured the situation. After a few seconds, Colonel Kuldip made the first move. Taking several steps forward, he raised his rifle and took aim.

Dubois checked his chamber and raised his rifle, too. Aiming at the bulky-framed man who had ended both of his lucrative poaching operations accelerated the deep loathing that he felt. Taking slow, steady breaths, Dubois concentrated on steadying his heart for an accurate aim. The distance and wind were going to make this easy target a tough shot. Tilting his head, Dubois aligned the notch, centering on Simon's chest.

Sizing each other up, the men felt the seconds linger for minutes. Both men held their stance, waiting for the breeze to change to insure a clean accurate shot.

Jon was standing a few feet behind Simon. His rifle was loaded and ready to fire. Watching the Frenchman take aim at his friend made Jon's heart race, though he had to stay out of the first round and let Simon do his job and take revenge for the loss of his nephews. Adding to the tension, the wind rustled across the field of tall golden grasses. Tossing and

349

swirling, the blades swayed back and forth in a wave of sound that imitated thousands of cheering voices.

Jon's eyes flickered from Dubois to his friend until a movement in the treeline behind the big Frenchman caught his attention. The shade obscured the source of the movement. Jon took a step forward and raised the stock of his old Holland & Holland to his shoulder. With rifle ready, he watched the thorny bushline, expecting to see more of Dubois' men.

As the wind began to drop, the old bull elephant emerged from the darkness of the forest into the bright, sunny field. Jon lowered his rifle and watched.

The breeze faded, and the Frenchman did not hear the elephant. A crooked smile slowly appeared on Dubois' face. Steadying his aim, he began to squeeze the trigger.

Jon laid his hand on Simon's rifle barrel, breaking Simon's concentration. Firmly, Jon said, "Wait." Lowering the rifle, Simon now saw what Jon was seeing; the old bull elephant sauntered up behind the poacher.

What's he doing? Dubois' mind raced. His finger again began to tighten against the curve of the trigger. The elephant was ten feet behind the poacher when his long wide shadow covered the man. The shape of the dark shadow on the ground captured Dubois' attention. As the poacher turned around, he was confronted with the same bull elephant he had been hunting. The long, stained ivory nearly touched the ground and mesmerized the hunter for a second. The elephant trumpeted a loud roaring blast.

The power of the trumpet startled Dubois, and he fired his rifle harmlessly into the air. The elephant paused as the echoing sound of the blast faded away. Gathering his wits, Dubois worked the bolt and raised his rifle as the big elephant shook his head, flattened his ears, and charged.

Dubois turned to run, but the old bull was close, and with a few quick strides he reached out and plucked the man like a wild flower. Wrapping his trunk around the man's waist, the elephant lifted the poacher high into the air.

Dubois screamed and cried out as the elephant tossed its head. Still clinging to the rifle, his grip tightened with pain. A shot rang out as the rifle was shaken from his hand. When the rifle struck the ground, the elephant dropped the man's body.

The old bull trumpeted again. Dubois tried to crawl away, but the elephant lowered his head and scooped his long ivory tusk under the tattered body. Wrapping his trunk around the man's waist, the elephant flung his head, casting Dubois like a rag doll into the tall golden grass.

Jon and Simon watched as the bull entered the high grass and retrieved the body, dragging it out by the man's foot. For several seconds, the man lay motionless, face down upon the ground, and then he moaned. Upon hearing the cry the elephant tilted his head and explored the body with his trunk. He rolled the Frenchman over, and the man weakly swung his arm at the elephant's trunk. Infuriated, the old bull tilted his head and then drove the tip of his tusk into the man's abdomen. Dubois' last breath gasped out. The bull then lifted the body up. Arms and legs dangled in the air. The limp body slid around the ivory cylinder, lubricated by blood and oozing entrails.

Annoyed, the elephant lowered his head, laying Dubois partially on the ground. Placing one of his huge front feet on the man's legs, the elephant stepped forward with all his weight. Lifting his mighty head, the curved tusk pulled through the man's side stringing out the man's intestines and other organs. As the body pulled partially apart, the intestines coiled and tightened around the ivory before bursting open.

The elephant ran his trunk over the broken bloody body. His fingered lip searched for any sign of life. Wrapping his trunk around the man's neck, the elephant lifted the motionless body. Still standing on the man's legs, the elephant pulled Dubois' torso apart with a loud champagne pop.

He swung the torso around by the neck, splattering blood and organs all around. The man's arms and body waved like a victory flag, until the neck finally snapped and the torso fell to the ground. The Frenchman's head popped out of the grip and bounced on the ground at the elephant's feet.

Picking the head up by the hair, the elephant curled his trunk up and looked carefully at the face. With pure hatred in his eyes, the elephant dropped the head at his feet. Raising his softly padded foot, the elephant squashed the head into the ground and trumpeted.

Then the elephant turned and mocked a charge at Jon and Simon. Both men stepped back quickly and raised their rifles. But the elephant stopped, so the men lowered their rifles. Turning away from the men, the elephant stopped at the mangled shredded pieces of the poacher who had been following him for weeks. His trunk fingered the body parts. Rolling over the lower half of the body, the elephant uncovered Dubois' weapon. Picking up the Mark V Deluxe Weatherby rifle by the barrel, the elephant twirled it overhead triumphantly and smashed it hard on the ground. Swinging hard, the old bull threw the remaining piece of the rifle into the thick thorny hedge.

EPILOGUE

A musk smell hung in the still air of the dimly lit airport terminal. The duty-free gift shops and food courts were closed as a plane full of tourists arrived. In a private office just outside the gate, Jon embraced MacKenzie on a dingy vinyl, duct-tape-patched couch. Her richly tanned skin glowed with health, and make-up hid the remaining traces of her black eye and bruised cheek. A wide bandage covered the shallow wound on her arm. Wiping away a tear, Jon kissed her forehead and asked once more, "Tell me again when you are coming back."

MacKenzie sniffled and chuckled, "For the twelfth time, just as soon as I can. I can't give you a date now. I don't know how long it is going to take to settle my dad's estate. I'm sure the lawyers of Sperry Pharmaceutical Research Laboratories will want to investigate this whole mess." Her voice trailed off, "It might take a year."

Jon pulled her in tight and whispered, "I keep hoping that I heard you wrong."

"Yes," she whispered back, "but I have to go. I need to be with Don and Henry when they see Mitchell's wife. They shouldn't have to face her alone."

"Do you think they will return to finish their studies?"

"Oh, I think so. With what they learned from Mhinga's uncle, there should be enough to warrant a return trip." Pulling back, she looked up at Jon, "You will keep me informed how Huffy is doing?"

Jon smiled and gazed into her dark hazel eyes. "Yes, of course. Huffy has an important job now, helping my mother educate the kids about the importance of wildlife conservation. In many countries, native kids have never seen a chimpanzee."

"I feel sad that he wouldn't stay in the forest."

"He had been through a lot of shock, and now he trusts people and that is very dangerous for a wild animal."

"What will happen to him as he gets bigger?"

"There are orphanages where he can live with other survivors from the bushmeat trade."

A tap on the door interrupted their conversation. Simon slowly opened the door and stuck his head in. "Mac, it's just about time to go."

With a nod and a deep sigh, Jon rose from the couch and reached out for MacKenzie. Rising up, she melted into his arms. Her body trembled and, burying her face in his chest, she cried. "Oh, Mac," Jon said softly as he rocked her in his arms, "Come on, it's just for a little while. A year will go by so quickly, you wait and see."

MacKenzie held tightly, "I don't know if I can ever come back." She sobbed back the tears and looked up at Jon. "When my dad was alive, and away on a study, I used to think of him working in some exotic place -- you know, some, some . . . debonair place. I used to think of Africa as debonair; wild and carefree. But then I came here, and now he's dead. I can never forget how he died or how this business of bushmeat has affected all of our lives." Tears rolled down her cheeks. Running her fingers through his hair she sighed. "Africa is nothing like I expected." She forced a smile. "It's not debonair at all. Not at all like they show in those old films."

Pulling her to his chest, Jon said, "Maybe it is like those old movies. All the great debonair actors had a dark side." Jon rocked her gently. "Almost everything has a dark side, Africa has its dark side too. It may not be like you expected," he pulled back and gazed into her hazel eyes, "but maybe in some ways it is better." He cupped her face in his hands. Wiping away the tears, he smiled. "You are strong. Get all of your things done and come back. Together we'll find a place that's debonair."

She nodded her head and took a deep breath. Forcing a smile, she reached up and ran her fingers through Jon's dark curly hair. Leaning over, he kissed her.

There was another tap on the door and Simon peeked in. "Mac, your plane is loading."

Their eyes locked on each other as the last boarding call screeched over the intercom. Tears welled up inside of her. Pulling her close, Jon kissed her passionately. Then whispering in her ear, he said, "I've never told you how I felt."

MacKenzie whispered back, "You don't have to, I can feel it." Pulling away, she forced a smile as tears streamed down her cheeks. Quickly she left his arms and darted through the doorway.

DARKSIDE OF DEBONAIR

The Bushmeat Crisis

Bushmeat in its simplest definition means: The meat of animals taken from the forest. Any forest, any animal, this includes threatened and endangered species. Elephants, chimpanzees, and gorillas are just a few species that are being hunted for human consumption. It is estimated that over 1 million metric tons of forest animals are killed in a year. That is equal to nearly 4 million cattle. Most prominent in central African countries, the bushmeat crisis is also occurring in Asia, India and South America.

The backbone of the bushmeat crisis is the timber industry. They are supplying local people with transportation, weapons, ammunition and wire for snares. It is estimated that 80% of the animals caught in snares rot there; never leaving the forest, never making it to market. Drought and currency devolution has made farming unprofitable, so it is poor who has turn to commercial hunting. The meat surplus is sold in markets to the wealthier urban people at 4 times the cost of beef and pork. But the meat of these endangered animals have reach far beyond their native borders. Across Europe, bushmeat is beginning to appear on menus.

If the demand for bushmeat continues to grow, some experts believe that in less than 15 years, there may not be any primates left in the wild. This could have a major impact on our health, as wildlife carry diseases that can jump to humans.

This is particularly true when it comes to our closets living relative, the chimpanzee. Sharing about 99% of the same DNA as humans, chimps are carriers of such diseases as Malaria, Ebola and SIV virus, which is believed to be the grandfather of HIV-1. Some scientists believe that by losing the forest, and the animals, we may be loosing one of our best chances for finding a cure for AIDS and opening the possibility of new plagues.

The bottom line is that the bushmeat crisis is being driving by economics. The key will be to find a balance for sustainable hunting, curbing the commercial trade in this exotic meat, while meeting basic human needs without future risk to the culture and wildlife. People need to be educated on the health risk and the important roles diversified groups of animals have in maintaining a healthy balanced forest.

The purpose of DARKSIDE OF DEBONAIR – The Bushmeat Trade, is to educate people about the aspects and effects of the bushmeat industry in an entertaining way, and to create mainstream controversy by exposing Africa's dirty secret.

www.bushmeatcrises.com

BARBARA DAVIS

All her life Barbara Davis has been driven to create, to build, and to learn. Whether using power tools on home improvements, drawing, painting, sculpting, or learning a new equestrian event, Barbara is always on the go. It was just a matter of time before her eye for detail and her wild vivid imagination evolved into the art of the written word. Barbara believes that all things happen for a reason, both the good and the bad, and that one can learn and grow from both. With painstaking research, clear and focused vision, colorful and riveting style, enhanced by her personal travels to Africa, she has brought forth an inspiring first novel to remember.